Two IN THE Bush

Book 1 of the Branwell Chronicles

Judith Hale Everett

Evershire Publishing

Two in the Bush © 2020 Judith Hale Everett

Cover design © Rachel Allen Everett

Published by Evershire Publishing, Springville, Utah
ISBN 978-1-7360675-0-5
Library of Congress Control Number: 2020921922

Two in the Bush is a work of fiction and sprang entirely from the author's imagination; all names, characters, places and incidents are used fictitiously. Any resemblance to actual people (living or dead), places or events, is nothing more than chance.

To Joe
my knight in shining armor

Two IN THE Bush

Chapter 1

IN VAIN DID the countryside of Hertfordshire burst forth in all the glory of autumn, gilding the rolling hills with fire and ennobling its manors and cottages, castles and ruins alike with golden hue. Sir Joshua Stiles merely urged his pair to a canter—unmoved by the charm of a lane overhung by ancient beeches, a valley of charmingly walled fields, and a burbling stream forded by a neat stone bridge—while inwardly cursing his own perverseness in accepting Amelia's tiresome commission.

Indeed, he had suspected the existence of a plot from the moment she had, with studied nonchalance, presented her request to him. He should immediately have demurred, but if he felt he owed nothing to the rest of the female race, he did owe brotherly obligation to her, so he had merely signaled his disapprobation with a raised eyebrow.

She had been moved to protest. "I felt sure you should have no objection to obliging me, Joshua," she had said, "for Branwell

Cottage is a mere step from Aylesbury, you know, and it would be such a kindness to my poor friend, and such a favor to me!"

With this last point, he had been in full agreement, and condescended to say so. "I've no doubt of it, my dear, but—you will pardon my curiosity—has something occurred to disrupt the Mail?"

"What can you mean?" she had cried, blinking. "No, of course not, but it would greatly relieve my mind to know the letter had been delivered into her hands, and not misplaced somewhere along the way, the post being as it is nowadays, what with all one hears of footpads and highwaymen, and young bucks tooling the coach! Oh! I have spasms at the very prospect!"

"Very disturbing, indeed," he agreed drily, knowing full well that, thanks to Mr. McAdam, the roadways had never been safer than in the present day. "One wonders how anyone finds courage to repose their trust in the Royal Mail at all."

"To be sure!" she had said, gratified at his quick comprehension. "And that is why I find it most providential that your journey takes you so near Branwell, for Cammerby may give you the direction, and I declare you shall not grudge the extra distance one bit, with the country being so lovely this time of year, though it has been so wet, and a jaunt of a few miles off your path will break up the tedium of your drive."

As she had hoped, Sir Joshua's sense of duty did not disappoint, and with a long-suffering sigh, he had accepted the commission. But if Amelia had had any notion of what was to befall him, she should have instantly repented her request, and forfeited her letter to the caprice of the Mail, and her plan—which indeed she had hatched—to a more favorable future.

The two days preceding Sir Joshua's journey had brought torrential rains, but as this morning had dawned as bright and as warm as could be possible—given that it was October, and given that it had been the dreariest and coldest year for weather he could remember—he had set forth in his curricle, letter in hand, with no more presentiment of evil than that the detour necessitated by his brotherly kindness would in all likelihood make him late for a nuncheon appointment with an old schoolfellow in Aylesbury.

Indeed, the condition of the King's highway gave him no cause for concern all the way to Chesham, but after Berkhamsted, where he turned out of his way and into the unknown territory described to him by his brother-in-law, the state of the roads rapidly deteriorated, becoming so horridly muddy in places as to try even the spirits of his matched bays, whose mincing progress ill-befitted their magnificence, and that of the well-sprung equipage they led. Sir Joshua, his eye on the rapidly moving sun overhead, at last resorted to a detour on a likely road that ran toward rising ground, only to be rewarded by a bone-rattling ride over deep, rocky ruts.

Another detour proved more propitious, however, and he made good time over several miles of even roads, until his path was suddenly blocked by a group of milk cows who apparently considered the right-of-way to be their own. The cowherd, having the effrontery to grin in response to Sir Joshua's civil desire that he bestir himself, merely shooed his charges forward along the road, rather than to one side or the other, and the cows, apparently sensing no urgency, either from their master's prodding or from Sir Joshua's blistering glare, consumed nearly a quarter of an hour of precious daylight in their progress.

The continuation of a smooth road after this obstacle served to stem the tide of Sir Joshua's deprecatory thoughts of sisters who could do nothing but fuddle the well-ordered lives of their brothers with frivolous errands, but just as he had begun to trust that he might join his friend in Aylesbury in time for dinner, he was obliged to pull to the side of the road to attend to a lame leader. The execution of this simple task so aggravated his temper that he jobbed at the horses' mouths when they were set to, and his subsequent self-reproach quickly fanned into hot recrimination against all localities whose inadequacy had precluded their establishing a turnpike trust—a conviction that was unimproved by the sudden commencement of a succession of pot-holes on the tightly hedge-lined road.

When, at long last, an obliging side road appeared, he set his pair at a gallop along it, keeping an eagle eye open for the signposts Lord Cammerby had described, until a dip and a turn brought him face to face with a mass of bleating sheep. At sight of this bucolic prospect, Sir Joshua—though at no time possessed of an aversion either to sheep or to their masters—was seized by an overwhelming desire to wring the shepherd's neck with his bare hands. This violence of feeling exercised such an exhilarating effect upon him that, snapping his reins, he plowed without ceremony through the startled animals, parting them as effectively as Moses had the Red Sea, and the curricle bowled along at a rate which should have been purgative to his anger, had it not, less than a mile down the lane, come abruptly upon a stationary wagon angling across the road.

Sir Joshua was not, in general, a man given to extremes of emotion. Taciturn by nature, even his wit was so dry as to burst upon the unsuspecting with startling effect. But the loss of his young wife ten years earlier had dealt him a stunning blow, from which he had never quite recovered, and though the impenetrable shadow of grief had at last receded, it had left behind a veneer of cynicism that was as deceptive as it was brittle. While his male associates were apt to turn a blind eye to this alteration, his sister, with the insight unique to the female sex, ever more devoutly hoped that something should occur to reanimate his tenderer feelings, and return him to himself before it was too late.

In fact, she had pinned all her hopes for his future felicity upon the success of this journey, for his unhappy circumstances were a problem which continually exercised her mind. This proposed visit to an old schoolfellow had coincided so wonderfully with the necessity of a timely reply to her dear friend that she was persuaded the occurrence was nothing less than the harbinger of his redemption, and had instantly set her ingenuity to work.

Had she been privileged to witness the effect of her labors she may well have lost all hope. For, coming upon the wagon, Sir Joshua was forced to pull up his team so sharply that they sat halfway on their haunches, and as they danced to a standstill, he surveyed the scene before him in formidable silence. The driver of the errant vehicle was nowhere to be seen and, unable to perceive immediately why the wagon was thus positioned, he swung down from his curricle, striding forward through the mud and challenging the quiet countryside, "What dashed nonsense is this?"

A figure popped up from behind the wagon near the front wheel, and Sir Joshua's angry step faltered. It seemed that the owner had not, in fact, abandoned the vehicle, and, to complicate matters, was a female. Unfortunately for the lady, these facts did little to soothe his temper, and he barked, "Do you not realize you are blocking the entire roadway?"

The lady's already heated countenance blushed hotter, and she brushed several wayward strands of hair from her cheeks. "Of course, I realize it, sir," she said with some asperity, gesturing impatiently to the wagon. "How could I not?"

This agreement of temper hardly mollified his own, and he

retorted, "And what, other than hiding behind the wheel, do you propose to do about it?"

"I was not hiding, sir!" she cried, her eyes flashing, but she closed her lips with a visible effort at civility before continuing, "I have been trying my utmost to correct it, but the wagon will turn the wrong way, no matter how I back the horse, and now the front wheel is mired!"

Even his jaundiced eye could see the justice in her predicament, but it obstinately searched for fault as he gazed narrowly at the lady. She was a mature woman, probably near in age to himself, and though she gave an impression of elegance, she was not at all attractive at the moment, with her shabby coat and skirts inches deep in dirt, and her dark hair escaping from its bonnet and whisping wildly about a perspiring and flushed countenance.

His better nature—which his sister hoped but could not be sure he still possessed—stirred with Herculean effort and, aided partly by his innate sense of duty and partly by the fact that any more delay should cost him his dinner, moved him to wrap the reins on an obliging branch, tossing his whip on the seat of the curricle. "Stand aside, ma'am," he said curtly. "I will see what can be done."

The lady, her head high, looked for a moment as though she would demur, but he shouldered himself between her and the wagon, leaving her little other choice than to move out of the way as he bent to inspect the wheel. It was indeed mired, halfway up to the axle, but his inspection was arrested by the sight of several stones thrust into the mud before the wheel, and he raised his head to cast a more appraising glance at his companion.

"Did you place these stones here?" he asked gruffly.

Her blue eyes regarded him dispassionately. "Certainly I did, sir. You cannot believe they moved there of their own accord."

He grunted at this, slightly appeased by this evidence of her intelligence—and of her determination to help herself, which he had always approved of in a female—and went to the cob's head. Taking the bridle firmly, he urged the animal forward, and through the physical effort of working with the horse and the novel and ennobling awareness that he was providing help to one in need, the brooding thundercloud about him gradually eased. By the time the wheel came free, Sir Joshua's patience was, if not wholly restored, at least once more in evidence, enabling him to endure the necessary tedium of maneuvering the cob forward and backward at the optimum angle to the wagon, several times, while the vehicle's owner, her affronted air forgotten in observing the skill with which he brought the cart into alignment, tried without much success to tuck her loose hair back into her bonnet.

When the wagon had been righted, she stretched out her hand to him in goodwill. "Masterfully done, sir! Though I am persuaded I should have succeeded by and by on my own, I cannot grudge your able assistance. You have my thanks."

"Pray do not regard it, ma'am," Sir Joshua responded, irked by this somewhat back-handed gratitude. "It's a devil of a place to lose control of your vehicle."

The civility stiffened on her face. "One does not always have the good fortune to choose when and where one loses control, sir."

"May I inquire, ma'am, or would it be impertinent," he said, coolly regarding her, "whether you slowed at all at the corner?"

She bit her lip and stared back at him, a humorous twinkle leaping into her eyes. "If I did not owe you my gratitude, such an inquiry would be impertinent, as you well know, but as you have earned, through your usefulness, a certain right, I will own to you that I was in a hurry, and made poor work of the turning."

Further annoyed by her sudden levity, Sir Joshua said baldly, "I am only amazed at your intrepidity, ma'am, for attempting a corner at speed in a wagon, and in such conditions."

"I fear I must amaze you further, sir, for it was not intrepidity but vice that drove me to it," she replied, without a trace of penitence. "As we are making confessions, you may as well know that I as much as laid odds with my cook that I could be to the village and back before dinner, and you see how well I am served for my reprehensible conduct."

This admission, made as it was in complete disregard for the inconvenience she had caused him, should have incensed him, but her playfulness of manner touched something forgotten in him, and he regarded her with wrinkled brow. She was so unlike the females with whom he was used to associate that he was conscious of a desire to know her better, but she had little else to recommend her, and the hour being far advanced, he quickly resolved that if he desired to reach his destination before dark, it would be to his advantage to close the interview.

Bowing to the lady, he said briskly, "It is, no doubt, as you say, ma'am, but I believe we are both eager to be on our way—"

"Pray, do not give me another thought, sir, as you have done your duty and must assuredly have better things to do," she returned sweetly. "Indeed, when I first took your measure, I doubted whether you should offer your assistance at all."

Sir Joshua—who considered himself, despite everything, to be a gentleman—was shaken, and took some moments to assimilate this unwelcome picture of himself. His better nature—which, having been roused, refused to go tamely—stifled his immediate tendency to discount her assessment by very helpfully bringing to his mind several points of their interaction which clearly supported it. Bereft of this defense, he was obliged to beg her pardon, which he did in a rather gentler tone than he had been apt to use, and prayed her to allow him the honor of handing her into her vehicle, and to accept his very best wishes for her good health and safety.

The lady lowered her eyes in acknowledgement of his apology, and quietly accepted his assistance, but showed no unwillingness to part ways. With a brief nod to him, she set the cob in motion down the road, and Sir Joshua watched her reflectively for a few moments before returning to his curricle to wipe the mud from his boots with an obliging stick. A strange female indeed, he thought, as he retrieved his reins from the branch and, shaking more thoughts of her from his head, was soon on his way.

His subdued mood did not survive the discharge of his sister's errand, for though the roads improved, the directions which he had received from his brother-in-law—who was fast becoming, to Sir Joshua's mind, the most shatter-brained nincompoop of his relations—were sadly lacking in precision. After twice passing the turning which Lord Cammerby had assured him would be on the south, Sir Joshua should then and there have consigned Amelia's commission to the devil if he had not, in pure desperation, turned north and thus discovered, nearly hidden by a profusely thriving hedge, the address board for Branwell Cottage.

The sight of the neat house set back from the lane was a balm to the soul of as fastidious a landowner as himself, and it was almost with pleasure that he surveyed the well-kept grounds as his curricle swept up the drive. But as he came to a stop in front of the low steps, and no groom came to greet him, a disturbing premonition crept upon him, which was not put to rout when his knock upon the door, though loud and firm, was unanswered. A frown creased his brow as he stepped back from the porch, darkling thoughts blooming in his mind on the respectability of a lady who did not—or could not—employ a servant to answer the door, and the advisability of his sister's continuing such an acquaintance.

He had just determined on abandoning his errand, and was composing in his mind a firm recommendation to his misguided sister, when faint strains of singing reached his ears, coming from the direction of the garden on the side of the house. His distaste for this troublesome errand was once more overcome by his strong sense of duty, and he resolutely strode around the corner of the house and onto a stone path, which was overhung by trellised vines and lined with late-blown roses and which, in another lifetime, would have enchanted him. In his present state, his only desire was to rid himself of that blasted letter and be on his way.

Emerging from the walk, he followed the leftward curve of the path, glimpsing a well-kept farm on some further acreage, and the silhouette of a manor house in the distance. These sights were noted only in passing as he continued around the periphery of the house, the path ending at a small herb garden, where a middle-aged servant of comfortable proportions knelt in the dirt, cheerily clipping parsley and chives.

He had nearly reached her before she glanced up and, recognizing a stranger—and a gentleman at that—leapt to her feet, dusting her skirts and bobbing a nervous curtsey. "Oh, sir, begging your pardon, sir, I didn't hear you come up!"

"It seems the entire household is afflicted with deafness," he remarked curtly. "Is your mistress at home?"

The servant, in agitation, wiped her hands on her apron, darting alternate looks at an upper window in the house and out across the fields. "No, sir, it's only Miss at home, with the master at the farm with Matthew and the mistress gone to the village. If you please, sir, we weren't expecting visitors. It's the maid's day off," she explained, as if the circumstance normally precluded unexpected company. Sir Joshua merely grunted, and the servant, with a visible swallow, added, "The mistress is expected back at any moment, if your honor should like to step into the house?"

Loathe to be one minute longer on his errand, he held out the letter. "No need. I trust I may leave this note with you, with the understanding that you will deliver it into Mrs. Breckinridge's hands immediately upon her return."

The letter was accompanied by half a crown, and the servant, receiving such unanticipated largesse from this very imposing gentleman, was stricken dumb, managing only several vigorous nods of the head and a double curtsey, and at last achieving the disjointed utterance of her gratitude for his honor's trust and the assurance that his honor's correspondence would be guarded with her life.

Sir Joshua, caring very little at this point whether or not his sister's letter would, indeed, be delivered, bestowed upon the fluttering woman a brief bow, and turned and strode back down the path to the drive. Shaking off the dust of his feet, he leapt into his curricle and turned it, without a backward glance, toward civilization.

Chapter 2

Upon reaching Branwell Cottage, Genevieve Breckinridge stopped to hang her coat in the hall to dry—mentally rehearsing her explanation to Sanford, her maid, for its deplorable state—then continued down the narrow passage, a parcel tucked under one arm. In the kitchen, she was met by the wide-eyed cook, who had been chopping herbs, but who at once dropped her knife to hasten her bulk around the table toward her mistress.

"This came for you today, ma'am. Delivered by hand, ma'am!" the cook announced breathlessly, diving a hand into her apron pocket and pressing a sealed billet writ on heavy, hot-pressed paper into Mrs. Breckinridge's hands.

"Thank you, Sally," her mistress said, taking in the cook's agitation with the ghost of a smile about her lips. "You did very well to give it straight to me. It looks excessively official, does it not? Who could it be from, I wonder?"

Sally shook her mob-capped head. "Oh, ma'am, he never left a name, and begging your pardon, ma'am, I forgot to ask for it!"

"My, he must have been intimidating indeed."

"Oh, he was, ma'am, ever so!" cried the cook, relief at her mistress's ready understanding plain on her face. "Tall and dark and—"

"If you say handsome, Sally," Mrs. Breckinridge cut in archly, tugging off her gloves, "I shall feel very ill-used at having been on your errand rather than being at hand to behold him myself."

"No, ma'am, I wasn't going to say that," Sally hastened to reassure her. "He was well enough, I suppose, ma'am, but it would be too much to say he was handsome!"

"Oh, in that case," said Mrs. Breckinridge, handing over the parcel to her, "I have nothing to regret, for tall and dark men are five a penny, I daresay. You are welcome to your merely tall, dark, and well enough stranger."

The cook, who had taken the parcel automatically, looked scandalized. "As if I would ever take on so, Mrs. Breckinridge! Shame on you!"

"Well, Sally, you mustn't put such shocking thoughts into my head by raving on about a tall, dark—"

"I was going to say imposing, ma'am," Sally hastily interpolated, "for he was, like a judge!" The memory of the stranger overpowered her once more, and she closed her eyes, the parcel pressed to her bosom. "Oh, it fair gave me shivers to have him glowering down at me, as if I was a common criminal or some such, and him not knowing me from Eve!"

"Good heaven, Sally! Was it so bad?" Mrs. Breckinridge laid a reassuring hand on the cook's shoulder. "Then I must count myself indebted to you for keeping me away, and sparing me such an interview. I shouldn't wonder at my bursting out with something shockingly uncivil, and giving him the most disgraceful notions of me."

Her eyes grew wide at a sudden realization. "You are nothing less than heroic for averting that disaster. Lenora will be positively green when she hears of it!"

"Oh, no, ma'am!" cried the cook, pink with pleasure. "She could never, not of me!"

"Never underestimate your powers, Sally," said Mrs. Breckinridge, her lips quivering. "However, you may be right. Lenora's preferred variety of heroism smacks less of confrontation and more of long-suffering, I believe. And when one comes to think on it, you did not, after all, rescue me from ignominy, for though I escaped your tall, dark, imposing gentleman, I did meet an angry, disagreeable one on the road, who most unwillingly helped me to free my wagon from the mud, and made no secret of his disdain for such a cow-handed driver as I proved to be." She shook her head grimly, remembering his coldness. "The sun, I fear, descends too rapidly upon the day of chivalry. My only consolation is that I shall probably never see him again."

"I should hope not, ma'am!" Sally's eyes had taken on a martial light at this disclosure. "What is he about, I'd like to know, to judge you as soon as clap eyes on you? And the man who don't see fit to render service to a lady in need ain't no gentleman, I say."

"Oh, Sally, but he did render me service," Mrs. Breckinridge said, her conscience requiring that she be just, "though he grumbled about it. And in the end, he apologized for his temper, rather inadequately, to be sure, but quite properly. So, we cannot, as Christians, give him up for lost."

This pious attitude did not seem to impress the cook, for she huffed, "A true gentleman would never have lost his temper, and not needed a trumpery excuse."

"Well, in all fairness, I did nothing to ease his disgust of me. No sooner had he helped me out of my embarrassment than I revealed to him that the cause of it was my yielding to a most despicable vice. I was obliged, you see, to tell him about our bet, which I have deservedly lost." She sighed. "I fear he did not approve the tone of my mind."

"And you the best lady I ever did know!" Sally then favored Mrs. Breckinridge with a detailed opinion of modern gentlemen in general, and tall, dark ones in particular, with an extremely vivid description of the set-down she would give one should he dare to insult her mistress within her hearing.

With becoming gravity, Mrs. Breckinridge attended to this diatribe until the cook drew breath, during which pause she gave such evidence of her unqualified approbation that Sally blushed rosily, and her mistress was able to escape the kitchen, her thoughts bent on the very interesting missive in her hands.

Mrs. Breckinridge could not imagine who the daunting gentleman could be who would deliver so very urgent a letter to her, for all her late husband's cronies had ignored her after his death, and all his creditors had been satisfied for at least a twelvemonth. In the privacy of the hall, she took a good look at the letter's florid direction and was at once seized by a dreadful memory, of the one man Bertram had known whose handwriting flowed like a woman's, and whose reintroduction to her society would be most painful. But the letter could not be from him. Surely, Lord Montrose had forgotten her very existence, as soon as Bertram's last obligation to him had been paid!

With trembling hands, she broke the seal and opened the note, her eyes alighting on the signature: Lady Amelia Cammerby. Her relief knew no bounds; indeed, her feelings underwent so abrupt an alteration that she was obliged to steady herself against the hall table, and with soaring hope she eagerly digested the note's contents. So satisfactory were they that no sooner had she read the last line than she hastened to the narrow staircase and up to the first floor, tugging impatiently at her bonnet strings and calling to her daughter.

Miss Lenora Breckinridge was to be found curled on the armchair in her bedchamber, engrossed in a novel she had borrowed from her dearest friend, Miss Elvira Chuddsley, who held a subscription to a circulating library in Berkhamsted. Having just reached the point of an alarming revelation that the insane monk was in actuality the heroine's long-lost father, Lenora's ears were understandably deaf to any sounds in the temporal world, and the precipitous entrance of her mother into the room wrenched her most distressingly back into reality. With admirable presence of mind, she thought to hide the book in the chair cushions, though this action proved unnecessary, for her mother was reading again a particularly enchanting line in the letter she held before her as she advanced into the room. Mrs. Breckinridge's inattention was to her own peril, her path being strewn with two bandboxes, a stool, and a carelessly discarded pelisse and hat, and it was with bated breath that her daughter watched her precarious approach, while shoving the novel deeper into the cushions.

"Oh, my love," breathed Mrs. Breckinridge, miraculously navigating to her daughter's side unharmed. "Our prayers are answered. This letter is from Lady Cammerby, and bears the most delightful news."

The novel was instantly forgot, the magnitude of this long expected and often despaired-of news such as to reduce even the most terrifying monk to obscurity, and Lenora clasped her hands to her breast, within which wild hopes now fluttered. "Mama! Mama! Oh, tell me at once! Has she agreed?"

"Yes! Oh!" sighed Mrs. Breckinridge, giving over the letter while sinking ecstatically onto the stool. "I cannot tell you how this news relieves me. A veritable world of weight off my shoulders!"

Lenora raised rapturous eyes from the hastily perused letter in her hands. "And she will bear the expense as well! Oh, Mama! I never dreamed!"

"I must say, I did dream it, my dear," replied her mama, eyeing her askance, "for I know not how we could have borne it. Indeed, we could not have, and would rather have been obliged to postpone your debut."

Lenora gasped. "Oh, Mama! Not another year! It would have been infamous to do so! I should have locked myself in my room, and—and gone into a decline!"

"An interesting fate, to be sure, my love," replied Mrs. Breckinridge, patting her daughter's hand sympathetically, "and I don't doubt but that you would have enjoyed it prodigiously, but through the excellence and generosity of my dear friend, you shall never know such suffering!" She passed a hand over her eyes. "Nor shall I. Oh, my dearest, the dreadful worries I have had, waiting and wondering!" She clasped her daughter's hand triumphantly. "But Providence has provided, and you shall have your London season!"

"Mama! Oh, I cannot speak for joy!" She bounced in her chair, but her passion was abruptly checked by a most lowering thought. "But will Tom agree to it?"

Her mother pressed her hand encouragingly. "He must, my love, for he is the last of all brothers to stand in the way of his sister's happiness."

"Indeed, I am the first to acknowledge his kindness to me," Lenora hastened to reassure her, "and he is generous above all things— and I love him dearly, and should never wish to appear ungrateful."

She paused, as if experiencing an inward struggle, before blurting out, "But you must own that in matters of pride he can be quite odious."

"It is true that pride has become somewhat of a sticking point with him, Lenora," acknowledged her mother, gently, "but it is also true that Tom's odious pride has kept us from an even more odious fate. Without his pride, a London season would be as unthinkable as it would be pointless." She stood, straightening her skirts. "Never mind about Tom. I shall have a word with him, for you know I can always bring him round my thumb."

Lenora's attempt to stifle a giggle was unsuccessful, and her mother cast a significant look at her. "I have great expectations for you now, young lady, so you must trade that horrid novel with Elvira for her latest fashion plates, and decide which of my old dresses we shall make over, for though dear Amelia has offered to stand the nonsense, we shall not overstep her generosity. We must at least make a push not to appear encroaching."

This elicited another gurgle from Lenora who, with heightened color, withdrew the offending book from its hiding place and laid it on the end table, pausing only to kiss her mother's cheek before bounding out of the room to plunder the depths of various trunks in the attic.

Depositing her hat and gloves in her own room, and putting off her soiled dress for a fresh one, Mrs. Breckinridge descended the stairs in time to see her son, Mr. Thomas Breckinridge, lay his hat and gloves on the table in the hall.

Hurrying forward to assist in divesting him of his driving coat, she asked, "Why does Matthew not help you? I thought him with you."

"He's taking care of the horses, Mama, which he can do much

more creditably than this sort of thing." He grimaced as he straightened his coat. "I never missed Budley so much."

"Nor I, dear." She hung his caped coat in the hall beside her own. "But I am persuaded he is happier where he is now, no doubt managing St. Matthew's staff with an iron hand and maintaining awful order among his supplicants. How does the farm?"

His look darkened. "We've hardly anything to put by, Mama, even for ourselves! Curse the wretched weather! Who knew it could rain so much? As if we lived in a downpour, and it carried half our soil down the canals."

"Well, it is no more than I expected," his mother said with a sigh. "But we shall contrive! We always do."

The grimace softened, and Tom drew his mother's arm through his, leading her toward the sitting room. "Though the farm has not done well this year, I have high hopes that the breeding season will be successful, and if that is the case, Mama, I trust that we shall be able to hire not only a new butler, but a housekeeper as well, and perhaps even a maid for Lenora."

"Oh, Tom, after this setback you mustn't worry about that. We do very well with Cook and Sanford."

"That's flim-flam, Mama, and you know it!" he retorted amiably, holding the sitting room door open for her. "Just because Sanford and Sally would go to the ends of the earth for you, and do it every day, doesn't mean you do anything very well!"

"You injure me, Tom!"

"That's enough of your flummery, Mama! You'd work yourself to the bone before you'd admit to discontent, and our loyal retainers may any day determine that working below their station is not, after all, desirable to a higher wage elsewhere," he said. "I'd liefer obviate that eventuality, if I may, ma'am."

She turned fond eyes upon her son, and pressed his arm. "You take such care of us, Tom. Of course, I'd prefer to hire a housekeeper and maid, but surely there are other expenses that take priority."

"No, Mama, there are not." He bowed her onto the sofa. "Even with the loss of income from the farm this year, your excellent son has eliminated all other pressing needs, and now looks forward only to regaining the comforts of our position."

She watched him thoughtfully as he went to the sideboard to pour himself a brandy. "Every day, I cannot believe my good fortune that you are so unlike your papa."

He glanced keenly back at her. "I should hope I am not, Mama."

"You are the very image of him, you know. All your growing-up years, I waited in terror for his vices to manifest themselves in you, because of that likeness. But you have proven me to be a great ninnyhammer, and I can be nothing but proud of you, Tom."

He smiled rather pensively as he sat in the winged chair by the fire. "I confront his face daily in the mirror—a most effective deterrent to any temptation, I must say."

"I have long ceased to anticipate excess in you, Tom, but now I fear you are in danger of falling too much to the other extreme. You spend so much time at business, and you are not yet even of age."

"Oh, Mama, never fear," he said with a mischievous glance. "You know I am not above a quiet card game, or a good ride to hounds, or standing up with a pretty girl at the assembly. And the investment of my time at business is beginning to pay off, with the promise of more time to spend at leisure when I do come of age."

"Perhaps you should consider going up to Oxford after all, Tom," suggested his mother. "All your friends are there."

"I can't deny I've thought of it," he said, then leaned forward eagerly, grasping his glass between his hands. "But nothing equals the enjoyment of turning this land to account, Mama! Causing soil that has lain fallow for so many years to yield plenty, and watching our debts disappear as our stability grows—it's beyond anything great! Even with this horrid summer that was more like winter, I'm more determined than ever to persevere. I must sound like the greatest bumpkin alive, but I wouldn't change my position for the world. I love country life! I own I never thought I'd settle to it as I have."

His mother's eyes twinkled. "There is the proof that you are not, and never will be, like your papa. He could not abide the country. He stayed only when he could no longer afford a house in town, and could not rid himself of the land, for the entailment. Little did he know his constraints would be your legacy."

"The only legacy I should have accepted from him." Tom turned to smile ruefully at his mother. "I never thought to be grateful to Papa, for neglecting to mortgage this cottage, so we could rent the manor, and save such expense."

"We must all be grateful." She dropped her eyes, unhappily aware of the truth that the only good Bertram Breckinridge had done for his family was to die before he had sold or mortgaged every brick and stone to his name.

Tom sat brooding, and his mother perceived in the following silence that the mood must be lightened if she wished to broach the subject of London. "If you do not wish for a change, I do, my love. I wonder if we could bear the expense of a holiday."

"You wish for a holiday, Mama?" asked Tom, a note of anxiety in his voice. "It would be the very thing! It's a shame we can't afford much at present, but you could—you could take Lenora to Bath, I suppose."

"But what of you?" she asked, smiling at his ready willingness to humor her. "For all you say of enjoyment, you work very hard. But the farm will be quiet during the winter, and you needn't stay. We may go somewhere as a family."

"But I am perfectly happy at work, Mama! And my accompanying you should only add to the expense. I have more than enough to occupy me at home." He caught the skepticism in her gaze and said on a laugh, "What must I do to convince you? I'd as lief stay here and tend to the estate than traipse around the country on muddy roads, staying in second-rate inns."

She raised an eyebrow, blinking imperiously at him. "If that is the extent of the holiday Lenora and I are to have the pleasure of anticipating, then you'd best not consider it at all."

"Mama!" he cried, throwing up a hand. "It is only the truth! But if you cavil at it, then I can promise you a lovely holiday, perhaps to Brighton, in the spring, when travel is easy and accommodation moderately priced."

She laughed, a musical ripple of sound. "Here is Bertram Breckinridge's son, preaching patience and economy! What a glorious irony!"

His lips twisted in a smirk, but his eyes danced as delightedly as his mother's. "Well, I intend that you will have your housekeeper, and will make what shifts I must to do so."

"I know it, dearest Tom," she said, reaching a hand impulsively toward him. "Forgive me for twitting you. But I think we may contrive a holiday of sorts this winter after all, and with very little expense." At his interested look, she gathered her courage and threw herself into the close. "My dear, I've had excellent news from my school friend, Lady Cammerby. She—" She faltered as his countenance became wary, but determinedly pursued. "She has ever so kindly offered to present Lenora this season."

"Mama!" cried Thomas, setting his glass down in dismay. "You didn't ask her—you couldn't!"

"Well, I did, for you have borne the burden of this family alone for long enough, and it is not uncommon for able friends or relations to give this kind of assistance. It was the only way I could think of to help."

"It does nothing to help me, Mama! It mortifies me!"

"Oh, Tom, you must be reasonable—"

"Mama, I've done my utmost to bring this family about, and you must needs go like a beggar to your rich friend, and have it out that we're still all to pieces!"

"But we still are all to pieces, my love."

"Not for long! The weather this year was the strangest we've ever seen, and set us back, but it must be better next year. We are so close—we will come about!" He pushed out of his chair. "I can conceive of no reason why some rich old tabby I've never met must bring out my sister, like she's some dashed charity child, when I can manage it well enough in a year or two!"

"But Tom, your sister is already eighteen, and a year or two—"

"Will hopefully bring her more commonsense and countenance!" he cried, throwing over his shoulder, "She's a feather-headed pea goose and you know it, Mama."

"Oh, she can be silly, and she reads far too many novels, but I shouldn't call her a pea-goose."

He stalked toward the fireplace, biting out, "She would be better-served if we waited until she is older."

Mrs. Breckinridge watched her son pace stormily about the room. "Oh, dear. I've made a muddle of it, haven't I?" He did not respond to this rhetorical question, and she sighed. "Of course, you must be right, dear, that Lenora is too young. I suppose I felt she was not, because she is two years older than I when I married your papa, but we know how well that turned out."

Tom stopped his pacing abruptly, turning to gaze in consternation at his mama.

She tipped her head in acknowledgement. "Lenora is rather foolish, but she is also a very good girl, and I have begun to question whether keeping her home to fill her head with gothic romance and tragic fantasies is truly wiser than bringing her out into the real world. Our society in the country is so limited that I cannot but be convinced that a wider range of flesh and blood gentlemen, with the accompanying lessons of town life, would turn her head in a more proper direction."

"Your head was turned in your season, Mama, but not for the best," Tom said quietly.

"To be sure," she answered, without rancor, "but I was much stronger-willed than Lenora, with the encouragement of a guardian who cared little what sort of man I married, as long as the dibs were in tune."

He lowered his eyes, but said only, "You sound like Papa."

"Yes, I know," she sighed. "I've expunged so much of the heartache, but the habits still remain. It seems no matter how I try, little bits of him refuse to disappear." She glanced ruefully up at him. "I suppose it is my reminder, every day, just like your mirror."

With a sigh, Tom came to sit with her on the sofa, taking her hand in both of his own. "Dear Mama, forgive me. I know you love us dearly. You are anxious to provide for Nora, and you are persuaded that marrying her off will relieve me of a great burden, but I should never forgive myself if she were to end unhappy—" Here he paused, as if searching for words to express himself. "If she should be hurt, simply because I could not afford to protect her."

His mother brought his hand to her cheek. "My dear son, nor could I, and it horrifies me that you think I mean to give her to the first man who will have her. Marriage from this season is not even in my mind. I wish only to give her the experience, and the care, that was denied me."

"But it mortifies me to not be allowed my right to provide the experience."

"Oh, Tom, you will be allowed! Young girls hardly ever have just one season. In giving Lenora a season this year, she realizes the wish of her heart, and there is nothing to keep you from giving her a second season, which would be in earnest. This season, she will be brought up to snuff, acquire a little town-bronze, and perhaps even lose her taste for those horrid novels!"

He shook his head, but smiled. "You are, as ever, wise, Mama, and I anticipate your prognostications will be fulfilled. But I suspect even greater depths to your reasoning." He gazed knowingly at her. "Elvira Chuddsley comes out this season as well, does she not?"

A dimple peeped in Mrs. Breckinridge's cheek. "She does, and you know life would be unendurable if Lenora were forced to wait after Elvira."

"Very well." He kissed her cheek. "My pride is checked, and you may have your season in peace. I may even come up for a week or two and squire you to the assemblies."

"But I depended upon your coming with us!"

"My dear Mama, the farm will not wait for an entire season! And I shall only be in the way," he insisted, patting her hand. "A week or two will be enough holiday for me, and will satisfy me of your comfort."

Seeing the wisdom in accepting this generous compromise, she threw her arms around him. "Oh, Tom, you are the best of brothers and sons!"

Chapter 3

LENORA BRECKINRIDGE FLUTTERED into Miss Elvira Chuddsley's bedchamber, her countenance aglow. Her hostess, following in her wake in a state of almost painful anticipation, pressed the door closed behind her.

"Well?" Elvira demanded of her rapt visitor, who was presently engaged in the singularly needless—not to say frivolous—task of loosening the ribbons of her hat. Receiving no response, she stamped her pretty foot. "Lenora, if you do not instantly tell me what has sent you into transports, I vow I shall choke you!"

The offending maiden turned wide eyes upon her. "I declare I know not how to begin!"

"Then you must try, Lenora Breckinridge!"

Lenora gave a delicious chuckle and cast her hat onto the bed. "Elvira, I am the happiest person alive!"

Perceiving from her guest's faraway look and rapturous sighs that more information was not immediately forthcoming, Elvira expostulated, "And I am the most mystified, for I am persuaded I shall never know the reason for your sudden elevation of spirits!"

"Oh, Elvira, you goose!" relented Lenora. "Pray, forgive me, and content yourself that you shall presently know the whole! My mama received a letter today. She has a dear friend, Lady Cammerby, whom she knew at school, oh, ages ago, in Bath. You know she attended a select seminary there, of course—"

"Lenora! What do I care for select seminaries?"

"Oh! Well, Mama had written on my behalf to this excellent female—for her husband is quite rich, you know, and has a large house in Berkshire, I believe—"

"I wish he lived at Jericho, so you had nothing to say of him and could get to the substance of the letter!"

Lenora giggled. "Oh, Elvira, the cream of it is that Lady Cammerby lives in the first style of elegance in London—" Elvira gasped, pressing her hands to her mouth and staring round-eyed at her friend as the truth began to dawn. Lenora continued, "And she has answered my mother's letter today, and says that she always wanted a daughter to present, and—and to be plain, I am to come out this season after all!"

"She will sponsor you?" asked Elvira breathlessly.

Lenora, speechless with joy, nodded, and her friend squealed, running forward to clasp her to her bosom. "My dear," cried Elvira, "we shall have the grandest adventure! The beaux we shall have, the balls we shall attend, the gowns we—" Elvira abruptly stopped as a distressing thought occurred to her. "But dear, what shall you do for—how will you—the expense—"

Lenora pressed her hands reassuringly. "My mother has a dozen lovely gowns from her London season—"

"What!" exclaimed Elvira. "You'll never wear those fusty things!"

"But they're perfectly good, for they've been stored up in camphor all these years—"

"Exactly! For a hundred, million years!"

Her friend giggled. "Stupid! What a quiz I would look! Of course, I shall not wear them as they are! We shall make them over. To think I should wear gowns from the last century!"

"Oh!" Elvira pressed a hand to her thankful bosom. "I had such horrid visions of you!"

"Frightening away all your beaux, no doubt!"

"I simply should not have acknowledged you," said Elvira, her nose in the air. "Of course, I was a goose to suppose that you would be so nonsensical as to ruin your one chance to cut a dash."

"Yes, you were! Even if I am buried out here in the country, I have at least enough sense to know what is dowdy and what is all the crack."

"Well, you would not, if I did not share my periodicals with you!" rejoined Elvira tartly.

"You know very well that I should be nothing without you, dearest," Lenora said in a coaxing tone, and taking her friend's arm. "It is precisely for that reason I've come to see you. For, when it comes to making up the gowns, you know, between Mama and me, with a little assistance from Sanford, we shall do very well with the hand-sewing, but may I borrow your fashion plates, for the patterns? Mama said I might, if I returned your novel." She pulled the book from the pocket of her pelisse and handed it, somewhat wistfully, to her friend.

Elvira's annoyance was not proof against such a sacrifice. "But Lenora! You can't have finished it! I only gave it you yesterday!"

"No," admitted Lenora, gazing longingly at the book. "I had just reached the unveiling of Father Caraggio, and Stephania had fallen into a swoon, when my mother interrupted me."

With great resolution, Elvira gave the book back into her friend's hands. "Then you must keep it, if your mother will allow it, for I could not bear for you to be denied the satisfaction of such an ending as it has!"

"Oh, Elvira!" cried Lenora, pressing the book to her heart. "I had despaired of ever discovering the identity of the prisoner in the oubliette, and I declare I should have died for the suspense!"

"None of my friends shall despair at my hands," declared Elvira, then waved the book away impatiently. "Enough of Caraggio and Stephania! We have more pressing matters!"

The all-absorbing story was tossed onto the bed as Elvira towed Lenora into her dressing room, where a pile of periodicals lay tucked into a corner. Elvira sifted through them, muttering to herself. "Those are nearly a twelvemonth old! If only Mama would allow me to bind them—" She sneezed. "I must remind Mary to dust here... But where are the—oh, here. They've slipped behind." Emerging triumphant from the corner, Elvira spread the latest issues of The Ladies' Monthly Museum on the floor.

Lenora pounced on them, flipping through to the illustrated descriptions of ladies' fashions. "Peach silk under white sarcenet, and split sleeves, how interesting. That would do well with cornflower blue I think, do not you? What a quantity of beading, and look at all the rosettes!" She set the periodical to the side and flipped open another. "Oh, Elvira, isn't this stunning! Peacock plumes! And Chantilly lace? Oh, how shockingly expensive it would be!"

"Yes, and you'll never wear it, in your first season, goose! What a show you would make, and have only the rakes admiring your brazenness."

"To have a rake admire one!" Lenora shivered deliciously. "Oh, but how romantic if he were to seduce me!"

"Lenora!" cried Elvira, staring wide-eyed at her. "What a wicked thing to say!"

Lenora shrugged a heedless shoulder. "I daresay there are several rakes among the ton, for my papa knew ever so many, and they were used to move in the first circles! So even if Lady Cammerby is not acquainted with any, we are sure to meet some!"

Elvira pressed a hand to her mouth as Lenora mused on. "I'm sure they are, in general, very handsome, for rakes always are, and charming, too. And I am sure to attract their attention, for a rake loves nothing better than a penniless girl, without a father to protect her."

Elvira blinked in bewilderment. "But they always try for heiresses, Lenora! It's in all the books!"

"Oh, only for marriage, my dear," Lenora remarked carelessly. "A rake loves to dally with girls for whom he cherishes no honorable intentions."

Elvira gasped, her eyes alight with terrified excitement. "Oh, it is true, Lenora!"

"And I, being innocent, will suspect nothing when he makes me an object of his gallantry, for rakes, you know, are subtle, else they should have no success among genteel females."

Her friend nodded solemnly, leaning breathlessly forward to catch every word that fell from her friend's lips.

Lenora continued blithely, "But when he presses his ardor far enough, and I am forced to give him a rebuff—for my heart would never respond to such impropriety as he would show, and would detect him as soon as he pressed for my favor—he is thrown into a towering rage and resolves then and there to have me or die!"

"Oh, no!" cried Elvira, her eyes round.

"He must be an evil Duke, of course," pursued Lenora, "and will, as a matter of course, carry me to his castle tower, where he vows to keep me until I allow him to steal my virtue!"

"But you have an admirer, a poor and handsome gentleman—with a stammer" supplied Elvira, entering into the spirit of the story, "whom you have held dear, but for whom you have never known your true feelings. He follows after you and, bravely enduring hardship and suffering untold, he reaches the castle and climbs the ivy vines to the tower window, rescuing you from the evil Duke's clutches at his own peril!"

"And when he has vanquished the Duke, he kneels at my feet," said Lenora in tragic tones, "and with his pitiful stammer, claims undying love for me, revealing that he has always loved me from afar, but his impediment and his poverty have kept him from a declaration!"

Elvira's eyes fluttered sympathetically closed. "But you cannot be wed, for you are both too poor, and you part in great sorrow." Then her eyes flew open again, dazzled with hope. "But when it is discovered that he is the long-lost heir to a vast fortune, he returns to throw himself at your feet!"

Lenora threw out a staying hand. "But he finds me in a decline, for love of him, and all despair of my recovery. But not he! Tenderly nursing me, he is rewarded with my return to health, and though I am fragile ever after, we are wed in a gothic cathedral, as my hero stammers out his vows of everlasting fidelity!"

"Oh!" cried both girls together, falling to the floor in rapture.

After Lenora had recovered herself sufficiently to rise, she propped her chin on her elbows and regarded her friend. "I don't suppose any Dukes shall seduce me, Elvira, Chantilly lace or no, for my mama has such stuffy notions of propriety that I am persuaded she would never countenance such a thing."

"Well," admitted Elvira, if reluctantly, "I should think she would not."

"But if you had known how she was when she was just out, dear, you would not think it!" Lenora leaned close to her friend, lowering her voice. "My mama was the most shocking flirt, and had so many beaux on a string that all the other girls positively hated her!"

"No!"

Lenora nodded with authority. "Yes. And when she discovered that my papa was the most sought-after bachelor in London, she instantly set her cap at him, and let nothing stand in her way, until she caught him."

"But she could not have known—at first—what he was like—" Elvira hardly dared to say what she knew to be scandalous history.

Lenora waved away her friend's concern. "Oh, no, not precisely. But she told me once that she knew very well he was dangerous, and pursued him nonetheless."

Elvira gasped, her eyes wide.

"So, I cannot comprehend why she should be so against my meeting a rake, or any dangerous gentleman, if she went so far as to marry one!"

"But—Lenora, you know he was—you know they were not—" Again Elvira hesitated. "She only wants you to be happy, Lenora."

Lenora pursed her lips, wishing she could deny the assertion but, being a truthful girl, knew she could not. She sighed. "It is too lowering. Why must dangerous men be so exciting, if they are to be inaccessible?" Elvira put a sympathetic hand on her friend's arm, but Lenora only shrugged dispiritedly. "I oughtn't to repine, for I shan't attract such a man at any rate, for I lack both fortune and beauty."

"You do not, Lenora!" Elvira cried, putting an arm around her friend. "The fashion is for dark hair and eyes, which you have, and put my fair ones to shame, and your figure is—"

"Gangly?"

"It is elegant," stated her friend positively, "and your eyes are very—very speaking! Any Duke would be a fool not to wish to seduce you!"

Lenora cast a grateful, if tolerant, glance at her friend. "And you, Elvira," she said, handsomely including Elvira in her felicity. "You must take great care, for you possess both beauty and fortune, which combination is the strongest attractant to an evil Duke."

"Oh, my!" sighed Elvira, momentarily dazed by her prosperity. But before being carried away, she chanced to catch Lenora's eye, and they both were sent into cascades of giggles.

Returning to her perusal of the fashion plates, Lenora gave another sigh. "Oh, Elvira! Though I know very well we have not the least chance of it, I still fancy it would be romantic, do you not, to be seduced, or at the very least abducted?"

In answer, Elvira shivered. "Oh, that London were like the Italian countryside, and full of mysterious monks and evil Dukes who reside in sinister castles with oubliettes and hidden passages!"

"You must not forget penniless, stammering heroes, dearest," added Lenora. "They are indispensable."

"They are, but it makes no odds. Our mamas would never bring us to such a place. No," she said mournfully, "we go to reside in bright and spacious townhomes, and meet with upright gentlemen of honest fortune."

"How insupportably flat!" cried Lenora, a twinkle in her eye, but after a glance at her friend, whose imagination had become so entirely absorbed by this depressing scene that she was drooping apace, Lenora hastened to ask, "However shall we endure the balls, and theaters and parties? We shall be forever fatigued, for there must needs be shopping as well. Oh, the endless tedium!" Eyeing her friend askance, she suggested, "Perhaps we ought to stay home."

Elvira instantly turned an outraged stare on her. "And miss perhaps your one chance at a London season? You ninny! Of course we shall go, and take the town by storm! And we shall wring delight from every moment!"

"And if we are fortunate," Lenora put in, "we shall meet with an unprincipled rake at a private ball, or in the gardens after a concert."

"And he shall prove to be an evil Duke after all."

"And one of the courteous gentlemen will prove to be quite heroic, despite his having been born hosed and shod, and come to the rescue." They giggled together at that, and then bent eagerly once more over the fashion plates.

Chapter 4

SIR JOSHUA STILES accepted a glass of Madeira from Lady Cammerby, leaning his shoulder against the mantelpiece. "No, the lady was not at home, nor, I may add, was the footman, or the butler, or even the housekeeper. The awed kitchen maid, or cook, or some such, at last served me, when I had found her round the back, knee deep in the garden." He sipped his wine, turning grave eyes upon his sister. "What kind of scrape have you gotten yourself into, Amelia?"

Lady Cammerby furrowed her brow. "Whatever do servants have to do with it, Joshua? I have merely offered to present my good friend's daughter to society, which I shall vastly enjoy, having no daughters of my own, and with Cammerby gone next month to the Continent for Heaven knows how long, I presumed you would be glad of my having company."

"Good company is what I'd be glad to know you shall have. What I'd like to know, sister, is why the chit's family doesn't present her. No matter how enjoyable it may be for you, it'll be a deal of trouble and expense."

His sister looked surprised. "Only a few hundred pounds, Joshua! You know Cammerby is well able to afford it and, what's more, he's given his consent. I don't know how you should have anything to say, for it's none of your business at all." She eyed her brother darkly. "If there's anything I abominate, it's wealth that is hoarded. I have a conscience if you do not, Joshua! There is nothing better than to use one's money for good, and I'd do anything for Genevieve, poor woman."

He humphed. "Poor is exactly what I suspected. You say she knows you well?" At her affirmative, he took a ruminative sip of his wine. "As I thought. She sounds like a spunger to me. With all your high-flown expressions of good will, are you certain you wish to be so intimately aligned with such a woman?"

"Genevieve Breckinridge is no spunger!" cried his sister, bridling in defense of her friend. "She is the most delightful creature, and always has been, though she was a bit high-spirited when she was young, but I never knew her to be unprincipled! It was her detestable husband who is entirely to blame for her present circumstances. He gamed away all his money, and then hers, and left her unpardonably situated. Oh, how we all were deceived in that man. It makes me livid just to think about him, taking such a jewel and reducing her to ruin."

Sir Joshua settled into a chair, placing his empty glass on the table at his elbow. "Almost you convince me of the lady's quality, seeing that she was willing to marry such a man."

"How odious you are! She's a Wainsley, so you know as well as I she comes from the best stock, for all her father was a gamester and a gaddabout, and forever in his cups! You may take it from me his daughter never inherited any of that!"

"You relieve me excessively."

"And I told you Bertram Breckinridge had us all fooled," she pursued, not conciliated by his dry response. "I had an eye to him myself, if you must know, and if Genevieve hadn't outshone the rest of us, I may be the one in her shoes even now."

"That you would not," said Sir Joshua, "for he'd have had to convince me, Amelia, and I would not have been taken in like a gudgeon. I expect her wastrel of a father had no reservations about the match?"

Lady Cammerby's mouth became prim. "Settlements were all that hateful Lord Kimmeridge cared for. Yes, he was well enough pleased with the match, you may be sure, for Breckinridge had a fortune, you know, and the offer for Genevieve came at a most opportune time for his lordship. Of course, I never knew at the time how things were, but since then I have learned a thing or two about That Man, things that would make your flesh crawl—but I am not one to gossip," she ended virtuously.

"So, the angel married a devil," her brother observed, "and now offers her child up from the ashes. Forgive me, Amelia, but I've witnessed better tragedies in Cheltenham."

"What a horrid mood you are in, Joshua! You put me out of all patience!" said Lady Cammerby, eyeing her brother with distaste.

His mouth twisted in a rueful smile. "You're right, Amelia, I am in a horrid mood. I have had my fill of designing females, and have no wish to be forced into acquaintance with yet another."

This enlightenment interested, but did not engender much sympathy in his sister. "Is that Orping woman still thrusting her spotted daughter at you? Poor Joshua."

"On the contrary, my dear, it is precisely because I am not poor that she thrusts her daughter at me. As do Mrs. Weller and Lady

Castleton—though," he said fair-mindedly, "neither of their off-spring has spots."

"I trust you do not mean to offer for any of them, for I should be most averse to be connected with such brass-faced girls," she sniffed. "But one could not expect any different, with such parents as theirs."

"And yet, you associate with a woman whose parentage is equally poor," reflected her brother, with maddening acuity, "and whose daughter may very well prove to be as ramshackle as her father."

"If you cannot be civil, I would you should go away," Lady Cammerby muttered in considerable annoyance. "Every family has their dirty laundry, Joshua! Heaven knows we have our own! But the stains do not always filter through the generations, and I am confident that Genevieve's daughter is unspoiled." Her brother only gazed cynically at her, and she adjusted her seat uncomfortably. "But we were speaking of your prospects."

"I have no prospects."

"But you have any number of prospects!"

"Pardon me. I had mistaken you to mean appealing prospects."

"Joshua! Come, now, be serious! What of Miss Pickering? Or Miss Whiteshead—she's quite a beauty, despite her chin! Or—or Miss Tipton, who is more mature, to be sure, but still very eligible!" He only shrugged his shoulders, and his sister sighed in exasperation. "Surely there is a lady who appeals to you?"

"Several have appealed to my fortune, but never to me."

Goaded, Lady Cammerby said acidly, "I expect you are too nice in your requirements. You must take some responsibility, you know, and at least try to present yourself as agreeable. Such a sneer as you are always wearing! At your age, you must realize that your fortune may be the only attraction you have left." He lowered his eyes in apparent dismay, and she was at once remorseful. "Really, Joshua, you must try at some lightness, if you wish to attract the right kind of female."

He snorted derisively. "I fear my fortune quite overshadows any other desirable qualities I might possess."

"You know full well you are quite good-looking," she returned, "but you cannot expect a lady to be inconsiderate of fortune, no matter her age. Every woman wishes to be comfortably settled, but it does not follow that they all must be mercenary."

"Yes, it does, and they are." He stood and refreshed his glass from the decanter, gesturing with it to his sister. "Not even my advanced years seem to deter them. Perhaps I should put it about that I've lost my fortune on 'Change."

"But it would ruin you, Joshua! Please be serious. Think of your reputation!"

"I do, my dear," he said casually, though his countenance was grim. "At present I am known only as a matrimonial prize."

Lady Cammerby's demeanor softened as she regarded him. "It is not wonderful that you are cynical, Joshua. I truly pity your circumstance, for I know how lonely you are." Her brother glanced quickly at her, but said nothing. "Would that I could find you another Rachel."

"That I forbid you to attempt, Amelia. She could not be matched, nor do I wish her to be." He bent and pressed his sister's hand. "I have no wish to eclipse her memory, my dear."

She sat in stunned silence at this revelation. "But, Joshua, you have put yourself about these three years, as if you wished—"

"I do wish—at least, I thought I did." He looked ruefully at her. "I had thought to add to her memory, if I could." He glanced down. "Since I put off mourning for Rachel, I feel an emptiness. I should like to find a woman to fill that emptiness, if she exists." He shook his head, emerging quickly from his reverie. "But I have little faith left in the notion, for every woman who has been forced into my acquaintance has proven insipid, calculating, or ridiculous." He nodded at her. "As I shall no doubt find your friend, and her daughter."

Lady Cammerby huffed. "Genevieve Breckinridge is nothing of the sort, and you do her a great injustice even to think it. You would be justly served if you fell in love with her."

"She must be nearing forty." He tsked. "Wouldn't fadge, Amelia. The quizzes will inform you that I am hanging out for a young wife." He bent and kissed her cheek. "I wash my hands of the business, but wish you joy of drawing the bustle with your new protegee." He turned back at the door. "And Amelia, inform Cammerby the next time he engages to give me directions, I shall box his ears."

Chapter 5

THE BRECKINRIDGES' JOURNEY to Hill Street the following February was accompanied by quite as much adventure as any young lady of sensibility could desire, if not a trifle more. Lenora, having ascertained from the groom the unlikelihood of a brush with highwaymen on their journey—as neither Hounslow Heath nor even Finchley Common lay along their way—resigned herself to an uneventful drive, and settled bravely against the squabs of the post chaise to stare the next four hours at the scenery. But the unanticipated circumstance of a broken trace—which necessitated a stop at an out-of-the-way hostelry just outside Watford—awakened hope in her breast, and she stepped eagerly down from the carriage into the humble yard, to await events. These rapidly transpired in the guise of two rival farmers, who had converged upon the inn to brangle over the merits of a prize pig, the countenance of which was claimed by the owner to be uncommonly similar to that of the Prince Regent.

The ladies, obliged to wait in the coffee room—the inn boasting only two guest rooms and no private parlor—were witness to the subsequent scene, wherein the first farmer, having been unsuccessful in proving the superiority of his animal by mere posturing, had the happy notion to introduce the pig to the inhabitants of the coffee room, to illustrate his point. The burly proprietor, who had been sedately polishing the bar for the entirety of this interaction, grunted, which was enough encouragement for the owner of the pig. But no sooner had the animal been fetched and shepherded into the room than the proprietress entered, bearing a tray of freshly baked cheesecakes, which she surrendered into the air with an unholy shriek at the sight of a large, smelly animal in her house. The pig, taking immediate exception to such goings-on, hastily made use of the most evident retreat, which happened to be the passage into the kitchen.

The empty tray was shoved into Lenora's hands as the outraged proprietress surged after the fugitive, closely followed by the pig's owner, and to the high delight of his rival. This gentleman, startling the ladies with a deafening guffaw, joyfully begged pardon with a pull at his hat brim and, slipping thumbs behind his braces, sauntered out the door to succumb properly to his mirth in the stable yard.

Lenora, regarding first the door, then the empty tray in her hands, uttered, "What a waste of perfectly good cheesecakes!" But as she looked to her mother, whose handkerchief was pressed desperately against her mouth, the distress in that lady's countenance undermined her own composure, and they both went into most unladylike whoops under the disapproving eye of the proprietor, who continued stolidly to polish the bar. The proprietress entering at that most inauspicious moment, the ladies were forced to endure with humility her muttered aspersions on they that profess to Quality, and were at last rescued by the timely summons of their post boy, with the news that the trace had been repaired, and they could be on their way.

Settling rather regretfully back into the chaise, Mrs. and Miss Breckinridge spent a delightful hour reviewing their adventure, and had no sooner worn the subject out than, just short of London, the coach lurched unceremoniously to the side, and the ladies were thrown against one another.

"Good gracious!" cried Mrs. Breckinridge, righting herself and her hat. "Lenora, love, are you alright?"

"Perfectly, Mama, I believe," she said, blinking as she pushed herself away from the side of the coach. "But what can have happened?"

Mrs. Breckinridge craned her neck to peer past her daughter out the window, remarking, "I'd not be surprised at footpads, my dear."

Lenora, gleefully letting down the window, put her head out, but saw, with no little disappointment, merely the post boy regarding with disgust a splintered back wheel. But, as experience had taught her to hope, she took this turn of events philosophically, and again stepped down from the carriage and to the side of the road while the post boys discussed what was best to be done. The ladies were presently informed that they must wait while one of the boys rode a leader into the next town to arrange repair and to fetch back a vehicle to convey them to comfort while this took place.

The sound of hoofbeats roused them all to look around and, to Lenora's absolute enchantment, a smart curricle, pulled by a gorgeous pair of greys and driven by a dashing gentleman in a many-caped driving coat, rounded the bend and slowed to a stop beside their carriage.

"You seem to be in some distress, ma'am," the gentleman said to Mrs. Breckinridge, gracefully sweeping off his tall beaver. "May I be of service to you?"

As Lenora stood transfixed with rapture at their good fortune, Mrs. Breckinridge explained their predicament to the gentleman, who smilingly offered to take them up in his curricle. "For it is only a few miles to Kilburn, where you may await repairs."

This offer being gratefully accepted, the ladies squeezed their slim persons into the curricle, wherein they whiled away the next half-hour by regaling their rescuer with the tale of the pig at the inn. Mr. Ginsham, as he introduced himself, set them down at a small but respectable-looking hostelry in Kilburn, crowning Lenora's delight by requesting the honor of calling upon them in London. She then felt her happiness was complete, and could conceive of nothing more to ask for the whole of the season.

But her adventure was not yet over. Their coach, arriving in Hill Street four hours later than expected, had just drawn up, and Lenora just alighted, when a link boy sauntered down the pavement, followed closely by a gentleman in a startling waistcoat and innumerable fobs and seals. As the boy was passing the horses' heads, his hire let out an exclamation which caused the boy to turn quickly, flashing his torch too close to the near animal's head. The horse reared and started forward, jerking free the halter, and the postilion at his head, who had been distracted by the rather fantastic dress of the gentleman, fell off balance and to the curb as the horses and the chaise bowled forward. Mrs. Breckinridge, still on the step of the coach, was flung to the side, but as she had a hold on the strap inside the door, she did not fall, but swung alarmingly outside the chaise as it jolted up the street, the link boy and his hire gaping and Lenora, terrified, watching helplessly from the base of the townhouse steps.

The chaise had thankfully not time to attain much speed, for another gentleman, walking down the pavement away from them, turned back at the commotion, and instantly jumped to seize the collar of the offending horse as it drew alongside. He threw his weight forward, aided by the nearest post boy, who had gotten his wits and also leapt after the coach, until the horses slowed to a halt. Leaving the handling of the animals to the post boys, the gentleman lost no time in rendering assistance to the dangling lady.

"Are you hurt, ma'am?" he asked as he set her, trembling but upright, on solid ground.

Mrs. Breckinridge, gripping the lapels of his coat, took several seconds to reply, her face hidden to him by her bonnet as she tried to steady her breathing. "I—I don't believe so, sir. I am only—a bit rattled, I think."

He waited until her grip loosened, then drew away from her, watching to be sure she could stand, but when she lifted her face to utter, "Thank you, sir," he stared in as much surprise as did she.

At that moment, a shriek echoed from the door of Lady Cammerby's house. "Joshua! Oh, you have saved her! Good gracious, Genevieve! What a blessing of providence!"

Sir Joshua's eyes narrowed at the lady before him. "Mrs.—Mrs. Breckinridge?"

Her eyes fluttered closed, her pale cheeks flushing. "Ah, Fates! My mortification may not end in anonymity." She drew a deep breath and looked again at her savior. "You have the advantage of me, sir. Though I believe I may assume you to be Amelia's brother."

"I am Sir Joshua Stiles," he said coolly, his civility once more falling prey to darkling suspicions.

Lady Cammerby, meanwhile, had sailed down the steps and nearly collided with the other post boy, upon whom Lenora, having observed in rapidly reversing emotions her mother's peril and rescue, could do nothing more proper than to fall in a swoon.

Mrs. Breckinridge, perceiving this circumstance in dismay,

accepted Sir Joshua's assistance to walk, and in reaching her daughter, she bent to pat the girl's cheek, gently at first, then more sharply. "Lenora! No need for theatrics, my love!"

Having fainted more out of propriety than necessity, Lenora's swoon was not deep, and her eye lids flicked open. "Mama! That hurt!"

Collecting with some disappointment that Miss wasn't dead, the postilion heaved Lenora up to her feet and Mrs. Breckinridge put an arm firmly about her waist, turning to regard her hostess and her rescuer, who had stepped away from the group and stood viewing the proceedings through hooded eyes, his countenance disapproving.

"Good evening, Amelia!" Genevieve said in a bracing tone. "What an exciting entrance we've achieved! And Sir Joshua, I must sincerely thank you again."

He bowed slightly to her, but Lady Cammerby forestalled anything he may have said by pushing forward to clasp her friend to her bosom. "Oh, Genevieve, my heart was in my throat! I am still all of a tremor, and can hardly speak! Cottam had only just informed me of your arrival, and no sooner had I come to the front window than the horses bolted, and I daresay I should have fainted dead away had Joshua not caught them! To think that he had just started out to his club after dinner here!"

"A lucky chance indeed," said Sir Joshua, smiling cynically. "Your obedient servant, Mrs. Breckinridge."

The lady blushed, but her eyes danced. "Yes, it seems that you are destined to be so, Sir Joshua." He raised an eyebrow and she took his meaning, quickly making her face as grave as his. "We must put a stop to it."

He blinked rather quellingly at her, and transferred his somber gaze to Lenora, who had been gazing at him in bemusement during this entire exchange. "Are you quite well, Miss Breckinridge?"

Lenora started. "Oh! Oh, yes, thank you, sir! Perfectly, sir!" She curtseyed to him, smiling brilliantly. "We are indebted to you, sir!"

Sir Joshua, regarding her somewhat doubtfully, gave an infinitesimal bow that included all the ladies. "I shall detain you no longer, then. Good evening."

"But, Joshua, they have just arrived, and you have been waiting to meet them!" cried his sister.

He bowed again, fixing his hat firmly on his head. "And we have met, Amelia. But I have an engagement which has already awaited me these two hours, and which I am unwilling to put off longer."

Lady Cammerby could only regard his retreating figure with consternation, but firmly dismissed his incivility from her mind in favor of shepherding her guests into the house, calling orders to her servants between exclamations of dismay.

"I daresay you are completely overset! Cottam, tea at once for our guests in the Blue Saloon. Four hours late! I cower to think what trials kept you on the road, and then such a calamity! Gerald, take the trunks up to their rooms. Come this way, my dears, upstairs. Such a near thing with that horrid link boy!"

She maintained this tirade as she saw her guests installed in the saloon, with the tea things set before them, then sank herself into a wing chair, groping for her vinaigrette.

Genevieve chuckled at her friend. "It seems you are the one to be overset, my dear Amelia! I shall pour out the tea while you recover."

This heretical suggestion instantly revived Lady Cammerby, who sat up in her chair. "You shall do no such thing as a guest in my house, Genevieve! Only give me a moment." Breathing deeply of her vinaigrette, she resolutely put it aside, declaring herself to be fortified against further weakness, and well able to do her duty. This she did, solicitously asking their preferences for milk and sugar, and entertaining small talk while Lenora gazed about in amazement at the grandeur of her surroundings.

Having been born in a manor house, Lenora had some experience of the elegancies of life, but it had been many years since her family had commanded the majority of these, and she had never, due to her father's propensity to throw money to the four winds, experienced such comfort as she collected her hostess could afford. Upon entering Lady Cammerby's house, she had counted two footmen, a butler, and two maids, and felt certain that several more maids, a cook, a housekeeper, and more footmen were most likely in residence. The entry hall of this London townhome was more spacious than that of Branwell Cottage, and the stairs swept up in graceful curves to the floors above. They had passed a well-appointed music room with a pianoforte and a harp in the corner, and a comfortable drawing room on their way to the Blue Saloon, which was furnished in the first style of elegance. Lenora had no doubt that the rest of the house, including the room in which she was to pass the next several months, was fitted up in just such a style, and her good fortune took her breath away.

When the tea things were removed, Lady Cammerby leaned back again in the chair with a gusty sigh. "There," she said. "Now we are comfortable and may look upon the evening with composure."

"I have always believed that tea heals all ills," said Genevieve, twinkling at her hostess.

"That may well be true, but still, there was a deal of trouble for you tonight!"

"Oh, ma'am, but it was such an exciting day!" put in Lenora, whose awe of her hostess's magnificent home did not extend to its owner, the lady's motherly manner upon their reception having banished all discomfort. "Only imagine, we met a man whose pig had won a prize for most closely resembling Prinny!"

"Good gracious!" uttered Lady Cammerby, grasping her vinaigrette once more.

"I thought it a most handsome pig, Amelia," offered Genevieve. "I am persuaded that the Prince Regent himself would have been honored by the distinction."

"Well!" said their hostess, but the mischievous glimmer in her friend's eye elicited a reluctant chuckle. "For shame, Genevieve! One would think you a seditionist, from the shocking things you say! But it was ever so with you, was it not?"

"I have never done well with authority, it is true, but I fear I lack the spirit to topple an entire monarchy, Amelia. The Prince Regent is safe from me. The pig in his image, however, must beware. There is not much I would not do for a good ham."

Lady Cammerby expostulated further over Lenora's giggles, and the conversation moved to a description of the other adventures that had delayed their arrival—notably, the kindness of the engaging Mr. Ginsham.

"It seems, dear Amelia, that we are beset by Galahads," observed Genevieve. "And only a few months past I had bemoaned the fate of chivalry to my cook."

Lenora sat forward in her chair. "Oh, Mama! I had no notion such things happened outside the covers of a novel! When the horses bolted, I was so shocked that I hardly knew what to think! I cannot comprehend how you ever kept your footing!"

"Nor can I, my dear, except that I am incurably tenacious, if only for a few seconds, which is exactly as long as I was in any danger."

"I will tell you," inserted Lady Cammerby portentously, "that

Joshua left this house only minutes before, I daresay just as you drew up. It was the hand of Providence." She pressed a hand to her heart, which she declared to be palpitating as much with the memory as at the time of the incident.

"Your brother is very brave," breathed Lenora, round-eyed. "Such presence of mind, and disinterested response!" She turned to her mother. "He saved your life, Mama!"

"Possibly, my dear, and I am enduringly grateful to him," Genevieve answered ruminatively, "But my pride is a trifle injured that he did not appear the least gratified by the circumstance. Is he always so frigidly civil, Amelia?"

Lady Cammerby, uncomfortably aware of her brother's opinion, however unjust, of her friend, valiantly attempted to explain away his coldness, and succeeded merely in satisfying her friend's rather unflattering idea of his character.

"I see," remarked Genevieve, looking thoughtful. "If I am to retrieve my standing with him, I must take care not to require his assistance."

Her ladyship was greatly distressed. "You must not think so ill of him, Genevieve, for he truly is a gentleman!" she cried.

"I have no doubts on that head, my dear Amelia," soothed her friend, "and quite consider him my knight errant, for though his reticence has rendered his armor a bit rusty, he did not, after all, hesitate to aid me."

"How right you are, Mama!" declared Lenora, much struck.

"Your sentiments do you credit, Genevieve," conceded Lady Cammerby. "And in the same spirit of good will, I shall endeavor to present you next to him in a more felicitous light, for I am determined that neither of you should, from cruel happenstance, wrong the other."

Chapter 6

ALL THE LADIES were late to the breakfast table next morning, the rigors of the previous day having rendered them exhausted. But a new day brought renewed vigor, and they each made a hearty meal as they entered energetically into plans for the season's success.

"The gowns must be ordered first," declared Lady Cammerby, cutting her toast into strips for dipping, "for dear Madame Francome will be beset with work before the week's out and we cannot risk a delay to Lenora's ball."

Genevieve waved a hand. "Oh, but dear Amelia, we have provided for Lenora's gowns already."

Her friend blinked, a piece of toast poised over her teacup. "But Genevieve, how—"

"I have saved all my lovely gowns, from my season, the half of which I wore only once or twice, before Bertram whisked me away into the country."

The toast fell from Lady Cammerby's suddenly nerveless fingers, splashing into the tea as she stared horror-struck at her friend. "My dear, you cannot be serious!"

Genevieve caught Lenora's eye, which gleamed appreciatively. "Why ever would I not be serious, Amelia?" she said, all innocence. "They were perfectly good!"

"You wish me to launch Lenora in your old dresses—"

"She is just my size, and has my coloring, too!"

"Dresses from the last century?" Lady Cammerby's voice achieved an octave that rang in the glassware. "What can you be thinking?"

Delighted laughter bubbled from Genevieve, and Lenora covered her grin with her napkin. "Oh, Amelia, how can you be such a goosecap?" She wiped tears from her eyes. "I did save the dresses, for the *fabric*, and we have made new, and they turned out beautifully. I am convinced they shall meet with even your high expectations."

"Well!" Lady Cammerby pressed a hand to her bosom, her lips pursed. "What a schoolgirl prank to play upon one, Genevieve!" She pushed her teacup of soggy toast away and went to the sideboard for another cup, glancing in disapprobation from one to the other of her mirthful guests. "I vow I never imagined you would be so rag-mannered as to—as to—" But in the face of such good-humor, her umbrage failed, and her lips began to twitch, and then her stiffness vanished altogether. Joining in their laughter, she said, "The tables have not turned, have they, my dearest Genevieve?"

"Not in the least." Genevieve smiled mischievously at her. "I promise I shall endeavor to be more grown up from now on, but I could not resist when you almost begged for such a trick, you know I could not!"

"No, you never could." She rejoined them at the table, her look becoming reflective. "Though, I wonder that your humor survived—well, everything, my dear."

Her guests' mirth was stifled, as if a jug of cold water had been tossed over them. Lady Cammerby lowered her gaze. "Oh, pray, do forgive me! It was unfeeling of me, and—and—"

Genevieve reached quickly to press her friend's hand. "There is nothing to forgive, my dear Amelia. That my marriage was an unhappy one is universally known. But perhaps it was because of good humor that I survived it."

The other two ladies' eyes sought relief in the pattern of the tablecloth, and Genevieve tossed her napkin onto her plate. "But enough of ancient history! We have much more agreeable things to discuss. Gowns we are sure of—"

Amelia put up an imperative hand. "Made-over gowns may be good enough for picnics and parties, but I depend upon providing Lenora's ball gowns, my dear. I shall brook no arguments on that head! I have no daughters of my own, and if there is one thing for which I have an eye, it is fashion, and one derives only so much satisfaction from the dressing of oneself!"

"Oh, but Amelia, the expense!"

"No, I insist upon it, Genevieve!"

Genevieve cast her daughter a droll look, and answered, "You are too, too good, my dear friend."

"Oh, pish! A mere trifle, and it will give me far greater enjoyment than it will either of you, I'll warrant!"

Thus, rising from the breakfast table in perfect charity with one another, the three ladies set forth on a week of dissipation and extravagance the likes of which at least two of them had never before experienced, but if one of the three was afforded more enjoyment than the others in this, none was the wiser. Lenora emerged from this experience the dazed possessor of not only three new ball gowns—which would be delivered as they were completed—but also three pair of long, white satin gloves, a silk net shawl, and a dainty silver reticule, all of which her hostess assured her were indispensable to her toilette, and so must be purchased.

Within the week came Miss Chuddsley to add to Lenora's pleasure, and no sooner had the two been reunited than a scheme arose to take them to the new but already legendary Soho Bazaar where, Elvira assured her friend in an awed undertone, one would find the most incredible bargains on everything required for the happiness and success of a young lady embarking upon her first season in London. Mrs. Breckinridge and Lady Cammerby being engaged to visit an old school acquaintance, the two girls were given use of the carriage and a footman to carry their purchases, and set out together with every expectation of enjoyment.

"Lady Cammerby seems a most agreeable hostess, Lenora! Much better than my stuffy Aunt Isobel," confided Elvira as they sorted through a dizzying array of reticules at one of the tables at the Bazaar. "If she gives a single party this season, other than my ball, which Mama nearly had to extort a promise from her to give, I shall count myself shocked and amazed. Oh, Lenora, wouldn't this be just the thing for my figured muslin?"

"But surely your aunt won't need to put herself out! You've told me of three invitations you've received already this week, and you have hardly set foot in town!"

Elvira giggled. "It is gratifying, to be sure! But it is all Mama's doing. Though little George's health will not permit her to stay long after the ball—she will stay for yours, of course—all her friends have engaged to take me in hand, so she need not worry for my success. And Mama has already received a promise from Lady Jersey to permit me a voucher for Almack's! Has Lady Cammerby procured one for you?"

"Oh, she has spoken of it, but I doubt she has had the time to pursue it, so busy has she been about my gowns and things. I have no doubt but that she will, however! She has been all that is generous, and I could never be happier! Look, Elvira, I declare this is the exact pattern I saw in that expensive modiste's shop last week! And at such a bargain!"

The girls moved from reticules to gloves to trimmings for hats, entranced by both wares and prices, and the footman who followed dutifully behind them became steadily laden with parcels. A particularly charming shop man helped them find the perfect gift for Elvira's younger brother, and the girls sighed together as they left his table—as did the footman, but for quite the opposite cause.

"Do you not find London delightful, Lenora? I declare if I have not seen more handsome gentlemen in one day here than in my entire lifetime at home," observed Elvira.

Lenora, put in recollection of the dashing Mr. Ginsham, regaled her friend with the story of his gallantry. "But he has not yet paid a call," she said wistfully. "I suppose he offered only to be civil."

"Do not say so! It has only been a sennight, which is nothing to a man!" Elvira pressed her arm. "And even if he does not call, I daresay you will not miss him once you come out, for then all the amiable gentlemen you meet at your party will call."

Lenora's irrepressible smile dawned. "I do hope so, my dear, for you are right—there are ever so many fine gentlemen about. But some of them ogle one so!" She lowered her voice. "I fancy one would have no trouble discovering an evil Duke among them."

Elvira covered her mouth with a gloved hand, glancing surreptitiously at the few men in their vicinity. "Oh, Lenora! It is too true! And among so many gentlemen, there is sure to be a hero as well. I only wish I knew how to recognize him."

Lenora gripped her friend's arm, at once recalling another occurrence she had neglected to share. "Oh, Elvira, I have met a paragon!"

"Mr. Ginsham?"

Relegating the unfortunate Mr. Ginsham to the ranks of the merely gallant, Lenora proceeded to tell the tale of Sir Joshua's heroism in rescuing her mother from the runaway carriage. Elvira's mouth formed an O as she listened, her eyes widening nearly as much, and she gripped the nearest table, swaying as if she may swoon at any moment. "It is just like Valancourt in *Udolpho*!" she breathed. "But how comes it that you have had all this good luck, Lenora? And how inexcusable, to keep such a tale to yourself!"

"London has put my head in a whirl, as well you know! Perhaps it is a more romantic place than we had imagined."

"Oh, Lenora," cried Elvira, grasping her arm, "tell me at once, does Sir Joshua have a stammer?"

Her friend giggled. "No, he speaks very well, if a trifle stiffly."

"But surely, he has a limp?" asked Elvira, gamely pursuing.

"He has not even a squint, my dear." At Elvira's look of disappointment, she said, "But I fancy he must have a tragic past, for he is very grave and serious."

"Grave and serious? Surely you mean broodingly sensitive." The prompt negative checked Elvira's enthusiasm for some moments. At last she shook her head. "I cannot discover how gravity could be romantic, Lenora. I fear we must pass over your Sir Joshua."

"But, Elvira," cried Lenora, whose loyalty was offended, "what rule is there that says gravity cannot hide a tormented soul, that privately pines for love?"

Elvira instantly embraced this enlivening notion. "His past injuries have steeled him against the pitfalls of sensitivity, and he hides behind walls of gravity!"

"But his chivalrous instincts cannot be hid, and will prove the re-making of his happiness, for how can any heart stand against the gratitude of another?"

"Oh, Lenora," Elvira gazed imperatively at her. "You must only tell me that he stands on the brink of poverty, and I shall be satisfied."

Lenora blinked at her, brought suddenly back to reality. "Dearest Elvira, I cannot. I believe he is rather rich."

Elvira's mouth drooped in disappointment, and it was some moments before she could rally herself. "Perhaps he has only recently inherited, Lenora. Perhaps in his tragic past he was poor."

"That would certainly redeem him," agreed Lenora, but she now felt it incumbent upon her, in recognizing the folly of leading her friend on in such a way, to disabuse her friend's mind on another point, and began to add, "But Elvira—"

Elvira, however, did not attend, rushing on impetuously. "If he is Lady Cammerby's brother, then you will see him often, and he will fall passionately in love with you, but will never show it, because of the disappointments of his past. His heart will not bear it!"

"I have no doubt you would be right, Elvira, but—"

"Oh, Lenora, it needs only an evil Duke to make the story perfect!" insisted her friend, turning excitedly toward her.

"Elvira," cried Lenora, grasping her friend's wrists. "I must tell you that Sir Joshua is rather old."

"Old? But—how old?"

"Of an age with my mother, at least."

"Oh." Her friend wilted a bit. "It is a pity, but older men can still be romantic, can they not?"

"Certainly, but recollect, advanced age is more often a characteristic of the villain."

Elvira grabbed her hand. "Do you think he could be a villain in disguise, and his rescue was merely a ruse to gain your trust?"

Lenora's eyes widened. "His reserve could certainly hide evil intentions. Oh! What danger may be lurking in the future? We will be thrown together often, as you said. I must be on my guard!"

Elvira met her friend's wide gaze, and they stared horrified at one another for a pregnant moment, then they burst into giggles, and went on to make their purchases, which they were obliged to hold themselves, as the footman's arms had overflowed—giving them to feel exceedingly satisfied by the success of the expedition.

When the young ladies came out of the bazaar, they perceived Lady Cammerby's barouche drawn up down the street, and in making their way down the crowded flagway toward it, Lenora was jostled by a passerby, and a parcel was knocked from her arms. With a cry of dismay, she attempted to shift the rest of the parcels so that she could bend to pick the one up, but a gentleman close by, recognizing her plight, retrieved it for her.

"Allow me, ma'am," he said, holding it out, but as Lenora tipped her face up to meet his gaze, his eyes narrowed, and he stared at her with an intensity bordering on incivility.

Unaccustomed to garnering attention from members of the male sex in general, and especially when her pretty golden-haired friend was nearby, Lenora blushed and took the parcel with downcast eyes. "Thank you, sir," she said, peeping up at him through her lashes. He was an older man, but well-preserved, with good shoulders, a handsome, if lined, face, and a decided air of fashion.

Her words broke whatever spell had seized him and, sweeping off his hat, he bowed gracefully over it. "Forgive my rudeness, ma'am, but it is not every day that I meet with such loveliness."

Lenora's color deepened and she looked away, but Elvira gasped, "You are impertinent, sir."

Affording barely a glance at her friend, the gentleman favored Lenora with a charming smile and began to expostulate, but the appearance of Lord Cammerby's footman, who had been signaling the coachman, checked him mid-sentence. The young ladies surrendered their parcels to be packed into the chaise, then turned back to the stranger, who had schooled his countenance to one of polite indifference and, replacing his hat, bade them a civil farewell, and took himself off.

Elvira craned her neck to watch his progress down the street, and tugged at Lenora's arm. "What do you think of that?" she whispered urgently.

Lenora bid her hush, allowing the footman to help her into the coach, but as soon as they were settled, their packages filling the forward seat and spilling onto the floor, Elvira nudged her. "Well?"

Lenora looked askance at her friend, still pink with pleasure. "He was an exceedingly fine-looking gentleman."

"And he could not tear his eyes from your face!" declared Elvira. "I do not know whether to be shocked or gratified, for I did say you have beauty, did I not, Lenora? Does this not prove me right?"

Lenora's eyes danced as she returned, "Indeed, dearest, but he was old enough to be my father."

Taken out of stride for only a moment, Elvira pointed out, "Did we not just agree that older men can be romantic?"

"Yes, but we also came to the conclusion that, more often, they are villains."

Elvira put out her hand to grip Lenora's and turned bodily to face her, her eyes round. "Oh, do you think it can be possible? Is he our evil Duke?"

"With such a rakish air? I should say, undoubtedly. Why, he flirted with a complete stranger in broad daylight!"

"Good heavens!" whispered Elvira, changing color. "What must we do?"

"Elvira! You look as though you did not wish to find our Duke!" When her friend's answering glance told her this was exactly so, Lenora laughed, putting an arm about her. "There is nothing to fear if, indeed, he is our evil Duke, for we shall surely never set eyes on him again!"

Not quite put at ease by this piece of common sense, Miss Chuddsley required the whole of the ride to her aunt's house, where she and her numerous parcels were put down, to be persuaded that the romance of the meeting was of far greater moment than the possible danger of it. Lenora, on the other hand, felt only giddy satisfaction, and when the coachman drew up in Hill Street, she snatched one of the bandboxes and tripped up the stairs, leaving the footman to contrive transport of all the remaining parcels into her apartment.

Lenora found her mother in the drawing room, a billow of muslin over her lap and her sewing box much disturbed by her side. The young lady collapsed into a chair, sighing dramatically.

Unmoved, Mrs. Breckinridge continued sewing. "I trust that you do not intend to throw yourself about the room when in polite company, Lenora."

"Mama! Indeed, I do not. Only Elvira and I have had such a day at the bazaar, and I am quite done in!"

"Is it too much to hope that you recollected my errand?"

"Mama!" she cried again, in an injured tone. "Have you no curiosity?"

"On the contrary, I have a great curiosity to know whether you have procured the ribbon I need for your dress."

Sighing gustily, Lenora opened the bandbox on her lap, extracting a length of ribbon and handing it over to her mother. "They had not any pale blue, but I am persuaded this will do, Mama."

Mrs. Breckinridge took the ribbon, inspecting it critically. "Indeed, it will do better. Well done, my dear." She placed the ribbon in the sewing box and took up her needle again. "Now, what has happened to do you in?"

"The strangest thing!" Lenora started in, sitting up with sudden energy. "I dropped a parcel on our way out of the bazaar, and a gentleman picked it up for me."

"That is not strange, I hope."

"No! It was not that, Mama. But when he saw my face, he positively stared in the rudest way. He tried to cover it with a compliment on my beauty, but I know that to be a plumper," she said with maidenly modesty.

"Lenora, love, far be it from me to administer to your vanity, but you are a very well-looking girl, and, I think, not far from beautiful." She held up the dress she had been stitching—a white muslin walking dress with a scalloped hem and puffed Marie sleeves. "What do you think?"

Lenora, gratified, so much forgot her fatigue as to spring up, taking the edges of the skirt into her hands and spreading it full before her. "Oh! Mama, it is lovely! You do such fine work! You always have, you know."

"Not always, my love. I fancy even you would have groaned at my samplers." But she smiled complacently. "You are merely the happy benefactor of necessity, which has taught me to persevere. Did you find gloves to match it?"

"I did!" Lenora cried, her spirits entirely restored, and the two ladies happily whiled away the rest of the afternoon with plans for toilettes, and in discovering any accessory that may still be wanting.

Chapter 7

THE NEXT MORNING, feeling the loss of the country for the first time since coming to town, Mrs. Breckinridge and Lenora betook themselves to the Green Park, intent on fresh air and exercise, independent of shops. As they wended their leisurely way past the lodge and beside the reservoir, they encountered few people, it being early yet, excepting the milkmaids who were to be found tending their little herd. The ladies stayed a while to sample the fresh milk served to them in tin cups, delighting in the merry tinkling of bells as the cows plucked up the tender grass, turning serene bovine eyes upon them as they went on their way.

Following the perimeter of the park, they turned toward Buckingham House then, unwilling to complete the full circuit of the park just yet, struck out across the lawns toward the pond. On the other side of a small hill, they came to a tree, upon the lowest branch of which, nearly two feet off the ground, they found a small boy scrambling to reach another branch well over his head.

"Young man, what do you think you are doing?" Mrs. Breckinridge ran to him, plucking him down from his precarious perch.

The boy squirmed in her hands until she put him down, then he pointed up into the branches of the tree. "My ball!"

Mrs. Breckinridge followed the direction of his pudgy little finger and saw a small ball wedged neatly into the crook of a branch about ten feet off the ground. "It's too high for you to reach, my young man. Too high for anyone, I daresay! I'm afraid you shall have to give it up."

"But I need it!" he cried, his face puckering.

Lenora came forward to pat his shoulders comfortingly, while her mother looked about with concerned eyes. "Where is your nurse? Or your mama?"

"Nurse is with baby," the boy said, pointing to the rise of the hill on the other side of the tree.

"Then we must do what we can not to upset her, for she has enough to occupy her," said Mrs. Breckinridge, and she turned to consider the tree. The branches were fairly evenly spaced, and she felt sure she could easily climb two or three and reach the ball down. It would be simple and quick, and no one need be the wiser. Casting a look about at the deserted vicinity resolved her, and she leaned down eye-level with the boy. "If you stay just here, like a good boy, I shall retrieve your ball for you."

He nodded solemnly, and Mrs. Breckinridge approached the tree, setting her foot on the lowest branch. Lenora inhaled sharply. "Take care, Mama!"

"I used to climb the trees in the park at Crandon." She looked over her shoulder at her daughter, her eyes twinkling. "There is no danger, I assure you, Lenora. The simplest thing in the world."

She pulled herself up to the second branch, stretching out her fingers toward the ball, but it was still out of reach. Stepping onto the third branch, she heard it creak ominously as she laid her full weight upon it, but the ball was almost within reach, and when she stretched her fingers up, they pressed against it. But the ball would not dislodge. She hopped onto her tiptoes, poking firmly at the ball, and had the satisfaction of feeling it move, but as it rolled free there was a tremendous crack, and the branch gave way, and Mrs. Breckinridge found herself draped by the waist over a high branch, about eight feet from the ground.

Lenora shrieked, "Mama!" her hands flying to cover her mouth, but the little boy went happily to his ball, catching it up in his hands and running off to rejoin his nurse, whose calls, tinged with panic, could now be heard on the other side of the hill. Mrs. Breckinridge twisted herself and, with an effort, came to a seat on the branch, blinking down at her daughter below.

"Oh, dear," she uttered, a little breathlessly. "What have I done?"

Lenora took an agitated step closer to the tree. "Are you hurt, Mama? Oh, how will you ever get down?"

"Only my pride is hurt, dear love. To think I am bested by a tree!" This attempt to lighten the mood did not seem to impress her daughter, who continued to gesticulate ineffectually beneath her. Reflecting that it behooved her to find a way down, if only for the well-being of her daughter's mind, Mrs. Breckinridge looked up and down the trunk of the tree. The branch that had caused her predicament had cracked near the trunk and hung down from a small nub. "Perhaps if I can—" she said, reaching her toe toward the nub.

But Lenora shrieked again, "Mama! Don't, I beg you! I shall swoon if you fall!"

Mrs. Breckinridge pulled back her foot. "Such solicitude would comfort me immeasurably, my love," she said firmly, "but it would do neither of us any good. Do not fear, we shall brush through this." She scrutinized her situation once more, musing, "How we shall, I do not yet know, for I can see no safe route to the ground, apart from risking a broken ankle, and a shocking display of my legs."

Though she kept her tone matter-of-fact, she was fully cognizant of the impropriety of her situation, and inwardly chastised herself for acting so rashly in such a public place. If anyone were to see her—but someone must see her, for she could not rescue herself, and Lenora was in no way capable of doing so.

Resigned, she looked down at her flustered daughter and said, "I fear I shall need assistance to descend, my love." But Lenora stood transfixed, eyes wide and face pale. Her mother raised her voice and clearly articulated, "Lenora, my dear, you must go to Lady Cammerby and ask her to send help."

"I—Oh, I cannot leave you, Mama!"

"But you must, love," Mrs. Breckinridge patiently pointed out, "for that is the only way you are to rescue me."

"Oh!" The tragic look on her daughter's face was replaced by one of wide-eyed wonder, as the realization that she had been granted the opportunity to play a heroine's part at last penetrated her brain. "Of course, Mama. I shall endeavor—Oh, my! I—I shall return presently, Mama."

Somewhat belatedly, her mother charged her with the utmost discretion, and she hurried away, stumbling a bit on the damp grass.

Mrs. Breckinridge, determinedly trusting to Lenora's competence, pushed all thoughts of a pessimistic nature aside and distracted herself by attempting to find a comfortable pose. In this she had, in the end, to make do with simply staying in balance on her perch, one hand on a branch overhead, and the other against the trunk of the tree. Lenora was gone for some time, and Mrs. Breckinridge whiled away the minutes by gazing out over the park, enjoying the peaceful views of grazing milk cows and barefoot milkmaids amid rolling green grass and graceful trees, and composing in her mind an explanation to anyone who should happen to discover her in this ridiculous predicament.

At last, she heard quick footfalls on the grass, and Lenora's voice panting, "Here is the tree!" Her daughter rounded the periphery of the tree, and Mrs. Breckinridge sat up straight, prepared to face her rescuer with fortitude, but when her daughter's companion came into view, her resolve fled, for it was none other than Sir Joshua Stiles. Mrs. Breckinridge bowed her head, covering pained eyes with one hand, while the other clung to the overhead branch.

Sir Joshua, having met with the little boy whom he had assumed at first to be fictitious, but whose nurse's adjuration to thank the kind lady for retrieving his ball had allayed his suspicions, gazed up at her. "How do you do, Mrs. Breckinridge?" he said, with meticulous politeness.

She could only shake her head, her face hidden in mortification.

"You must pardon my feelings of astonishment when I was apprised of your present situation, ma'am," he said in a conversational tone, "for though my previous knowledge of your adventures has persuaded me that you would be intrepid enough to attempt such a thing, I could not bring myself to credit it."

She peeked down at him from between her fingers. "Oh, sir! You behold me humbled beyond anything. It seemed the simplest thing, and it is not as though I have never climbed a tree! Of course, that was years ago, but I am far from incapable, and I never imagined the branch would break!"

Sir Joshua surveyed the damaged branch, his gaze travelling up the tree and back to her. "You must forgive my plain-speaking, ma'am, for I am shocked that no alternative to climbing a tree like—again, I beg your pardon—like a hoyden, presented itself to a lady of such resource as yourself. One or two occur to me even now! For example, one might have thrown something at the ball to dislodge it."

Rendered speechless for a moment by this simple good sense, she blushed, but presently gathered her wits to exclaim, "How could you suggest anything so poor-spirited, sir, as to stand on the ground, hurling things impotently into a tree? For I am a terrible shot, you know, and should have missed. My plan was far superior in sense and in execution, for whatever the consequences, my object is achieved."

He gazed blandly at her. "If your object was to be stranded in a tree, I can do no other than agree with you."

Effectively silenced, she bit her lip and averted her eyes, and he removed his hat, handing it along with his cane to Lenora, who had been attending to their dialogue with some awe.

"As you have fetched me here," he said, "I shall do my poor best to assist you, a circumstance I trust you shall not presently regret, for I perceive only one way out of your predicament." He straightened his coat. "You must jump."

Mrs. Breckinridge stared at him for some moments, frantically grasping in her mind for any alternative. "Surely there is something else that can be done!" she cried.

"I fear not, short of summoning the Guards, which would bring upon us all the most painful embarrassment." He stepped forward, extending his arms. "Come now. You must jump."

She blinked, but upon somewhat agitated reflection, was compelled by her own good sense to concede. With a sigh, she brought her legs up enough to cinch her skirts tightly around her ankles, pressing her feet together to hold the fabric, then she inched forward to the very edge of the branch, clinging to the bough above and the

TWO IN THE BUSH

trunk beside her. The ground seemed very far below, perched so precariously as she was, and she found it necessary to take several calming breaths before bracing her hands on the branch and pushing off. Sir Joshua caught her neatly, and without obvious effort, placing her gently on her feet on the grass.

He stepped back, his hands steadying her waist. "Well?"

She met his gaze a trifle uneasily, then pulled away, straightening her skirts and her bonnet. "As well as can be expected, sir, for one whose dignity can never seem to recover."

She thought his lips twitched, but he turned to the tree, examining the broken branch more closely. "It seems it was unstable at the outset. There are signs it had been cracked previously."

"Then it is just as well that I broke it, rather than that poor child, or some other," said Mrs. Breckinridge in a stout tone.

"Even had you broken your neck?" returned Sir Joshua coolly.

"Especially so! When put in that light, I feel rather heroic, actually," she said with spirit. "A sacrifice to a worthy cause."

"Mama!" protested Lenora, but Sir Joshua merely gazed at her. "A most interesting view of the situation, ma'am." He turned to Lenora. "And are you quite recovered from your fright, Miss Breckinridge?"

She looked gratefully up at him. "Yes, with Mama safe, I am quite well, thank you!"

"By all appearances, you were very brave. You did not even swoon!" he added, nodding gravely at her. Lenora blushed prettily and ducked her head, which caused her to recollect that she still held his hat and cane, and she instantly gave them up to him.

He took the hat, placing it on his head, and leaned upon his cane, looking from daughter to mother. "I trust you will be safe from here?"

Mrs. Breckinridge, wishing to oblige Sir Joshua no more than absolutely necessary, put her arm through her daughter's. "You needn't be troubled, sir. We are going to the confectioner's on Bond Street, and I will readily promise to attempt no more perilous feats."

"I hope it may be so," he answered, as if unconvinced.

Her eyebrows went up, a challenge in her eye. "Well, sir, if you cannot be satisfied, I shall engage to meet you next without emergency."

He regarded her steadily. "Do you intend to lay odds?" With something very like a twinkle in his eye, he bowed to them both and walked away across the park, leaving them to gape after him in astonishment.

It was with dismay that Lady Cammerby heard of their adventure, for she had determined upon endearing her friend to her brother, and the account that reached her ears did not bode well for her success.

"I recall most vividly, Genevieve," she said, in tremulous accents, "a promise from your own lips that you should act your age! How can you betray me by—by climbing a tree in the Green Park?"

"I promised to endeavor, my dear Amelia," responded her friend in her most soothing tone, "which I have most faithfully done, I assure you."

"Yes, but climbing a tree? I can only be grateful such gross impropriety was witnessed by no one else!"

"But you must allow that my motivation was not a disregard for propriety!" cried Genevieve. "The poor little boy, Amelia—one must not discount the urgency of his plight! I had no other choice."

Lady Cammerby had recourse to her vinaigrette. "Oh, what must he think of you?"

"The boy?" asked Genevieve, settling herself onto the sofa. "I fancy he thinks me a right one."

"Oh!" her ladyship cried, closing her eyes in agony and uttering, in accents of doom, "Genevieve, I fear Bertram has ruined you!"

"Oh, dear, no, Amelia, I was a hoyden long before Bertram carried me away." In a reflective tone, she added, "Indeed, I count myself fortunate that my marriage did not entirely stifle what spirit I had to begin with."

Her friend's harassed expression melted into one of compassion. "Dear Genevieve, how right you are. You were ever a free spirit, and we all loved you for it!" She sat upright, swallowing her own disappointment, and said, with tolerable composure, "There shall be no more talk of blame, my dear. This—this occurrence was merely unfortunate, and we shall put it behind us."

"Oh, Amelia," said Genevieve, chastened at last, "you bear so bravely with my ridiculous starts! Truly, I never meant to cause you anxiety, and I am a monster to have teased you. Forgive me."

Lady Cammerby was much mollified and expressed her willingness to do so, but, after a short struggle, she said abruptly, "It is merely that I wish my brother to have a good opinion of you, for you deserve anyone's respect, Genevieve, and as you are both to be thrown much together during the season, I will be more comfortable—indeed, we all will be—if there is nothing to set you against one another."

"Well," said Genevieve, gleaning much of the truth from this speech, "you may rest easy in the knowledge that I promised your brother not to be in need of rescue the next time we meet, and I feel certain you may depend upon my keeping that promise, if you recollect that I was a pattern of propriety for our first fortnight in London, and there is not even that between now and Lenora's ball. I shall be too busy to get into a scrape."

With this assurance, Lady Cammerby had to be satisfied, and turned without demur to finalizing plans for the upcoming ball.

Chapter 8

SIR JOSHUA'S PART in their adventure in the park could not but captivate Lenora, and she lost no time in sharing the story of it with Elvira, who was suitably impressed, even going so far as to forgive him some of his years.

"For he cannot be so very old, Lenora, if he can run after wild horses and catch fully-grown women jumping out of trees, without so much as a strained muscle. My papa, you know, would've been winded after two steps, and he'd as soon have dropped your mama as caught her!"

Lenora giggled. "How can you think to compare Sir Joshua with your papa? His notion of action is any motion belonging to anyone or anything else, my dear, and I should have been very much surprised if he had thought it his duty to move at all." At Elvira's look of chagrin, Lenora patted her hand. "I am persuaded that he would have valiantly looked about him for someone else who could help."

"Oh, Lenora, I love my papa, but his malaise tries the patience of a saint! I vow I shall marry someone who will leap without hesitation to my rescue, whenever, and wherever I need him!"

"And you will!" Lenora assured her. "Indeed, I prophesy that you will meet him at your coming out next week."

This turned the conversation back into enjoyable channels, and the girls instantly began to discuss the length of their respective guest lists, the enormous quantities of champagne that had been ordered from Gunter's by each house, and the great good fortune that Lenora's mother had succeeded in dissuading Lady Cammerby from festooning her ballroom in pink silk.

"Only think, Elvira, how insipid! And my hopes should have all been dashed, for who could admire me against such a background? I've never shown to advantage in pink."

"I don't know, dearest," said Elvira, who had always looked lovely in the color. "I think pink would have been charming."

"You would!" replied Lenora. "And as an accent, I am sure it should have been, but Lady Cammerby meant to turn the ballroom into a tent of it! We should all have been sick of pink by the end. But my mama had the lucky notion of turning the room into a bower, with bunches of fresh flowers in urns all around."

Elvira clapped her hands. "Oh, that will be lovely, like a fairyland!"

"Won't it just? Lady Cammerby was quite taken with the idea, and handsomely agreed that pink ribbons in with the flowers would be just the thing. Oh, Elvira, I was simply terrified that all the gentlemen should take violent exception to dancing in a pink tent, and would make the flimsiest excuses just to get themselves off!"

"But they shouldn't, Lenora! My mama says it isn't done, for leaving early from a party is very bad *ton*."

"But they could never wish to return to a house that lived in their nightmares as a florid pink prison! We would have been snubbed from that day on, and my season wasted."

Elvira laughed, throwing her arms around her friend. "You take on so, Lenora! I know you cannot be serious. Surely Lady Cammerby had meant to choose a pale pink, not a florid one, and all the gentlemen should have been too captivated by the lady of honor to be offended by something as paltry as decoration."

Lenora blushed, returning her friend's embrace. "I've never captivated a man before, Elvira."

"Yes, you have, Lenora! I have not forgotten that fine gentleman outside the bazaar, if you have!"

Lenora's eyes gleamed, but she shook her head. "I am persuaded that that man did not admire me, precisely, Elvira."

"I cannot think what you mean!"

"Never mind, dear. But I also have not forgotten Mr. Ginsham, who said he would call, and he has not."

"But he may have any number of reasons for not having come, and none of them to do with his lack of admiration for you."

Elvira's explanation was waved aside. "For all you say, I am nothing out of the common way, and without a fortune to tempt a man, what hope do I have of making a good match?"

"Dearest! You are far from ordinary!" Elvira sat back, regarding her friend keenly. "For one, you are delightful company—even Harry says so!"

"But he is your brother, Elvira, and only said so because I was used to follow him like a puppy. I daresay my worship administered to his vanity, but he should be of a very different mind now."

"Yes, he should. He will like very much to court you when he sees how pretty you've become."

"We must leave off appearance, Elvira," cried Lenora, "for I fancy I have been long enough in London to know I am not a beauty, and I am very much mistaken if Harry, or any gentleman for that matter, should look twice at such a beanpole as me."

"You do yourself an injustice, Lenora! Your figure may be slender, but you are far from a beanpole!" Elvira at once seemed to be taken by a wonderful notion. "On the contrary, Lenora, you are very near to fragile, and men cannot resist fragility! A maiden whom an errant wind would wither rouses all their protective instincts, and they will fall over themselves in their attempts to shield you from the least danger."

Impaired as her sensibility was by anxiety at present, Lenora considered this eventuality with little enthusiasm, pointing out that she'd prefer not to have a train of suitors who would never allow her to see the sun or feel the wind again.

Elvira blinked at this. "Well, I suppose you are right. Perhaps— perhaps stately grace is more fitted to your character!" Quite taken by this fancy, she expatiated, "You will greet every gentleman with polite indifference, and each, pining to be the one to inspire passion in your breast, will woo you with such devotion that you shall be forced to break all their hearts!"

"All their hearts but one, I hope!" cried Lenora. "That is the point, is it not, Elvira, to have one suitor left?"

Elvira sought in some confusion for an adequate amendment to her scenario. "All resign themselves to despondency but one, who, in spite of his broken heart, will love you from afar until he is able to render you a signal service which melts your heart of ice and makes you his own!"

"That's better," sighed Lenora. "Though, I have never been inclined to indifference, and all may fail if I cannot stand firm against so much devotion. It is more likely that I shall melt at first sign of it."

"Exactly, Lenora! You instantly fall in love, at first sight, but hide your feelings until the crucial moment, when his sufferings and yours have unalterably bound you together, and the revelation of your true feelings reclaim him from a disastrous course, and he hails you as his beloved angel!"

With a rapturous sigh, Lenora relinquished her anxious hold on reality and allowed herself to enter fully into Elvira's schemes for her future happiness. But as the date of the ball drew nearer, she discovered that she was unequal to Elvira's expectations. The role of Ice Maiden was not so easily assumed, for Lenora simply could not refrain from smiles, or laughter, or other such displays of genuine pleasure, especially when confronted with the gorgeous gown Lady Cammerby had ordered for her on that first frenetic shopping spree. The gown arrived with only a day to spare and, when paired with the long, white kid gloves and reticule her hostess had so kindly provided, and the simple pearls Mrs. Breckinridge had thoughtfully brought along from Branwell Cottage, was deemed by all three ladies as the loveliest toilette imaginable.

Lenora was a tall girl, but demurely proportioned, and the tucked bodice, cut modestly across the bosom, joined to a flowing silk skirt under a spangled gauze overdress, lent her a fairy-like appearance, which gave Lenora to think that, stately grace being unattainable, and fragility undesirable, perhaps maidenly could be made to answer. But when Lady Cammerby's own maid dressed her hair in a dashing new style, and dabbed the tiniest bit of rouge on her lips and cheeks, turning her charge exultantly toward the mirror, Lenora felt anything but maidenly, for no shy maiden's eyes ever sparkled with excitement as did Lenora's at that moment, and she could find within herself no desire to shrink. On the contrary, she knew a desire to flirt outrageously, and to conquer hearts, a desire not at all foreign to her, but until that moment, one she had unquestionably supposed impossible. She felt, in short, powerful—an emotion very far from her romantical ideal—and had a strong notion that in feeling so, she stood to disappoint not only herself, but Elvira as well. However, she was patently unable to feel sorry for this, and went down to dinner, intent upon enjoying herself to the fullest.

The evening was a success. Lady Cammerby's acquaintance including numerous fashionable members of the *ton*, young and old, her drawing rooms were soon filled with splendid company, including several handsome and eligible gentlemen who had come—or so her hostess congratulated herself—prepared to admire Miss Breckinridge. Lenora had the felicity to sit out only one dance, and that with a gentleman who had begged her hand for the dance and then genially complied with her entreaty to instead provide her refreshment and a breath of air. Her mother watched with complaisance as Lenora bloomed under the attention of so many amiable gentlemen of address, and she was grateful to observe that the damsel never seemed anxious to consider if her actions were worthy of a romantic heroine.

Mrs. Breckinridge, finding among the company many old friends, was herself honored by multiple requests to dance, the most surprising of which was from Sir Joshua Stiles. He had claimed Lenora's hand for the cotillion, and Mrs. Breckinridge had watched their very graceful progress with pride. But when he had relinquished his fair partner at the end of the set, to her astonishment, he had come to stand by her, and had engaged her in conversation.

"I must own to disappointment, Mrs. Breckinridge," he said.

Having fulfilled her promise to him faithfully, as she had supposed, she answered in no little surprise, "I can only say I am sorry, sir, though I hardly know why."

"You will pardon my not reposing any faith in your ability to meet me without emergency, ma'am. I steeled myself for an eventful evening." He flourished a hand to indicate the relatively peaceful state of the room. "I feel a trifle let down."

Her mouth twitched treacherously, but she said with admirable gravity, "Please accept my apologies, sir, for keeping my word so unexpectedly. I trust you have learned your lesson?"

"Only that I am glad you did not lay me odds."

Collecting that Lady Cammerby had grossly misjudged her brother, Mrs. Breckinridge barely managed to control herself enough to say, "Just so, sir."

After receiving a negative to his offer to procure her some refreshment, Sir Joshua said, "I trust your first month in London has been satisfactory, ma'am?"

"Satisfactory is too tame a word, sir. I would say, rather, intoxicating." He looked askance at her but she went on, unabashed. "Your sister is a most generous and energetic hostess, and we have enjoyed ourselves far beyond what we deserve, to be sure. Indeed, while I am most grateful to Amelia for her hospitality, I cannot help feeling the concern that Lenora will go into a decline in the quiet of the country after all this dissipation."

"You must not despair if she does, ma'am. It is not uncommon for young girls to be overcome by the pleasures of London."

A faint flush came into her cheeks. "That I know too well, sir. But you may rest assured that I shall do all in my power to forestall her."

"I have learned to have faith in your powers, ma'am."

She acknowledged this tribute with equanimity, and they were silent for some time, watching the dance. Mrs. Breckinridge expected him to draw politely away at any time, but he suddenly said,

"Your daughter dances delightfully, Mrs. Breckinridge. You must be very proud."

"Thank you, sir, but I must own I have never seen her dance so well before tonight. She had not the benefit of masters, you see, and her brother has not much patience for teaching." She smiled archly up at him. "I was her partner more often than not."

He looked down at her with raised brows. "But you said she had not the benefit of a master. You surely must be a master to know both the men's and the women's steps."

"What a pretty compliment, sir," she said, warily gratified. "I hope you do not find it a waste, for you cannot be sure that I know the women's steps. Perhaps I know only the men's after all."

He looked away to survey the room. "Some men would take that as a rather clumsy attempt to extort an invitation to dance."

She was taken aback, and was deciding whether to give him a set-down or to retort in humor, when he looked back down at her and continued, "But I hope I know you better than that, ma'am. I have been watching you very gracefully execute the women's steps all evening, and long since resolved to try if I may enjoy the benefits of your skill myself." He held out his hand and bowed. "May I have the honor, ma'am?"

It was Mrs. Breckinridge's turn to raise her brows, for she felt as much surprise as pleasure at this speech, and she took his hand, letting him lead her into the new set that was forming. He was a fine dancer, as she had earlier observed, and seemed truly to enjoy the dance as he had intended, so much so that his lips turned up in a smile once or twice.

Chapter 9

IT WAS NOT surprising, from the success of the ball, that the ladies in Hill Street enjoyed a flood of invitations and visits from that date on. No morning passed without the introduction of another young lady or gentleman into one or another of Lady Cammerby's saloons, and very few afternoons were spent idly, unless through design. One unexpected visitor was the Honorable Mr. Gregory Ginsham, whose full title burst upon the ladies with quite startling effect, rendering at least Lenora speechless. As his card was brought in while they were entertaining Miss Chuddsley, that damsel was obliged to bite her tongue on her curiosity, for no sooner had they exclaimed over him than he entered the saloon.

"Good day to you, Mrs. Breckinridge, Miss Breckinridge. I hope you will forgive the tardiness of my visit, for I was detained on business on my father's estate." Sweeping off his hat, he bowed gracefully over their hands, and then turned to allow Mrs. Breckinridge to present him to Lady Cammerby.

"You are the kind gentleman who attended my friends when the post-chaise wheel shattered!" she cried, smiling graciously while taking in his coat of blue superfine and pale-yellow pantaloons.

"Ah, yes, it is on the strength of such a long acquaintance that I impose upon you today, your ladyship."

He turned to greet the fourth lady in the room and was arrested by his first full vision of the blue-eyed, golden-haired Miss Elvira Chuddsley. Lady Cammerby performed the introduction and Elvira, a naturally modest girl, held out her hand to him in artless uncon-cern for the spell under which he seemed to have fallen.

"How do you do, Mr. Ginsham?"

Bid by her voice, Mr. Ginsham flowed into movement again, bowing over her fingers and returning her greeting as if he had never frozen at all. He disposed himself in a chair nearest Lenora, but with an exceptional view of Elvira, and smoothly initiated a lively discussion of the merits of the Metropolis as opposed to the virtues of the country, only the younger ladies unaware of the adroit-ness with which he drew certain personal details from them. His half-hour went comfortably by, and put him happily in possession of several facts which he no doubt intended to put to good use in the near future, and when he had gone, both Lady Cammerby and Mrs. Breckinridge thought they knew in which quarter the wind lay, though Lenora merely pronounced him a most amiable man, and Elvira that he was excessively conversable.

Satisfied of Lenora's social success, Mrs. Breckinridge aban-doned herself to the enjoyment of London society, the pleasures of which she had been denied these many years. As Lenora enlarged her acquaintance, her mother renewed her own, sped on by the ser-vices of Lady Cammerby who, thrilled by the triumph of launching a hitherto unknown into the *ton*, kept up her momentum by hosting as many card parties and soirees as her schedule would allow.

It was at one of these that Mrs. Breckinridge was reacquainted with Caroline Tenningbury, a rival from bygone days, who had become Lady Wraglain, but who now seemed less than inclined to air past offenses, and rather more likely to become a bosom friend. This somewhat surprised Genevieve, who had been persuaded that the former Miss Tenningbury, who at two years her senior had openly rankled at Genevieve's success, would rejoice in whatever misfortunes had afflicted her erstwhile competitor; however, it was borne in quickly upon her that just as the vicissitudes of life had altered her, so had they altered Caroline, and each found herself more and more satisfied with the other.

Sipping tea together while some dozen other guests played at cards, their reacquaintance began cautiously enough, with the usual polite inquiries into the separate events of the last twenty years of their lives. But when Lady Wraglain offered her sympathy regarding the loss of her husband, Genevieve responded with perfect unconcern, "You are very kind, but I assure you, I do not consider Bertram's passing a loss."

There was a stir at a nearby card table, and Genevieve glanced that way to see Sir Joshua frowning over his cards. She had the distinct impression that he was frowning at her, and she could not refrain from adding to Lady Wraglain, "You may think me monstrous, but I gained more that day than on any day of our marriage."

Her ladyship took a meditative sip of tea. "We all of us would have given our eyes to be in your place, once." Setting her cup back on its saucer, she shrugged gently. "I suppose we all make mistakes."

To be met with so much compassion from a woman she had expected to cordially dislike affected Genevieve with enough gratitude as to determine her upon fixing Lady Wraglain's friendship.

She accordingly confided various details of her struggles since her husband's death, and was rewarded with complete understanding.

"I am glad he left you with at least the house and the land, my dear," commented Lady Wraglain, "Poor Valeria Pynnstone, who married that no-account Langford, you know, was still in mourning when the bank took possession of Langford House."

"Yes, Bertram very thoughtfully neglected to sell off the cottage as well, though I cannot say he should not have recollected himself had he lived a month or two longer. Letting the house and land has brought us enough income to pay off the mortgages, and perhaps we may actually live in our proper home again soon."

"Which is more than Lady Langford can boast. She's now the drudge of her odious sister Lucretia."

"Poor Valeria," Genevieve sighed, in true sympathy. Aware of someone's eyes upon her, she turned and caught Sir Joshua just looking away. It occurred to her that if he listened, it was to find fault, and she pointedly turned away from him, unapologetically continuing her conversation. "At least she esteemed her husband, which must have sustained her during her embarrassments."

Lady Wraglain looked askance at her friend. "If Lord Langford had respected Valeria even half so much as she esteemed him, he would have left her provided for, rather than lining his worthless friend's pockets with the proceeds of his mortgages."

Genevieve smiled wryly. "One does not often respect another when one does not respect oneself, Caroline. I have often thought that if men made friends of their wives more than they did of other gentlemen, they might get on better with themselves."

"Ay, and the world would be a better place. Indeed, if females had charge of society, I daresay all problems would be at an end, would they not?" She sipped the last of her tea and set down her cup. "How did Bertram die, Genevieve? One hears rumors, of course, but one can rarely place one's dependence upon their veracity."

Feeling Sir Joshua's eyes upon her once more, Genevieve airily answered, "It was the hunt, Caroline. He took a toss into a gravel pit and broke his neck. He was killed instantly, which was distressing, to be sure, but imagine my relief when we found his hunter entirely uninjured; I sold the horse for enough to purchase another month's solace from the cents percent!"

Lady Wraglain, by this time, had observed Sir Joshua's interest in their conversation, and lifted her nose in his direction. "That gentleman seems disturbed by what he overhears."

"I have been given to understand that that gentleman does not approve the tone of my mind," replied Genevieve sapiently.

Her friend huffed, remarking loudly, "Anyone who cannot take truth with the bark on it is unwise to listen in on what don't concern them."

Genevieve nearly choked on her tea, but with great presence of mind, she safely deposited the cup and saucer on a side table without upsetting its remaining contents while she succumbed to an attack of coughing. After some judicious slaps to her back, obligingly administered by Lady Wraglain, she recovered sufficiently to beam upon a rapt audience consisting of all persons in the room.

"All is well, I assure you!" she said with ragged throat and streaming eyes. "Beg pardon for the disturbance; pay me no mind, pray!" The room resumed its low hum and, her shoulders shaking gently, Genevieve turned once again to her companion. "Caroline, how glad I am to have met with you again. You will think me selfish, but I wouldn't give you up for the world!"

There was another old acquaintance, however, that Genevieve did not value, and he most painfully obtruded himself upon her notice at a rout party held some days later in the home of a new acquaintance. The room being hot, Genevieve had drawn herself apart into a small alcove with an open window, and stood there, breathing in the cool night air and fanning herself. All at once, the fan was plucked from her grasp and employed by an unknown hand, and a lazy voice drawled in her ear, "My dear Mrs. B, you haven't aged a moment from when last I saw you."

She turned quickly, dreading that the person who addressed her so familiarly was who she thought, and found herself uncomfortably close to a finely-dressed gentleman of medium height, whose handsome face showed all the signs of a life of dissipation, paid for, Genevieve knew all too well, by her husband's addiction to gaming. She stiffened, and her disdain could not be hidden. "Lord Montrose."

She put up a hand for her fan, but he held it out of reach. "What luck to finally meet!" he said, pressing closer to her. "I've long suspected you to be in town, but with no sure knowledge of your whereabouts, I have despaired of renewing our acquaintance, never having found myself in the same room with you these many weeks. And yet here we are." His eyes flitted down and up her person, and his lips curled in a smile she could not like. "Yes, you are looking well, Mrs. B."

Momentarily paralyzed by revulsion and fear, she could only gaze speechlessly at him, memories of his inhuman unconcern for her family pulsing through her brain. How dared he approach her, much less speak to her, after his merciless actions during the years after Bertram's death? Anger at last freed her from stupor and, stepping quickly to the side, she retrieved her fan and, under the pretext of placing it back in her reticule, found time to recover herself, and she was soon able to smile upon her unwelcome companion.

"The years, I am grateful to say, have been kind to me, since last we met. But you, my lord! Forgive my inability to return the compliment, for you are so altered that I confess at first I did not know you."

Instead of offense, appreciation flashed in his eye, and he possessed himself of her hand. "You always did have such engaging manners, Mrs. B. But you must allow me to call you Genevieve."

He bent to drop a kiss on her fingers but she snatched her hand away, her smile unabated. "I must do no such thing, my lord."

He stepped back, affecting a wounded look. "Surely, with all our history, we must not stand upon ceremony, you and I."

Glad of the space, Mrs. Breckinridge took the opportunity to slip around him as she said, "On the contrary, my lord, our history requires that we stand very much upon ceremony. You will excuse me." With that, she slipped from the alcove, back into the safety of the crowded and stuffy room, and presently found an excuse to leave the party.

But many days passed before she could rid herself of the perturbation of their exchange, for she met him again, and again. Lord Montrose seemed after that to be everywhere, at this card party or that museum, with a box at the theater just opposite Lady Cammerby's, or astride a showy chestnut in Hyde Park—despite Genevieve's forsaking the fashionable hour of the Promenade and driving there at very different times. He did not attempt such cavalier treatment as previously, however. Now, he was unfailingly polite when he met her, but insistent upon a greeting, no matter how she slighted him. And though she took care not to seem to regard it, their meetings invariably left her shaken, for she did not know what he meant by it.

Not once did she deceive herself that Carlisle Dupray, Lord Montrose, had any honorable interest in her. He had never cared two straws about her before, whenever he had come to entice her husband away "for a game or two, among friends," which never ended before many hours and several hundred pounds had been lost. Even at Bertram's death, he had shown no consideration, only coming to Branwell to retrieve a pistol which he had lent some months previously, and expressing brief and trite condolence while in the act of presenting her with a stack of Bertram's vowels. These she had paid as quickly as possible, though it had taken many months to scrape up the money, only to get the vile reminders of him out of her sight. And she had never heard of him since.

Genevieve could not think why he would be courting her acquaintance now, when she had nothing of value to tempt him. Her fortune he had stolen, through Bertram, years ago, and her society she owed entirely to Lady Cammerby, so he could not hope to further himself in any way by her association. This sudden, public claim to her acquaintance worried the widow exceedingly, for he must have some end in view, and all her experience of Lord Montrose had taught her it would be only to his benefit, and to her detriment. But she could not find out what he wanted, and though she affected to not regard it, a shadowy, insubstantial foreboding haunted her.

Two consolations only did Genevieve find in spite of his unwelcome attention: that he had not been introduced to Lenora—and likely didn't even know of her existence—and that he was never to be found in Hill Street.

"I quite detest the man," cried Lady Cammerby, after she and her guest had met him in Hyde Park. Common civility had obliged them to pull up and exchange greetings, but the gentleman received no encouragement from either of the ladies in the barouche, and both parties directly moved on. "Such vulgar manners, to press his acquaintance upon you, Genevieve, when all the world knows he almost single-handedly ruined Bertram. I know not how you bear it, my love."

Assuming an air of unconcern she did not feel, Genevieve said, "I comfort myself with most unladylike visions of his comeuppance, dearest, and work to devise ever more clever set-downs."

"But he seems inured to them. I fear you waste your time."

"It is not a waste if it keeps my mind clear of dread," answered Genevieve airily. "One cannot fear what one makes ridiculous."

Lady Cammerby murmured agreement, but she could not keep herself from dropping a word in her brother's ear. "For Lord Montrose was your contemporary, was he not, Joshua? Do you not know him to be a dangerous man?"

Sir Joshua thoughtfully sipped his Madeira. "He is dangerous to any young flat who will take him up, but I have never known him to be a threat to a well-bred woman."

His sister was moved to expostulate. "Such a man does not confine his villainy to the card room, sir! I am persuaded that the same vice that drives him to delight in a man's ruin must manifest itself in all his dealings, to some degree."

"I agree, Amelia, but if Mrs. Breckinridge does not respond to him, he has no dealings with her. What damage a nod from him in a public place can do, if it is not reciprocated, I cannot see."

"Then you feel that nothing will come of his odious attentions to Genevieve?"

He set down his glass. "I did not say that. I merely recommend you do not refine too much upon it. Such men like to make a show, and without encouragement, he will most likely lose interest."

"Indeed, you must be right," answered his sister, without conviction.

Genevieve, however, took rather a more active approach, in the interest of forestalling as much danger to her family as possible, remarking off-handedly to Lenora one day, "I wonder if you have ever met Lord Montrose, my dear."

"Lord who, Mama?"

Her mother pulled gently at the thread on her needlework. "Lord Montrose. He was a friend of your papa's. Have you met him?"

"No, Mama," answered Lenora, in a tone of such mildness that her mother was instantly set on guard. "Should I have?"

"Oh, no," said Mrs. Breckinridge, "He does not move in our circles. He is quite beneath our touch, I believe."

"Oh." Lenora took up *The Mirror of Fashion* and turned over its pages. "If such is the case, I wonder why you should have brought his name up to me."

"I mention him only because I have had the misfortune to meet him here in town myself, and I fear he may push his acquaintance upon you, my love, on the strength of his friendship with your papa."

"How alarming," said Lenora politely.

"Not alarming, dear, only tiresome," Mrs. Breckinridge replied, with the greatest calm. "For, you know, such an acquaintance would surely jeopardize your very enjoyable place in society, and we should be obliged to give up the season and go home."

There was a pregnant silence, fraught for one lady with suspense, and for the other with consternation.

"Then I shall certainly cut him, if he is so disagreeable as to push for an introduction," Lenora presently declared. "I own I've longed to have a reason to cut someone."

Mrs. Breckinridge snipped her thread. "It is unfortunate, dearest, but you must. It is the only thing to do."

Lenora nodded obediently, and Genevieve, unsure if she had averted disaster, or invited it, merely smiled her approbation and continued her needlework.

Chapter 10

LENORA, BLISSFULLY IGNORANT of her mother's discomfiture, whether through the general self-absorption of youth or because her mother's manner was exceedingly convincing, felt herself very ill-used. That a former crony of her father, who would undoubtedly prove to be just the villain for whom she and Elvira had been on the look-out, should be in town and seeking their acquaintance, and that her mother should be beforehand enough to obligate her to cut him, was too cruel. Why could not Fate have placed him in her way before he had made himself odious to Mrs. Breckinridge? It was too provoking, for now Lenora must obey her mother, no matter how little she was disposed to do so.

Her youthful spirits could not long be depressed, however, for there was too much contentment to be had in each day's entertainments. If it was not an al fresco picnic, it was an outing to Sadler's Wells, or to Astley's Amphitheater. A fine day in early April found her with Elvira part of a gathering at Hampton Court comprised of no less than eighteen young people, and chaperoned by the gregarious Lady Timmington, whose genius in collecting about herself persons of youth, beauty, and interest was legendary. Lenora and Elvira felt all the honor they had received in the invitation, and were left only to wonder if they had been included for their beauty, their interest, or merely for their youth.

But all such considerations were swept aside by their introduction to Mr. Samuel Barnabus, who was brought to their attention by Mr. Ginsham. That gentleman's interest in Miss Chuddsley having become marked enough over the preceding weeks for even Lenora to notice, Mr. Ginsham had managed to appear at nearly all the social functions that had Elvira, and had begun refining his skill at extracting her from any large groups and securing her attentions to himself. Though somewhat disappointed to discover that he was not, as she had hoped, the younger and impoverished son of an earl, but the heir of a fairly well-to-do viscount, Elvira had not been unresponsive to his advances. Today, he approached the two ladies with Mr. Barnabus in tow, to solicit their company into the maze, which had begun to claim several of the party already.

"I know two adventurous young ladies such as yourselves will be wild to conquer the maze," he said, "therefore, I offer my poor experience, and that of, if you will permit me, Mr. Barnabus, here."

Mr. Barnabus politely took each young lady's hand in turn, saying, "Your m-most obedient."

Both girls stared hard at him, Lenora the first to recover. "Delighted, Mr., em, Barnaby."

He smiled and graciously corrected her. "B-barnabus, ma'am."

"Oh, pray, forgive me!" Lenora exchanged a speaking look with her bosom friend as she nodded to their new acquaintance. "Mr. Barnabus."

"We were just pining to enter the maze, Mr. Ginsham," declared Elvira, her eyes flitting to Mr. Barnabus as she spoke. "How timely is your invitation!"

If Mr. Ginsham noticed how his friend had eclipsed him with only a few words, his winning smile gave no indication. Holding out an arm to Elvira, he said, "Shall we, Miss Chuddsley?"

She took his arm readily enough, for although Lenora had the good fortune to be attached to Mr. Barnabus, she had thoughtfully maneuvered him between herself and her friend, and the four walked abreast to the maze. Entering the maze was impossible all side-by-side, but Elvira was able, through the expedient of allowing Lenora and Mr. Barnabus to go before, to keep the couple in sight, and so not miss any halting word that fell from Mr. Barnabus's lips.

It was not long before the young ladies had learned that Mr. Barnabus was just come down from Oxford, was the third son of a baronet, and had nearly decided to study law—three facts that resonated deeply within each female breast, attesting as they did to his heroic likeness—and they peppered him with so many questions that the young man was obliged to mutely appeal to his friend to aid him in redirecting their attentions. To his relief, through Ginsham's adept handling, the attractions of the maze soon supplanted the young ladies' fascination with stammering and hopeless poverty, and led them to fully enjoy an afternoon with the two very amiable young men. Elvira did not even cast a third glance at Mr. Barnabus, after the first and second, while she made her farewells to Mr. Ginsham, and Lenora made both young men feel so equally responsible for her present felicity, that all were smiles as they parted.

As soon as the young ladies had attained Lady Cammerby's carriage, however, Elvira grasped her friend's arm. "Oh, Lenora! He is the ideal, is he not?"

"Ginsham? I think him as agreeable as ever, but—"

"Oh, do not rally me! You know very well I speak of Mr. Barnabus!" With a sigh, Elvira collapsed onto the squabs. "I believe him to be the most attractive man in the world!"

"Next to Ginsham?" retorted Lenora, who thought it quite unreasonable of Elvira to wish to lay claim to yet another young man's heart. "You are either blind, or you have windmills in your head, my dear."

"Speak no more of Ginsham, if you please! I wish only to think of Mr. Barnabus's perfections!"

Lenora eyed her askance. "Who knew that a stammer could make invisible a hawk nose and stooping shoulders!"

"Oh, unfair, Lenora!" Elvira cried out. "His nose is not hawkish at all, merely—aristocratic! And *if* I noticed a deficiency in his posture, I would rather call his shoulders sloping, than stooped!"

Recognizing that her ploy had failed, Lenora abandoned all pretense at criticism to agree with her friend. "The obvious result of diligent study, by candlelight, in a tiny boarding room at the college. Oh, Elvira, he will make an excellent lawyer! I foresee him defending the poor and abused, without thought of reward."

Her friend sat bolt upright at this inspiring vision. "His elocution alone will excite such sympathy with the judge and jury! But they must also be impressed by his earnest expression and sober air."

Disregarding that this description was an absolute departure from the young man who had exhibited enough liveliness with them in the maze to impress a judge only with disfavor, Lenora leaned intently toward her friend. "But how will he measure up against the evil Duke?"

Elvira's eyes widened. "How could we know that, until we have met the Duke?"

"Which we may never do," Lenora sighed mournfully, resting back against the squabs as her mind revolved on her mother's stricture against Lord Montrose.

Elvira said, after some hesitation, "But perhaps it is Sir Joshua after all."

"Oh, no, Elvira, it cannot be he!" cried Lenora. "The thought revolts!"

"But why not? We know little enough about him—"

"We know enough to acquit him of villainy, Elvira! Consider! He is Lady Cammerby's brother, and moves in the best circles. He came to my ball, and danced with me, and my mother, and never showed the least sign of rakishness. I am persuaded that the town would be talking of him if he were the least questionable."

Elvira bounced in her seat. "But the Duke is often virtuous in public, and it is only when he steals away the fair maiden that he is found to be black at heart!"

"That is true," said Lenora, suddenly struck. "Like my father!" A furrow appeared between her brows as she pondered this revelation. "Only, I believe he was not evil, precisely. It was his friends who—" She threw up her hands, falling back against the squabs in defeat. "Oh, Elvira! We shall never meet the evil Duke, though I know who he is!"

"You what?" shrieked Elvira. "Lenora Breckinridge, how could you hide such a thing—tell me who it is at once, Lenora, at once!" she cried, tugging at Lenora's arm.

Lenora merely groaned. "You do not know him—I do not even know him, and it is too vexing, but I know his name!"

"What?" Elvira let go her arm in disgust. "Anyone can know a name, Lenora. If all we needed was a name, we could imagine to ourselves any number of villains, and call them whatever we wished!"

She turned stern eyes upon her friend. "We must find a real villain, and we must meet him to be sure of the depravity of his character!"

Lenora despondently waved away this assertion. "Elvira, I have found a real villain, for my mama warned me against him, but we cannot meet him, for she most straightly charged me to avoid him— but he was a friend to my papa," she added hastily, perceiving a look of skepticism creep into her friend's face, "so you see, we are assured that his character is most black!"

Elvira's interest was regained. She shifted nearer to her friend, round-eyed. "And what is his name?"

"Lord Montrose," Lenora said, in sinister accents.

"Lord Montrose," Elvira repeated, tasting the taint of the name on her tongue. She shivered and turned half frightened, half shining eyes on her friend. "Perhaps it is enough to simply know his name. Though we may never meet him, I have the most dreadful feeling that our worst fears will be realized!"

Chapter 11

B UT ALL DREADFUL excitement was forgot with the arrival of Mr. Thomas Breckinridge in Hill Street. Never having been keen on meeting the demands of fine society, Tom had nevertheless faced his duty with fortitude, and set out for London on horseback alone, for Matthew was needed on the farm. He broke his journey at his friend Humphrey Twindale's estate, where he was sufficiently reinforced by fellow-feeling and excellent wine to face the exigencies of the coming fortnight, but the fine weather, aided by a gouty attack sustained by Humphrey's father—which rendered the old gentleman mightily disagreeable—resolved Tom to put his journey forward a day, and he therefore reached Hill Street without notice.

Tying his horse in front of the house, he took the steps two at a time, and rapped smartly on the door. It was opened by the footman, who, at Tom's inquiry, was just entering upon the merits of a stable to be had nearby, when Lady Cammerby sailed into the foyer and stopped dead.

"Bless my soul, but you must be Tom Breckinridge!" she cried, one hand to her bosom and her face white as a sheet.

Confronted by this shocked female, who proceeded to stare at him in the blankest astonishment, Tom forgot the speech he had glibly prepared to explain away the impropriety of his coming a day ahead of his time, and only just managed to bow creditably, and assume what he hoped to be his politest expression. "Your servant, Lady Cammerby."

Her ladyship, recollecting herself at his words, swept forward, her hands out to grasp his. "Oh, my dear boy, forgive me, but you are the image of your father. It took me quite twenty years back!" She pulled him into the house, volubly explaining that his dear mother and sister were out at the moment, having not expected him until the next day.

With mixed feelings at her reference to his father, Tom made an effort to recall the gist of his speech, and made his apologies. "The weather is so fine, you see, and travel was easy, and I determined that rather than dawdle, I'd best come along and get it ov—that is, join my family sooner than later!" he finished with aplomb.

"To be sure!" cried his hostess, without hesitation. "You are welcome at any time in my house, I assure you, and we shall get you settled so there will be no more bustle to attend to when your family returns."

"Thank you, ma'am," he said, the sincerity of her words dispelling his discomfort. "I only must find a stable for my horse—"

"Nonsense! Cammerby keeps the best stables hereabouts, and shall never be known to turn away a guest's cattle. I will brook no arguments on that head, for if you are anything like your mama, you will have the impertinence to question my hospitality! No, no," she said, imperiously waving away his objections. "Cottam will see to your horse." She nodded to the butler, who bowed as she shepherded Tom upstairs to his chamber.

An hour later saw him unpacked and changed, and possessed of perfect charity for his hostess, toward whom his heart had earlier been softened by the contentment and gratitude of his mother's and sister's letters, and regarding whose disinterested goodness in throwing about her money on his sister's behalf he was now perfectly satisfied. He was soon very happily ensconced with his mother, sister, and hostess in the Blue Saloon, and regaling them with the particulars of his journey.

After satisfying herself of his good health, and that of Humphrey Twindale, whom she had known since he was in short coats, Mrs. Breckinridge sat back, listening complacently to the spirited argument that presently sprang up between Tom and his sister regarding the superiority of London to the country. Tom refused to imagine that a city could afford more amusement than the country, while Lenora maintained that the country had never been in any way exciting.

"There are infinitely more engagements to be had in town than in the country, Tom," insisted Lenora. "I congratulate myself that I have never been obliged to spend an evening at home above once in a week."

Her brother harrumphed at this. "If all one lived for was to be amused, then I suppose a never-ending string of engagements might be something on which to congratulate oneself! But *some* minds are of a more serious stamp, and could never find satisfaction in having no discretionary time, whereas the country offers such persons plenty of leisure."

"I suppose if one does not enjoy society, the country must be pleasanter," observed Lenora handsomely, "however, if one wishes to mix with more than a few of the same families one has seen forever, one cannot argue that town society is superior."

"There is plenty of good society in the country, if one desires to have it—or have you forgotten the house parties, and assemblies—"

"I was speaking of new and fresh society, Tom," Lenora said.

"And I was speaking of good society, Nora," returned her brother.

When they had come to an inevitable stand, their mother considered it wise to intervene. "In one way, I must agree with Lenora that the city does outshine the country," she said, her eyes twinkling, "and that is in the assemblies. Your arrival is most opportune, Tom, for we had just determined on attending the assembly at Almack's this evening, and a party of females is never so unexceptionable as when augmented by a handsome young man."

"Indeed, you are right, Genevieve," put in Lady Cammerby, "and I have sent around to invite my brother Joshua to dine, expressly so I may present him to you, and shall desire him to come along with us. He is a most accomplished dancer, and will round out our party admirably."

Tom, whose countenance had assumed an almost wooden politeness, rolled a distressed eye in his mother's direction, and she hastened to reassure him. "Sir Joshua is Lady Cammerby's only brother," she said, stressing the solitariness of her friend's relations, which seemed to comfort her son. "He is a perfect gentleman, and I have every expectation of your getting on famously."

Thus soothed, Tom managed a wan smile to his hostess. "I am all delight, ma'am."

But once alone with his mama, as they ascended the stairs to dress for dinner, he whispered tightly, "I've come to do my duty by you and Lenora, Mama, and I knew full well that would mean dancing and doing the pretty, for I have not forgotten my promise to squire you to assemblies, but I will tell you to your head that if you'd warned me I'd be thrown in head-first, I'd have spent an extra day at Twinny's."

She patted his hand affectionately. "And we would not have blamed you one bit, dear, but what has me in a puzzle is how you supposed me to have warned you, when I had no notion of your coming before your time, until you had come." He was visibly consternated by this just remark, but she went on serenely, "I would cry off this evening, my dear, to make you more comfortable, but Lenora is so looking forward to it—your sister is simply wild about dancing!—and tonight is to be her first time at Almack's. We were unable to attend the opening night of the season, you see, but if you do not care to go, and Lady Cammerby is unsuccessful in securing Sir Joshua's escort, I hardly know how we shall contrive, for we would be left quite unprotected."

Affronted by the insinuation that he would put his comfort before that of his family, Tom did not think to question why a party of two matrons and a young lady had need of protection at Almack's. "What do you take me for, Mama? I am not such a care-for-nobody that I'd thrust a spoke in your wheel just to save myself annoyance! We shall all go to Almack's, and dance, and do the civil, and shall enjoy ourselves immensely!" he said with dignity.

Mrs. Breckinridge pressed his hand and beamed upon him. "How good you are, Tom, and for that, I give you my promise that I'll not to throw you in head first again, at least while you are in London."

He grinned at her. "If I know you, Mama, something—entirely out of your control, of course—will occur to throw me on my ear, no matter how faithfully you promise."

They parted in the corridor, and Tom, never one to fuss overmuch about his appearance, arrived in the empty drawing room with several minutes to spare. After glancing over the pages of the day's newspaper, he took a moment to peruse the paintings on the walls, of much younger versions of Lady and, he assumed, Lord Cammerby, and two fine young boys. He was absorbed in this task when the door opened behind him and he turned to find a tall gentleman with a rather stern countenance, whom he fancied he recognized as the man both Mrs. Breckinridge and Lenora had described in their letters.

"You must be Mr. Breckinridge," said the gentleman, extending a hand. "I am Sir Joshua Stiles."

Tom acknowledged this, shaking Sir Joshua's hand, and they stood back, taking each other's measure.

Sir Joshua said, "I see little of your mother in you. You must take after your father."

"I do, sir," answered Tom, stiffening slightly.

Correctly interpreting this alteration in Tom's manner, Sir Joshua remarked, "I did not know your father personally."

His unintentional emphasis on the last word impressed Tom to disclaim, "I take after him only in appearance, sir."

"I have no doubt," Sir Joshua said, smiling in a disarming way. "You have nothing to fear from me, young man. All I know of your father is hearsay, and I seldom rely on such stuff."

Put off his guard, Tom admitted, "I would I could say he was wronged, sir, but I haven't heard a rumor about him that wasn't true."

At that point, Lenora and Mrs. Breckinridge entered the room, and the conversation was necessarily diverted into less awkward channels, helped on by Mrs. Breckinridge's resolution to be on her best behavior in Sir Joshua's presence. The talk centered on Lenora's expectations of a fantastical evening, her visions of Almack's Assembly Rooms having been embroidered by Elvira's rapturous description of opening night. None too soon for more than one person in the room, Lady Cammerby entered, and the butler announced that dinner was served.

The group being small, and the elders indulgently willing to remain silent, Lenora's running account to her brother of all the delightful outings she had attended quite dominated the conversation. When she turned to a list of all her expectations for his visit, Tom's eyes began to bulge, and Mrs. Breckinridge thought it expedient to try and save him, but Sir Joshua anticipated her by turning the conversation, abruptly but politely, to the farm at Branwell, and Tom's plans for breeding.

"Have you been to Branwell Cottage, sir?" inquired Tom, no more surprised than pleased.

"Briefly. I had the honor of losing myself in the country a few months ago, and ended at your door." Tom and Lenora both stared at him, and his handsome smile lit his face. "I had a letter to deliver from my sister, but I was at the mercy of the most abominable luck, and wandered for what seemed like hours. I was even beset by no less than two herds of recalcitrant animals, a lame leader, and—" with a meaningful glance at Mrs. Breckinridge, "a wagon stuck in the mire."

"One may imagine your temper must have been sorely tried, sir," said Mrs. Breckinridge, in deepest sympathy.

"It was, ma'am." He turned his eyes to her, reassuming his grave demeanor. "But if I was so ungentlemanlike as to be uncivil, even in so vulnerable a moment, I should hope that I have been forgiven."

She blushed, caught unawares by this sincere apology, and suddenly found the contents of her plate vastly interesting.

"You delivered the letter!" cried Lenora. "But Sally said you found her in the garden!"

He cleared his throat. "I believe my arrival was unanticipated."

"No one was there to receive you at the door!" pursued Lenora, leaning forward over her plate in her chagrin. "And you being lost, and weary to the bone, I am sure. Someone should have been there to offer you refreshment, and rest! Oh, sir, it was unforgivable in us!"

"Do not give it another thought, Miss Breckinridge. Sally, I believe you said her name was, received me very kindly, and far from being tired, I was pleased to have the delight of traversing your garden path, which afforded me a view of a most pleasant farm, and sheds on the property." He turned to Tom. "What do you plan to do with them, Mr. Breckinridge?"

Needing no further encouragement to enlarge upon the theme dearest to his heart, Tom readily expatiated his plans for the farm and animals, and Mrs. Breckinridge's eyes flew from one to the other as they carried the conversation for the remainder of the dinner, with only a few interjections from an eager Lenora. Sir Joshua's interest was gratifying, and Tom's knowledge left nothing to shame, but Mrs. Breckinridge felt a twinge of pain watching them. This was a conversation that Tom could have had with his own father, but had not, and never should have, even had Bertram lived. But the megrims could not flourish in light of Tom's evident enjoyment of the interchange, and she ended the dinner quite satisfied with everything.

After dinner, they set out together to Almack's, walking in the mild evening, and again Mrs. Breckinridge's pride in her son was justified when he offered his arm to Lady Cammerby, and the other to her, and walked with them, giving such assiduous attentions to his hostess as to make a most pleasing impression. Her attention was divided, however, between admiration of her son's excellent manners and an itching desire to hear what Lenora and Sir Joshua were talking of. The low murmur of their conversation pulled at her ears, and it was only with great self-control that she did not turn her head to hear what was said.

Almost immediately upon their entering the ball room, Mr. Ginsham came to greet them, along with a Miss Diana Marshall—one of their numerous new acquaintance—a circumstance which proved to enliven Mr. Breckinridge exceedingly. When Elvira joined their party, the evening promised to exceed expectations, but the young ladies sought for Mr. Barnabus in vain. After inquiry, Ginsham confirmed that the stammering young man "was no dancer, desiring rather to study his books against the time he stood for exams." This information could not but injure him in the eyes of his admirers, and it was only with much whispered discussion and general large-mindedness that the ladies were finally able to acquit him of unheroic character. This was accomplished by their discovering that devotion to the future public good was, in fact, more romantic than spending every available moment in agreeable activity with one's heart's desire, because, of course, one's devotion would be torn between the two occupations, thus enhancing one's tragic attractions.

The preservation of Mr. Barnabus's character thus accomplished, neither Elvira nor Lenora had cause to repine his absence, for both young ladies were soon surrounded by their admirers, who gave their minds little opportunity to wander. Tom, partaking of the attractions of Miss Marshall, in addition to those of several of her pretty friends, found the assembly far more enjoyable than he had thought possible, and began to congratulate himself on the great good sense of his coming a day ahead of schedule. Though he was not in general keen on dancing, he possessed a natural talent for it that distinguished him as a most desirable partner, and neither Miss Marshall, nor any of the other ladies he stood up with were made to regret the circumstance.

Seeing her children so happily engaged, Mrs. Breckinridge settled into a seat along the wall with the other chaperones, and thought to spend the evening in conversation, but a certain set of broad shoulders kept catching her eye, and she found herself unable to focus on the vapid chatter of the matron beside her. The lady did not seem to recognize Mrs. Breckinridge's lack of attendance, but prattled on as if she were reciting a laundry list, leaving her companion free to observe, fascinated, the machinations of two ladies in particular who seemed to be vying to gain Sir Joshua's attention for their very plain daughters. No matter how forbidding his aspect, or strained his civilities, the girls took turns chatting in what looked to be the most hen-witted manner, giggling and simpering and gazing up at him through their lashes. Consternation was writ plain on his face, but neither the girls nor their mamas—one of which Genevieve recognized as Lady Castleton, a rival from bygone days—heeded it, instead gaining encouragement, perhaps by imagining the other as the cause of his annoyance.

The press of bodies hid Sir Joshua from her view from time to time, but she spied him dancing with each of the girls and then with their mamas, with no visible enjoyment, until at last he ducked into the refreshment room, and did not reappear. As the minutes lengthened, Mrs. Breckinridge smiled to herself, envisioning him hiding under the refreshment table rather than endure the overtures of these fair maidens—or their mamas.

She was surprised, then, to find him at her elbow, requesting the honor of a dance. Smiling archly, she said, "How low you stoop to ask a matron such as I! Surely there is some young thing wishing most sincerely to dance with you."

Tension bled through his polite mask. "But I have asked you to dance, have I not?"

At that moment she chanced to see Lady Castleton bearing down on him, her face set, and taking pity on him, allowed him to lead her into the set. They moved through one or two figures of the dance in silence, but she could not long refrain from quizzing him. "It must be difficult to bear, being so much in demand as you are."

"Perhaps you may now understand why I am not often available to escort my sister to the assemblies."

An attempt to hide her smile only revealed a telltale dimple. "I confess I had imagined you taking refuge behind a handy curtain somewhere, sir, but I suppose such extremes will not always answer."

She thought she saw his cheek twitch. "They are most determined ladies."

"And you are too much the gentleman to give them the cut direct," she observed, assuming a thoughtful expression. "Perhaps I may be of service to you, for a change, sir. I am not averse to giving rather more pointed hints. You must only say the word, and I shall do my poor best on your behalf."

"I would give your offer some serious consideration, ma'am, but I am persuaded your efforts would be in vain, merely clearing the field for a new onslaught. I fear that until I am no longer viewed as a matrimonial prize, I shall continue to be a victim."

"If that is the complexion of the matter, sir, I can still hope to be of use to you. I must only think of some way to destroy your character."

"Oh, no, that will not answer, ma'am, unless you divest me of my fortune as well. For as long as the worth of a man is great, his sins are counted as negligible."

"Then you must gamble away your fortune. I have it on the best authority that it is easily done at White's or Watier's, or even more expeditiously in any number of quiet little houses in St. James' Street."

"An interesting notion which I shall forego, ma'am."

"You have no aspirations to waste your substance, sir? How odd in you. I had accounted it all the rage for rich men to outrun the constable."

"No, somehow I wish to end my days in comfort, having never dipped in a certain infamous river, and with something more than debt and dishonor to leave to my posterity."

"Then endurance is your only recourse, sir, for age and infirmity must surely discourage at last."

He chuckled. "It has yet to deter the most dogged, ma'am. I fear they shall badger me until I am dead."

"Or married, sir—although to some it is one and the same. But, their opinions notwithstanding, marriage could prove the more desirable fate for you. Perhaps you ought to look about you for some eligible spinster with whom you would not be too disgusted to spend the small remainder of your life."

"There are far too many for my liking, ma'am, but I do not scruple to tell you that I'd as lief take my chances with death. At least while I wait for the end, I may hope for happiness."

"Hope is but a dream, sir, if such delightful females as there are here do not entice you."

"I did not say *all* the females here did not entice me, ma'am, but only those with mercenary mamas."

She smiled graciously and said, "You may feel secure in the knowledge that I will never throw Lenora at your head."

He looked down, meeting her eyes. "I flatter myself that you will never have the need to, ma'am," he said evenly. The dance ended, and he led her off the floor.

Something about his last words had disturbed her, but as he bowed her to a chair she said lightly, "Perhaps if you danced with

Lenora, your admirers would be more effectively deterred."

"Your solicitude is most moving, but I am unable to dance with Miss Breckinridge, though not for lack of trying. The happy effects of your tutelage, ma'am, are that she has been engaged all the evening."

Smiling warmly, he bowed, and left her to consider why her spirits felt suddenly impaired.

Chapter 12

IT WAS NOT before many more outings with Mr. Ginsham and Mr. Barnabus that Lenora and Elvira began to chafe at one another, for ownership of the hero naturally belonged to the heroine, a role each was more than eager to assume, but that neither wished to relinquish, even to her bosom friend.

"Ginsham makes no secret of his admiration for you, Elvira, and you cannot deny that you like him," said Lenora one day, as she walked with her friend in the park.

"I like him, Lenora dear, but so may any number of young ladies. Liking has nothing to do with love, you know." Elvira nodded prettily to a passing gentleman. "I may like several gentlemen, but will bestow my heart upon only one."

"Poor Ginsham," Lenora said reflectively. "His heart will be quite broken, you know."

Elvira glanced quickly up at her. "Surely not. If he does feel strongly for me, it is only calf-love, and he is such a lively fellow that I cannot believe he could ever be long cast down."

"But the sunniest optimist may suffer from disappointment, my dear." Lenora sighed gustily. "He is destined to join the ranks of broken men, ghosts of their former selves, bravely concealing their tragic pasts from heedless eyes."

Elvira's pace slowed. "You refine too much upon his attention to me, Lenora, depend upon it. He could not suffer so on my account."

Perceiving a note of uncertainty in her words, Lenora pounced. "You do not see his eyes upon you, Elvira, when you are not looking. I, who am in a position to see all, could not be more convinced that he pines for you."

"Oh," said Elvira, her cheeks flushing pink. They walked in contemplative silence for several minutes, brightening only to acknowledge an acquaintance or two as they passed. Suddenly, Elvira straightened and said, rather hurriedly, "It doesn't signify, Lenora, if he pines for me, for I feel nothing but friendship for him. Oh, it is tragic indeed that his love must be unrequited, and I would not hurt him for the world, but my heart has been won already, and I cannot give it again, can I? Poor Ginsham must find his true love in another, for I am destined for Mr. Barnabus!"

With pursed lips, Lenora hastened to catch up with her friend, whose pace had quickened as she spoke, but she did not deign to reply to this idiotish speech. Clearly, her dear Elvira was deluding herself as to her feelings for Mr. Barnabus or, at the very least, his feelings for her. For Lenora could not be more certain that their hero had chosen neither of them—yet—and if only Elvira could be made to know her own heart, the way would be clear for Lenora to win Mr. Barnabus.

The remainder of their outing being singularly unproductive, she parted civilly with her friend, but entered the house on Hill

Street with a determination to take matters into her own hands, for Mr. Ginsham, amiable though he was, had proven himself absurdly cowhanded in his courtship of Elvira. He was only a man, after all, and could not be expected to understand that to capture a young lady's heart, he must captivate her imagination, but with the odds against him, his time was running out. She pulled off her bonnet and set it on the dressing table with decision. She would simply have to guide him, for his own good.

Thus, Lenora entered into the noble cause of dissolving the scales from her bosom friend's eyes, by endeavoring to show the Honorable Mr. Ginsham in his best light. Selflessly placing her immediate enjoyment behind the cause of her friend, Lenora strove tirelessly at every opportunity to enhance Ginsham's romantic qualities, and to diminish the impact of such vulgarities as fortune, title, and excellent health, of which he was so unhappily possessed. In addition, Mr. Barnabus, whose attractions far exceeded Mr. Ginsham's, must be cast into the shade whenever the two gentlemen were in Elvira's company together—which was more often than not—and Lenora required all her ingenuity to accomplish this without offending her poor victim. Such machinations were exhausting, but Lenora, committed to effacing herself for the greater good, was undeterred, even successfully recruiting her mother's genius without harboring suspicion—which would sadly have necessitated an explanation of her motives.

For this cause, Mrs. Breckinridge was made to yield to her daughter's entreaties to chaperone Lenora, Elvira, Tom, Miss Marshall, Mr. Ginsham, and the indispensable Mr. Barnabus, to the opera, taking Lady Cammerby's box at the dear woman's insistence, as she had caught a chill and was laid up in bed, for fear of being carried off by the putrid throat. The young people were in high spirits, every one eager to impress the others with their refinement. The music was, thankfully, exquisite, and at the interval, the gentlemen, ready to stretch their legs, expressed their willingness to take the young ladies for refreshment. Mrs. Breckinridge readily agreed, declining to join them on the grounds that she wished to let the last aria ring in her mind without their endless babble and chatter. Grinning at this, the noisy group left her to the relative peace of the box, and after procuring lemonade for their companions, Tom drew Miss Marshall away to a window, while Ginsham and Barnabus hastened to expound upon the artistic merits of the performers.

"Catalani may not be much to look at, but her technique cannot be matched," insisted Ginsham.

"I w-will allow her technique to b-be s-superior, but M-mombel-li's voice holds s-such ethereal beauty that it cap-ptivates the soul!"

Elvira's eyes shone as she gazed with adoration upon Barnabus. "I cannot agree more, sir. Such a voice attests to an inner purity that is far more compelling than technique."

"What is technique but the expert guidance of natural talent?" proposed Lenora, perceiving her protegee on unsteady ground.

"Exactly, Miss Breckinridge," cried Ginsham, eager to recover his position. "Without pure, natural talent, technique is mere posturing. But Catalani marries the two for a truly glorious result."

Elvira gazed at him with new respect, but Barnabus crossed his arms over his chest. "Glory b-belongs to heaven, and M-mombelli's voice is that of an-n angel."

Elvira's eyes flew back to him, her attention arrested by that last, evocative word, and Ginsham rather desperately burst out, "Pure and innocent, I'll allow, but a mere whisper to Catalani's power—" He faltered under Elvira's look of outrage.

Lenora gritted her teeth, resolved. "Do not angels speak with trumpets as well as with whispers? Perhaps both orders of angels are represented here." All eyes turned to her and she added, "One may be stately, while the other is fragile, but you must own both to be inspiring."

She had the satisfaction of watching Elvira's assimilation of her metaphor, and her subsequent, and very thoughtful, sideways glance at Mr. Ginsham.

Meanwhile, Genevieve, glad for a respite from her beloved but energetic offspring and their friends, placidly gazed out at the milling throng in the pit, grateful that dear Amelia had placed her box at their disposal. She glanced over the occupants of the other boxes, raising a hand to some few acquaintances and wondering idly if any would come to visit her. However, when the curtain behind her did part, serenity all but deserted her as Lord Montrose entered.

Concealing her discomfort under a mask of indifference, she regarded him coolly, waiting for him to make known his intentions, for though fairly confident that he did not mean to accost her physically in the broad public view, she knew full well that the majority of her box was in shadow, and could not be seen from the other boxes, or the pit.

Her guest paused at the threshold to afford her a bow. "Mrs. B, again we are thrown together. It is the hand of Fate; there can be no other explanation."

"I have been used to consider the practice of shortening surnames to mere initials vulgar in conversation, my lord, and the vehicle of contempt." She swept a disdainful gaze over him. "But if you insist upon it, I shall not scruple to call you Lord M."

He smiled appreciatively and disposed himself in the seat next to her, leaning toward her over the chair arm. "Your readiness to address me so discreetly excites the imagination, madam."

Astonishment held her frozen for an instant as his meaning registered in her brain but, rejecting the impulse to jump up from her chair and flee the box, she kept her features impassive, eyeing him with bored contempt. "Only in the basest imagination could one find gratification in the degradation of one's character, my lord."

He chuckled. "Bertram's widow, so high flown! I trust you know not what you say, for surely your experience has taught you that the height of one's character has nothing to do with gratification."

"It is not surprising that one who finds enjoyment only in the disgrace of another's situation should feel thus. Let me assure you that I know exactly what I say, and will thank you to leave this box immediately."

He pulled back, lifting his quizzing glass and considering her through it. "You seem ignorant of the already disgraceful state of your situation, ma'am. It is well within my power, I assure you, to either elevate it or to degrade it further, according to my satisfaction with your wishes."

"You mistake, my lord," she answered, gazing unperturbed at his ridiculously magnified eye while inwardly she seethed. "My situation is not in the least disgraceful, and I have no interest in your satisfaction. If I had possessed any notion you were laboring under such a delusion, I should have employed less subtle measures to convince you, for you are sadly unresponsive to gentle hints."

"I can be very responsive," he let his gaze slide down her face to her bosom, which rose and fell more quickly than she would have wished, "under the right inducements."

"Someone, I am sure, somewhere, pines to provide you with such inducements, my lord," she returned sweetly. "May I encourage you to leave off this empty hope with me and find her, or him, without further waste of time?"

His eyes snapped back to her face, and he tapped his mouth thoughtfully with his glass. "It is a wonder that Bertram ever tired of you, my dear Genevieve."

"An observant man would discover no mystery in that, my lord," she said silkily. "When one is routinely bled, one not surprisingly finds oneself easily tired by otherwise desirable interests."

The tell-tale sounds of a noisy young party returning brought him to his feet, but his eyes did not leave her face, an unsettling smile twisting on his lips. "I regret even more strongly that I have for so long grossly underestimated your worth, Mrs. Breckinridge." He gracefully bowed. "Until we meet again."

He quit the box in two strides, and then the young people returned, chatting animatedly as they settled again in their seats, and none seeming to notice the silence of their chaperone as the lights were dimmed and the orchestra struck up for the second act.

It was not to be supposed that the state of Genevieve's mind should admit of her attending to the music, but while she could not afterward give her opinion as to its excellence, its subconscious effects were felt in the rapidity with which her emotions were set in order. Her foremost sensation was indignation that he should offer her such an affront, but this was closely seconded by apprehension, for she hardly knew what he meant by it. That he could be truly attracted to her, even in so vulgar a manner, was a notion that she quickly dismissed, for she cherished no illusions regarding her personal charms. She allowed herself to be a good-looking woman, but a matron, and a widow, and far removed from the vivacity and daring that had given her success in her youth. No, Lord Montrose had another reason for his attentions. That he had followed her snub with a threat supported the notion that he believed her to be an easy prey, as her husband had been, and that he desired merely to show his power. But she could not be satisfied with this explanation, any more than the other, for there was something in his manner that made her very much afraid.

Her fear did not stem from money, for she and Tom between them had paid all Bertram's outstanding debts, and neither she nor Tom were in any way addicted to gaming; Lord Montrose could neither purchase nor induce them to create a debt for him to hold, which had been his chief method of enslaving Bertram. But Genevieve had a weakness that had never plagued her husband, and which Lord Montrose, if he was not already aware of it, could guess with little trouble: Genevieve loved her children, and would protect them at any cost.

She felt little anxiety over Tom's safety, his feelings being very strongly expressed against every vice that had possessed his father. Lord Montrose may try his hand at seducing Tom into low company, or into gaming hells, or to strong drink, but she would hold herself exceedingly shocked if he succeeded at all. But Lenora's safety was an entirely different matter. Lenora, having no experience outside their restricted country circle, could not be depended upon to recognize a dangerous man when she saw him, especially one with such a gentlemanlike appearance, and so well-versed in the arts of flirtation. And to complicate matters further, Lenora, as borne out by her reaction to her mother's warning, had entered into that stage in her development when everything dangerous is alluring, and every warning becomes a challenge.

No, Lord Montrose must not be allowed to meet Lenora, for having already tested her curiosity, Genevieve had no doubt that no sooner met than he would swiftly dominate the girl's imagination. Once part of her acquaintance, Lord Montrose would flirt so skillfully with Lenora as to convince her that only such a girl as she could catch him, while preserving an uncertainty of her power over him, leading her along until she was so firmly under his spell that what good sense she did have would be supplanted by the romantic notion of enslaving a Bad Man.

She could not even be sure that he knew of Lenora's existence, but while they were in London, Genevieve could place no dependence on Lenora's never exciting the notice of such a resourceful man as Lord Montrose. Though he did not move in the same circles as they did under Lady Cammerby's aegis, Genevieve was forever meeting him, in the park, at the theater or opera, on the street. She could fairly fob him off, but only with the force of ingenuity, and Lenora was not proof against his style. It was true that under the strictures of London society it would be difficult for him to force an introduction onto Lenora in any but the most extreme situation, but Genevieve had no doubt Lord Montrose could readily contrive such a circumstance.

Yet, they could not quit London. Besides giving rise to undesirable gossip, to leave precipitously in the middle of the season would not only make Lenora feel excessively ill-used, which could bring on an even more unpleasant situation at Branwell, but would be an act of cowardice likely to entice Lord Montrose into following them. What better evidence of his power could she give him than a show of fear? No, he must be dealt with, at the very least until Lenora could be made to understand her danger, and be trusted to comport herself sensibly.

How to accomplish this, Genevieve little knew, for Lord Montrose had made it plain to her that he had no intention of discontinuing his attentions, however little she welcomed them. He thought, perhaps, to wear her down, to flatter her into submission to his whim, and while she was resolved never to submit to such a man, in any way, she could also foresee much unpleasantness ahead.

Strangely, this thought served to revive her, for she, of all females, was inured to unpleasantness. Alone she may be, fearful and uncertain she may be, but of one thing she was sure: persistent, indeed, would be the man who could succeed in such tactics against the widow of Bertram Breckinridge, and he should find himself forced to endure every bit as much unpleasantness as would she.

Chapter 13

AS IT TRANSPIRED, Mrs. Breckinridge was not immediately called upon to test her resolve, for Tom proved a ready replacement to herself as chaperone, suddenly anxious as he was to be in Lenora's company. Where Lenora went, Elvira was sure to go, and there needed very little coaxing to ensure that the lovely Miss Marshall would attend them. And Mr. Ginsham, having recognized in Mr. Barnabus a veritable snake in the bosom, found a most suitable alternative to him in Tom—toward whom Elvira cherished only sisterly feelings—and the two were soon found to be almost daily together, concocting schemes for the young ladies' entertainment.

This happy circumstance left Mrs. Breckinridge with a choice hitherto unavailable to her: that of becoming inaccessible to Lord Montrose. Tom proved equal to almost every outing Lenora wished for—with the notable exception of the occasional, but essential, shopping expedition—and these, in addition to attending an evening at Almack's here and there, Mrs. Breckinridge did not grudge.

Indeed, she had discovered, after the bustle of the previous several weeks, that she required these periods of respite, having become aware of a growing fatigue occasioned by her unaccustomed pace in town. Lady Wraglain commented upon it one day—"my dear you look worn to a frazzle"—and Genevieve, in a blinding flash of brilliance, seized the opportunity to retire for a time behind the imminently useful screen of ill-health.

Lady Cammerby, while entering fully into her dear friend's desire to rest herself, could not feel that a withdrawal at this time was necessary, or prudent.

"I cannot conceive of what you hope to accomplish by shutting yourself up in this house," she said rather pettishly one day, after Genevieve had declined yet another invitation. "For anyone can see that you are in the best of health, though you profess to be out of sorts."

"Exactly, my dear Amelia," replied Genevieve placidly, setting another stitch in the petticoat she was mending. "If I were to show myself about, no one would be in the least deceived, and I should get no rest at all!"

Lady Cammerby pursed her lips at that, and plumped herself into a chair, pouting, "And while you sit here, heedlessly sewing, Lenora gambols about town, free to catch any rascal's eye!"

"But she is not free! Do not forget that Tom is constantly her escort, Amelia, and has a very good sense of his duty."

Tom's credit was swept away like a fly. "His eye is all for that Marshall chit, and while she is by, I should be very surprised if he has one thought for his sister."

"Dear me, Amelia! Do you think me so irresponsible as to entrust my only daughter to such a niffy-naffy creature? Tom may appear to be serving his own interests, but he takes good care to protect

Lenora, either by himself or through the services of Mr. Barnabus, or another of his friends."

"Very well, if that is the case," said Lady Cammerby, gamely pursuing, "you need not sacrifice your own enjoyment, if Lenora is so well disposed."

Genevieve took her friend's hand with a smile. "But I do not sacrifice enjoyment, my dear friend! I am not such a fidgety one as I used to be, always game for entertainment. I have been used these many years to live quietly, remember, and there are times when I feel nothing is better than solitude. I assure you that it is a passing sensation, however, so you need not fear it will last long."

Her ladyship was still uneasy, but showed her good-will by unashamedly perjuring her soul to create or support any rumor that may forward Genevieve's interests and keep her peace. Lady Wraglain, however, was not to be fobbed off, stating pithily, "You never could tell a fib, Amelia, but I could, and I shan't scruple to do so if it's what Genevieve needs, but I can't render her assistance if I'm not put in possession of the facts."

Lady Wraglain still had full access to the house, for she had made both ladies in Hill Street acquainted with a movement to ameliorate the circumstances of female prisoners, and this pursuit, being as it was indispensible to the comfort of others, could not be laid aside for the frivolous purpose of ill-health. Indeed, Genevieve had no wish to discontinue their meetings, for though she had been obliged to leave the funding of such an operation to others, she wished nothing more than to be useful, and share her skill in the needle arts, which could provide the prisoners with much-needed income and occupation in their many idle hours.

Having little desire to share her many worries, however, Genevieve bent all her attention upon this project whenever her friend came to call, but Caroline, being both sensible and wise, merely bided her time until she felt it was expedient to give her friend a hint.

"It was never like you to hide yourself away, Genevieve," she said one day over tea.

Genevieve hesitated before replying, "It is not hiding to forego a few trifling events."

Caroline, who took her tea with copious amounts of sugar and milk, observed blandly, "Those who forego life's enjoyable trifles will soon find themselves with more regret than is reasonable."

"And what would you say is a reasonable amount of regret, Caroline?" asked Genevieve, regarding the half-empty sugar bowl with awe, bordering on respect.

"Only what is entirely of one's own making, my dear. We spend our lives being acted upon, and all too often feeling such helplessness in the consequences, when in reality, one has only to determine one's own actions, and accept those consequences. All else may be disregarded." She waved a dismissive hand in the air. "The resultant reduction in regret is enormously liberating."

Genevieve smiled behind her teacup. "I have often wondered if it has been callous of me to attempt to leave Bertram behind, one memory at a time, but I see now that it is completely sensible."

"Do not let anyone persuade you otherwise, Genevieve, including yourself. What good is it to cling to shadows?"

"None whatsoever." Genevieve sipped her tea reflectively, darting a glance at her wise companion. "But when the shadows cling to you, what then? There can be real horrors in the darkness, you know."

Lady Wraglain eyed her shrewdly. "I knew there was more to your supposed indisposition than Amelia would say. He's come back to haunt you, eh? Some ghost of Bertram's past has been threatening you?"

"Yes," admitted Genevieve, recognizing that her companion was not to be deceived. "Lord Montrose has discovered me here, and has made himself mightily disagreeable. Do you know him, Caroline?"

Her friend snorted. "Only a bowing acquaintance, I'm happy to say. Wraglain took care of that."

"Bertram was not so wise." Genevieve considered the depths of her teacup. "Nor was he so considerate. But Lord Montrose took little enough notice of me as Bertram's wife, and after Bertram's death, I had not expected to see him again. But he has inserted himself into my life quite unavoidably, and though my instinct has been to repel him, I do not know if I ought to persevere." She looked up at her companion. "If I force his eye from myself, I fear it will too naturally alight on Lenora."

"It's like that, is it? Then you are in a hobble." She sipped her tea meditatively. "Wraglain was wont to call Lord Montrose the most persistent scoundrel ever to blight the world. I knew Bertram was in his toils, but he's had many victims over the years, and he's as clingy as a limpet, if half of what I've heard is true." She gestured with her teacup toward Genevieve. "I can tell you that he is more likely to move heaven and earth to break you, than to accept defeat, much less let his interest waver."

Genevieve took another sip of her tea. "Yes, I expect you are right. Why are some men so perverse as to take rejection for a challenge?" She knit her brows at a sudden, disconcerting thought, and set her cup and saucer down in disgust. "If I had had my wits about me on our first meeting, I should have flirted madly with him, then I would only have had to endure a fortnight's gallantry before he'd have bored of me. But now—" She sighed in annoyance. "And I cannot even take comfort in fobbing responsibility for the whole onto Bertram, for I cannot deceive myself that my stupidity has not lent enough weight to the present circumstance as to be entirely blameless."

With a darkling look at her friend, she added, "Whether or not I shall be liberated by the acceptance of my regret remains to be seen."

A day or two later, she sat considering this problem, among others, as she mended a torn flounce on one of Lenora's gowns—a green silk that was apt to fray—when Sir Joshua was announced. He paused on the threshold and glanced about, as if to discover anyone else hiding in the corners of the room.

"I did not expect to find you alone, ma'am," he said.

Suddenly aware of a heightened sensation throughout her limbs, Genevieve set aside her mending, clasping her hands together to hide her disquiet, and smiling politely. "I cannot understand how that is so, sir, for Cottam must have known there is no one else in the house. Your sister has gone on an errand, and Tom has taken Lenora with some friends to Astley's Amphitheater."

Advancing into the room, he said, "But Miss Breckinridge has seen the horses already, has she not?"

Wondering how he should be aware of such a fact, she answered, "But that was merely *The Flying Wardrobe and Various Acts*, and Tom discovered yesterday that there is a new show. You could not imagine that they would forego such a high treat as *The Blood Red Knight!*"

"Certainly not," he said, his brows going up. "I am only astonished that you did not wish to see it as well."

"I should have," she said, inviting him with a gesture to sit, "except that I find myself sadly out of twig, and find I have no taste for amusements just now."

"I had heard that you were unwell, but I suspect that I have been misinformed." He had been watching her as she spoke, a little crease forming between his brows. "You will allow me to say that I perceive you in good health, but perhaps you are not quite in spirits."

This expression of genuine solicitude brought a rosy color to her cheeks. "I see that you are not to be deceived, sir," she said composedly. "The truth of the matter is that I am in hiding."

"You shock me, ma'am. I had not suspected cowardice in one so intrepid as yourself."

"That is only because you do not know me well, sir. I am not in the least brave, I assure you."

He shook his head gravely. "That, if you will pardon my saying so, is a bouncer."

She laughed. "Again, you give more credit than what is due. I own I can be valiant in a pinch, to be sure. But show me the means of escape from any distasteful situation, and you may depend upon my availing myself of it without compunction."

"Do not we all?" he said, his lips turning up in a fleeting smile, but at that moment, Cottam brought in a tray with wine and two glasses, depositing it on a side table before discreetly withdrawing.

After his offer of a glass to Genevieve had been refused, Sir Joshua refreshed himself and leaned back in his chair. "May I inquire what distasteful situation it is from which you wish to escape?"

Lamenting that she had not been more guarded, she delayed her answer, taking up her mending again while searching for an excuse. "Merely, I find London society somewhat more tiresome than I had supposed."

"You cannot imagine my relief to find that your ailment is not physical, ma'am, but I do not apprehend as yet why it should confine you to the house."

She chuckled, inwardly delighted that he seemed to care so much that she had sequestered herself. "I perfectly recall referring to the effects of intoxication at Amelia's ball, if you do not, sir, and your unfeeling references to my robust health are excessively painful to me. I should think that one who has had the good sense to succumb to exhaustion during the dissipation of a London season would be treated with more sympathy, even by you."

This brought an actual smile to his face as he sipped his wine. "Believe that I am merely glad that Miss Breckinridge is in no danger of catching your disease." She looked up sharply at this, and he added, "It would be a shame to end the enjoyment of her first season in such a shocking way. And so, you need have no scruple in relinquishing your duties as chaperone to poor Tom."

"None, sir," she said, a little shaken that he had had occasion to observe this circumstance, but she continued in a light enough tone, "And he should consider you a great gudgeon to think him thus, for, owing to the timely introduction of Miss Marshall to our midst, Tom has found escorting Lenora an admirable means to his own end."

"Any young man would find satisfaction in the escort of not one, but two agreeable young ladies, even if one is his sister. Lenora is a charming companion in her own right."

She agreed with some asperity, bending her head to set two or three stitches in the torn flounce. Conscious of a desire to turn the conversation away from her daughter, she said rather suddenly, "You were kind to take an interest in Branwell Wednesday last, sir. Redeeming the farm, and thus our livelihood, has been Tom's life's work since his father died."

After a slight pause, Sir Joshua accepted her thanks with a nod. "His knowledge is impressive, and I saw the effects of his practice, though superficially. But surely, he has not spent so long at it. He must have been still a child when his father passed."

"He was but thirteen, but was as determined then as he is now to put things to rights," she answered, taking to the subject with enthusiasm. "He was my shadow as I met with our land agent and our lawyer, and so grew up learning management. As soon as he could, he took the whole out of my hands, and by the time he comes of age, we shall be able to hold our heads up again, all through his endeavors."

His brow lifted. "As one whom you have justly claimed does not know you well, I nevertheless would be surprised to discover that you have not always held your head up, ma'am."

She smiled. "You are right. I fear I have a terrible lack of pride, sir."

"I would say, rather, that you have an incredible degree of resilience," he answered, with his sincere smile.

She looked at him, pleasure at odds with the wariness in her mind. "My, Sir Joshua, but you have a disconcerting habit of coming out suddenly with very pretty compliments. I am never certain how to take them."

"I would be honored if you took them at face value, ma'am."

She bowed over her work to hide the color rising in her face, and after some more desultory talk, he rose and took his leave, leaving her to consider the very inexplicable emotions she had experienced during the visit. That she had pleasure in his company, she could not deny. Their conversation was never stilted, and the discomfort of their first interactions had been replaced by an easy understanding, not disagreeably spiced with satire. She had an uneasy feeling that she rather liked Sir Joshua, a discovery that was all the more disturbing because of the emotion that crept over her when he so much as mentioned Lenora's virtues—an emotion that was distressingly like jealousy.

Chapter 14

MEANWHILE, TOM HAD enjoyed the outing to Astley's prodigiously, their party was so well-suited, and perfectly balanced with the last-minute addition of Mr. Barnabus to its ranks. The journey to the theater was accomplished in Lady Cammerby's barouche, with Ginsham driving his curricle. There was some commotion at the start of the expedition in regard to which lady Mr. Ginsham should have the honor to drive, both Elvira and Lenora expressing themselves willing to ride in the less dashing barouche, wherein Barnabus should be seated. But Lenora having the fortune to truthfully declare herself able to abide the forward seat without motion sickness, and Miss Marshall already comfortably ensconced beside Tom in the back, Elvira gave in with a good grace, and was handed by a beaming Ginsham into his vehicle.

Upon arrival at the theater, another disturbance was avoided by the happy chance of the couples entering their row exactly so as to place Elvira between Ginsham and Barnabus, with Lenora next, leaving Tom very satisfactorily placed beside Miss Marshall. Their enjoyment of the spectacle was then so complete as to suspend all considerations of a competetive nature until they rose from their seats. But as they approached the vehicles once more, Elvira took firm hold of Mr. Barnabus's arm, guiding him inexorably toward the barouche, and compelling him by an unceasing dialogue to follow her into it.

When Ginsham was made to understand that Miss Chuddsley should not prefer to ride with him back to Hill Street, his expression fell so ludicrously that Lenora felt it incumbent upon her to rescue the shattered remains of his hope if she could. Leaning out of the barouche, she whispered in Tom's ear, and after a brief conference, he turned to suggest to Ginsham that he ride with the others and give Tom the chance to drive Miss Marshall in the curricle.

"For you know," Tom said, with every evidence of conviction, "you've been dangling the promise of letting me drive your chestnuts these two weeks and more. I've begun to wonder if you'll ever come up to snuff!"

Brightening, Ginsham good-naturedly assented, taking his seat beside Lenora while Tom handed Miss Marshall into the curricle. But the drive was not to be as refreshing to his spirits as Lenora had hoped, for Elvira kept up a continual flow of conversation with Mr. Barnabus, only occasionally allowing a comment from the other occupants of the barouche, and scarcely otherwise acknowledging them at all.

When the two parties drew up to Elvira's Aunt's house, and the gentlemen alighted to wish Miss Chuddsley good day, it was with some surprise that Tom, who had spent a most pleasant quarter of an hour in Miss Marshall's company, perceived that Ginsham had fallen into a fit of the sullens. Indeed, Ginsham parted so grimly with each of the young ladies on their doorsteps, and most bitterly with Barny, that Tom felt impelled to take him in hand, dragging him forcibly to the Green Man, where, at a table in the corner, and with a glass of daffy before each of them, he encouraged the young man to unburden his soul.

Ginsham stared at his glass for some time before growling, "I should never have introduced him to her."

Tom waited for further elucidation, but getting none, he pressed gently, "Introduced who to whom, my dear boy?"

"Him. Barny." The name was little more than a snarl. "I was a gudgeon to let him meet her, and now she's forgotten me completely."

"Who, Miss Chuddsley?" Tom laughed and took a swallow of his blue ruin. "You are a gudgeon. She hasn't forgotten you! What gammon! It's not forgetting you that drives her to accept every invitation you throw at her."

Ginsham banged his fist on the table. "It is when she thinks he'll be there! Whenever I leave him out, or he doesn't come, she's moped to death, like I'm a dead bore. The only thing that'll animate her is to talk about him! How I met him, what he was like in school, what dashed plans he has for the future!" He gripped his glass so tightly that Tom felt some anxiety. But the fit passed, his shoulders sagged, and he looked up at Tom in flat despair. "It's no use. He's taken my place in her affections, Tom."

"It ain't so, Greg," said Tom, giving his shoulder a reassuring pat. "You're exaggerating, I'm sure of it! You can't refine too much upon a few trifles."

"They're not trifles, I tell you!" cried the afflicted young man. "She never so much as looks at me anymore!"

Tom took a sterner tone. "Nonsense, man! Why, she rode in your curricle today, and I know for a fact she looked at you! Didn't seem a bit unsatisfied with the circumstance, either. You've just let yourself become blue-devilled."

"She seemed a little too satisfied on the ride home with Barny," muttered Ginsham in a recalcitrant tone.

"Dash it, she can't always be with you!" A new notion bloomed in Tom's brain. "Perhaps she doesn't know her own mind, yet, Greg. Perhaps she's just being prudent, and spreading a little canvas."

Ginsham's bleak eyes lit with fire. "She knows her mind. Her canvas is all at Barny's feet! She hangs on his every word, she dotes on his every whim! Before I was such a clunch as to introduce him to her, I flattered myself that she was in a fair way to becoming attached to me, but no more! Now, I don't hold a candle to him, and I don't know why!"

Drawing his brows together, Tom bent his mind to the problem, cogitating some minutes before saying cryptically, "I'd not think it of Elvira, but it is her first season, and all the ton parties may have gone to her head." In response to Ginsham's grim stare, he explained, "That is, and I hate to mention it, Greg, but does Barny stand to inherit a higher title than you do, or a bigger fortune?"

Ginsham instantly leapt to his feet. "I'll not hear you impugn her character, Tom! She's the sweetest girl that ever breathed, and as innocent as a babe! There's not a mercenary bone in her body, and if you dare to think it again, I'll make you wish you hadn't!"

"Oh, take a damper, Galahad! I know better than you Miss Chuddsley's innocent. She's like a sister to me, and I tell you I wouldn't put it past either Lenora or Elvira to go swoony over a fortune. It's just the sort of gooseish thing those girls would do."

"I tell you, it's not!"

Tom pushed Ginsham's glass deliberately toward him. "You don't have sisters, you clodpole, so don't go standing there telling me what girls will or will not do! If they read it in a novel, then it's the very thing they'll be itching to do next, and that's the whole truth."

"But it's not that," persisted Ginsham, who had sat down and recruited himself at his glass. "She knows he's a third son, and she knows dashed well he don't have a fortune. I can't understand it, Tom! For all he's a right one, he's as boring as a bluestocking when he starts prosing on about the law, and I thought nothing of introducing him to her, but I was dead wrong!"

Tom's eyes narrowed and he stared into space for some minutes. "Shame I wasn't here when you met Elvira. Is she the first female you've tried to fix your interest with?"

Ginsham glared at him. "Yes, but if you think I muffed it, you'd be advised to think better of it before I plant you a facer, Tom."

"No need to get nasty, I'm only trying to help. I'm sure things were going swimmingly before Barny came along, so it must be all on him," said Tom, kindly. "Not sure what there is to do."

Ginsham tossed off his drink, banging the glass back onto the table. "Your solicitude overwhelms me, Mr. Breckinridge."

Tom laughed, slapping his friend on the shoulder. "Take heart, my friend. You will rise again."

"I don't want to rise again. I want Miss Chuddsley." He stood then, with alarming decision. "There's only one course left to me. I will challenge Barnabus."

"Ho, there, sir, gently, gently." Tom pressed his honorable friend back into his seat. "Barny ain't done anything wrong. You can't go challenging him or your case will be worse, my boy, for as sure as check, no matter how quiet we try to make it, the ladies always hear about a duel." He called for another drink for his friend and waited while he tossed it down. "Now, listen to me, Greg, old boy. I've just had the devil of an idea. But I'd do better to run it past Lenora to make sure of it. If you promise not to challenge Barny, not only will I engage to find out just what maggot has got into Elvira's brain, but I will pledge myself to promote your cause with her."

Ginsham's fingers tightened around his glass. "I'll promise, but I tell you to your face that I won't wait forever."

"No need, Greg. I've a feeling it may be a simple thing, after all."

Tom received no answer, for at that moment, a shadow fell over them. Two pairs of eyes turned up to stare at an exquisitely dressed older gentleman, who smiled suavely.

"Unless my eyes deceive me, I behold the offspring of my former protegee." He held out his hand to Tom. "Mr. Breckinridge, I believe."

Tom warily shook the hand, but refrained from offering any other encouragement as a tiny suspicion crept into his brain that he knew this man, and would rather he didn't.

The gentleman pulled a chair from an adjacent table and settled into it. "I am Carlisle Dupray. Your father and I shared many adventures together. He is greatly missed."

Ginsham sat up straight. "You're Lord Montrose."

Tom's eyes narrowed as Montrose flicked his gaze to Ginsham. "Of course, I am. I do not believe I've had the pleasure."

Ginsham snorted. "No, you haven't."

Dismissing him, Montrose turned back to Tom. "Your resemblance to your father is striking, young man. I have no doubt you have inherited his best qualities."

"What qualities would those be, my lord?" inquired Tom coldly.

"Boldness, courage, and determination, I would say, were his most outstanding strengths."

Tom's lips pressed tight, and Ginsham's fascinated gaze flicked from one to the other.

Montrose signaled over his shoulder for a drink. "I hear you have made incredible strides in recouping your family's fortune. You are to be congratulated, young man. Your father would be proud."

"I doubt that, my lord," said Tom, with an appraising look at Montrose. "He never showed any pride in the fortune of his family."

"Ah, yes, it is too true, young man. I thought so myself." He shook his head mournfully. "Bertram had strengths, but he also had weaknesses. He was imprudent, I fear."

This drew a snort from Tom.

Montrose took his gin in one gulp. "But you have learned from his mistakes, I have no doubt. I admire that in you." He toyed with his glass. "I would like to offer you my help."

Ginsham's gaze snapped to Tom, who sat back in his chair, eyeing Montrose narrowly. "And why would I need your help, sir?"

"I was never as imprudent as your father, though he would not be guided by my advice. His determination and courage drove him to make many rash decisions and, while some rewarded him, others doomed him," he said regretfully. He paused, as if in somber reflection, then continued slowly, "If you have indeed learned from his mistakes, and are willing to be guided by me, I could show you how to play your cards wisely."

Tom's jaw worked as he gazed intently at Lord Montrose. After several tense moments, he glanced at Ginsham. "You know, Greg, I have never heard a snake speak until now, and if they're all so silver-tongued, there's no wonder Adam and Eve were deceived. Well, my lord," he said, taking up his gloves and hat. "I was not born yesterday, and you will not find me a pigeon ripe for your plucking. I am not so much like my father that I will sit here to be worn down by your double-edged words."

Montrose, far from taking offense, merely shook his head with a sorrowful smile. "You have, no doubt, heard your father blame me for his losses. He became exceedingly bitter over the years, and could not take responsibility for his own rashness. But I forgive you, my boy. I will not hold a grudge."

"This is rich," Tom cried, pushing to his feet, and Ginsham with him. He fixed Montrose with a smoldering glare. "I watched my father leave his family time and again, to go where you would take him, to be in the safety of your company, to play at the games you taught him, and always at his return—always, sir—he was worse in every way. You are wrong, my lord. He did not blame you for his misfortunes. But I blame you. My father may have been ill-suited for card play, but his companions did nothing to curb his indiscretion. His friends did not keep him from vices they knew him too weak to refuse. No, they nurtured every one of his weaknesses and turned them to their own advantage."

His lordship rose from his chair. "What are you trying to say, pup?"

Tom pushed face to face with him. "I am saying that my father was a flat, sir, just as you are a sharp."

The room was silent. Montrose glanced to the side, then back at Tom. "Do you wish to repeat that insult?"

Ginsham stepped forward, gazing down at Montrose from his superior height. "He has no need to repeat it. Everyone who has heard of you knows you for what you are. Nothing he has said has altered your reputation a whit."

"I will have satisfaction," spat Montrose.

But Tom laughed. "You already have the satisfaction of having driven a man of unknown potential to his grave, and of leaving his wife and children nearly destitute. Congratulations, sir. May that satisfaction comfort you on your way to hell."

He pushed past his lordship, and Ginsham, favoring Montrose with a look of disdain, turned and followed him out.

Chapter 15

TOM'S FIRST INCLINATION was to keep his meeting with Lord Montrose a secret—at all events, from his mother and sister—but the more he turned it in his mind, the more he realized that Mrs. Breckinridge must know the whole. For it had become clear to Tom that Lord Montrose was not one to be put off, and if he had tried to take in Tom, it would be only a matter of time before he tried for his mother or Lenora.

On his arrival back in Hill Street, he found his mother in the drawing room, sewing, as she seemed always to be, and she looked up when he came in, a smile lighting her features. "Tom! Did you have a good chat with Greg? I do hope he is feeling more the thing. Lenora said he was blue as megrim, and made her more than glad to be out of his company, poor boy."

He sat in the wing chair near the fire and regarded her pensively. "Greg will do, Mama, but I must tell you who else I met at the Green Man."

His manner arrested her attention and she put down her needle. "What is it, Tom? Whom did you meet?"

"Lord Montrose."

Her mouth tightened, and she took up her needle again with agitated fingers. "What did he have to say to you?"

"He claimed that he wanted to help me."

"What fustian! I trust that you did not believe him."

"No, I'm not such a clodpole as that, Mama."

"I never thought you were, my dear. But I also never thought to warn you against him."

"There was no need. I remember what he did to Papa, and to us, and that is enough."

She put her needle down again, sighing deeply. "Thank God." She held out her hand, inviting him with the gesture to come sit by her on the sofa.

He did as she bade him, watching her keenly. "Did you know he was in London, Mama?"

"I did, my dear. He has met me, oh, nearly everywhere. It is such a bore!" she said, a tight smile flitting over her lips.

"You should not have kept this from me, Mama. The strain has been wearing you, I know."

"I am not such a poor creature, Tom!" she said, though smiling at his thoughtfulness. "There is nothing he can do to me but vex me with his odious attentions, and no one ever died from vexation, I assure you."

"No, but I am persuaded he means no good."

"Indeed, Tom, he could mean nothing else. But there was not the least need to worry you while I could manage him perfectly well. I own I had hoped we would be gone from London before you knew anything about him, or he you."

"Are you such a goose, Mama, that you could believe such non-sense?" said Tom baldly. "He was bound to find us out."

Mrs. Breckinridge directed an affronted look at him. "He cared so little for Bertram's family that it was not too much to hope that he would not recall specifics, such as the sex or number of our children, and so be unable to discover you or, even more importantly, Lenora."

"Mama! How could he not find us out? I could be Papa's twin, and Lenora looks mighty similar to you, and we are forever going out together." He stood abruptly and strode to the sideboard to pour himself a drink. "I would you had told me, Mama, so I'd have been on my guard. Now I've snubbed him, he'll go after Lenora!"

She clasped her hands tightly together in her lap. "We cannot be sure of that, love. He has known of my being in town for many weeks now, and though he has found occasion to come in my way, he has not yet sought out Lenora." She looked down. "I own it is a blow to me that he has sought you out, when I thought him ignorant of either of you. Now that he has met you, we must redouble our efforts to prevent his becoming acquainted with Lenora."

"Dash it, Mama, it would have been better to have warned her before now!"

"Oh, I did, dearest, but she instantly became so incurious—you know her way—that I thought it best to treat him not as dangerous, exactly, but as undesirable."

Chastened by this motherly wisdom, he came to sit with her again on the sofa. "But will it serve, Mama? He is such a man that I cannot be persuaded it will be enough. If you had heard how he spoke to me today..."

"He is disastrously charming. Almost as charming as was your Papa," she said, in a tone too forced to be light. "We are in a hobble, Tom, and I know it, but we must do what we can. I have warned

Lenora against him, and I know she will not disobey me, for I most strictly adjured her not to allow an introduction to Lord Montrose. Beyond that, we must simply never leave her to be alone, anywhere." She saw the consternation on his face and leaned toward him, placing her hand on his arm. "I know it is trying to be forever in your sister's pocket, my dear, but it is for her safety."

He covered her hand with his own, his features resolutely set. "I know it, Mama. I may not like it overmuch, but I daresay I'll get used to it. I must." He squeezed her hand reassuringly. "Think nothing of it, dear. I'm yours to command."

She smiled gratefully at him, picking up her needle again. "You and Sir Joshua. I vow I never thought to be so lucky with such knights errant at my fingertips!"

Tom left her to go in search of Lenora, whom he found picking out notes for a new piece on the pianoforte in the music room. She glanced at him as he leaned his elbows on the instrument. "I trust you talked Mr. Ginsham out of the sullens?"

"Well, I urged him not to give up hope, but we neither of us know the answer to his problem."

She turned her head to regard him. "You can't guess?"

"Oh, we know Elvira prefers Mr. Barnabus, but only I have the slightest notion why."

"And what do you think, Professor?"

He smiled and came around behind her, bending over her shoulder to look at the music pages. "I think that Barny is irresistible because he is an object of pity."

She turned to shove him away. "Oh, you odious creature! He is not to be pitied, unless you are a heartless wretch, and set store by looks and titles and fortunes!"

"You asked what I thought," he cried, hands up to defend himself.

"Yes, but I never imagined you to be such a gudgeon!"

"Well, why does Elvira admire Barny, then?"

Lenora played a few more angry chords, her lips pursed, then gave it up, casting her brother an exasperated look. "Very well. You are the teensiest bit right, Tom."

"Oh, ho!" he shouted, thrusting a finger at her.

"Only the teensiest bit, mind you!" disclaimed Lenora, removing from the stool and flouncing over to the chaise. He took her place on the stool and waited with eyebrows raised. With a withering look, she turned her head away. "He is attractive because he is romantic, Tom, not because he is to be pitied. The attributes upon which the world looks down are the very ones which females like Elvira—and myself," she turned to glare a challenge at him, "find appealing."

He grasped the edge of the stool and leaned forward, a skeptical gleam in his eye. "You think his stammer appealing."

"Yes."

"And his lack of title, and his poverty."

"Amazingly," she said, with a toss of her head.

"Most amazingly," he agreed.

"Oh, Tom, how can you be so horrid? I tell you that a man who must fight against all odds is far more romantic than a man who is born hosed and shod, who must only throw out money to get his way, and who never struggled in his life." She crossed her arms with a huff. "You may believe me or you may not. I do not regard it."

"So," he said, spinning around on the stool, "a man who is so unfortunate as to be born wealthy has no chance with females such as yourself, and Elvira?"

"That is not the matter at all! Why must you be so provoking?"

He started back, blinking in astonishment. "Pray, forgive me, ma'am! What have I misapprehended?"

Taking a deep breath to calm herself, Lenora stated, with icy hauteur, "We do not judge a man by his weakness, Tom. We judge him by his character!"

"So, wealthy men must needs be possessed of bad character."

She threw a cushion at him. "No! But wealthy men presume that they must only drop the handkerchief to get their bride."

"Ah," said Tom, raising a finger in enlightenment. "So, they are in need of a good set-down."

She eyed him with hostility. "Humility is a virtue of unsurpassed attraction, I will have you know. A vain man too easily forgets to whom he owes his happiness, while a humble man will fight for his beloved, through deprivation of every kind, and will never take glory to himself."

"I see," Tom said, still quite at a loss, but put in recollection, by this talk of fighting through deprivation, of a scene from one of Elvira's novels that he had come upon one day, quite by accident, when it had dug painfully into his ribs upon his nestling into the sofa for a nap. Wresting the book from its hiding place, he had stared blankly at the cover, then flipped through its pages, and read a most edifying passage about just such a humble man as Lenora had described. That man had taken a wound, in a very chivalrous act, and had nearly fainted from loss of blood, but had stoically refused to take honor for his actions, even at the hands of his beloved.

Nauseated by such exaggerated virtue, Tom had immediately consigned the novel to the depths of the wing chair cushions and carried on with his nap, thus relinquishing all hope of knowing our hero's fate, but the connection effectively set the wheels turning in his mind now. Considering Lenora's hitherto bewildering expostulations in light of the book's passage, it occurred to Tom that what Lenora and Elvira desired was a man of action, but one who would make his way without wealth or title. Presumably, allowances were to be made between the romance of novels and that of real life, for Tom had never known Barnabus, dubbed romantic, to engage in any heroic activities. Additionally, he had gathered from long association with his sister that the heroines of novels constantly flitted in and out of the clutches of villains, which Lenora had never done in her life, and nor had Elvira, and yet they deemed themselves worthy to ally with such romantic men as they could find. The attraction seemed to be in a man's beating the odds.

But the issue of humility Ginsham may be unable to circumvent, wealth and pride apparently being one and the same in Lenora's mind—yet he had a vague notion that all the humble men in the novels Lenora read ended up the long-lost heir to some vast fortune anyway, and though he could not depend upon Elvira's accounting for that, he was shrewd enough to suspect that in the appeasement of some of their scruples, though ridiculously impractical, the others would be forgotten.

"So," he said, standing from the stool with exaggerated resignation, "shall I give poor Ginsham the hint that he has no chance with Elvira?"

Lenora turned sharply toward him. "No! Oh, no, Tom. He has every chance with Elvira."

"But he has a title and a fortune, Lenora," he said, ingenuously. "You have informed me—"

She got to her feet. "That is neither here nor there! Gregory Ginsham is just the man for Elvira, if she could only be brought to comprehend it! It is the veriest coil, Tom! She is besotted with Barnabus, who doesn't give a fig for her, while poor Ginsham truly loves her, I know it!"

Less experienced gentlemen may have reeled under this display of feminine logic, but Tom had not passed the greater part of his life in the confidence of a youthful sister for nothing, and he merely uttered a noncommittal acknowledgement while Lenora turned about the room, deep in her cogitations. "He would have her for the taking, if only he was more romantic."

"Do you mean romantic like Barnabus?" inquired her brother.

"To be sure! How else could I mean it?" she replied, opening her eyes at him.

"Never mind. So, how do you propose to bring Elvira to imagine that the Honorable Gregory Ginsham, standing to inherit six thousand a year, and without physical defect, is romantic?"

"It is a quandary." Her shoulders slumped. "Oh, Tom, if he could only be made to look sensitive, or brooding, or something to justify his birth! I've tried my possible to help him, but he cannot say the right things, not with Mr. Barnabus there to say just what he ought."

Deciding the time was right to play his cards, Tom said, "What about humility, and fighting through deprivation?"

"If I could but arrange deprivation, or even a fight against insuperable odds, I am persuaded it would be just the thing!" cried his sister positively. "But I cannot!"

"My dearest Nora," he said, putting an arm around her, "you should have come to me. Who better to arrange a fight than your brother?"

"Oh, Tom!" She looked at him with glowing eyes, hands clasped at her bosom. "Would you? I know Elvira simply does not know her heart, and Mr. Ginsham is just the man for her. If she could only see him as the man of her dreams, she would be fairly caught!"

"Leave it to me, Nora. I'll not fail you."

Chapter 16

ON WHAT WAS thought to be Tom's last night in London, Lady Cammerby had contrived a cozy little party with just their family—which she took to include herself, the Breckinridges, and Sir Joshua—planning to take in Yates's latest play, with dinner at the Piazza afterward. The play was quite good, if one forgave the rather unfortunate lisp of the leading lady, and the evening, though threatening rain, remained dry throughout the walk to the Piazza. As they were guided to their table, Mrs. Breckinridge was waylaid by an old, and very chatty, acquaintance, and while extricating herself, was separated from the group. She was standing on the edge of the room, scanning for her party, when a hand took her by the elbow.

"What a lovely gown, Mrs. Breckinridge," said a most hated voice in her ear. "I flatter myself that I recognize the pattern, but perhaps I am mistaken."

She turned, freeing herself from his grasp with the movement, and gazed impassively at Lord Montrose. "This is perhaps the one instance in which you do well to flatter yourself, my lord. It is from the gown I wore the night of my betrothal party, and of course, as Bertram's closest friend, you were in attendance."

"Ah! Then my memory has not yet deserted me."

"No, even I must be made to admit that your memory, at least, has not yet deserted you, my lord," she said, sweetly.

His brows raised at this snub, but he let it pass, merely observing, "I wonder that you should wish to retain a reminder of such a day, ma'am."

"But that is precisely why I chose to refigure the old gown, my lord," she said placidly, "so that the memory could be reconstructed. I cannot forget that I was betrothed, and even married, because those events shaped my life, introducing other events that I will never desire to forget—"

"The birth of your children, for example."

Mrs. Breckinridge hesitated, but continued to regard him coolly. "Yes, one is always grateful for the birth of a child, no matter one's feelings for a late husband."

He smiled. "I understand why. I have recently met your most charming son. I found him, if you may forgive me for saying so, exactly like Bertram."

Her eyes sparked. "Then you must forgive me for saying, my lord, that I cannot believe you to have truly met my son, for he is nothing like Bertram."

"But he is the very image of Bertram. His looks must give you trouble in reconstructing those abhorrent memories you speak of."

"You will have much to forgive in me, my lord, for again, I will contradict you." She tipped her head to the side, in the manner of a mother addressing a child, her tone deceptively mild. "But you must not feel ashamed, for as a man, you really can have no knowledge of these things. I will attempt to explain it to you simply." She fingered the skirt of her gown. "Consider that a gown is made of fabric which, cut into rather ridiculous shapes, could not to the inexperienced eye be fitted together to make anything even comprehensible. But skilled fingers fashion from this chaos a thing of beauty, admired by many and for many reasons." She lifted the side of her skirt to fan it out. "When time and experience alter perspective and taste, what was once desirable becomes unappealing, but a proficient will tear it apart, cut out the undesirable bits, and create an entirely new thing of beauty from the pieces—pieces which, you have observed, my lord, still retain much of their original appearance."

"A fascinating lesson, ma'am." He bowed his head to her, but his eyes were mocking. "You seem to have many hidden talents."

"I do not hide them, my lord," she answered in a dispassionate tone. "Anyone who knows me may see them."

"Then, may I be so bold as to say," he said, possessing himself of one of her hands, and kissing it, "I wish to know you better, ma'am."

"How disappointing for you, my lord." Resolutely reclaiming her hand, she gathered her skirts with the greatest calm. "One often wishes for what one will never attain—it is a misfortune of life. You will excuse me."

Sweeping past him, she disappeared into the crowded coffee house. Her party had remarked her absence, and when she found her way to their table, Tom immediately stood and, in the guise of helping her to her seat, whispered, "What do you mean by conversing with Lord Montrose?"

"I could not very well avoid it, Tom! He approached me and positively constrained me to talk with him. He would not be brushed off."

"You did not seem too keen upon brushing him off, Mama," he hissed.

"I meant nothing but to avoid a scene in public."

He had taken his own seat beside her by this time, and was obliged to respond to a request of Lenora for the menu before speaking quietly once more to his mama. "You cannot think me such a gudgeon as to believe there was nothing to your conversation! For heaven's sake, Mama, you stood talking with him for ages, as if he were a friend! He kissed your hand!"

Darting glances at the other members of their party to reassure herself that they were not attending to her words, she answered him in a low tone, "I could not help that, you must believe me, and if you had heard our conversation, my dear, you would have known it was not genial."

"Better to nod and move on than converse with him at all," he insisted. "Dash it all, Mama, you can do nothing but encourage him with such attention! I have a fair mind to stay longer, rather than to let you carry on in such a hen-witted way!"

"You hardly need my actions to justify you in that, my dear," she said wryly. "I suspect Miss Marshall's attractions have long since decided you."

Stymied for a moment, Tom retreated into his wine glass, but presently bent toward his mother's ear again. "I still say this kind of encouragement will lead to trouble, Mama."

"I perfectly comprehend your concern, Tom, but if conversing with Lord Montrose for two minutes here and there will keep him tolerably content, then I will do it, for I have not yet thought of a better way to tame his roving interest."

He followed her gaze to Lenora, and struggled for several minutes with consternation, but at last nodded his consent. "It's a devil of a risk, Mama. But it may well serve. At least until we are gone home—until all of us are gone home."

Genevieve was convinced that it must serve, and though Tom did extend his stay, she resolutely resumed chaperonage of Lenora, and if she was disinclined to meet with anyone in particular, none in general were aware of it. Lenora's engagements were kept to drives with unexceptionable gentlemen, parties with only young people and their chaperones, and hand-picked outings where unintentional meetings were unlikely, but still Mrs. Breckinridge kept an eagle eye open, driven not by fear, but by sheer determination to beat the devil at his own game.

So it was that, finding herself in need of sundry articles, she boldly submitted to Lenora's request that they visit once more that unrivaled of all bargain houses, the Soho Bazaar, in the belief that even such a dandy as Lord Montrose would not be caught dead within its precincts. They sallied forth from Hill Street with Lady Cammerby, who had offered to convey them there in her barouche, and she set them down within sight of the doors. Armed with an umbrella and the resolution to purchase a new pair of kid gloves and some ribbon to furbish up a hat that otherwise must be considered unfit for wear, Mrs. Breckinridge indulged herself so far as to purchase a reticule for Lenora and a particularly pretty lace cap for herself, and Lenora happily found a table selling absurdly inexpensive silk stockings. They had nearly escaped the place when Lenora spied a lovely shawl that she was convinced Lady Cammerby must have, but as she had not the means to purchase it, she applied to her mama, whose lively awareness of her debt to her hostess, and the bargain price of two guineas, determined her not to hesitate.

The ladies bent their steps toward Hookham's library and, their purses considerably lighter than they had intended them to be, wandered along Bond Street, peering into windows and mourning their lack of funds, until Mrs. Breckinridge was startled at the sight of Lord Montrose just descending from his carriage not forty paces away. Wasting no time, she whisked Lenora round a corner and onto Grafton Street, telling that outraged damsel, who had been inspecting a hat whose style she wished to copy, that this was a shorter and less alluring way to the library, and so safer to their depleted purses.

Turning onto Albemarle Street, with the intention of rejoining Bond Street by Stafford, Mrs. Breckinridge was jostled by a ragged boy, and one of her packages knocked to the ground. This would not have overly distressed her had he not, at the same time, slipped her reticule from the arm that was now empty. Alarmed, she grasped at the urchin's sleeve, but he tugged free, sprinting away from her down the flagway. Lenora screamed, but was unheeded, at least by her mama, as Mrs. Breckinridge experienced a panicked and overwhelming desire for the restoration of her property which precluded any thought for her own or her daughter's welfare, and prompted her to give chase. After only two paces, however, the impracticality of running in long skirts, while bearing parcels, was borne in upon her and, with more desperation than foresight, she heaved the largest of her parcels—the bandbox containing Lady Cammerby's shawl—at the thief's head.

Somewhat to her surprise, it was a dead hit, and the boy went down, sprawling sideways into the street with the bandbox bouncing after him, and the reticule flying from his hands. An instant later, he had jumped up and fled through the traffic and into the busy thoroughfare beyond, and Mrs. Breckinridge, pursuing as quickly as she was able, reached the place where she had hit the thief in perfect time to witness her bandbox being crushed under the wheel of an advertiser's cart.

A cry of indignation burst from her lips as the gaudy vehicle rolled past, its pasteboard tent desiring onlookers to partake of the wonders of the Spectacle at Sadler's Wells, and its driver wholly indifferent to the distress of the woman on the side of the road. When the cart had at last gone by, Mrs. Breckinridge rushed into the street to snatch up the remains of her property, but as she put out her hand to retrieve her reticule, another hand picked it up, and she discovered that its fellow was extended toward her in aid. Taking the proffered hand, she stood and looked up into the rigid countenance of Sir Joshua Stiles.

Her face flushed hotter than it had already become from the exertions and frustrations of the last several minutes, and she was unable to utter more than "Thank you," as he led her back to the flagway, where a kind passerby had restored her dropped parcel to Lenora and was providing that pale maiden support. Mrs. Breckinridge, instantly conscious of the scene she had caused, was necessarily ashamed that she had so thoughtlessly abandoned her daughter, and for a course whose outcome had been as predictable as it had been unsatisfactory, and her mental perturbation was made all the more acute under Sir Joshua's grim observation.

Valiantly resolving to master the situation, she first determined to absolve herself by owning to her fault and, turning to Sir Joshua, she said, "I might have known it would be you to assist me, sir! You will pardon that I take it as a personal affront that you are ever present during my most ridiculous moments!"

His eyes flickered with something that might have been appreciation, but his countenance remained grave as he answered, "It must be the perversity of Fate, ma'am, but if you will insist upon impulsivity, you will be justly rewarded."

"The boy stole my reticule, sir!" she responded, goaded by the justice of his reproof. "Would you have me stand idly by while it was done?"

"One hoped you would take more thought for your daughter, ma'am!"

This rebuke—merely an echo of her own self-recrimination—stung her pride into rearing its head, and she retorted, "Such a view is typical of a man! If I were a male, my actions would have been applauded, but no! Females must remain quivering in fear, while they are put upon by thieves! Forgive my progressive views, sir, but Lenora was safe enough while I exerted myself to retain our property!"

"You cannot pretend there are more than a few guineas within this purse, ma'am," he said, holding up the reticule and shaking it slightly, so that the faint jingling of the few coins inside could be heard, "and you will not persuade me that the other contents are worth a risk to your personal safety."

"As my safety was never at risk, sir," she said with some asperity, reclaiming her reticule with heightened color, "and as I am used, out of necessity, to abide by the strictest economy, the loss of *a few* guineas, as you say, beside that of a perfectly sound, and, I must point out, practically new reticule, would be a shocking waste."

His jaw worked. "Not so shocking, it would seem, but you must follow it with a bandbox full of purchases."

"Bandboxes I have in abundance," she bit out through clenched teeth, "and if that horrid boy had had the sense not to fall into the street, my purchases would never have landed where they could be wantonly crushed by that—that devilish cart!"

She turned on her heel and, possessing herself of Lenora's arm, marched her down the busy street, head high, and the dingy shawl, still encased in its crushed bandbox, clutched to her chest. She had not gone five steps, however, when Sir Joshua passed her with quick strides and stopped them, his hat held to his chest in an almost submissive gesture.

"I must beg your pardon, Mrs. Breckinridge," he said in a softened tone. "I meant no offense, and would be honored if you will allow me to assist you both."

She put her chin up. "Contrary to what has, no doubt, become your expectation, sir, we do not require rescue."

"Mama!" whispered Lenora, still pale from her fright.

"This is no rescue, but a mere civility, I assure you," said Sir Joshua, gently but firmly taking from her the tattered bandbox. Lenora gladly relinquished her parcels, smiling up at him as he added, "I am on my way to Hill Street. May I escort you?"

Uneasily aware of Lenora's desire to accept his kind offices, Mrs. Breckinridge said rather stiffly, "It is kind of you to offer, sir, but we were on our way to Hookham's library."

"As I am in no hurry, I would be pleased to accompany you there."

Wilting under this persistent civility—and under Lenora's pleading look—and wishing to be done with the matter as soon as may be—she consigned their other errands to another day, and her pride to the devil. "It will not be necessary, sir," she said with a weary sigh. "I suspect Lenora has no more desire for another errand than do I." After a moment's struggle, she added, "Your escort home would be most appreciated."

They walked for some minutes in silence, Mrs. Breckinridge rapidly sinking under the mortification she felt, and laboring against a gnawing dissatisfaction in her breast. Her companion's disapproval caused the recent scene to replay over and over again in her mind, and her guilt grew as the justice of his censure became more plain. She should not have left Lenora alone, especially with Lord Montrose still at large. Anyone, including him, could have set upon the girl while her mother was busy flinging parcels at a thief. And the thief, too, was to be pitied, for he likely had no home or parents, and was forced to steal to survive, and she was the veriest monster to not only keep him from his livelihood, but to injure him as well, all for the sake of a few coins.

With such increasingly critical thoughts, Genevieve was well on her way into a depression when Sir Joshua suddenly observed, "I do not believe I have ever seen a thief dealt with in such a way, Mrs. Breckinridge."

Lenora giggled. "I am sure I have not, sir."

Mrs. Breckinridge blinked up at him, and discovered what looked like a slight smile playing on his lips. She felt herself plucked from the depths. "You must own it was effective, in its way."

"It certainly caused him to reconsider." He looked down at her. "But you misled me, ma'am. I distinctly recall your owning to imperfect aim."

She blushed and hurriedly disclaimed, setting down the hit to sheer luck.

"Perhaps," he allowed quietly, "but if that is so, it was even more of a risk."

She was forced to avert her gaze, the very gentleness of his rebuke striking her to the heart. "I own you are right. I cannot claim any cause for my actions, sir, except what you so rightly termed my impulsivity."

He took a moment to answer her. "You must pardon me, ma'am. I misspoke. I am sure I meant intrepidity."

"Are you certain you wish to allow me such a compliment in this instance, sir?" She looked prim. "For you also spoke of just rewards."

He opened his eyes wide at the recollection. "Indeed, I did, ma'am." He again paused. "But if you cannot see anything rewarding in the end of that adventure, I can."

Unsure how to take his meaning, she turned to look searchingly at him, but he did not return her gaze, merely showing her a side view of the charming smile that could so suddenly and handsomely transform his features. At the same time, she caught the admiring look her daughter cast up at him, and with a lowering feeling, Mrs. Breckinridge believed she understood them both.

Chapter 17

Having invited Elvira to spend the afternoon at Lady Camerby's house, ostensibly to be the first to admire a new hat, Lenora wasted no time in pouring into her friend's ears the story of Sir Joshua's most recent act of chivalry. Her story could not have found a more interested audience, and Elvira sat spellbound throughout.

"I do not think I will ever meet a more heroic man, Elvira!" breathed Lenora, at the close of her tale. "Such poise, and yet such passion! He was more romantic than words can describe!"

Though she wholeheartedly agreed, Elvira required some minutes to assimilate all the details of the story, and she discovered, to her chagrin, that her sensibility was ruffled. "But to take your mother to task, Lenora, and in your hearing! I should have been mortified."

"Oh, no," said Lenora, quick to defend her hero. "If he was strict, it was only due to his concern for our welfare, which I found unutterably moving."

Elvira observed obliquely, "But you told me he is rather old."

"I had not then considered! He is exactly the right age, Elvira, with such experience and knowledge to exactly suit, as evidenced by his perfect handling of the situation."

Her friend sighed. "Then he is most assuredly not the evil Duke. As there is no hope of meeting the real evil Duke," she said, casting a sigh heavenward, "I had hoped he might yet turn out to be just such another."

"I told you he would not fit the role, Elvira," Lenora said, sublimely unaware of anything but Sir Joshua's perfections. "He is too good, too heroic!"

"Next you will be saying that he is our hero, Lenora," Elvira chided. Her friend looked much struck by the notion, and Elvira quickly exclaimed, "But he must not be the hero, Lenora! Mr. Barnabus is secure of that role! No, Sir Joshua must be—" She bent her thoughts to the problem, but to no avail. "Oh, he must play only a supporting role."

"Well, Elvira, Sir Joshua need not be your hero, but he most definitely deserves a heroine of his own. You will not like my mentioning it, I warrant, but even Mr. Barnabus has yet to prove himself so wholly heroic as Sir Joshua. Such a man must be rewarded."

Elvira, though unwilling to relinquish Mr. Barnabus's perfections, could not deny the justice of this claim, and struggled to find a compromise. Offering up several entirely unsatisfactory scenarios, she was suddenly struck with inspiration, and cried triumphantly, "He will be the foil to the evil Duke! To, oh, what's his name—Lord Montrose!"

"Yes!" Lenora clapped her hands in delight. "Oh, Elvira, what a perfect notion! Every hero must have an ideal to follow, and though the hero must ultimately defeat the evil Duke by his own merits, it stands to reason that he would be inspired by another great man."

Elvira perceived the very good sense of this reasoning, and entered into Lenora's feelings on the matter. "Sir Joshua is the King Arthur to our Galahad! I see it all! Rumors of his exploits spread like wildfire through London, and our hero takes them to his bosom, espousing those virtues for his own! He will treasure up Sir Joshua's example against the time that he shall rescue the heroine—of whose identity I am persuaded we are both sure." She looked demurely down on these words, and so missed the quick, uncertain glance Lenora darted at her.

"I wonder if Sir Joshua is acquainted with Lord Montrose," mused Lenora, guiding the conversation back to the pertinent point.

Elvira dismissed this necessity. "As the foil, he need not come into contact with the villain. It is enough for their characters to be exactly at odds."

"I would that we could be sure that Lord Montrose truly is the evil Duke. We neither of us know him but for hearsay, and it would be a pity if we had misjudged him. Such a mistake could be the ruin of our story!"

Alarmed, Elvira whispered, "But surely your mama can be trusted that he is a despicable man! He was a crony of your father's was he not? And that alone—I mean—I need not mention—" She fumbled, embarrassed, to a stop.

"I do trust my mama, and my papa had only the horridest friends, it is true," Lenora said, unoffended. "But there are many kinds of horrid, are there not?"

Elvira uttered some incomprehensible sounds indicative of agreement, and Lenora, encouraged, continued. "As the creators of our adventure, it behooves us to be sure of our villain, else how can we be certain he is capable of the conduct we expect? Should we not at least make a push to acquaint ourselves with his character?"

Elvira stared dumbstruck at this defiant attitude, which roused a righteous spirit in her breast. "But your mother—she charged you most straitly—you cannot!"

Silence greeted this declaration, silence that stretched for several taut moments. At last, Lenora sighed. "Indeed, I hardly know how I could do it, being so carefully guarded as I am." In a rallying tone, she said, "We shall just have to make do with what we know of Lord Montrose, and hope for the best outcome."

"I trust we shall not be disappointed, Lenora!" cried Elvira with the utmost relief.

"We have, after all, the perfect hero—and heroine," spoken with emphasis, "and foil to our villain. It really is all that we had wished."

Elvira hastened to agree. "Yes, yes! How perfectly all has fallen into place!"

Mrs. Breckinridge, passing by the door at the start of this very interesting conversation, found herself caught in place for several seconds—though by principle not one to eavesdrop—her ears straining of their own accord to hear the whole. The intensity with which her daughter expressed her feelings for Sir Joshua could not but grip her with a feeling that she knew was most unsuitable for a mother to entertain, but when the talk moved to Lord Montrose, that feeling changed to dread. The close of the conversation awakened her to the impropriety of her remaining where she stood, but it was only with the greatest effort that she conjured up the strength to unroot her feet and move along down the hall to her intended destination.

The agitation caused by the first portion of the conversation she gladly allowed to be suppressed by the alarm caused by the second, which still rang in her mind that evening when she and Lenora retired to bed. Alive to the absolute necessity of stifling Lenora's curiosity to meet and interact with the evil Duke, she resolutely followed her daughter into her bedchamber.

Closing the door behind them, Mrs. Breckinridge sat on the edge of the bed, plunging directly into deep waters. "I hope you will forgive me, dear, but I overheard some of your conversation with Elvira today."

Lenora blushed scarlet. "Oh, Mama, how could you!"

"A thousand apologies, darling, but I was passing in the hallway, and heard something about finding an evil Duke! How could I not stop to listen?"

"Oh! That!" Lenora regained her color. "We are only being silly, you know."

"But 'all has fallen into place?'"

Her daughter smiled impishly. "Well, it is strange how we have come upon all the characters in a first-rate romance, Mama. We have the heroine, which is—well, to tell truth, we have not yet settled between Elvira and me—and we have the stammering hero, which is Mr. Barnabus, and—well—you told me of Lord Montrose, and who else could be the evil Duke?"

"Ingenius, my dear," said Mrs. Breckinridge with the utmost affability. "And are there supporting characters, in this romance of yours?"

"Indeed, Mama! There is Mr. Ginsham—he is the disappointed suitor, I fear, unless Tom and I can contrive a way for him to be Elvira's hero—"

"Thus, opening the way for you to be Mr. Barnabus's heroine?" interpolated her mother, not unhopefully.

Lenora giggled nervously. "Perhaps, Mama. That remains to be seen."

Her mother, deciding not to belabor the issue by grasping at this straw, went on. "My, but your cast of characters seems prodigiously well-picked. Are there any more members?"

"Oh, well, you, Mama, to be sure, and dear Lady Cammerby, and Tom, and—and Sir Joshua."

"Mmm, yes," she agreed, as if contemplating the gentleman's suitability to high drama. "Sir Joshua is quite romantic, isn't he, with his grave demeanor and sober conversation. We cannot do without him."

Lenora bit her lip, then burst out, "He is romantic, Mama! You must see it!"

"Yes, dear, I do." Lenora's face lit up, and Mrs. Breckinridge had to look away. "But the evil Duke, my love. He is the only member of your cast unknown to you. How shall you contrive?"

Taken unawares by this solicitous inquiry, Lenora said eagerly, "May I know him, Mama? I declare it is my dearest wish!"

"No, Lenora, I fear not," her mother answered gently, but with a firmness that could not be mistaken.

Patently disappointed, Lenora pouted, "I really think it is too bad of you not to allow me to decide for myself if I should know him, Mama!"

"I fear I know you too well to entrust such a decision to you, my love. You see, he is quite as villainous as you could wish, and more. You would be much better served to imagine yourself an evil Duke."

"No! That would never do, when all the rest are real!"

Aware from Lenora's recalcitrant tone that the discussion had moved to unsteady ground, Mrs. Breckinridge smoothed the coverlet beside her, choosing her words carefully. "An evil Duke is excellent when safely tied up in the pages of a book, my love, his character neatly bound by black and white. But such men as Lord Montrose, when they are to be found loose in society, with no writer's pen to curb their villainy, would not scruple to injure a girl, without waiting for the hero to arrive."

Lenora did not answer, but her silence was more grave than pettish, encouraging her mother to continue. "Men such as Lord Montrose do not wait to steal their victim's virtue, or spew forth involved speeches whose length enables the hero to reach the heroine in time to avert tragedy." She paused to let Lenora absorb this. "Such men take what they will, when they will, and are so cunning as to ensure their own safety at any cost—even that of another's reputation. They are dangerous, my love, and cannot be trusted within arms-length, at any time."

"This is serious, indeed, Mama," said Lenora, in a half-hearted attempt at lightness.

"It is most serious, my love." She took Lenora's hand in her own. "You must believe that I am in deadly earnest when I say that you must not court the acquaintance of a dangerous man, be he Lord Montrose or some other who comes into your way, simply to fill a character in an imaginary game."

Lenora sat down quietly beside her mother. "Mama, you did not tell me he was so dangerous before."

"I am telling you now. Do I have your assurance, Lenora?"

"Yes—yes, Mama, of course."

Mrs. Breckinridge pressed her hand. "Then I will reward you with this: Lord Montrose was the principle instigator of all that drove your father to ruin. He led your father to gamble away a fortune and mix in degrading society, all to his own profit. He feels no remorse, and he has already forced his presence upon myself and Tom, here in London, with the undoubted intent to do us harm. He must not be allowed to know you."

Lenora's eyes had grown wider during this speech. "No, Mama. No, I—I most solemnly promise not to seek out Lord Montrose, and—and to avoid him if ever I find myself in his vicinity."

"Thank you, love," said her mama softly, then, striving for a heartening tone, she added, "There! You have your evil Duke, and you may imagine his evil deeds to your heart's content, but he must remain bodily in the wings forever if we are to have a romance, and not a tragedy, on our hands."

Chapter 18

Thoroughly sobered by her mother's warning, Lenora rivaled even Sir Joshua's gravity for the next few days, but it was not to be expected that her spirits should be dampened long, especially as the season was still in full swing, and there were so many parties and outings to be had. To Mrs. Breckinridge's great relief, Lenora continued to submit meekly to the careful vetting of her invitations, in greater part because there were few that met with prohibition, as Lord Montrose, happily, did not move with the younger set.

Lenora did not find anything unaccountable in Tom's extending his stay another fortnight, for though some of his motives were quite otherwise than she supposed, Tom's obvious enjoyment of Miss Marshall's attractions was reason enough for her to believe his stay was entirely a matter of self-indulgence. Indeed, she blithely assumed Lady Wraglain's ball, which augured well to be quite a squeeze, and happened to fall within his extended time, to be the chief excuse for his stay, and he did not deny it, having ascertained that Lord

Montrose would not be invited, but that the Marshalls had been.

The ballroom at Wraglain House was bedecked with flowers, a fact which gratified Lady Cammerby into fond and vocal remembrances of her ball, which must of course have been the inspiration. In response to this, Lady Wraglain merely expressed to Mrs. Breckinridge her wish that the next *ton* ball would usher in a new kick of fashion in ballroom decoration so as to allay her overwhelming desire to depress some persons' pretensions.

Brought into the ballroom on Tom's arm, Lenora was quickly discovered by a young dandy, who had made her acquaintance fairly recently, and who begged her hand for the first set. Tom, eyeing the height of the young gentleman's shirt points sternly, bade fair to dampen the entire evening by suggesting that sprigs of fashion were notorious for loose morals. But when Lenora twitted him on being a bulldog, he couldn't help but laugh, and spoiled the effect of his speech. Lenora left him quite contentedly, but Tom knew his duty, so, leading a young lady into the same set, kept an eye on his sister, to the end that Lenora took him aside after the dance.

"What do you mean by following me, Tom?"

"I'm not following you," he said, all innocence.

Her eyes narrowed. "Did Mama set you to watch me?"

"I don't know what you can mean, Nora," he said, twitching his cuffs with studied nonchalance.

She eyed him in annoyance. "She'd not the least need to set you to watching me, as she has already counted this ball as safe, for she knows there will be no evil Dukes present."

He stared at her. "Evil Dukes?"

She laughed. "You know, from the novels. The villain who will stop at nothing to claim the heroine as his own."

He snorted. "Lord Montrose is no Duke. Though he is evil."

"Precisely, and he was not invited, as Mama particularly discovered, so you may be at ease."

"Lord Montrose isn't the only Bad Man, Lenora."

"To be sure, however, you cannot hover over my shoulder all evening trying to discern who is and who is not. We must trust Lady Wraglain's choice in her guests, and in every gentleman's sense of propriety."

He pursed his lips and grumbled, "Well, I don't."

"Tom, don't be provoking! You must own that in the six weeks since I have come to this town, which everyone knows is teeming with rascals, I have never once been in the company of a man who has gone over the line. While I am sincerely grateful to you for your protection, I'd liefer go home than have you guarding me like the Black Monk."

He gazed narrow-eyed at her, but at last seemed to accept the practicality of her words. He folded his arms over his chest like a general. "Very well, little sister, I will let you free, but you will conduct yourself with propriety, and you will not let yourself be taken in!"

She rolled her eyes at him but shook his hand with as much sobriety as he could wish, and he left her to her next partner. As she spied him leading Miss Marshall into the next set, and seemingly oblivious to anyone else, she felt fairly certain he had taken her words to heart, leaving her to the full enjoyment of an excellent ball, until she was made to wish that Tom had not given in so easily.

Asked to give him the honor of accompanying her down to dinner by young Lord Castleton, a buck with a florid waistcoat and a profusion of fobs and seals—and whose wriggling eyebrows gave her a feeling of acute discomfort—she politely refused, saying that she had already promised the honor to another nameless young man. He was teasing her for the name of this unknown gentleman when suddenly Mr. Barnabus appeared and asked if she was ready to go down. Lenora, gazing at her savior in both amazement and admiration, waited only until Mr. Barnabus had swept her off before crying, "How famous, Mr. Barnabus! Thank you, a thousand times! But how did you know?"

He grinned, leading her to an empty table. "I overheard your m-mendacity, Miss B-breckinridge, and was only too glad to ob-blige. B-besides, that's Castleton—a s-slimy toad if there ever was one."

She giggled. "But why are you here, sir? I was given to understand you do not dance."

"I d-don't, ma'am. B-but the Oslows, with whom I'm staying, were invited, and felt s-sure you'd be here, so I d-decided to come along." He bowed his head graciously. "You see, I leave town tom-morrow."

"Oh!" Lenora looked at him, astonished. "But I thought you did not attend Easter term! Have you determined to sit for exams early?"

"N-no, I am sum-moned to the ancestral home." He widened his eyes meaningfully. "M-my poor father fears m-my knowledge should s-suffer from all this dissip-pation, and I feel sure he means to d-drill me until June."

Assimilating this alteration of plans with her own hopes, Lenora was slightly taken aback by her lack of emotion. To lose her hero should have prostrated her with grief—in the very least should have brought on a swoon—but no such fate assailed her, and they both quite easily talked of his home in Devonshire, and of his hopes in the Bar, until dinner was ended and they joined the other couples returning to the ballroom.

In the hall, he bowed. "Here I leave you, Miss B-breckinridge. I have an early s-start in the morning."

With very little qualm, Lenora offered her hand to him. "You will be missed. If your father will spare you, we are settled here through the season, and will always welcome you. But if not, I wish you good luck on your exams, and hope to meet you again, perhaps next season."

He had bowed over her hand, but straightened and glanced behind into the ballroom. "I n-nearly forgot. Is Miss Chuddsley here tonight? I m-made sure she would be, b-but have not seen her."

Shaken by a tiny spasm of jealousy, Lenora's smile wavered. "No, she is not. Oh, she will be disappointed. Can you not pay her a call before you leave?"

"As I leave b-before sunup, I think she would rather b-be annoyed." He grinned. "Would you b-be so kind as to carry my r-regrets to her?"

"Of course, I will, gladly!"

"Well, then. Goodb-bye!"

She watched him go with a warm glow, brought on by the certainty that he valued her companionship more highly than that of Elvira, but blinked at herself for feeling little else at his departure. This disquieting realization forced her to sink back down onto a chair, and she mused over the interactions of the last several weeks, to see if she could discover the depth of her feelings. These, after some probing, proved depressingly shallow, and based on fairly flimsy footings. Her romantic tendencies, however, rejected these findings outright and, after some mental gyrations, she was able to conclude that her lack of despondency must stem from an innate confidence in his fidelity to her, and only a ninny would be so ill-bred as to resent his obedient return to his family. The more she reflected on the excellence of Mr. Barnabus's character, and the certainty that he was the hero of the story she and Elvira had so painstakingly constructed, the more the circumstance of his being taken from their circle took on a desolate hue, and she began to feel positively low. This, she concluded happily, was proof of her devotion, and she found herself able to return to the gaiety of the ballroom without compunction.

Immediately upon entering the crowded room, however, she was accosted by Lord Castleton, whose apologies for his rudeness and professions of contrition at offending her were so effusive that she accepted his invitation to dance merely to halt his tongue. This gambit was only partially successful, however, as he left off abusing himself to take up cataloguing her virtues, which was embarrassing enough, had not his blandishments been contingent upon his own superiority. Already regretting her rash decision to stand up with him, Lenora resolved upon preserving a civil countenance and leaving him as soon as she was able, but at the end of the dance, not ceasing his encomiums, Lord Castleton proceeded to lead her out onto the balcony, where he was sure she would enjoy the fresh air. As his actions were accompanied by many winks and a squeeze at her waist, Lenora quickly forgot her resolve to be civil, and when her desire that he instantly take her back into the ballroom was ignored, indignation suffused her person.

An angry attempt to remove herself from his company was greeted by a rush of rather moist proclamations of his undying love, and an attempt at a loose-lipped kiss thwarted only by Lenora's being able, due to his lordship's eyes being closed in ardor, to side-step, causing her cavalier to career into a tall shrub growing at the edge of the balcony. She had taken only two steps back toward safety, however, when she felt his hands close about her wrist and she was wrenched into the shadows and into a tight embrace. Over his lordship's shoulder, Lenora's eyes sought desperately for Tom, but the press inside the ballroom was too great, and her outraged cries were not heard over the noise. She thought frantically that if she could only break free of her tormentor, she could flee from him into the garden, but this train of thought broke off abruptly when a tall figure suddenly appeared in the doorway.

"I see you are in need of assistance, Miss Breckinridge," said Sir Joshua, firmly removing Lord Castleton's arms from Lenora's person. In a trice, he had shoved his lordship bodily into the shrubbery, and was offering her his arm. "I believe your brother has been looking for you, ma'am. May I take you to him?"

She murmured something, too overcome to order her mind properly, and walked a little unsteadily with him back into the crowded ballroom.

Once surrounded by the press, Sir Joshua leaned his head down to her. "Are you alright, Miss Breckinridge?"

She clung to his arm with both hands. "Yes, thank you, sir. I am only angry and—and—"

"It is very understandable how you feel," he murmured, patting her hands comfortingly. "You will drink a glass of lemonade, then I will take you to your brother. He ought to have been watching over you."

"He—he was, sir, but I told him not to worry so. I never imagined that—"

"One does not, to be sure, ma'am. Indeed, if you have any of your mother's blood in you, you could not." He handed her a glass of lemonade and stayed by her side until she had recovered her color. Taking her glass, he smiled down at her. "Now, I do not think you are very worse for the experience, do you?"

She exhaled and shook her head. "Indeed, I think I am better, for now I shall know how to go on, if ever I am accosted so again."

"Good. To learn from adversity is wisdom, and shows you to be very mature indeed."

She blushed, looking gratefully up at him, and let him lead her to Tom. Her brother was outraged by what he deemed "that pup's dashed insolence," but after a quiet conference with Sir Joshua, he declared his intention to meet with Lenora before every dance, to satisfy himself as to her safety, and as to the propriety of her partner, but to leave her to enjoy herself otherwise. With another speaking look to Sir Joshua, Lenora went with Tom to find a suitable partner.

Sir Joshua, having seen his two young friends safely into the next set, made his way across the room to Mrs. Breckinridge. She, interrupted in dull conversation with a matron whose sole purpose in life seemed to be to enumerate the many ills of her children, happily excused herself at his approach, and rose to greet him.

"Sir Joshua, I had not thought to see you here."

"Mrs. Breckinridge. I had a previous dinner engagement, but assured Amelia I meant to come afterward." He bowed over her hand and murmured just so she could hear, "Am I come in time to rescue you once again?"

Keeping admirable control over her countenance, she said brightly, "Ah! Your timing is excellent, sir!" Then, to repay him, she glanced pointedly over his shoulder and murmured, "Or do I owe the pleasure to Lady Castleton? Does she hunt you again, or is it her daughter?"

His eyes widened and he cast a quick glance around, which brought an impish smile to Mrs. Breckinridge's lips. He returned a rather cold gaze to her. "That was not kind in you, ma'am, and now you will do penance by standing up with me."

"Oh, surely you must know that would be more a punishment to you than to me, sir," she said, her eyes still gleaming.

"I know nothing of the sort, ma'am. Do you waltz? I have a particular desire to see you waltz, and how better to do it than to dance with you?"

She stared at him, taken completely out of her stride. "You behold me speechless, Sir Joshua. One of your startling compliments again! But I have determined to take you at your word, so, yes, sir, I will dance with you."

The already heady feeling of being so close to a man for the entirety of the dance was heightened by the fact that, as she had admitted to Lenora only days before, Genevieve really did know that Sir Joshua was a romantic figure. She had been increasingly aware of it these past few weeks, and as their friendship had grown, so had her regard for him. She had quickly recognized that his solemnity sprang merely from a solidity of moral character that was, to a woman of her experience, vastly preferable to the more common carelessness of gentlemen of fashion, and it hid a ready sense of humor that exactly fit Mrs. Breckinridge's ideal. His person was attractive as well, and within the circle of his arms, and responding readily to his enjoyable conversation, she forgot herself so far as to fantasize that he was not like a brother to her.

But her pleasure in the evening was to end with the waltz, for as Sir Joshua led her back to her chair, she noticed Lady Castleton in reality bearing down upon them, and reluctantly advised Sir Joshua of this impending danger. As she had foreseen, he bowed quickly over her hand, murmuring something about the card room, and was gone, leaving her feeling slightly bereft.

Lady Castleton, rather than sailing by, deigned to pause beside Mrs. Breckinridge, looking her up and down through beady eyes. "Well, little Genevieve Wainsley has unburied herself at last!" she said in her brusque manner. "Though, you cannot be blamed, my dear, for keeping hidden so long, society being so unforgiving as it is. Anyone with any sensibility will agree that you were right to wait."

"Ah, Cassandra, what a pleasure! Yes, I have risen from the ashes of my deplorable marriage and come to cast myself at the feet of such liberal persons as yourself. And as you see, the prodigal has been welcomed with open arms!" Genevieve placed a hand over her heart and said, with an ingratiating look, "I am overcome."

Lady Castleton's sneer deepened into a frown. "Less generous persons would say you got your desserts, but I should never say so. No, I cannot imagine the distress of watching a hard-won fortune disappear before one's very eyes, and one's idol proven to be the veriest brute, and I would never wish such revelations on anyone." She lifted a cynical eyebrow. "Even you, Genevieve."

"It is very odd in you, for I seem to recall you wishing me the very thing just after my wedding day. But memories are tricky things, you know. For example, I vividly remember marrying Bertram for love, but you are not the first to assure me that I married for money. I confess I cannot find it in me to thank you for undeceiving me, for it is excessively lowering to believe oneself possessed of virtue, and then to discover one has been all along a viper." She had the satisfaction of watching the color rise up into her ladyship's face.

"Some Persons find it easy to persuade themselves into love, when there are greater inducements at hand. But it is all of a piece, dearest Genevieve. I cannot conjecture why I should have entertained the expectation that your sufferings must have altered you."

"Nor can I, my dear Cassandra, for how can one who has not changed a whit hope to perceive change in another?"

Her ladyship reared her head back, assuming the posture of a Great Lady. "Despite your impudence, I feel it incumbent upon me to put a little word in your ear, my dear. My Dulcinea has fairly captivated the very gentleman you seem to have in your eye. I should not wish you to make more of a fool of yourself than you must, and so I trust you will look otherwise to recoup your losses."

This speech fell a trifle flat, for Genevieve's attention had been arrested too early in it to pay the heed it deserved. She blinked rapidly, her lips twitching with the urge to let forth a most ungenteel laugh. "D-dulcinea? Oh, what—what a lovely name!" Her inner devil, on such a loose rein, rather unsurprisingly unfurled its genius, and she clasped her hands ecstatically before her. "My dear Cassandra, you are to be congratulated! Such perspicacity to bestow so magnificent an appellation upon an infant, and so be prepared for just the eventuality in which you find yourself. You behold me in awe."

"What can you be insinuating?" demanded Lady Castleton, looking thunderous. "Shameless creature, you will tell me at once!"

"Oh, my dear," said Mrs. Breckinridge, executing a flowing curtsey, "it is only that in clothing your daughter in such beauty from birth, you have made liars of all who consider her plain."

Her ladyship, bereft of speech, swept away, and Genevieve gracefully resumed her seat, too well-bred to outwardly revel in her victory. Indeed, she could not, for though she had affected not to heed her, Lady Castleton's barbed hints that she had set her cap at Sir Joshua had struck home, and thrown her mind into a state of perturbation she was at much trouble to resolve.

It had never been her intention to catch anyone for her daughter this season, but she could not pretend to be unaware of Lenora's admiration for Sir Joshua, and the knowledge that others had observed it as well, and had accorded it such a despicable motive, deeply mortified her. There was no denying Sir Joshua's being a matrimonial prize—Lady Castleton herself had set her sights on him for her daughter—and hopes of a match between him and a portionless girl like Lenora would be considered the height of pretention. But another, less defined sensation strove in her breast, one which loudly deprecated Lenora's right to Sir Joshua's heart, and she cravenly put it down to Lady Castleton's insinuations.

Her ruminations were here interrupted by Tom, who came to sit beside her with a sigh. "What an evening, Mama."

"Are you not enjoying yourself, Tom?"

"Oh, yes, hugely, despite Lenora." He caught her worried look. "Oh, don't fret for me, Mama! I've had a capital time! That Miss Marshall!"

She smiled and took his hand. "She is a lovely girl, Tom. I like her very much."

He looked down bashfully, but rallied her with, "And you've been cutting a dash tonight, Mama! Don't try to deny it. I saw you dancing with Sir Joshua—the waltz, no less!"

She colored, a flood of contradictory emotions threatening to overpower her. She wisely turned the subject. "I think Lenora has enjoyed herself as well."

Tom grimaced. "Yes, though it's been dashed exhausting for me!"

"How so, dear?"

"It's no easy thing to keep an eye out for any rum touch who may present himself."

"But surely you saw no need to put yourself out tonight, Tom! Lady Wraglain assured me—"

"Well, she didn't tell you she'd invited that commoner Castleton, who thought it good sport to get Lenora alone on the balcony!"

"Oh, dear. No doubt he was foxed. I suppose you gave him a set-down?"

"Didn't have to, Mama. Sir Joshua did it for me, and I'll be honest with you, I'm glad he did."

Mrs. Breckinridge had suddenly succumbed to a sort of numbness, and could not comment.

"Sir Joshua's as good a fellow as ever breathed, Mama. Can't say I don't wish he would quit beating about the bush and—" He broke off with a conscious little smile. "Well, I'm sure you know what I mean." Then, spying Miss Marshall alone nearby, he made his gallant excuses to his mama and took himself off to beg a second dance.

As soon as she was able to mobilize her thoughts, Mrs. Breckinridge stridently suppressed the nameless sensation that had suddenly assumed the mien of a suspiciously green-eyed monster. She could not be jealous of Lenora—Sir Joshua was a brother to her, an uncle to her children, and a man who, with half the eligible maidens at his feet, would never even think to throw his attentions away on a worn-out woman. Indeed, she did not wish him to, being herself inured to the idea of romance. She had her children to care for, and her home to reclaim, and—and not a thought to spare for such frivolous notions as twilight love. Firmly rejecting the wry thought that she had windmills in her head, she squared herself to dispassionately consider the evening's revelations in light of Lenora's happiness.

Though Lenora surely cared for Sir Joshua, she also had a marked interest in Mr. Barnabus which, as the recent overheard conversation attested, strongly suggested that she did not know her own heart. She was young yet, in body as well as in mind, as Mrs. Breckinridge very well knew when she laid her plans to bring Lenora out this season. Only a conviction that Lenora was not ready to pledge her life to one man had given Genevieve the complaisance to move forward with her plans, but that conviction, she now realized, had not taken into account the emotions Lenora should possibly excite in male breasts. Mr. Barnabus she was fairly sure meant nothing by Lenora but friendship, and until tonight, Sir Joshua's manners toward her daughter had appeared to her so staid that she had experienced only moments of distress, and generally only from Lenora's open admiration of him. But as an attachment to him would leave Lenora's heart vulnerable, Mrs. Breckinridge dutifully acknowledged that it behooved her to ascertain the degree to which Sir Joshua returned Lenora's affection.

This resolution reached, Mrs. Breckinridge could do nothing better than to put the matter out of her head, and she did so, only descending into a brown study twice before turning to the chaperone next to her and engaging in conversation wholly appropriate to responsible and aged matrons. She signally failed, however, to recall more than two of Tom's childhood illnesses, being distracted by reminiscences of Lenora's sunny disposition from a child and the development of her lively sense of humor, and so was forced to doggedly attend to her companion's much more comprehensive saga. The ploy ultimately failed to prevent her from entertaining morbid thoughts, so she excused herself from this particular purgatory and marched purposefully to the refreshment table in search of something to recruit her stability. But when she reached for a glass of champagne, another hand lifted it for her, and she turned, and stared in plain astonishment at the most unwelcome gentleman beside her.

He tutted. "What a greeting for an old friend, Mrs. Breckinridge! If it were not you, I should be affronted, but I believe I know you well enough to comprehend your feelings."

"My Lord Montrose," she said, with sufficient calm. "I did not know you were to be here."

"Or you should have stayed at home?" he said knowingly. "By happy chance, I am the guest of young Lord Castleton at the moment, so it is to his pity that you owe your discomfiture."

"Oh, I am not so small-minded," she said, recovering enough to take out her fan in an effort to keep from glancing about for Lenora. "How lucky for you to have found such a friend."

"Yes, I should say so." He took the fan from her, offering her the glass still in his hand. "It is insufferably hot," he said, plying the fan for her.

She laughed and took a judicious gulp of the champagne. "Yes, though one could not expect less, with such attendance. I declare you must be only one of many who have come uninvited."

"Yes, and a great many of them too superstitious to open a window!" he said, his eyes never leaving her face. "I happen to know the way to the gardens, however."

"What an excellent idea, my lord." She set down her empty glass and plucked the fan from his grasp. "Do not you let me keep you."

He possessed himself of her hand as she turned away. "No, you must come see the gardens, Genevieve. They are lovely in the moonlight."

"I apprehend it is the moon that calls you, my lord," she said smoothly, "in which case, I should be a fool to accompany you. I've no doubt others of your kind will respond to its call, and it should be horrific to find myself surrounded by your fellow creatures."

"Your fears are entirely unfounded, ma'am," he said in a low tone, pulling her toward him. "My intention is to protect you from any and all danger."

"As you are blind to my greatest danger, my lord, you must excuse me if I place absolutely no dependence on your protection." So saying, she broke from him and turned to flee, only to be met with Sir Joshua Stiles.

"Mrs. Breckinridge! I have found you at last." He bowed, taking up her hand. "They play another waltz, and you know I will waltz with only one lady here."

"How pleasant, Sir Joshua," she said, aware that her cheeks were blazing. "Let us go and find her."

He chuckled unconvincingly and swept her away from the refreshment table and into the ballroom. Leaning his head slightly down to her, he murmured, "I am at a loss to understand why you should encourage such a man as Lord Montrose."

"I am at a loss to understand why you should think I encourage him!" she hissed back.

"You stand talking amiably with him for several minutes, allowing him to fan you and give you refreshment. Is this not encouragement?"

"I hardly know whether to be affronted or diverted at your staying to observe me so long, sir! But if this is so, and if you were in the least astute, you would have seen that he stole my fan, that he obliged me to take the glass, and that *his* part in the conversation only was what you would call amiable."

His jaw tightened. "Then you should be all the more careful."

Painfully conscious of the little leap of her heart at his solicitude, she stifled it. "I appreciate your concern, sir, but I know what I am about," she said.

"I hope you do, for you have Lenora to consider."

His words felt like a slap, and for some moments all her energies were bent upon retaining some semblance of composure. They stood without speaking on the side of the room while the previous dance finished, and she half expected him to leave her again, but when the orchestra struck up the waltz, he led her onto the floor. His face remained grave throughout the dance, however, and though his claim that he would waltz with only one woman flitted enticingly into her mind, she easily dismissed it as the excuse of the moment, to bring her away from Lord Montrose, and she could not enjoy the second waltz as she had the first.

Chapter 19

AFTER THE BALL, Tom met Mr. Ginsham at Limmer's, an appointment the latter found strange, as the former was most eager to secure it on that night and at such a late hour. They were met, however, and Ginsham was made even more wary by Tom's tightly wound mood.

"What's made you so rusty, Tom?"

"I'm worn out by care," said Tom grimly. "Too young by half to be looking after my sister like that. What she needs is a husband," he said, taking his drink in a gulp and signaling for another. "Not only must she dance with half the loose screws in town, she's so green she lets one of 'em take her out on the balcony alone! It's enough to fret me to flinders! I'll tell you truth, I could use a good turn up after this evening."

Mr. Ginsham gauged his friend's potations with an experienced eye. "At that speed, I'd say you're likely to get your wish!"

"Devil a bit, my friend," said Tom, as he tipped back the second drink without a pause. "But with a sister like mine, none could blame me for going a little up in the world."

"Well, I would!" answered Ginsham bluntly. "What the deuce makes you drag me out here just to watch you get drunk? Dashed waste of my time!"

Tom disclaimed, and though his protestations seemed fully comprehensible, Ginsham looked indecisive, but as he had been on tenterhooks regarding his future happiness, he relented after a moment. Leaning forward and gripping the edges of the table, he said urgently, "Were you able to speak to your sister about Miss Chuddsley and—and—you know," he finished impatiently, unable even to speak the traitor's name.

Tom sat up straight in his chair. "I have, and you, sir, have been going about it all wrong," he said, punching a finger toward Ginsham's nose. "That hunch I had was right—well nearly—and what it comes to is this: you ain't romantic enough."

"Ain't romantic enough?" cried Ginsham incredulously. "Well, I ask you, what more can I do? I take her to the theater and the opera and to al fresco picnics and for drives in the park. I bring her flowers and treat her like a queen—"

"No, no, that's all well enough for everyday love making, and I daresay you do it very creditably," said Tom, waving away his friend's exclamations like so many gnats, "but you, sir, *you* are not romantic enough."

Mr. Ginsham's mouth turned mulish. "Well, if all you've got to tell me is that I'm not good enough for Miss Chuddsley, I'll thank you to keep your mouth shut, or I'll be obliged to shut it for you." He pushed stormily to his feet. "Good night, you—"

"Must I always beg you to take a damper, Greg?" Tom rolled a long-suffering eye at his friend, tugging at his immovable elbow.

"If you'll only attend to what I've got to say—But see, if you want to go, I'll bear you company as far as Berkeley Square." Ginsham was inclined to object, but Tom put a hand firmly through his arm and walked him from the hotel and onto the street. "Now, where was I? Oh, yes." He gesticulated largely as he spoke. "After wading through mountains of flummery—all on your behalf, I'll not scruple to remind you, Greg—I have been made to understand that females of Miss Chuddsley's stamp define 'romance' differently than such gudgeons as you and I, my friend."

Mr. Ginsham gave a low moan. "What am I going to do?"

Tom patted his shoulder bracingly. "No need to despair. Possessed as I am of new knowledge, I am equipped to enlighten you."

"Then I wish you would," was the sullen response.

"Stand buff, man!" Tom poked his finger into his friend's chest. "Lenora tells me that you have every chance with Miss Chuddsley," his friend's head came up with a start, and he stared hungrily at Tom, who continued with a smile, "provided you humble yourself."

The eyes widened. "Humble myself?"

"Yes. Humble yourself. Miss Chuddsley has no interest in a man whose title and fortune make his way easy."

"You're shamming it."

Tom went on without mercy. "You must struggle."

Mr. Ginsham halted, glaring at his companion. "You're foxed."

"I assure you, I am in complete possession of my senses, sir."

"But you're talking fustian!"

"If what I say is fustian, it is because I repeat the words of a goose of a female," Tom replied reasonably. "Be that as it may, what I say is true. You must humble yourself through struggle. Oh," he said, raising a finger into the air, "and you must not take glory to yourself for any heroic deed you may be called upon, by honor, to perform."

Mr. Ginsham curled his hands into fists, but before he could rid himself of his most deservedly gathered spleen, two shadows flew forward from the darkness of an alley, brandishing weapons and hurling themselves at the two gentlemen. Ginsham, though taken utterly by surprise, was by this time perfectly ready for a good set-to and, thrusting away from Tom, he threw up an arm to block the blow of a cudgel aimed at his head, while Tom was made to grapple with an assailant armed with a glinting knife. Mr. Ginsham, who regularly boxed at Jackson's Saloon, made quick work of his attacker with a series of solid jabs, but upon dropping the man to the ground, he turned to find Tom dodging the wide swings of his attacker's knife.

Leaping to his aid, Ginsham seized the man's knife arm and tried to wrench the weapon away, but the assailant spun with astonishing dexterity and plunged the knife toward Ginsham's forearm. Ginsham blocked the blow, but not before the tip of the knife penetrated into his muscle, and an outraged yell escaped him. Tom jumped toward them and grasped the attacker's knife hand, wrenching it up and back, and Ginsham thought, but could not be certain, that he heard Tom hoarsely whisper to the man, "Enough!"

The fight seemed to go out of the man, and he turned, fleeing into the darkness, and a scuffle and pounding of footfalls behind them proved to be his accomplice on the run as well. Tom strode to Ginsham's side and examined the blood that welled alarmingly from the wound, and Ginsham was disturbed to see his friend's eyes light.

"Thank God! I thought he'd overdone it—" Tom said rather breathlessly, then he grinned. "It's a capital wound, Greg! Just the thing!"

"You're mad!" gasped Ginsham, pulling his arm out of Tom's grasp and taking off his coat. "Why the devil did they attack us?"

His friend shrugged, helpfully tearing off the tattered sleeve of

Ginsham's shirt. "I expect we seemed likely victims. Here, I'll tie it up. The bleeding's already slowed."

"You don't seem at all put out, Tom," Ginsham observed, a disquieted frown on his face. "Almost as if you expected it."

Tom's eyes flicked up to his for a brief moment, then back at the makeshift bandage he was tying over the wound. "I told you I needed a good turn up tonight."

Ginsham's eyes narrowed. "What's your game, Tom?"

Satisfied with the bandage, Tom turned an innocent gaze on his friend. "You'll want to put some basilicum powder on that, Greg. Lucky thing it's not deep."

"Yes, very lucky," said Ginsham, his jaw tight.

Tom draped Ginsham's coat over his shoulders. "Now, we'd best get you home."

Ginsham whirled on him. "I won't budge an inch until you tell me what you're playing at, Tom! You thought he'd overdone it?" he sputtered. "This was a setup, clear as day! And don't tell me to take a damper!"

"Well, you'd better take one or you're going to faint, you cawker!"

"Out with it!"

Tom put up his hands in resignation. "Alright, alright! I've made you romantic, Greg, that's the long and short of it." Ginsham gaped at his mentor, who took a bow. "You've struggled through adversity, and now all you need do is puff it off as nothing, a mere scratch, and if a certain young lady must know, if she drags it from you, it was done to save the life of the young man who is almost a brother to her."

Finding his voice, Ginsham gasped, "You—those men—plunged a knife in me—could've been killed—" His eyes rolled back and he wilted.

Tom caught him by the shoulders, holding him up. "Now you've gone and made yourself light-headed." Ginsham swayed a bit more, but he blinked his eyes, and Tom congratulated him. "That's the dandy! You'll be all right and tight, no harm done." Supporting his beleaguered friend around the waist, Tom turned him in the direction of his lodgings. "We'll get you home, get some brandy into you, and then off to bed."

As they shuffled along, Ginsham's strength gradually reasserted itself. "You're a rascal, Tom," he said.

"That I am," Tom replied cheerfully. "But only for the greater good."

"What if they'd killed me?"

"Well, I'll own I was a trifle anxious for you, but they're professionals, after all."

"You ought to be ashamed."

"I'm sure I shall be, but not yet. I feel rather heroic, actually."

Ginsham eyed him with dislike. "You'll never persuade me you're not drunk as a wheelbarrow, Tom."

"It don't signify. You'll thank me after Miss Chuddsley sees you."

"Best not lay odds," said Mr. Ginsham, darkly.

Chapter 20

THE NEXT MORNING found Miss Chuddsley and Miss Breckinridge together in Lady Cammerby's sitting room, where Elvira
rather mournfully received her friend's exciting description of the
previous evening's ball. Other than a few rather pointed animadver-
sions on Lord Castleton's unwanted attentions, Lenora had nothing
but raptures to share.

"There were dozens of amiable gentlemen there, Elvira, and even
though Tom was horridly protective, I never lacked a partner. Indeed,
at one particular moment, no fewer than three gentlemen asked
me to dance! I felt like a queen, with dozens of suitors at my feet!"

"Oh, I wish I had been there!" said Elvira wistfully. "But my aunt
is not a friend of Lady Wraglain."

Lenora pressed her friend's hand. "I'm ever so sorry you were
not, Elvira, for I would have enjoyed it more had you been—but
you know that!"

"Indeed," answered Elvira, looking as though she very much

doubted it. "You are my bosom friend."

Her bosom friend at last perceived that Elvira was not in spirits, and asked her the cause.

Miss Chuddsley toyed with the tassels on a cushion nearby. "Have you heard that Barnabus has gone from London?"

"Yes, he told me he was to go." At Elvira's look of surprise, Lenora hastened to explain. "Did I not mention it? He was at the ball last night."

Elvira gaped. "But he does not dance! Mr. Ginsham told us, ever so long ago! That is why we have never seen him at Almack's!"

"Nevertheless, he was there," Lenora said, acknowledging Ginsham's authority with a toss of her shoulder. "Barnabus came with the Oslows last night, but he did not stay long. And he most specifically asked after you, and wished he could have seen you, to take leave, for he planned to go this morning early."

Elvira plucked harder at the tassels under her fingertips. "It was Ginsham who told me Barnabus had gone. Perhaps I should have expected that he would deceive me."

"He must merely have been mistaken." Lenora plumped herself down on the sofa next to her friend, perceiving danger to Mr. Ginsham. "He is the perfect gentleman!" she said soothingly. "He would never knowingly deceive anyone."

"But he told me Barnabus was gone home, so he might not join our party yesterday to Hyde Park, but we both know he was not yet gone! And he insisted Barnabus does not dance, and yet, why else would a young man attend a ball?" Elvira turned brave but brimming eyes toward her friend. "If that is not deception, what is?"

Lenora bit her lip. "It is black against him, indeed, but—Elvira, Mr. Barnabus did not dance last night. Indeed, he told me his only purpose in coming was to take his leave!"

Her friend's face wore a stubborn frown. "Perhaps he simply did not wish to dance with you."

"Perhaps not," Lenora conceded, though nettled, "but he did ask me to go down with him to supper!"

"And I suppose he took leave of you?"

"I told you he did."

Elvira could not hide her envy at that. "Then you have made the conquest, my friend! Let me be the first to congratulate you! Though why you should feel the right to him, I don't know, as I was the first to meet him!"

"You are wrong, my dear, for he was first introduced to me!"

"*You* are wrong, my dear, for Ginsham introduced him to *me*, and you very rudely spoke first!"

Lenora leapt up. "Because you could do nothing but stand and gape at the poor man!"

The cushion on her lap fell to the floor as Elvira jumped to her feet. "Mr. Ginsham brought him to meet me, no matter which one of us responded to the introduction!"

"Mr. Ginsham obviously intended Barnabus for my escort, as he knew you would not attend him alone into the maze!"

"I distinctly recall his referring to the both of us in his invitation into the maze—"

"And as he had so flatteringly paid you particular attention in the previous weeks, it was to be expected that he would bring a stammering, stoop-shouldered, poverty-stricken young man to guide you into the maze, while he intended to squire me!"

"Oh!" Elvira stamped her foot. "That you could pretend preference for dear Mr. Barnabus with one breath, then with another refer to him in such a way! For shame!"

"You only admire him because he stammers!" Lenora retorted.

Flushed, Elvira gathered her things. "I will not stay another minute to hear such a noble young man's character belittled." She stopped at the door to fling back, "I never thought you, Lenora, of all people, could be possessed of such a cold heart."

Slamming the door, Elvira flounced from the house and rushed home, flying to her aunt's drawing room in search of comfort. But here she was drawn up short—Mr. Ginsham sat in conversation with her aunt, and as he stood to greet her, all her feelings of anger and hurt became focused on the hapless young gentleman. Fortunately, the excessively uncivil words on her tongue died unspoken when she glimpsed Mr. Ginsham's arm reposing interestingly in a sling.

"Ginsham, you are hurt!" she cried, dropping her reticule in her shock.

Ginsham, justly discomposed by the baleful stare he had first received, managed, "It—it's nothing, Miss Chuddsley. A—a mere scratch. Do not regard it, I pray you."

"But will you tell me what happened?" she asked with such melting sympathy in her eyes that he was quite unmanned, and allowed himself to be led to the sofa and pulled down to a seat beside her.

Much flushed, Mr. Ginsham put even Barnabus to shame with his stammered responses to her searching inquiries, encouraged by the dawning realization that Tom had been absolutely correct in his assertions that a mere wound would prove the turning point in Miss Chuddsley's affections.

Her eyes glowed as he haltingly described his adventure of the night before, and she paled dramatically when he explained his poor part in saving Tom's life at the hand of the desperados. When he reached the point of his taking the wound, her hand reflexively darted out to clasp his own, only to release it in a flutter of pretty confusion.

"Oh, Mr. Ginsham, how thankful I am that you are safe!" she uttered, pressing hands to her glowing cheeks. "What courage you displayed, and under such duress! I cannot imagine how Tom feels toward you at this moment!"

Knowing exactly how Tom felt about him, Ginsham's feelings of chivalry suddenly revolted at the thought of continuing the deception of his innocent love. He stared helplessly into her adoring eyes, striving within himself, then lowered his gaze. "I must tell you, Miss Chuddsley, that I discovered afterward that Tom had orchestrated the whole. So I am no more a hero than I was yesterday."

"Oh!" uttered Miss Chuddsley, obviously taken aback. "But why would he do such a thing?"

Exceedingly uncomfortable, Mr. Ginsham muttered something about cock-brained fools and romance, unable to meet Miss Chuddsley's gaze as his words dwindled to a stop. It took Elvira some minutes to digest this revelation, and her eyes began to blaze, while poor Mr. Ginsham, swallowing rather convulsively from time to time, tensely waited for her verdict.

"Oh! The perfidious wretches!" she cried at last, startling both Mr. Ginsham and her aunt, who had been reading quietly in the corner. "I never knew they were so black at heart! But I should have known it would be so, for Lenora has behaved outrageously to poor Mr. Barnabus, courting his good opinion while nourishing the most callous feelings—she had the impudence to tell me that she considers him to be nothing better than a gargoyle, if you please! Which I know to be the most shocking untruth, for she fairly fell over herself in trying to disengage my affections for him, all so she could attach him to herself!"

She jumped to her feet and began to pace about the room, both her companions regarding her with the utmost astonishment. "And

Tom—employing common thieves to pretend to endanger his life, to lure you into a farce of the most odious kind—and for what? To make a fool out of me! I, who have been like a sister to him! I, who have never done him the least harm—excepting when I made him break his arm because I was too afraid to go for help when he was caught in Sir Wallaby's tree, but it was his fault for hoaxing me into stealing the apples, so that is neither here nor there—But it is all of a piece! I am persuaded they have no thought but for their own amusement, no matter the cost, and I will stand for it no longer!"

She stamped her foot. "Lenora may have cheated me out of Mr. Barnabus's affections, for I fancy it was she who kept him from calling to take leave—indeed, I should not be surprised at her having pretended not to care for him at the last out of pique, for he was becoming most assiduous in his attentions to me, I assure you, and must have expressed his ardent wish to see me once more—but she has merely the satisfaction of seeing the back of him, for he left her just as well as he left me!"

She rounded on Mr. Ginsham, who shrank back into his chair as she shook her little fist at him. "And Tom, who was ever a disagreeable boy, thinking to bamboozle me with this horrid trick, fancying me to be such a goosecap as to swallow such a story! And that he caught you up in the trap as well—you, who have ever been his truest friend!—Oh, I could choke him!"

This ferocity drew a startled exclamation from her aunt, to whom she directed a curt apology, but continued to hold forth for several minutes on the scandalous dealings of two such false friends, until she had torn the two young Breckinridges' characters to shreds, and finally her anger seemed to burn out. Still, she paced back and forth in grave silence, her brow furrowed, while two pairs of wary eyes followed her.

At last, she stopped in front of Ginsham, her blue eyes intently searching his own. "But you did fight those men."

Mr. Ginsham, having run the gamut of emotions during her tirade, from shock to disbelief to awe, was startled out of his admiration of the hitherto unknown fire his love possessed to say, "I did."

"And you were, indeed, wounded."

He nodded, glancing at the bandage on his arm as if to satisfy himself of its reality. "Yes."

"And you did mean to rescue Tom."

"Not that he needed it, the dev—" He shut his lips tight and cleared his throat, gazing with great humility upon her. "That was my intent, yes, Miss Chuddsley."

She smiled, and it was like a beam of sunlight through the clouds. "Then you are a hero, Mr. Ginsham! And I daresay you have been one all along, and I never knew it." Mr. Ginsham's heart thumped with relief and hope as she held out her hand to him. "We were both deceived, but you deserve honor for your part, for you acted, I am persuaded, from the purest motives."

He stood, taking her hand and bowing reverently over it, then looking into her eyes with wonder at how he had never seemed to have truly seen her before.

Miss Chuddsley, responding to his worshipful gaze with heightening color, seemed at last to recollect herself, reclaiming her hand and glancing away. "It is a pity Mr. Barnabus was not there with you last night."

"Barnabus?" repeated Ginsham, stunned out of his dream.

She glanced at him with an arch look in her eye. "Yes, Barnabus. 'Tis a pity he had quitted town for, had he been present, he may have seen through the nonsense and put a stop to it."

Mr. Ginsham's heart plummeted, and his jaw tightened

infinitesimally, but he took the blow with fortitude. "Perhaps you are right. It is a pity I mistook his day, or he could well have been present at the farrago last night, for he did not depart until this morning."

She looked quickly up at him. "But you told me he had gone yesterday."

"So I did," he said manfully, "and I'm terribly sorry, for it seems he missed his chance to take leave of you. I had the deuce of a surprise when he sauntered in yesterday afternoon to bid me farewell."

Several emotions flitted across her face, chagrin and relief among them, and Mr. Ginsham, unable to read her mind, felt certain that she was lost to him at last, and all through his foolishness. With this belief, he prepared to take his leave of her, but she said suddenly, "It doesn't signify," and favored him with such a sweetly apologetic look from under her lashes that he could not repress a flutter of hope.

She shrugged a pretty shoulder. "I'm sure he will be missed, but I should always regret the loss of any of my friends."

This last was said in so conciliatory a manner that Mr. Ginsham dared to fan his hope. Grasping his hat and gloves to his chest, he said, "I had planned to ask you to go driving with me this afternoon, Miss Chuddsley, but as my arm is—well, you know—I wonder if you would do me the honor of accompanying me on a walk in the park? The bluebells are lovely just now," he added with rare inspiration.

"I can think of nothing more delightful, Mr. Ginsham!" she answered, smiling angelically.

Receiving approbation from her aunt, who seemed still to be in shock at the revelation of her mild niece's true character, Miss Chuddsley took her dazedly beaming suitor's arm and went with him out into the sunshine.

Chapter 21

Tom, oblivious to the consequences of his actions upon his character, departed two days later for Branwell, confident that he had left things well in hand with his friend and, having received certain assurances from Sir Joshua, that his mother and sister would be excellently safeguarded.

Sir Joshua had taken Tom aside before leaving the Wraglain's ball, informing him of Lord Montrose's appearance, and of Mrs. Breckinridge's interaction with him. Tom had not hesitated to share his exact feelings on the matter, and there followed a hushed discussion in a quiet corner regarding the advisability of Tom's returning home and leaving the females of his family unprotected.

The outcome of this discussion was that Sir Joshua, on his own insistence, became almost a fixture in his sister's house, coming to drive out with the ladies, or turning up just in time to attend them on errands, and placing himself entirely at their service.

"My dear Joshua," said his sister one afternoon, primly pleased at his activities, "I begin to suspect an ulterior motive for your assiduous care of me."

"You need not scruple to ask if I do, my dear. Lord Montrose has proven himself dangerous to your guests, and by association, to you, and with Cammerby away, and Tom gone back to Branwell, you are none of you protected," he said, with disappointing honesty. "I am merely doing my duty as a faithful brother."

Her budding hopes quite crushed, Lady Cammerby was moved to remonstrate. "I did try to warn you about him."

"You did, dear, and I was unwise to heed it," he acknowledged handsomely. "Now I must bear the consequences."

"But you do not dislike the consequences, I am persuaded," she said, not one to give up easily. "None could believe you merely tolerant who has seen your enjoyment of my guests' company."

"I hope I am more the gentleman than to let my boredom show, Amelia," he said gravely.

She colored, biting her lip, and at last he relented, casting her a humorous sideways glance. "My dear, forgive me, but you are too easily gulled. Indeed, I wronged both you and the Breckinridges, on my first acquaintance with them, and I am at least gentleman enough to admit my fault in that." He turned, taking his sister's hands and kissing them. "I believe I shall have reason to count myself indebted to you in the not too distant future, for requesting me to deliver your letter to Branwell."

Eyes bright, Lady Cammerby beamed at her brother. "I knew how it would be, Joshua! I did tell you it would serve you right!"

"And I hope it does," he said, turning to straighten his cravat in the mirror. "But while you are congratulating yourself, Amelia, you must recall that *you* never suspected me of hanging out for a young wife."

Bowing politely, he left her blinking in consternation in the hall.

Mrs. Breckinridge, though seemingly resigned to Sir Joshua's chivalry, behaved in a punctiliously civil manner whenever he called. As he had gotten wind of Lady Castleton's speech with her at the ball, he thought he knew the reason for this formality, and made coaxing her out of it a kind of game.

"Allow me to help you with your pelisse, Miss Breckinridge," he said one day, as they prepared to depart on an errand, "for your mother seems to be in a terrible hurry today."

"I am in no hurry, sir," said Mrs. Breckinridge stiffly, arrested with her foot on the bottom step of the house.

"I see that I mistook the matter," he said from the doorway, patiently waiting until Lenora had donned her bonnet and gloves and preceded him out the door. "Miss Breckinridge and I are simply too slow." Mrs. Breckinridge maintained a dignified silence as they came down to join her, and just deigned to take the arm offered her. They had gone only a few steps when Sir Joshua asked civilly, "Are you cold, Mrs. Breckinridge?"

"No, I am not."

"I must beg the indulgence of our long acquaintance and declare that I do not believe you. Indeed, you must be frozen to walk so rigidly."

Her mouth tightened, but that irrepressible dimple belied her. "Your solicitude, though misplaced, is most appreciated, sir."

"As always, ma'am, you are all that is generous." He noted that her shoulders relaxed a trifle, but her chin remained decidedly up. "Ah, I begin to understand you, ma'am, and must beg your patience with my obtuseness," he said, still eyeing her askance. "You obviously fear a nosebleed."

His countenance remained only tolerably composed as she

turned glittering eyes on him.

"There can be no other cause for your holding your nose in the air," he said with an air of innocence, "for not even I have courage enough to accuse you of being stiff-rumped."

The glitter changed to a gleam and her mouth twisted in an abortive effort to keep from laughing. "Oh, you odious man!" she said at last, and joined him in a chuckle, while Lenora smiled affectionately on them both, and he was pleased to discover that once down from her high ropes, Mrs. Breckinridge found it nearly impossible to ascend beyond reach again—at least until solitude offered her a period of reflection.

Lenora betrayed no qualms in being in Sir Joshua's company, and especially seemed to enjoy driving with him in Hyde Park, or to various sites around the city, or even as far as Wimbledon. Having lost, so she believed, the companion of her youth—Elvira had most stubbornly persisted in not speaking to her—she had been in very real danger of a decline, until Sir Joshua offered himself as a most excellent confidante. He, in turn, was gratified by her trust, for she shared with him all her excitements and interests, and the joys she had experienced while in London, and she so artlessly encouraged him to speak that he found himself imparting his most cherished memories, and without pain, for the first time in many years.

"We were married only three years, when she was taken from me," he confided on one of their long drives.

"Oh, how tragic, sir! I am so sorry." She hesitated, and he could sense her desire to know more striving with an unwillingness to pry. "What was she like?" she at last enquired in timid accents, hastening to add, "Or does it pain you too much to speak of her?"

Touched by her sincere concern, Sir Joshua replied, "No, my dear. On the contrary, I imagine my feelings will experience some relief in sharing my Rachel with you." Encouraged by her smile, he continued, "She was a lovely woman, in all respects. She had hair the color of corn silk, and eyes as blue as a mountain lake. Her laughter was music, and she was as gentle and graceful a lady as one would wish."

"She sounds perfect," said Lenora in a small voice.

"I thought her so, indeed," answered Sir Joshua reflectively, "but I have lately considered that just as none could compare with her, none ought to be compared to her."

This notion seemed to enliven his companion, who observed, "Indeed, sir, there must be many kinds of love, to fit with the many kinds of perfection."

"Just so," murmured Sir Joshua, casting her a glance of approbation.

Lenora glanced up shyly. "Was she much younger than you, sir?"

"By several years, but I do not think that age has anything to do with suitability in marriage, do you?"

"I should think not, sir," answered Lenora, with decision. Again, she seemed to struggle for some moments before bursting out with, "Did you love her terribly?"

He smiled at her choice of adverb. "If you mean deeply, yes, I did. I do not mind telling you that it broke my heart when she died."

"As well it must!" she cried, looking up at him sympathetically. "I always knew you had a tragic past, sir." Instantly, she colored and turned away. "Forgive me! That was unfeeling."

"But there is nothing to forgive, Miss Breckinridge, because it is true." He bestowed a warm look upon her. "I do have a tragic past, but it is past, and I have had many years to grow accustomed to life as it is without Rachel."

Lenora kept her gaze trained on the horses' heads. "Are you—do you ever—could you think of marriage again, sir?"

"There was a time, not so very long ago, that such a thought was impossible." He glanced sideways at her. "But, more recently, it has not seemed so."

He was rewarded with a bright smile. Settling happily back in her side of the curricle, she said, "Tell me about your home. Wrenthorpe Grange, is it not?"

"It is. My estate is near Painswick, in Gloucestershire."

"Such a romantic county!" breathed Lenora. "In truth, I know only what I have heard, but I should think the countryside to be most beautiful. I should love to see it." A dazzling thought struck her. "Does your estate have a wood?"

He nodded. "While the demesne encompasses mostly fields, the Grange has a large park, which boasts a lovely wood."

"An ancient, mossy wood, with great creaking trunks and sinister shadows?" she asked with suppressed excitement.

"I have not been accustomed to consider them sinister," he began but, glancing down, perceived a look of disappointment rapidly displacing the rapture on her face, and hastily rephrased his negative answer. "But I am certainly biased, having been resident there my entire life—for upon reflection, I do not doubt my wood must certainly be sinister under the right conditions."

"Indeed!" she cried, once more entranced. "I, myself, have been deceived by a sunny day in an otherwise gloomy wood."

Entering into her feelings, he said, "I am persuaded that all that is needed to render my wood perfectly sinister is a howling wind and ominous skies."

"Just so." She nodded approvingly, bestowing upon the wood her approbation, and moved on to the romantic possibilities of the residence. "And is Wrenthorpe an old house?"

"Very," declared Sir Joshua, fully aware of her expectations by this time. "The original building dates from the sixteenth century, and you may depend upon its being utterly shrouded in vines and lichen."

Lenora shivered in delight. "Tell me at once if there are secret passages!"

Here, he was at a loss, for he was an honest man, and could invent no sufficient answer on the spur of the moment, and so was obliged to answer apologetically, "I do not believe the Grange boasts any secret passages."

"Then there must be a ghost," she declared positively.

"I do not know of one, but it is entirely possible that I have merely never seen it," he replied cautiously.

These unsatisfactory answers checked her enthusiasm for a moment, but she presently recovered enough to ask, "Is there by chance an oubliette?"

"Not to my knowledge," he owned with chagrin but, bidden by a sudden inspiration, he hastened to add, "But, you see, my dear Miss Breckinridge, that I have never looked for such things." Her gasp of astonishment produced an apologetic shrug. "I fear I lack imagination—a failing that must be mended, to be sure."

"An absolute necessity, sir!" cried Lenora, turning fully toward him. "That one could live one's entire life in such a romantic place as Wrenthorpe Grange, with ivy and lichen, and—and a sinister wood, no less—and never think to search for secret passages? It makes me shudder to think of it!"

"You have brought me to realize that I have made a perfect waste of dramatic surroundings," he said, gazing ahead with a lurking smile, "and would make reparation without delay but, in truth, I should hardly know the first place to look."

She sat back, pondering the problem. "I see. If one was used to have no inclination, one would not know where to begin, without an experienced person to guide you."

"Exactly my thought, Miss Breckinridge. Perhaps we may discover a secret passage or two, if you were to help me look."

"We?"

He smiled down at her. "Amelia plans to visit me at Wrenthorpe for a few weeks after the season, and it had occurred to me that she might invite your family along, if you should like it."

"Oh, sir! It would be perfect!" Lenora was visibly delighted. "I'm sure Mama would be thrilled to have us come." She tucked a confiding hand into his arm. "I am sorry I ever thought you were the evil Duke."

He blinked at her. "The evil Duke?"

"Oh! My wretched tongue!" She pulled away, blushing in confusion. "Oh, sir, forgive me. I cannot think how I came to rattle on so."

He looked stern and said, "I expect I can find it in my heart to forgive you, on the condition that you tell me what you mean, for I shall surely die of suspense if you do not." When she only covered her face with her gloved hands, he persisted gently, "Come, I will not eat you. Now, why did you think me 'the evil Duke?'"

She glanced anxiously up at him. "You will think me the silliest pea goose alive, sir."

"That doesn't signify in the least, Miss Breckinridge, for I have always thought so," he said, assuming his gravest countenance.

"Oh, sir!" she gurgled, responding most satisfactorily to this sally. "Well, I suppose I may as well tell you, for you'll find it out soon enough, I daresay. The case is that my dear friend—Miss Chuddsley, you know—subscribes to the circulating library, and she and I have read all of Mrs. Radcliffe's novels—"

"Ah! The case becomes clearer already—but I interrupt. Please, go on."

"And we resolved, only in fun, of course, that we should find ourselves in the midst of a romantic tale when we came to London, for there is so much variety here, among people, you know, and we thought it would be so thrilling if it did happen!" She leaned toward him again, wound up in her story. "And it did, sir! For, of course, Elvira or I would be the heroine, and we had not been out a fortnight when we met the perfect hero—Mr. Barnabus, you know, who has the most tragic life—"

"My heart is quite broken, Miss Breckinridge!" interjected Sir Joshua. "Am I not tragic enough to be your hero?"

She took his arm again. "But you are a hero of a different kind, sir! Still quite as important!"

"Oh, then I am redeemed," he said, accepting this explanation with perfect equanimity. "Pray continue."

She giggled. "We have many supporting characters," she squeezed his arm, "like you, and the disappointed suitor—"

"I see now I have escaped a terrible fate! I would much rather be 'a hero of a different kind' than the 'disappointed suitor.'"

"You shall not play that role, sir, not if I have anything to say!" she declared.

He looked ironically down at her. "But you did think that I might play the evil Duke?"

"I can honestly say that I never thought you to be such a man," she disclaimed. "Well, not very seriously at any rate."

"But you interest me excessively, Miss Breckinridge! What kind of man is the evil Duke?"

She gripped his arm with both hands. "He is capable of the most heinous villainy, sir! He seduces the unsuspecting heroine, cultivating her trust through the most insidious deceit, then abducts her and holds her in his crumbling castle, in the highest tower, until she is compromised and must sink to marrying him!"

"Goodness, you alarm me! And you thought me such a man, even for a moment?"

"Oh, sir!" She stared wide-eyed at him as the injustice of such a thoughtless fancy came home to her. "It was unpardonable of me! Please say you forgive me?"

"With all my heart, my dear girl," he said, his handsome smile lighting his face.

She sighed in gratitude. "Indeed, I would never consider you the evil Duke now, and have not a long time since!"

"My relief knows no bounds, Miss Breckinridge."

Chapter 22

HAD SHE BEEN privy to one of these conversations, Genevieve may have experienced the relief at least of facing the demon which seemed to have taken possession of the recesses of her mind. When Tom had apprised her of Sir Joshua's intention to take his place as guard over them, the feeling in the pit of her stomach she had put down to embarrassment at the need of placing such a responsibility on his shoulders. That her chest prickled hotly whenever Sir Joshua bestowed his wonderful smile upon Lenora, or chatted in low tones to her, she easily dismissed as the effects of too much indulgence at tea time, and would never give the least heed to that sly voice in her head that suggested she had more concern than a mother ought in Sir Joshua's friendliness to her daughter.

Sir Joshua might have relieved her mind one way or the other, but his intentions remained maddeningly elusive to her, even more so after she had determined to put herself in command of them. He treated Lenora with the same gentlemanlike manner as he did herself, and gave them almost equal parts of his time, with no distinctions that she could discover. If he preferred to take Lenora on drives in his curricle, and so be seen publicly in her company, he never missed a morning walk with Genevieve, which could be perceived as more intimate.

He most often took her on long, rambling walks through the Green Park, where they never neglected a sober inspection of the tree whose treacherous branch had precipitated her third debt to his chivalry, or to pause beside the sparkling water of the reservoir. Here, with the fresh air and quiet to clear her mind, she could forget how the man beside her had upset her peace.

"I think you must miss the country, ma'am," Sir Joshua noted one day. "Your spirits seem to animate whenever we walk here."

She squinted up at him, the sun glinting off the water into her eyes. "You must tell me how to take that remark, sir. Either you wish me away, or you think me blue-deviled."

"Or I find a kindred spirit in one who responds so palpably to nature."

"Pardon me, sir, for misreading you," she said, the dimple appearing in her cheek. "My nerves have been so over-stimulated by the bustle and noise of the Metropolis that when confronted by peace and tranquility, they are so dumbfounded that I become a trifle stupid."

"That must be why you are blue-deviled."

"That was no admission!" she cried, glaring askance at him. "Why should I be blue-deviled? I am perhaps a little tired, from all this gaiety and action."

"Then why do you stay?"

More than a little annoyed at his shrewdness, she masked it by pressing a hand to her heart, and saying in an injured tone, "You do wish me away!"

"Not in the least, ma'am. I merely wish to get to the bottom of your malady." He turned to face her, regarding her intently. "Since the Wraglain's ball you have been in the grip of a most persistent melancholia. I would I knew what I could do to cheer you."

She could not speak for several moments as her thoughts tottered from gratitude at his concern, to distress at the mere possibility of her true feelings bursting to the surface.

Reading her silence only slightly awry, he said, "Perhaps I am impertinent. I had hoped to have shown myself enough your friend to merit your confidence, but I have no wish to obligate you."

"Yes—I mean, no," she disclaimed, turning from him in confusion. "You have been all that is kind, sir, but I could not presume upon—" She stopped, the very thought of owning her struggles to him overpowering her.

He said quietly, "I will not press you, but will crave your indulgence on one matter." She glanced up, startled and rather fearful, as he went on. "I must beg your forgiveness."

"My forgiveness?" she echoed, completely at a loss.

"Yes. My behavior toward you at the ball, when I found you with Lord Montrose—"

"Oh," she murmured, coloring and looking away again.

He removed his hat and passed it from hand to hand, rather in the manner of a shy schoolboy. "Friend or no, it was none of my business. I have no opinion of Lord Montrose, or if I do, it is not what I ought to speak aloud. Suffice it to say that I shouldn't wish any female of my acquaintance to be in his company, and feeling as I do in some way responsible for—well, for your family, while you are guests in my sister's house, you understand—I lost my head."

It took some minutes for Genevieve to compose herself after this handsome and unexpected admission. "Well, sir," she said, a little hesitantly, "if you must beg my forgiveness, then I must beg yours for giving you any anxiety. I have never had the intention of obligating you in any way, though circumstances may have conspired to make you believe otherwise, and I can only say that your concern is felt with gratitude, and will be rewarded as conscientiously as may be."

Opening his eyes at this speech, he said, "I am put in my place again, I see."

"No, sir!" she cried. "It is only that I have no other choice in the matter." He gazed dubiously at her and, flustered, she cast about in her mind for adequate words to explain. "Though I dislike Lord Montrose excessively, he is an acquaintance of long standing, and our relationship is such that—I simply cannot cut him."

"You will pardon me, ma'am, but to keep the acquaintance of a man so low as Montrose simply because he was your husband's friend seems to me the height of folly."

"It does, sir, I know it does, but you cannot appreciate my situation. For a man, it would be simple enough to sever ties, but for a woman, it is not so easy. I must do what I can to keep relations civil between us, for fear of what revenge he may decide to take."

He seemed to digest this. "Very well, ma'am. I bow to your superior knowledge of him, and will engage to stay clear of your dealings with him."

She thanked him, though with some misgiving, and they walked on in silence until he said abruptly, "Now here is a sight I expressly wish you to see." Stepping off the path, Sir Joshua led her amongst the trees, then stopped, pointing with his malacca cane to a branch high above them. "There is a dove's nest there. If we are fortunate— yes! You see the female's head? She is at home."

Genevieve, quite ready to leave their former subject behind, craned her neck to see into the shadows of the leafy tree top. "Sir Joshua, how delightful! I suppose it is too much to hope for babies in the nest?"

"It must be too late in the year for that."

"Of course." She gazed a few minutes longer, then glanced up at him, and caught him regarding her intently. She blushed faintly and said, "However did you discover the nest?"

"Lenora told me of it, and two days ago I came to see it for myself," he said, with obvious satisfaction. "I thought it would be a sight to cheer you."

She quickly stifled the ruffling of her feelings and achieved a smile. "Well, you have gauged me rightly, sir, to fancy such a sight would cheer me. I declare I never felt better."

"If only all your worries could be gotten rid of so easily."

She dropped her gaze as they moved out of the shelter of the trees. "You must think me a poor-spirited creature, indeed, sir, if you believe I desire deliverance from all my cares. I am no fair maiden in distress."

That brought a tiny smile to his lips. "Woe betide me to think such a thing, ma'am!"

She was forced to chuckle. "What sort of woman would I be without my trials, I ask you?"

"A very uninteresting one, to be sure, ma'am."

After a few paces in companionable quiet, she said, gazing out over the lovely verdure of the park, "You were right that I respond to nature. I should be very sorry were these parks unavailable."

"So, you do prefer the country to town?"

"For the most part, yes. The country is more forgiving, with fewer pressures and more simple pleasures. But town presents challenges to one's intellect and habits that country life can never approximate.

It is good to put oneself to the test once in a while, but there are limits to all good things."

"Not all good things, Mrs. Breckinridge."

She glanced up to see a ghost of a smile on his lips, and she longed to know if his thoughts were here, with her, or with another, younger lady not far away. Shaking her head, as if to clear away such nonsensical thinking, she unconsciously quickened her pace. "And do you prefer the country, sir?"

"I do, when I have company. Being a widower, with no children, my country seat seems rather bleak when I am there for very long. Consequently, I find myself in town whenever I can be sure of good society." He turned to look down at her. "But I hope I foresee much satisfaction in coming home in future."

She forced herself to smile again. "I should like to see Wrenthorpe Grange, sir."

He seemed gratified. "I should like to see you there, ma'am. I have already mentioned a visit to Lenora, and she was not indisposed to the idea."

She thought her face would crack with the strain of her smile. "I am sure not. What a lovely prospect!"

His handsome smile brightened his face, and he offered his arm. "You are a wonderful woman, Mrs. Breckinridge. Lenora is a lucky girl to have you as a mother."

No longer able to maintain her mask of delight, she turned her face away and murmured many proper things about "so kind," and "much obliged," all the while cursing the sly voice in her head for being right.

Chapter 23

W^{ITH SUCH FEELINGS} jumbled in her breast did Genevieve
receive Sir Joshua's invitation to an intimate little supper
party at Vauxhall Gardens, to which renowned retreat he knew Miss
Breckinridge had yet to go, and to whose many delights he was persuaded Mrs. Breckinridge would not be loath to return. Her mood
half determined her to decline the invitation, to spare herself the
pain of an entire evening wondering and wishing, but after sober
reflection, she accepted it, and swiftly, delivering the note with the
sand hardly swept off, to teach herself not to deny her daughter any
opportunity for pleasure through selfishness on her own part. Then
she steeled herself not only to enjoy the evening, but to watch with
complaisance her daughter's enjoyment.

At first, her resolve seemed to no purpose, for Sir Joshua was all
amiability, greeting each lady with equal gallantry, and smilingly
making the introductions of his two friends, Sir David Granton and
Colonel Bunding, who had graciously agreed to enlarge the party,

and to whom Lady Cammerby was already well known. Genevieve rather despondently perceived that the gentlemen were much closer to her age than to Lenora's, and so were more likely to be meant as companions to her, leaving Lenora to Sir Joshua, but nothing in their behavior vindicated this notion. All three gentlemen attended the ladies down the steps to where Sir Joshua handed them into the carriage, then they all three rode behind the carriage to Vauxhall.

Arriving at the Gardens from Kennington Street, they were set down some way from the coach gate and, once all the ladies had alighted, were drawn eagerly on by Sir Joshua, who navigated through the crowded carriageway toward the entrance. Light spilled from the gateway as they approached, and once through, their eyes were dazzled by the myriad oil lights in colored glass lanterns, appended, it seemed, to every surface imaginable. Both Genevieve and Lenora sighed in wonder as they were led down the principle walks, barely able to speak, much less withdraw their gazes from the glittering lights to greet acquaintances on the way.

Genevieve glanced up at Sir Joshua to say, "They've cut down all the beautiful trees in the Grove, and replaced them with lights!"

"Do you disapprove?" he asked her.

"I hardly know," she said, gazing around her once more. "I suppose at this time of night I must not, for I have seen nothing to rival the sight of all these lights, but in the day I should be scandalized for the loss of such natural beauty. They were lovely old trees."

In answer, he drew her arm through his, further dispelling her fears of a painful evening, and led the party back into the Grove, where animated groups of people from all walks of society congregated here and there, mostly under a stately iron colonnade on their way into the Rotunda, or near the Orchestra in the center of the clearing.

They drew nearer this amazing edifice, whose tiered front was so bedecked with colored lights as to mesmerize the unwary onlooker, and as lively couples danced before them, the band worked away on the first tier, the music floating out to fill the Grove. Their party stood and listened a while, not a little bemused by such a bright display, until the gentlemen, inured to the sight from more frequent experience, urged the ladies to come along to the Rotunda, where the formal concert was to be played. Sir Joshua left them in the colonnade to bespeak a box for supper, then rejoined them in good time to see them to their seats.

After the bustle of settling had done, Genevieve found herself beside Sir Joshua, who showed no consternation at being separated from Lenora by Colonel Bunding, who was engaged with that damsel in eager conversation over the delights of the evening having taken place so far. Observing the general satisfaction of the party, Genevieve felt compelled to relax, and quickly succumbed completely to the enjoyment of good company and novel surroundings. For though she had been to Vauxhall Gardens as a young girl, it had changed so materially in the succeeding years that she felt almost as if she were in a strange place. She gazed with appreciation at the artfully embellished canopy above her, and the intricately carved scrollwork along the walls, which was much the same as she remembered, but the paintings around the room had been updated to rural scenes, which she thought infinitely suited to such a place.

The performance of the orchestra being exquisite, Genevieve, a true lover of music, sat throughout with her eyes closed, drinking in the sounds which reverberated pleasingly around her, and quite losing herself. When the last strains subsided, and the audience erupted in applause, she awoke from her blissful reverie feeling renewed, and, turning to her host to expostulate on her enjoyment—and to express her profound thanks for his kind invitation—she was disconcerted to find him regarding her with a secret smile on his lips.

Understandably, her former consternation returned, with questions as to his intentions flitting through her mind, but she was given little opportunity to ruminate upon them, as the group rose to leave the box to partake of supper during the interval, and the discussion that ensued, regarding the talent of Mrs. Bland in the sonata, engaged her interest. They ate finely sliced ham and roasted chicken, and a salad they dressed themselves, all the while comfortably conversing about London and its virtues and vices, upon which topic all were versed. Thus, the supper hour flew delightfully by, and when they had finished, they re-entered the Rotunda for the second half of the concert, which was equally good as the first.

By the close of the concert, Genevieve had again forgotten her anxieties, and the circumstance of Colonel Bunding's offering her his arm while Lenora walked with Sir Joshua, Sir David and Lady Cammerby bringing up the rear, served to keep her at ease as the whole of the party set off to wander the many walks until the fireworks at midnight. They went first to the Dark Walk, and immediately Lenora demanded to know the history of its name.

"The Dark Walks were purposely unlit to provide romance for those who craved it," offered Sir David. "But, as you can imagine, they very often, especially in the deeper hours of the night, were misused."

"There was a time when these walks became so dangerous to virtue that they were blocked off," confided Sir Joshua.

Sir David laughed. "Much good it did them! There was such a hue and cry over it that the very next season the blockades were torn down again."

"But was nothing done to—to protect—virtue?" cried Lenora, shocked by this misuse of romance.

"Vauxhall enjoyed an unsavory reputation for several years, my dear," said Lady Cammerby, "but by the time your mama and I were your age, the proprietors had managed to subdue most of the rumors through better management."

"They could hardly manage the whole place, though, Miss Breckinridge," added Colonel Bunding, "so do not you let just any man lead you down the Dark Walks, even today." He accented his speech with a squint-eyed look at Sir Joshua, who merely smiled, while the other gentleman laughed.

Genevieve, noting Lenora's blushes and confusion with her own share of discomfort, was relieved to hear the bell announcing the unveiling of the Grand Cascade, and she suggested they all go to see it.

"The Cascade has seen better days, I'm afraid," said Colonel Bunding. "It has lost nearly all its charm, with the spouts of tin so dented and dull, and the figures continually being handled by every curious urchin—they resemble mud men more than sylvan characters! It is a shame, but it is rumored they plan to tear it down and build a theater of some sort on the site."

With expressions of outraged dismay, Genevieve still insisted upon seeing it, and they joined the crowd already gathered just as the curtains were drawn away. The sight was not as dismal as the colonel had painted it, which went some way toward mollifying Genevieve's disappointment, but still melancholy enough that the elder members of the group joined in remembrances and lamentations over the spectacle that was lost, and in attempting to describe its past glories to Miss Breckinridge, until the curtains were once more drawn closed.

In an attempt to distract their depressed spirits, Sir Joshua led them to the Hermitage, which was still in good repair, and they were able to put aside their sorrow to admire the skill which had crafted it. The cutaway scene of the Hermit studying his tomes by candlelight in the close little room could not excite their attention long, however, and they were soon on their way again toward the firework tower at the south end of the walk.

Here a large crowd had gathered in expectation of the Ascent of Madame Saqui, and Genevieve gazed with wonder at the height of the tower, some seventy feet above, to which was attached a sturdy rope that inclined toward the ground for upwards of three hundred feet.

Lenora's feelings exactly matched her mother's, as she exclaimed, "She will never walk up that rope! She could not!"

"Ah, but she will, Miss Breckinridge," replied Sir David sagely. "And she will walk back down again, and as quick and as sure as a monkey!"

"But it seems we are far too early to be waiting about here to see her," said Colonel Bunding, consulting his watch. "It lacks over an hour to midnight. What are we to do with ourselves?"

This produced a murmur of opinions, but Lenora's ardent wish to explore the smaller paths among the trees became the general resolution of the party, and they all turned down the walk to find an opening. This proved more difficult than they had anticipated, for the press of the crowd around the tower and rope, being composed of several ungenteel and even rowdy persons, pushed and swayed rather than part for the ladies and their escorts, and it was some trouble to work their way with any degree of comfort away from the crowd.

At this moment Genevieve distinctly heard her name called, not only once, but twice, and with her Christian name. She turned quickly to look in the direction that she had heard it, only to be met with the sight of heads and bodies of persons whom she had no acquaintance with. In some puzzlement, she turned forward again to follow her party, and was dismayed to find that she had become entirely separated from them in the crowd.

A woman of strong resolution, Genevieve pushed forward through the press, excusing herself politely but firmly to those who would not move and whom she was obliged to put out of her way with rude force. She fairly quickly came to the edge of the crowd, and the side of the walk, but still could not glimpse her companions ahead. Knowing their destination to be the wooded paths, she hastened to the first opening she saw and plunged down it, uncomfortably aware of a small feeling of panic that had begun to stir in her breast. The darkness of the wood after the dazzling brightness of the walk she had just left caused her to slow her pace as her eyes adjusted, and shapes seemed to shift just outside her vision. She knew these paths were undesirable for unaccompanied young females, and hoped only that her age and experience would give any young buck pause in the contemplation of trickery.

She remained unmolested as her eyes adjusted to the dimness, however, and hurried down the path, until she was very deep into the wood, looking anxiously down several side paths as she went, until at last she thought she descried her party at the end of one of them. With a rush of relief, she turned down this lane, but quickly discovered the group at the end were none of her own, and she fled down a branching path to avoid meeting them. Her heart was beating dreadfully, and she had just determined upon returning to the tower to await their return, when a man's voice uttered her name behind her. She whirled about with the hopeful expectation of being greeted by Sir Joshua, but the man who stepped from the shadows was the last one she wanted to meet, here or anywhere, without protection.

"What luck to find you here, and quite alone, Mrs. B."

Her fingers clutched at her skirts as she backed away a few steps. "I am not alone, my lord." His eyes mocked her and she stood still, cursing herself for betraying fear to him. Straightening, she assumed a look of unconcern that she hoped would be matched by her voice. "Such a lovely evening for a stroll, is it not? My party is just ahead, so you must excuse me if I am uncivil. I do not wish to be separated from them. Good night."

She turned and had taken a step, but he grasped her arm, halting her where she stood. "Alas, you are already separated from them, I perceive. What a pity." He tutted, his eyes roving over her face as his grip stayed firm. "Allow me to bear you company awhile. I would not have you wander this place without protection. One never knows what kind of scoundrel one may meet in the dark."

"No, one does not, my lord," she said, with a pointed look at his hand on her arm. When he did not remove it, she added, endeavoring to keep her voice steady, "Your kind offer of protection is entirely unnecessary. My friends are just beyond that shrubbery—"

"No, my dear Genevieve, the truth is that they passed by here several minutes ago, and seemed distressingly unconcerned for your whereabouts. Are you certain they miss you?" She pulled against his hold, but he drew her closer to him. "They did not appear anxious for a third, as cozy as they were."

"A third, my lord?" She stopped struggling. "Were there only two?"

"Only two, and such a pretty couple they were."

She pulled against him again, to no avail. "Then they were not my party. I most sincerely wish to rejoin my friends, and desire you to allow me to go in search of them."

"Not your party, Genevieve?" He clucked his tongue and shook his head indulgently. "If that was not your daughter with old Sir

Joshua Stiles, then I am the Duke of Wellington."

She stiffened, staring wide-eyed at him. "What do you know of my daughter?"

She could smell the sour of wine on his breath as he chuckled unpleasantly. "What need I know of her, but that she is quite alone in a dark wood with a very experienced man?" Genevieve's face paled, and he narrowed his eyes contemplatively. "The more I consider it, the more I feel it would be a shame to interrupt their tete-a-tete, don't you agree?"

"I do not, sir, and trust that your understanding of the situation is imperfect," she said, putting up her hand to pry at the fingers on her arm. "I beg you will release me so that I may rejoin them."

His grip did not loosen. "But you protest too much, ma'am. What mother leaves her daughter unsupervised in such a place, unless she means to snare a fortune for her? Come, your purposes will be better served by your leaving them to themselves."

His insinuations both unnerved and infuriated her. Through clenched teeth, she said, "I am no more after Sir Joshua's fortune than you are after mine! Let me go."

"I will restore you to the care of your friends all in good time," he said, his eyes glittering, "but this night, this place should not be wasted."

Renewing her efforts to disengage herself, she cried, "It is already wasted, my lord, as is your time and mine. You will do me the honor of believing me when I say that I do not wish your company, now or ever."

She wrenched free of him at last and took to her heels down the path, but he too quickly caught her, grasping her by the waist and pulling her against his chest. "But you must satisfy me, Genevieve," he whispered in her ear, his sour breath hot on her neck. "Why pursue Sir Joshua's fortune when mine is yours for the taking? I lay it at your feet, along with my heart."

"If you are in earnest, my lord, then you surely intend to offer me your name as well, or is that assuming too much?" she spat.

"What good would my name do to a woman of your resource? I offer you all my worldly goods, my body and soul. What more could you want?"

"Dignity, my lord!" She pried at his arms around her waist, but they were like bands of iron. "And freedom!"

With a quick movement, he twisted her in his arms until they were chest to chest. "But you are too wild to be let free, Genevieve."

"Unhand me this moment," she hissed, pushing with her forearms against his chest.

"It is not to be thought of. So long have I wished for this, with you here in my arms, and no one to come between us. No, I do not think I will let you go."

She raised a hand, striking it hard against his cheek, but he only smiled, a gleam in his eyes that sickened her with fear. "My, how your eyes burn when you are angry."

Then his lips were on hers, trapping the scream that rose to her mouth, and a shudder of revulsion took the strength from her body. He held her tighter as she shivered in shock, pressing hot kisses down her neck, but when his mouth wandered toward her décolletage, her senses reasserted themselves, and she screamed.

Instantly, he pressed a hand against her mouth, his eyes sparking. "None of that, my love. You ruin the mood."

Beating at his head with her freed hand, she scratched and clawed to no avail, for he merely chuckled and resumed his exploration of her neckline, and she had begun to give herself up for lost when a sudden rush of footsteps sounded very near at hand, followed by a violent exclamation. Lord Montrose's hold on her loosened as he turned to confront the intruder, and the next thing she knew, he had been yanked away from her and felled by a thundering blow to his jaw. Blinking, she stared at his inanimate form on the ground for some seconds before her eyes traveled up the form of her rescuer, who stood over him, the most terrible expression of hatred on his countenance she had ever seen.

"Sir Joshua!"

He turned to her, his expression melting into something so like possessive concern that she thought her heart would burst. In two steps he was by her side, his arms reaching for her. "Genevieve! Are you hurt?"

"Oh!" was all she managed to say before she was enveloped in his embrace, and she found herself, for the first time in nearly twenty years, with a manly chest upon which to cast her troubles. Clutching at the lapels of his coat, she burst into tears.

After some time, she became aware that Sir Joshua was stroking her hair and murmuring soothing words, and that she would like to stay in his arms forever. He must love her, his look had said it all, and here she was, secure in his embrace, even in this—oh, this was a public place, and no matter how he felt about her, they ought not to be standing so long in such an attitude.

Reluctantly, but firmly, she pushed away from him, fumbling in her reticule for her handkerchief. He produced his first, and she took it with a trembling hand. "Oh, I am much obliged to you, sir! You must believe that it was my furthest intention to become a watering pot!"

"I am fully prepared to believe everything you say, ma'am, but I should be a brute indeed to fault you for giving way to emotion after such an affront."

She involuntarily shuddered, wiping at her eyes with the handkerchief. "You are too kind. And—and so timely!" She wrung the handkerchief. "I had been searching for you—all of you—and had nearly given you up, but you—you have a habit of appearing when you are needed!"

He bowed, but his look had become grave, and she felt as if the night had grown suddenly chilly. Putting her arms around herself, she looked at the ground, the hope that had bloomed at his first look wilting beneath such solemnity. That look! Had she imagined it? His manner now could never have produced such a look, and how could he have altered so quickly from tenderness to this?

She had misconstrued his actions, she must have. Rather than acting out of care for her, he had come to her aid out of concern for Lenora, properly unwilling to allow the mother of his love to come to harm. Any gentleman would have comforted her, even taken her into his arms as he had done, from sheer embarrassment at her explosion of emotion. No, he had not been tender, as she had at first believed, but merely kind to her in an impossible situation.

A moan from the ground caused her to start from her reflections. "Oh, he seems to be coming to."

Sir Joshua cast a disdainful look behind at the body on the ground, then guided her away, down the path. "We need no longer be concerned with him, ma'am." They walked to a wider path, turning out of sight of the recumbent Lord Montrose. "You ought not to have left our party."

As sensitive as her feelings were at that moment, this unjust remonstrance stung. "I did not leave of my own volition, sir. I was detained by the crowd, and by the time I had reached the path, you were all gone from sight." She put up her chin. "If you had not gone on ahead into the wood, I may have caught you up."

"We did not go on ahead into the wood, ma'am. How could you think we should go on without you, and you nowhere in sight?"

"But you were ahead of me, he told me—" She stopped, comprehending too late the extent of Lord Montrose's deception.

Sir Joshua's mouth was set in a grim line. "Your naivete regarding Lord Montrose is a constant source of wonder to me."

"I have mentioned many times that I know full well what that man is capable of, sir!"

He rounded on her. "Then when will you understand that by furthering your acquaintance you deepen your danger—Tom's danger—Lenora's danger?"

"I have never sought his company!"

"But when he forces it upon you, you welcome it!"

"On the contrary, sir, I am no more than civil to him, and most often less!" she cried.

He stepped closer to her, bending to look directly into her face. "I know that I engaged to stay out of your way, but I repent it. Someone must convince you that a man such as Montrose must not be encouraged, in any way."

She pushed her face closer to his. "A man such as Montrose needs no encouragement, sir! Here I prove my superior knowledge of him! I tell you he would seek me out the more if I fled from him, and that is the only reason I have not."

"With the outcome that he accosted you at the first opportunity," he returned, "and in the worst place. How was this more desirable than the alternative?"

"There was no alternative!" she cried, turning from him in frustration. She closed her eyes, breathing heavily to compose herself. "Perhaps I was foolish to proceed as I have done. I see now that I grossly misjudged his intentions toward me, in my anxiety for Tom and Lenora. I flattered myself that I knew how to handle him, hoping only to keep him distracted until we were gone from London, and could be forgotten, little suspecting that he would seriously propose—that he could have the effrontery to—" She could not bring herself to finish the statement.

She heard him move behind her, and then he had taken her hand. "Your intentions, as always, were for the best," he said with unwonted gentleness, "and this time you have nothing to regret. I am only glad I found you when I did." He brought her hand to his lips, then placed it within his arm, leading her onto the walk and toward the lights surrounding the fireworks tower ahead. "I believe Lord Montrose will not dare to further distress you, at least for an appreciable time. But Lenora will be wondering where we have got to, and must not be made to worry."

With that, he quickened his pace, and she could only keep step with him as they made their way to the base of the pole to which was secured the bottom end of Madame Saqui's rope. There, they met the remainder of their party, and scarcely had they heard Lenora's exclamations of relief at her mother's safe return, and given hurried explanations of what had happened to separate them—neglecting to make mention of Lord Montrose—than a cacophony of popping and whizzing was heard from the fireworks tower, and a glory of sparks burst upon their vision.

The night sky blazed with the fireworks, but Genevieve hardly saw them for the confusion in her own mind. Lord Montrose's attack upon her person had been a horrid shock, to be sure, but Sir Joshua's attack of words had cut her to the heart, and given her to understand that his disapproval of her was so deep-seated as to make their acquaintance only tenable for the sake of his attachment to Lenora, and his esteem for Tom, as his future brother. She could only be amazed that he tolerated her company as well as he so often did.

That her actions had endangered her children she knew, and she regretted it with all her heart, but she could never have discovered any way to keep them safe from Lord Montrose—of this she was convinced. But Sir Joshua would never see it that way. He was right that her plan had turned out faulty, but once she had started, there was no other way to proceed. Retreat after their initial encounter would have spurred Montrose the harder, and greater encouragement would merely have proven to him that she was an easy, if not a willing, victim. She was caught as soon as he had discovered her.

But her children had not been. They had been in some danger while Lord Montrose made her his object, but she had stood firm against him tonight, and prevailed. And because, as Sir Joshua had opined, Lord Montrose was not likely to bother them for some time after the humiliation and injury of this night, she must feel that her plan had been in some measure a success. If it had not been for the pain of Sir Joshua's judgment on her, and the mortification of her own feelings toward him, she should feel much of the joy of celebration that the fireworks seemed to invite.

Her thoughts were distracted by a figure that was climbing the ladder next to the pole. It must be Madame Saqui, who, as she had heard, was a wiry, mannish female, with little grace or beauty. Her costume, made up of garish spangles, fringe, and plumes, seemed designed to make up for her personal deficiencies, and indeed, the eyes of the spectators never left her small figure from the moment it was perceived.

So quickly as Madame Saqui had ascended the pole, did she ascend the rope, walking dexterously and without hesitation, upward toward the platform of the fireworks tower, with the rockets exploding all around her. The necks of all persons in the crowd below the rope were craned upward, all eyes watching aghast, as the slight form darted through smoke and fire, up the slender rope to the platform, and without even a pause, turned to descend again with equal rapidity. Even Genevieve's troubles were suspended for the few minutes Madame Saqui flitted through the air above her, and until the small acrobat reached the base pole and scampered down the ladder, disappearing into the crowd, Genevieve was merely a lady on the arm of a gentleman, watching an amazing sight, ostensibly without a care in the world.

Chapter 24

LENORA, KEPT IN ignorance of the danger her mother had escaped, retained only happy memories of their outing to Vauxhall, with its beautiful music and wondrous fireworks display. Sadly, however, she had no one with whom to share her joy, for her estrangement from Elvira continued. No notes had passed from one to the other since their argument, no visits had occurred between them, and if both had happened to attend the same party, Lenora, receiving only punctilious civility from her erstwhile bosom friend, was compelled to repay her in kind.

But Lenora was speedily tiring of this display of officiousness, for she missed Elvira, and after a fortnight without Mr. Barnabus—the object of their envy and thus their discord—she had come to the shocking conclusion that she did not care for that gentleman any more than she did any other young gentleman, and in many cases, far less. That she had made him, who had no claims upon her but those she had imposed upon him, into the hero of her fancy was a fact that caused her all the more mortification, because of the breach it had introduced between herself and Elvira.

Uncertain as she was that any olive branch of her own would be received by Elvira, she took what comfort she could find and, nearly a week after Vauxhall, made her way to Hookham's library with a footman in tow, where she lost herself among the shelves, in search of the perfect escape for a girl who had no bosom friend with whom to share her own adventures, and so sought relief through another's. Spying a likely volume, she took it down from the shelf, opening its cover to peruse the opening pages and, turning as she did so, took an unconscious step forward, to collide with a person she had not before perceived.

"Oh, pardon me! I did not see you—" she cried, stopping mid-sentence to gaze in shocked embarrassment at none other than Miss Chuddsley, who stood with amazement mirrored on her face.

Lenora recovered first. "Elvira! Oh—I did not think to see you here!"

Elvira, who had flushed pink upon these words, clutched her hands to her chest, her gaze fluttering abstractedly all around. "Yes. I came—I found I needed—how does your family, Lenora?"

"Very well, I thank you," Lenora mechanically replied, equally disquieted. "And—and your Aunt?"

"She is well, I thank you." Elvira shifted uneasily on her feet, until her eyes fell upon the title of the book in Lenora's hands. "Oh, *The Chronicles of an Illustrious House!* It is what I came to find!"

Lenora instantly held the book out to her. "You may take it, by all means!"

"Oh, no! You found it first—"

"But I had only taken it from the shelf by the merest chance. I had not determined upon taking it."

Elvira accepted the proffered book with a hesitant smile. "I have not yet read it. I hear it is most exciting." Her eyes flicked up to her friends' and back down again. "But this is only the first volume. It is one of five."

"I know nothing of the story," said Lenora, turning to the shelf to take down the other volumes. "Perhaps—" She peeked at her friend. "Perhaps we could read it together?"

The smile on Elvira's lips faded. "I do not know—I cannot say—" She averted her eyes, disquiet upon her face, and silence settled between them.

"Elvira?" Lenora said, almost in a whisper. "Please, let us be friends again. I am most desperately sorry that I offended you—"

"But it was not only me whom you offended, Lenora," Elvira returned in a hushed but bitter tone. "You spoke slightingly of Mr. Barnabus, and behind his back, too!"

"Did I?" Lenora asked, blinking and trying to remember her last words to her friend, which had long become garbled in the angry haze of her memory.

"Yes! You called him a 'stammering, stoop-shouldered, poverty-stricken young man!'"

"Oh. Yes, I recollect—" Lenora bent her head and went on bravely, "And it was very unfeeling of me, and shameful, and I would I had not said it, but it was only because I was angry, and I never meant a word of it, for he is an excellent young man, and a good friend."

Elvira, who had been regarding her narrowly throughout this speech, was visibly affected by it, and dropped her eyes to say quietly, "Perhaps we both were too hasty that day."

There was silence between them again, and at last Lenora offered, "Shall we borrow *The Chronicles of an Illustrious House* together, then, my dear friend?"

"Would it please you?" Elvira said, with a tremulous smile. "I—I would dearly love to read it with you, Lenora."

Lenora matched her smile and, with the sudden unreserve that accompanies the reconciliation of good friends, the two girls embraced, and then, with delighted giggles, proceeded to discuss the presumed merits of the new book, giving free reign to conjecture of how the story would align with their notions of romance. They were fast reaching the heights of exhilaration, their discussion accompanied by much gesticulation and generously interpolated with heartfelt sighs, when someone bumped into Lenora. She turned to see the older gentleman who had admired her—or so he had said—upon her first coming into town. He was looking aggrieved, his hand arrested in the act of reaching toward a book on the shelf.

"Pardon me, ma'am. I seem to be most clumsy! There really is no excuse—Oh!" he cried, his eyes opening wide with recognition. "Have we met? Yes, I am persuaded we have met—"

"We have not, sir, but briefly in the street," said Lenora, coloring prettily.

"Ah," he said, dropping his eyes. "Forgive the pretension." He perceived the books in her hands and smiled ruefully. "I see that I have been looking in vain, for you have my copy of *The Chronicles of an Illustrious House*."

Lenora blushed, looking in confusion from the books in her hands to the gentleman. "Oh, no, sir! There must be some mistake! I do not see how it could be—I took it from the shelf!"

"You mistake me, ma'am, and must pardon me once more. I should have said, you have the copy I had hoped to borrow for myself. But, no matter," here he sighed melodramatically, "I shall wait patiently until you are finished and I can at last satisfy my yearning curiosity."

As the fine tailoring of the gentleman's coat, his rather exquisite waistcoat and pantaloons, and his glossy Hessians had not escaped Lenora's notice, either at this time or the first time they had met, she could not but wonder what prevented him from purchasing his own copy of the book.

But Elvira put herself forward, her expression demure. "You are funning, sir, and with persons unknown to you. For shame!"

"You think me a coxcomb," said the gentleman, assuming a tenor of gravity. "Please accept my humble apologies." He swept off his hat and bowed low. "I will prove my gentility, and absent myself to live upon the hope that you will return those most interesting volumes in good time." He bestowed a winning smile upon both of them. "Good day to you."

The girls watched him go, then exchanged speaking looks.

"I believe you must revise your earlier opinion of that gentleman, Elvira," observed Lenora. "He seems to be given to levity."

"But so charming, do not you think?"

"Decidedly," replied Lenora, looking after him with interest.

But youth is easily distracted, and only a few moments more passed before the young ladies had dismissed the intriguing gentleman from their minds and, taking each other's arm, hastened to the desk to borrow their books. Once on the street, with an abigail and the footman following behind, Elvira tugged Lenora closer.

"I've missed you, dearest! My feelings are all commotion, and I've had no one to tell about it!"

Lenora felt nothing but surprise at this announcement. "For heaven's sake, Elvira, tell me at once! Has your Aunt been treating you ill, or—or have you received an offer?" She stopped abruptly in place. "Has Mr. Barnabus returned?"

Elvira colored, but shook her head. "No, none of that. My distress is all my own doing, and I feel so ashamed! Oh, Lenora, I have discovered how wrong I was to blame poor Ginsham for deceiving me about Mr. Barnabus's leaving town."

"But how came this about? Oh, dear, let us walk into the park."

Crossing Picadilly, they made their way into Green Park and came upon a bench where they could sit and chat comfortably.

"Now, Elvira," said Lenora, putting her arm round her friend, "tell me how Mr. Ginsham has been redeemed."

Elvira smiled self-consciously and began. "He came to see me the day after the ball, the very day you and I quarreled, and you know I was in such a black humor when I left you, and the ride home only made it worse. So, when I came into my aunt's parlor, and there he was, I nearly fell into hysterics! I thought him fully conscious of his deception, and could not believe his effrontery at coming so boldly to see me. In that instant I resolved to turn him away, and never allow him into my presence again, but then—oh, Lenora!—then I perceived that he was injured!"

"He was injured?" cried Lenora, baffled.

"Yes, his arm was in a sling. I was so taken aback that I hardly knew how to look, but presently, I wished him to tell me what had happened, and at first, he would say nothing about it, saying it was not to be regarded, or some such nonsense. When I pressed him, he said that it was a mere scratch, and that I shouldn't worry, and he said it so mildly, and humbly, that I was fairly chastened for even thinking the least ill of him before. So I sat him down, and offered him refreshment, and coaxed and pleaded, and practically begged him to tell me how he had come by his mere scratch, which cannot have been a mere anything if it left him without the use of his arm, and at last he admitted the truth!"

"Elvira! Well?" cried Lenora. "And what was the truth?"

Her friend turned to fully face her, eyes wide with the import of what she was to impart. "That he and your brother Tom were set upon by thieves, on their way home from the ball!"

"No!" was all Lenora could bring herself to say.

"Yes! They were attacked by two armed men, one with a cudgel who went at Ginsham, and the other who had a knife!"

Lenora gasped, but still could not interrupt, round-eyed and engrossed in the shocking tale.

Elvira needed no encouragement, however. "Mr. Ginsham had all he could do to ward off his attacker, but as soon as he had done so—by means which we have been wont to abhor, but for which I must tell you, Lenora, we ought now to feel gratitude—he rushed to Tom's aid, pulling the thief about and wrenching the knife away, but in the act was wounded himself!"

"But Tom never said a word!" Lenora cried. "I shall never forgive him for this! To be in mortal peril, and to be snatched from death! Oh, what an adventure!"

Primming up her mouth, Elvira said, "He is most likely too ashamed to tell you, Lenora, as well he should be, for Ginsham discovered after the fight that Tom had orchestrated it, for—well, for some trumpery reason I shall not stoop to recount."

This stopped Lenora's raptures abruptly; however, as the memory of a particular conversation with Tom, regarding Mr. Ginsham and Elvira, suddenly came to mind, she could only stare at Tom's cleverness. "The scamp! How brilliant!" she murmured, without thinking.

Elvira stared at Lenora, scandalized. "I had flattered myself that you should deprecate such thoughtlessness!"

"Oh! I do, most certainly," Lenora hastened to assure her, assuming a disapproving expression. "I spoke ironically, of course."

"I should hope so," said her friend haughtily, "and if I were you, I would have a word with my brother upon the propriety of such pranks, for poor Ginsham could have been killed, and very likely Tom as well!"

"But gentlemen are always discounting danger, Elvira," observed Lenora, "and are horridly backward in their notions of bravery."

Elvira, upon reflection, acknowledged this to be too true, then quickly revolved back to her admiration of Ginsham's heroics "Even had he known of the deception, I declare I should never have thought Mr. Ginsham capable of such a feat! In actuality wresting a knife from the hands of a ruffian! Just as if he were Antony grappling with the Black Monk! Oh, Lenora, never would I have imagined— but I am unjust, for I must own that he has never given me reason to believe him cowardly."

"No, he has not," agreed Lenora, "but I, too, have nevertheless misjudged him. How blind we have been! This event has entirely reformed my opinion of our Mr. Ginsham. I am now inclined to think him excessively romantic, for not only has he behaved with bravery, but he has done so with the utmost humility!"

"Indeed!" said Elvira, much struck. "From the start he wished not to flaunt his bravery to me. It was only after much coaxing that he even began to tell his story, and that reluctantly. And then, when he might have withheld Tom's perfidy from me, he willingly revealed the whole though, undoubtedly, he must have feared it would dim the gallantry of his actions!"

Lenora nodded approvingly. "It is just as it should be, and we must be moved by his heroism, and acknowledge his goodness. He has shown himself to be the perfect hero, and deserves our highest respect." She stood then and resumed walking, though slowly, Elvira chattering by her side.

"To be sure! I have entirely reformed my opinion, as you said.

According to Ginsham, the two thieves were so desperate that he was forced to fight with his bare hands for his very life—and although his life was never in any real danger, he could have no notion of that until after the fact." She shook her head ruefully. "And to think that I had deprecated his frequenting Jackson's Saloon, as he has more than once mentioned he has done, when now I see it was most necessary for his success, for though it was all a horrid joke of Tom's, the thieves were still desperate enough to wound him!"

"Oh, Elvira! Too true! What a mistake we have made in judging that pastime harshly. How little we must truly know of sport's necessity to a gentleman's well-being!"

Her friend blushed, looking at her feet as they walked along the flagway. "You may well imagine that after he had satisfied my curiosity regarding his injury, I remembered my argument against him, and mentioned Mr. Barnabus, only to prove that I had been just in suspecting him. And I hadn't, Lenora, for he said in all innocence that he had mistaken the day, and had a terrible fright when Mr. Barnabus came in to take his leave of him the afternoon of the ball. So." She sighed and Lenora squeezed her arm encouragingly. "I have forgiven Mr. Ginsham. But now I am at outs with Mr. Barnabus."

"Elvira! Whatever for?"

Elvira stopped her with a hand on her arm. "Lenora, you must speak honestly, and do not dissemble—did you indeed relay his exact message to me? Did you not, perhaps unwittingly, discourage him from coming to see me?"

Lenora, aghast at this suspicion, assured her friend that, quite the reverse, she had urged him to visit Elvira.

Elvira blinked, as if tears threatened, and lifted her chin in defiance. "Yet he left without saying goodbye to me, Lenora! As if—as if I were nothing to him at all! As if our relationship meant no more than—than the next person's!"

"But Elvira, he told you through me!" cried Lenora. "Do you not recollect, he sent his regrets—"

"Through you! Why did he not call upon me, Lenora?" cried her anguished friend. "Why could he not stop for ten minutes to tell me himself? It is not to be borne! If he could seek you out at a ball where he did not even intend to dance, why could he not delay for ten minutes more to seek me out, to take his leave properly?"

Lenora's conscientious defense of Mr. Barnabus died on her tongue, as she realized its probable repercussions against the only recently redeemed Mr. Ginsham. Perceiving that she must carefully choose her words, she said slowly, "Perhaps we have misread Barnabus, dearest. Perhaps his feelings are not so tender—"

"Lenora, you mistake me!" said Elvira, dashing the tears from her eyes. "Though I have fancied often that he has shown marked attentions to me, I do not believe him to be seriously attached, not yet, but such a man as he is ought not to leave such a civility undone, not for such a friend as I have been."

Feeling it would serve neither her suffering friend nor Mr. Ginsham to give a comforting answer, she answered, "Perhaps he is not the man we believed him to be."

Elvira turned to stare at her, astonishment written plainly on her face. "But we know him, Lenora! We know exactly the kind of man he is!"

"Are you quite certain of that?"

Elvira was quiet as they walked, taking the crossing and turning onto Berkeley Street. When they stopped at the corner where they were to part, she looked up with decision. "Though I respect your opinion, Lenora, I cannot abandon Barnabus to the ranks of the ordinary and heedless as easily as you have done. I do not fault you for your feelings—on the contrary, I honor you for them. But it is a strange business, fraught with complexity, and must be given due consideration before any judgement can be reached." She curtseyed rather formally, keeping her eyes down. "Goodbye, my dearest friend. I am indeed grateful for our reconciliation, and I shall hope to call upon you tomorrow, or at least very soon."

With that, she turned with her abigail toward her aunt's house, leaving Lenora to the dubious comfort of having regained her friend, only to distress her.

Chapter 25

I F GENEVIEVE HAD expected that Sir Joshua would shun her after
their heated discussion at Vauxhall, she was mistaken, for he not
only continued his frequent visits, but sought her private company
as often as before. She was understandably taken aback by this
behavior, especially considering the obvious disapproval of her he
had shown, and wished more than once, in light of her continued
attachment to him, that he felt less obligation. His constant attention gave her no opportunity to subdue her feelings, and her position
was made worse by the fact that he never appeared the least cold, as
he had at Vauxhall, but was so considerate and friendly that it was
increasingly difficult for her to remember that he had no opinion of
her. With every exposure to him, her heart was more susceptible to
fluttering at his compliments, and she found it impossible to stop
her tongue from responding to his wit—in short, she fell too easily,
even naturally, into flirting with her own daughter's suitor—and
was appalled at her own shamelessness.

She knew, oh, too well did she know, that she must keep him at a distance, but she simply could not deny herself entirely of the enjoyment of his company. If she refused one invitation, she could not refuse the next, her misguided heart convincing her that she only accepted so as not to offend him. And so, all willingly, she perpetually placed herself in a position that she must try, and always fail, to act the mother-in-law to a man she could not but see as her ideal.

For Sir Joshua was everything, and more, that Bertram had failed to become. Even at his best, Bertram had rather been sharp than witty, and persuasive than courteous. Sir Joshua was serious where Bertram had been charming, but so was he thoughtful where Bertram had been careless. And while Bertram had been lively and adventurous, Sir Joshua's gravity was the perfect foil to his clever humor, which had attracted Genevieve from the start, and caught her at last, because her own highly developed sense of the ridiculous had been nearly starved by a joyless marriage.

She sought in vain for a solution to her predicament. If she kept to her room, she only distressed Lady Cammerby and Lenora, who feared she was ill, and wearied her with their solicitude—and Sir Joshua invariably sent her flowers, which only heightened her awareness of his perfections. If she haunted the parks, alone or with Lenora, Sir Joshua was sure to find them somewhere or other. At last, encouraged by a rumor that Lord Montrose had quitted his lodgings, she approached Lady Cammerby with the suggestion that she return home and leave Lenora in her care.

Her friend looked appalled. "Are you unhappy here, Genevieve? Oh, I knew you were out of spirits, and yet I did nothing! I am ashamed! How can I make reparation? I've become remiss in your entertainment, I know. I ought to have held that card party last week, and invited Lady Wraglain and Emily Shepherd, which you would have enjoyed so much. But Cottam's mother was ill and I thought he was not equal to such an exertion. Was it a mistake? No?"

Genevieve denied any feeling of neglect in the area of her entertainment, but her hostess was not to be comforted. "What has happened to cast you down? You were so happy at first, but now you are forever in the dismals! I cannot imagine—leastways, I can, but I will not speak of it, for if I do, I vow I shall be cast down, and then what will become of the pair of us?" She looked up at Genevieve with tears sparkling in her eyes. "Oh, dearest, when I think of my hopes, dashed!" She pressed her lips tightly together and hastily wiped at her eyes with her handkerchief. "No! I shall not succumb to despondency! My nonsensical fantasies are my own folly, and will not add to your troubles. It is better for me to put my cares behind me and look to your comfort."

This speech, though enlightening, had rather the reverse of its intended effect on the hearer, but Genevieve could not fail to be moved by Lady Cammerby's concern, and with valiant effort, comprised of mendacious statements regarding her perfect contentment and solemn promises never again to suggest her early removal, she coaxed and cajoled her friend back into complacency. When they had both drunk their tea and talked of happy things, and Genevieve was convinced of her friend's complete revival, she retired from the apartment with the resolution to conquer her demons or die.

The weather becoming warmer by the day, Lenora's engagements seemed chiefly to consist of picnics and outdoor entertainments, and she was obliged to put away her pelisse and half-boots in favor of light shawls and slippers. So, it was with some disappointment that she awoke on the morning of a particularly exciting expedition to find it dismally raining, and a note at the breakfast table announcing the outing cancelled due to weather. After much bustling about, Lady Cammerby triumphantly announced that she had successfully obtained permissions for Lenora and a party to view the marbles newly on display at Montagu House, and that she would act as chaperone. Lenora, whose temperament was extremely elastic, hastened to compose the invitations, and not long after, found herself part of a lively group who were very happily squinting alike at guides and various bits of sculpture for the afternoon.

A good crowd had gathered in the museum that day, on account of the rain, and due to the nature of the activity, Lenora became separated a little from her group as they all wandered about the galleries in profound contemplation. She was reflecting on the rather gruesome sight of a carved horse's head, severed from its body and sitting on a pedestal, when a stranger's voice startled her.

"I see, ma'am, that your interests continue to run with mine."

She turned to behold the same mysterious gentleman who had twice before met her. "Good day, sir," she said, startled but not displeased. "I don't know what you mean by interest, however, for I cannot pretend to be attracted by this sight."

"Hmm, no," he said, tilting his head to regard the poor disembodied animal. "It is disturbing, indeed. But I find the friezes impressive."

"Yes, most impressive, I agree, sir. But the number of missing limbs displayed puts one in mind of a disaster, rather than of art, and quite harasses the contemplative mood. I cannot help but wonder in what state the rest was left behind."

He chuckled. "Indeed! Your honesty is refreshing! Most persons come here in the expectation of beholding wonders, and if they are disappointed, as you are, they are too mortified to make it known, lest they appear vulgar. I applaud your bravery, ma'am!"

She colored. "I do not pretend to any high understanding, sir, but I hope I am able to appreciate great works. I only question the wisdom in stripping them from their native setting."

"And you are not alone," he said warmly. "It is quite a controversy, and you are brave to state your feelings." She looked even more conscious, and he smiled, shaking his head. "Your position in no way detracts from your understanding, for appreciation must not always equal enjoyment or agreement. Indeed, I am of the opinion that your evincing a distaste for these particular great works, rather than betraying a lack of intellect, proves your discernment." He lowered his voice, glancing around the room. "Whereas the majority of these persons are so startled they have no thought whatever, and shall leave this place with only the vague notion that what they saw must have been magnificent, for so says the guidebook."

This surprised a giggle out of her, which echoed indelicately through the room, and though she moved quickly to stifle it, she was too late. Several sober onlookers cast glares her way, and the gentleman, smiling conspiratorially, bowed and walked away. Lenora watched him go, realizing too late that she still did not know who he was, and pleasantly intrigued that he should single her out thrice now, without offering an introduction. His manner, after their first meeting, had been almost fatherly, or more closely that of an uncle, so she did not suspect him of romantic motives, but he seemed very personable. Try as she might, she could not recall seeing him at any of the many functions she had attended during the season, which gave her to wonder if he was a Cit, or some other kind of social outcast—which merely intrigued her the more.

But here she was obliged to leave off her musings, for Elvira came round the corner on Mr. Ginsham's arm to exclaim in an excited whisper, "Lenora, they have no heads!" which brought on another fit of giggles, and more disapproving looks.

While the young people navigated the wonders of the Past, Sir

Joshua arrived in Hill Street, and was ushered into the drawing room where he found Genevieve mending a tear in one of Lenora's gowns, which this time was a ball dress of watered silk that had been trod upon by an energetic partner.

"I bid you good day on this dreary afternoon," he said, smiling.

She returned his greeting politely enough, while stridently stifling the fluttering of her heart at the sight of him, and determinedly continued her work.

"You must be an accomplished needlewoman, ma'am," he observed, "for I never see you at rest but you are sewing something or other."

Genevieve, having resolved that it was less painful to treat him as a brother, said in a very sisterly way, "It would be improper in me to own accomplishment, sir, but I will readily assent to being a needful needlewoman. I have discovered, or rather have recollected, since I had forgotten it from my own season so many years ago, that if Lenora attends one ball, I may depend upon finding as many rents in her gown next morning as there were hours in the evening."

He sat opposite her, saying, "But surely my sister employs a servant who could mend for you."

"Oh, she does, but it seems the older I am, the more I fidget if I am unemployed." She smiled pleasantly, adjusting the dress on her lap. "I find I am grateful to Bertram for giving me reason to exert myself in the needle arts, for, with all these servants to wait on me, I have not the least conjecture what I could otherwise find to do."

He seemed to hesitate for a moment before asking, "I collect that you employ only a few servants at this present."

"Yes, at present." She kept her eyes downcast, sewing nimbly as she spoke. "My maid and dear Matthew, the head groom, quite refuse to leave us, as does Sally, our cook. And our good butler outstayed himself, dear old fellow. But not every servant, loyal or otherwise, can afford to live on a pittance." She glanced up brightly. "But Tom assures me we shall have a new butler and another maid by the winter."

"Tom has borne his responsibilities admirably. He is a most impressive young man."

"He gets none of it from his parents, sir," she remarked candidly. "You know my flightiness, and you may count yourself fortunate not to have known his father's temperament."

"If it was such as would attract Lord Montrose, I do not need to imagine it." She darted a look at him, but his gaze was on her quick fingers as he continued. "I am happy to bear good tidings on that head, ma'am. His lordship does not appear to have plans to return to town for some time, at least. His house is shut up, the servants gone and the knocker down." He paused. "He seems to have fled, and I feel it safe to say we need not fear interference from that quarter again."

Genevieve raised her eyes to his face, waiting for the rush of relief his news would surely bring, but it did not come. Something teased her, and she recalled Caroline Wraglain's words: "He is more likely to move heaven and earth to break you, than to accept defeat." Her gaze dropped to the work in her lap and she said, "It may be premature to assume so, Sir Joshua. Somehow, I cannot think him—"

She broke off, and he leaned a little forward. "You cannot think him so poor-spirited?"

"In essence, yes," she answered, very seriously. "I would never think Lord Montrose poor-spirited. It would be thoroughly unwise of one who knew him well."

"Yes, but though I do not wish to give you pain, I must remind you that even you did not know him as well as you had before thought." She did not vouchsafe an answer, but began plying her needle with some energy, and he regarded her quietly before continuing, "If he returns to town, I shall know it. You may rest assured of that, ma'am." She merely nodded and was silent. He settled back in his chair and calmly changed the subject. "And where is Lenora this afternoon?"

Genevieve started as her needle pricked her thumb. She glanced at him in annoyance, sucking on the injured digit as she searched in her reticule for her handkerchief. "Dear Amelia has been so kind as to take Lenora with a group of young people to Montagu House. They had planned an expedition to Wimbledon, but it was not to be. I expect we shall see them back presently."

"Then you have snatched a few hours' peace."

She looked quickly up at him again, mollified a bit by his thoughtfulness. "I cannot imagine they would be so carried away by the marbles as to keep you waiting much longer, sir."

He shrugged. "I am not impatient for their return. It would do neither Lenora nor her friend Miss Chuddsley, whom I may assume has been included in the group, harm to be exposed to more culture."

"I must agree with you there, sir," she said, disarmed.

"Tom agrees with me, too, it seems."

She nearly dropped her needle. "Tom?"

"Yes. In his last letter to me, he expressed his conviction that his sister would be much improved by more serious study while in London, rather than the frippery amusements she has hitherto enjoyed. Of course, this came after he expounded his satisfaction in the very same entertainments, of which he seems to have freely partaken while in town, so I am not entirely certain how to take such sagacity."

She chuckled, but was moved to ask, "How comes Tom to correspond with you? I collect he has done so more than once."

"I have been honored with three letters from Master Tom. I flatter myself that he counts me quite one of the family."

"I am sure we all do, sir," she said, flushing slightly, "for you have shown such kindness to us all. Be that as it may, however, I cannot conceive of how he came to be such a faithful correspondent." She continued in a resolutely light tone, "I vow I've never received more than three letters from him in all my life."

"He consulted me on matters of business," he said in a conciliatory tone.

"Regarding his stay in London? You terrify me, sir!" she said tranquilly enough to hide a tiny prickle of worry. "Am I to understand that my Tom has proved to be as susceptible to the lures of town life as any other young man in his salad days, and has found himself in need of manly advice on the subject?"

"You know it is nothing of the sort, Mrs. Breckinridge, and mean only to wrest from me congratulations for his level-headedness. Unfortunately, I am unable to fully satisfy you on that head."

"Oh?" she said, her needle pausing.

"I infinitely regret to tell you that word has reached my ears of a most ill-advised prank he perpetrated against poor Mr. Ginsham."

"My maternal serenity is shattered, sir!" she replied, reassuming her composure. "Pray, what has Tom done to his friend?"

"Merely caused that he should be set upon and wounded by would-be thieves, in the name of romance. Do not alarm yourself, ma'am. Mr. Ginsham is quite recovered and will bear no long-term effects from his injury."

Shaken by this disclosure, Genevieve looked keenly at him before replying, for she was not a little anxious regarding his true feelings on the matter, but his countenance was grave as ever, and gave her no clue as to his innermost thoughts. In light of his open disapproval of her mothering, she feared this kind of escapade must reflect even more poorly on her, and in an attempt to recover herself, she said, "But, dear sir, even you must own that much may be forgiven in the name of romance."

He merely remarked, "I suspect Miss Chuddsley was somehow the object," in a very somber tone.

"I apprehend that Tom is then in a way responsible for Ginsham's prosperous love," she said lightly, in the hopes of soothing any censorious thoughts he may be entertaining. "For myself, I find the intervention quite timely. Poor Mr. Ginsham was in a fair way to throwing himself in the river."

"It is true that a man can withstand only so much indifference when his emotions are engaged. Miss Chuddsley, were she any less innocent, would have much to answer for. I sincerely trust Lenora will play no such games in her turn."

Genevieve bent industriously to her needlework again. "Though she does have a lamentable taste for fantasy and romance, Lenora is quite level-headed."

"Then one may depend upon her being steadfast once her interest has been fixed."

She found her vision obscured by sudden tears and, blinking rapidly, turned to search in her sewing box for thread she did not need. With strong effort and much inward remonstrance, she had presently composed herself enough to straighten and say, "You may be sure I depend upon it as well, sir."

Chapter 26

DESPITE SIR JOSHUA'S convictions, Mrs. Breckinridge could not lay the specter of Lord Montrose, to the effect that Miss Breckinridge knew no respite from her guardians. She thought little of the matter, however, having been assured by Miss Chuddsley that maidens never walked alone in town, and neither girl was possessed of enough worldly knowledge to comprehend the other as a fitting chaperone. With such an understanding, Lenora walked happily down Bond Street some days after her visit to Montagu House, arm in arm with Elvira, and followed dutifully by a footman.

Elvira was ecstatically relaying news of Mr. Ginsham. "He rode all the way to Richmond to get them, Lenora, fresh from the fields! Simply because I mentioned one day how I adore wildflowers!"

"A truly romantic gesture, I think," commented Lenora, secretly pleased at the young man's capabilities. A few more of such gestures and he would need no more of her help. "But perhaps they had wilted, after such a distance."

"Oh, they had, but not to signify!" Elvira hastened to assure her. "I thought them lovely, and put them directly in water, and will press them when they begin to wither."

"That will be the most fitting tribute to his sensibility, Elvira," approved her friend. "You may place them alongside those of Mr. Barnabus."

Elvira glanced quickly at her. "I have none from Mr. Barnabus."

Lenora glanced innocently at her friend. "Did Mr. Barnabus never give you flowers?"

"No," said Elvira, wistfully.

"He never—" began Lenora, in tones of amazement, then artistically clamped her lips shut on the words. "Well," she said, after some moments composing herself, "I have no opinion of men who court favor while withholding tokens of affection."

"But he didn't," murmured Elvira, with downcast eyes. With some difficulty, she said, "He never singled me out, Lenora, no matter how I wished he had. I see now that I imagined his partiality for me. He was always gentlemanly to me, but no more."

Lenora allowed this admission to hang between them in the air, long enough for it to sink in fully, then squeezed her friend's arm. "Well, I say flowers from Mr. Ginsham are better than none from Mr. Barnabus."

Elvira smiled shyly. "Of course, they are, Lenora! I'd have to be a simpleton to think otherwise." She looked down at her feet. "I think Mr. Ginsham very sweet."

"Only sweet? He seems excessively thoughtful as well."

Her friend blushed. "Yes, he is that. Only yesterday, at the Chisholm's picnic, when the breeze picked up, he fetched my shawl, without a word from me."

"And when he met us on the street Wednesday last, he turned

back only to carry our packages," Lenora added with a satisfied air.

"Yes, that was so kind of him." Elvira ducked her head. "I thought his new brown coat handsome, did not you?"

"Decidedly." Lenora smiled archly at her friend. "And while we are enumerating all Mr. Ginsham's fine qualities, I wish to point out that, unlike a certain other gentleman, he is settled in town for the remainder of the season, which, besides being a mark of great intelligence, is exceedingly convenient."

"Now you are quizzing me," Elvira complained laughingly, but she blushed more deeply.

"And we must not forget what a fine dancer he is, unlike a certain other gentleman," pursued Lenora mercilessly. "Has he reserved a dance with you yet for tonight?"

"Oh, yes! He has engaged me for two waltzes, Lenora! For Mama gave me permission, if Lady Jersey thought it suitable, and she did, you know, on the last occasion of our being at Almack's. Oh, how Mr. Ginsham sweeps one around the room! It's like to flying!"

Lenora hugged her friend's arm to her, smiling warmly and widely upon her raptures, and feeling in perfect charity with Mr. Ginsham and his great good sense.

A cough from the footman stopped the young ladies, and they turned inquiringly to him.

"Begging miss's pardon," he said, his cheeks ablaze as he snatched the cap from his head, "but I only just remembered I was to pick up a gum plaster for poor Oliver—the groom, that is, miss." He stood twisting his cap in his hands. "He's been so poorly that I'd hate to see him worse, which he would be if he's made to wait."

"Oh," said Lenora, surprised that she knew nothing about this errand, or the malady that occasioned it, but moved by compassion for the unfortunate groom. "He must certainly not be made to wait a moment longer than need be. John, you may turn back to the apoth-ecary and purchase the plaster, while Miss Chuddsley and I walk on. We are not so very far from home, and shall be quite safe together."

"Miss is very kind," he said, smiling shyly at her. "If you please, miss, the next turning will be a shorter way home."

Lenora inclined her head graciously. "Thank you, John. Do not you worry for us."

The grateful footman whirled abruptly and jogged back toward Bond Street, the young ladies gazing thoughtfully after him.

"I wonder that he did not think of his errand while we were in Hookham's," mused Lenora.

"It must have slipped his mind, with so much to look at," said Elvira, in perfect understanding. "There is such a bustle here, I declare if I have not forgotten my own head sometimes!"

Lenora laughingly agreed, and they turned the corner onto a short alley connecting to Curzon Street. They had walked only a few steps past a loafer lounging against the wall, when he pushed him-self upright and began to follow them. Lenora watched his move-ments over her shoulder with growing uneasiness, for he seemed to be watching them rather greedily.

"Perhaps we should move more quickly, dear," she whispered to Elvira, who had noticed the man as well.

With anxious glances behind and forward to the end of the alley, they hastened toward Curzon Street, but just before they reached it, the man grabbed Elvira's wrist, and pulled her backward. She cried out, letting go Lenora's arm, and Lenora turned back to see her friend tightly gripped around the shoulders by the man, who pressed an evil-looking knife to her side as he stared back with wild eyes.

"If you like your friend, you'll come with me quiet-like, love."

Lenora's heart leapt to her throat, but she found courage enough to demand, "Unhand her, villain."

The man laughed. "Villain, am I? That's rich. I ain't done nothing, not yet." Elvira whimpered, and he turned his head to sputter in her ear, "No squawking, you, or I'll have call to be nasty, and your pretty friend there won't have a friend no more."

Lenora stood her ground, but her face drained of color as the man dragged Elvira backward. "I shall scream," she warned, her voice high with terror.

"Not if you like your friend," he said, with an ugly chuckle.

Elvira's eyes widened with fear, and Lenora hazarded a swift glance behind into the street, but no one was near enough to whom she could signal. There did not seem to be anything she could do but follow the man, so she stepped once more into the alley, following with halting steps, and many frightened glances toward either of the streets where assistance might appear, as he backed toward a sinister-looking doorway.

Suddenly, a movement on Curzon street caught Lenora's eye, and she spun to see the door to the nearest house opening. A figure appeared, walking jauntily down the steps, and as all three tense persons in the alleyway watched, the gentleman glanced over at them, and Lenora was shocked to recognize the man as the stranger whom she had met on three separate occasions.

He stopped on the stoop, blinking at her in surprise, then tipped his hat and smiled, calling, "Ma'am! So, we meet again!"

Lenora's mouth opened but, under the injunction of silence, she dared only look in mute terror from him to the man who held Elvira. The stranger's eyes followed hers, and with lightning clarity seemed to grasp the direness of the situation. In a moment, he had leapt the railing and advanced with quick strides toward Elvira and her captor.

"What's this, then?" he asked amiably, withdrawing a short sword from his belt.

The man holding Elvira froze for an instant, the knife trembling against her ribs, but as his eyes flitted from the gentleman with the sword to the young lady nearly bursting to scream, he seemed to think better of pressing his case and, releasing his prisoner, he turned and fled down the alleyway. Elvira, swaying where she stood, gave a gurgle of a sigh and collapsed in a faint, falling neatly into Lenora's arms, who had stepped forward to catch her.

The stranger was at her side in a moment, relieving her of her fair burden. "Good gracious, ma'am! What a near thing!"

"Oh, sir!" cried Lenora, nearly overpowered by the relief flooding through her body. "Oh, thank you! That hateful man—he—oh!"

"It was nothing, dear girl, nothing at all. I am only glad you are unhurt." He laid Elvira gently down onto the flagway, where Lenora, having quickly knelt, received her head onto her lap. The man patted his pockets. "Have you any smelling salts, or vinaigrette?"

Lenora searched through her reticule, but to no avail. Instead, she began to chafe her friend's hands, all the while animadverting on the deplorable state of a city whose constables were forever ambling wherever they were not needed while dangerous cutthroats roamed at large on even the most civilized of streets. At length, she glanced up at their rescuer, whose head bent next to hers, and experienced a fair amount of astonishment at how worn and dissipated he looked at such close quarters.

The stranger met her gaze and smiled encouragingly. "She will recover soon enough, I'll wager. I wish I could offer somewhere to lay her until she regains her senses, but I am new to this district, and a man's lodgings are nowhere for a young lady, sensible or not."

"Indeed, sir, but I am much obliged for your kindness," said

Lenora, blushing. The thought occurred to her that here was another gentleman of heroic, if advanced, qualities. "If you would be so good as to call a hack to convey us home, my mother will care for her there."

"An admirable plan, young lady." Instantly, he rose and strode into the street, raising his arm to a hack just then coming up the street, and when it had stopped, hastened back to lift the still insensible Elvira into his arms. The jarvey opened the door and the gentleman deposited Elvira carefully on the seat, then turned to hand Lenora in.

"Oh, sir, how can I thank you?" she said, her fingers gripping his. "Such a providential thing for you to come out just as you did."

"I ought to say I felt a premonition, but as I am a truthful man, I will not. Merely, I am glad to have been of service, ma'am." He tipped his hat again. "If you will give me the direction, I shall command the driver, and speed you on your way."

Lenora pressed his hand with her fingers. "You are too kind, sir, and with so little inducement! We are strangers to you, but we are everlastingly grateful! I only would that I could repay you!"

"Oh, I have a very good reason for what I have done, ma'am," he said, smiling secretly up at her. "But as for payment, perhaps you will allow me to introduce myself."

"Without hesitation, sir! You have certainly earned the honor. I am Lenora Breckinridge."

The hat was removed and placed over his heart. "And I am Carlisle Dupray, your obedient servant."

Lenora smiled gratefully and, murmuring the direction of Lady Cammerby's house, she settled onto the forward seat of the hack and allowed the step to be folded up and the door closed. The hack lurched forward, causing Elvira to roll on the seat, and Lenora leapt across to support her friend. Elvira's eyes fluttered open.

Lenora took her hands. "Elvira, are you well?"

Her friend moaned and closed her eyes again.

Lenora patted her cheek. "Elvira!"

"Oh!" The girl opened her eyes once more and, absorbing her surroundings, struggled upright. "Lenora! Where are we? What happened?"

Lenora moved to the seat next to her, putting an arm about her shoulders. "You fainted, my dear, but that kind Mr. Dupray helped me care for you and called us a hack, because I had no smelling salts, and now we are on our way home."

"Mr. Dupray? Is that his name? How do you know him?"

"He met us on the street, and in Hookham's, do you not recall?"

"Perfectly," murmured Elvira, a hand to her head. "But I do not recollect his being introduced."

"He was not, though I have seen him once more after that, at Montagu House," admitted Lenora. "It is perhaps irregular, but I thought it proper that we should be introduced after he rescued us."

"Oh, yes, of course." Elvira shook her head as if trying to clear it. "Oh, dear, what an ordeal! I am convinced we should have been murdered, had that horrid man succeeded in dragging us into the doorway!"

"I have no doubt we should have been dreadfully harmed, if Mr. Dupray had not come out of his house just then. What a lucky chance!" Lenora shivered.

"To think that we happened to be there, on the street where he lived! Oh, Lenora, I'm trembling all over!"

Lenora rubbed her friend's arms and hugged her against herself. "Now, do not worry, Elvira, we shall be home in a trice, and Mama will set you to rights again. A little tea and some bread and butter, some cosseting and care, and you'll be right as a trivet!"

Elvira smiled thankfully, leaning into the welcome embrace. Presently, she said, "Mr. Dupray is quite heroic, is he not? Though he is rather old."

"Much like Sir Joshua."

The girls giggled, and Elvira said, "I suppose this proves we mustn't fancy only one kind of hero, or we should miss all kinds of romantic adventures!"

Sighing in agreement, Lenora was glad to relapse into silence for several minutes. As they swayed in the poorly sprung hackney, musing over their frightful experience, Lenora was unable to refrain from mentally following the awful possibilities had they been trapped in the alley, until an odd idea occurred to her. She said suddenly, "Would it not be strange if Mr. Dupray is actually the evil Duke? This could all be a take in, you know. Like with Tom and Ginsham and the fight. We could be playing directly into the evil Duke's hands."

Elvira laughed. "And next time we meet he will ravish us? Oh, Lenora, you must be funning. He would not rescue us and send us home if he meant to harm us. Such goodness as he has shown cannot be pretense."

"I am persuaded you are right, my dear." She looked out the window at the darkening street as the minutes passed by. "My, but it seems a long way home."

Chapter 27

GENEVIEVE HAD SPENT the afternoon harassed by excessive-ly uncomfortable thoughts. That Elvira Chuddsley was on the brink of making a very respectable match both delighted and disturbed her, for on the one hand, she liked Mr. Ginsham very much, and thought the couple extremely well-suited, and could no more wholeheartedly have approved the match had she been Mrs. Chuddsley. On the other hand, however, Elvira's approach-ing marriage would naturally increase Lenora's desire for her own, which would very probably hasten events of which her mother would rather not think seriously until absolutely necessary. Not all the forbearance in the world could resign her at any time within the near future to Lenora's marriage to Sir Joshua, and she did not trust herself as of yet to act with composure upon his applying to her for permission to address her daughter.

She had tried valiantly to suppress her feelings. Indeed, after Vauxhall she had been too mortified even to acknowledge them.

But Sir Joshua's continued friendliness to her acted as a perverse balm to her embarrassment, lulling her into comfort while in his presence, then abandoning her to disheartening reflection when he had gone. He always managed to disarm her when he visited, and in spite of her resolve to treat him as a brother, their conversations danced into the realm of what she considered to be flirtation far too easily for her comfort. When left alone, she knew that he could not view their interactions as she did—how could any man wish to flirt with a worn out, old woman when a vital, young girl welcomed his attentions? Surely, his aim was nothing more than to develop an easy relationship with his prospective mother-in-law. With this conviction, she tried to rejoice that in such a relationship, she could expect many more opportunities to join in delightful repartee, and strove equally to believe this was all to which she looked forward in his company. But the pleasure she felt in his notice, and the general depression of her spirits on contemplating the future, gave the lie to her hopes.

As the dinner hour approached, Genevieve left her workbox, but could not abandon her musings, to attend to her toilet. As she went up the stairs to her room, she passed a maid and asked her if Lenora had yet returned from her errands. Bobbing a curtsey, the maid informed her that she had not seen Miss, but would inquire if she was in the house. With a nod of thanks, Genevieve continued to her room, a little crease between her brows.

She dressed for dinner, stifling the temptation to dawdle because Sir Joshua was to dine with them and she had little inclination to make a fool of herself, as she would inevitably do. She finished in good time and went downstairs, enquiring of the butler if Miss Breckinridge had come in while she was dressing.

Bowing, he said, "No, ma'am, but John came in over an hour

since. Knowing that he was to accompany Miss Breckinridge, I took the liberty of asking where she had gone, and he told me she had met with a gentleman friend, and had sent him home, but as she had Miss Chuddsley with her, he saw nothing in it."

"Did he tell you the name of the gentleman, Cottam?" At his negative, she desired him to send John to her in the Blue Saloon, knowing that the dinner guests would be assembling in the drawing room.

The footman came into the saloon with trepidation, his eyes darting everywhere but to her face. With mounting concern, she asked him the name of the gentleman with whom Lenora had gone.

"He said as he was a Mr. Smith, ma'am."

Her brows lowered at this unlikely surname. "Had you seen him before, John?"

"Only in the pub, where we met, ma'am."

Shocked, she immediately demanded, "Did you arrange a meeting between this Mr. Smith and my daughter?"

Trembling, he wrung his hands before him. "No, ma'am, please, ma'am, I didn't mean to do wrong. Only he said as he had a passion for Miss Breckinridge, and he looked so forlorn, that she wouldn't never meet him, and he only wanted a few minutes of her time, to tell her how it was with him. I told him as she wasn't never left alone, and he said as how that was proper, and he wouldn't never be so ungentlemanly as to try to meet a young lady on her own, clandestine-like, but that if I could bring her with her maid to a certain place, he'd speak with her out in the open, and engage to get her home safe afterwards."

Words forsook Genevieve for several moments. When at last she could command her voice, she asked in a ragged tone barely above a whisper, "And you saw nothing wrong in this, John? Nothing suspicious in a strange man wishing to meet with a young lady over whom you were to guard?"

"No, ma'am!" he cried, his face white with fear. "Leastwise, he told me how he had known her all her life, and that they'd had a misunderstanding, and that was all that kept her from his company. He told me all about her, so's I'd know he really did know her, and when I told him she walked often with her friend, he named Miss Chuddsley, and didn't have no argument over having her with them while they talked. I saw no wrong in him speaking to her in public, with her friend by."

Before Genevieve could respond to this, the door opened, and a maid entered, a note on a tray before her. "If it please, ma'am, this just arrived."

These words struck foreboding in Genevieve's heart, and with a shaking hand, she took the note, dismissing the maid. The footman stood trembling before her as she stared for some moments at the folded note in her hand, her reeling brain somehow recognizing the hand that had written her name in florid characters across the front, as if it were an invitation—or a celebration. Almost in a trance, she broke the seal and opened the note.

"*My dearest Genevieve, you must forgive me for sinking beneath even myself, but you have given me little choice, and I must have my way. Your delightful daughter and her lovely friend find themselves in my company this evening, and will stay with me at Nordley until you, and only you, come to collect them. I have no doubt that you will have guessed by now the price for their freedom. I will accept no compromise. You may be assured of their safety—until I despair of your coming. Then, it will be beyond my power to dispel your fears. I trust you*"

will believe that I am made wretched by this course of
action, but I have no doubt that it is my surest path to
reward. Come quickly, my love. Carlisle"

Her free hand went out to grasp the back of a nearby chair for
support, and the footman took an agitated step toward her.

"John," she said, her voice dangerously low. "At what time did
you leave Miss Breckinridge with Mr. Smith?"

"Just past four o'clock, ma'am."

It was now a quarter past six. "That will be all," she managed.

The unfortunate footman fled from the room, leaving Genevieve
pale and shaking, clinging to the chair. Montrose had fooled them
all, even Sir Joshua. He had lulled them into a sense of security, pre-
tending to have left London, to have given up his pursuit of her, but
setting forth on this despicable plot instead. She had mistrusted Sir
Joshua's assertion that Montrose was beaten, and so had not lifted
the constant watch on Lenora, but had been too distracted by her
own worries to give proper consideration to her fears. And now, he
had taken Lenora, and Elvira as well! His estate was three hours or
more from town, and the girls had been left with him two hours
since. There was not a moment to lose. She must go.

Dropping the note in her haste, she rushed into the hall and
collided with Sir Joshua. He caught her shoulders, helpfully holding
her upright, his apology dying on his lips when he saw her face.

"Good heaven, Genevieve, you are white as a ghost! Tell me what
is the matter," he demanded. When she could only stare up at him
with a horrified gaze, he led her back into the saloon. Closing the
door behind him, he said, "Tell me, Genevieve."

"Something—something dreadful has happened—to Lenora—"
she stammered.

His hold on her arm tightened. "Is she hurt? Where is she?"

Such a jumble of emotions assailed her that, once again, she could not speak. Sensing this, Sir Joshua gently propelled her to the sofa, helping her to sit before going quickly to the sideboard to pour out some sherry.

"You are overcome," he said, pressing the glass into her hands. He waited until she had sipped it, then adjured her, "Tell me what has happened."

She knew she must tell him all. Even could she rid herself of him, she could not, and would not, rescue the girls by capitulating to Lord Montrose's demand, which was all she could hope to do if she attempted a rescue alone. She needed an accomplice, and she could choose none better than Sir Joshua. The story tumbled out of her then, and Sir Joshua listened quietly, but before she had done, he stood abruptly and strode to the fireplace, leaning against the mantelpiece and staring into the flames. Genevieve finished her tale and watched him, hating that she wished he did not feel so strongly.

"You say they were delivered to him two hours since?" he asked suddenly. At her affirmation, he murmured, "Then they are nearly at Nordley." He paced in front of the fire. "Even so, it is not too late. Not until—" He turned and came to her, taking her hands in his as he sat beside her on the sofa. "I will go, Genevieve. I hold myself to blame for this. I did not heed your warning. I ought to have been more watchful, more careful of Lord Montrose. I will not let him compromise Lenora."

She gripped his hands, ashamed of her littleness and determined to redeem herself. "If anyone is to blame, it is I. I hoped to protect Lenora by keeping her from him, but I failed utterly! I ought to have given her more information about him, not been so reticent—I ought to have refused his acquaintance, as you counselled me to do, and risked reprisal."

"But we should still have been right where we are, in that case," Sir Joshua said, gently. "You told me so, at Vauxhall, but I did not believe you. This despicable action of his has finally convinced me that nothing you could have done would have dissuaded him from his course. He is a villain, and will do as a villain does."

At that moment, the door opened, and Mr. Ginsham rushed into the room, halting at sight of their agitated faces. "Devil take that butler of yours!" he cried, then tried to compose himself. "Forgive me, ma'am, but I'm dashed if something is not very much amiss."

Genevieve let out a dismayed sigh. "Oh, dear. Mr. Ginsham, I had quite forgotten you were coming tonight." She rose with tolerable composure and held a hand out to him. "Pardon our confusion, sir. You find us in an uproar, for we have just discovered that Lenora and Elvira have met with an accident—nothing serious, I assure you—but I am quite distracted."

"I should say so! And you're not alone, ma'am," he confided, still upset. "Here's Miss Chuddsley's aunt in palpitations because her niece has gone missing, and I managed to convince her that the girl's got to be here. But that butler let slip that neither Miss Chuddsley nor Miss Breckinridge has been seen since four o'clock, then he tried to fob me off with some Canterbury tale about a sick relative!"

Genevieve raised eyes heavenward with a most unladylike wish regarding the disposal of all silly butlers. "Cottam is an excellent servant—too excellent sometimes, I fear. No, Mr. Ginsham, the girls are merely detained, and we intend to be off directly to rescue them."

"Good," he said. "I shall offer you my services."

"No need," interposed Sir Joshua. "I shouldn't dream of imposing upon you in this circumstance."

"But Miss Chuddsley—an accident, you said—"

Sir Joshua waved away his anxiety. "They are quite well, you may be certain. They need only to be fetched back home, which is no dire business."

"We are so very much obliged to you, Mr. Ginsham, for your kind offer," put in Genevieve, taking his arm and leading him toward the door, "and we shall certainly apprise you of their safe return and continued well-being."

He disengaged his arm from her grasp and eyed the two of them narrowly. "You're both acting dashed havey-cavey. I've a strong notion that butler isn't the only one trying to fob me off!"

"You're right, Mr. Ginsham," said Sir Joshua evenly. "We are wishing you at Jericho, for the longer we stand talking, the longer Miss Chuddsley and Miss Breckinridge await their rescue."

"Then why may I not go with you?" the young man demanded.

"The fact of the matter is, this is none of your concern."

Mr. Ginsham stepped hastily toward Sir Joshua. "I may not have your years, sir, but I've cut my wisdoms. Please! I wish you will stop shamming it, and tell me the truth!" With a side glance at Genevieve, he lowered his tone. "You know how I feel, sir. I will go mad if I do not know she is safe!"

This straw broke Genevieve's poise, and she threw up her hands. "Would that I had gone by myself!" she cried. "There is no help for it, I'm afraid, Sir Joshua." Turning decidedly to Mr. Ginsham, she declared, "The truth of the matter is that the girls have been abducted."

He stared at her. "You're bamming me."

"No, sir, I am not," replied Genevieve. "One of my husband's old enemies has, for reasons which we need not go into, taken the girls and holds them for—for ransom at his estate. If we do not redeem them before the night ends—you know the consequences."

Words seemed to fail Mr. Ginsham. He goggled first at Genevieve, then at Sir Joshua and, receiving comfort from neither, tottered to a chair and sank into it. "I don't know what to say."

"Speech is unnecessary, sir," said Sir Joshua dryly. "If you still wish to be of service, you may stay to protect Mrs. Breckinridge."

That lady turned indignantly to him and declared in an undertone, "I go with you!"

"That is out of the question," he said shortly.

She angled in front of him, her chin up. "The note stipulates in no uncertain terms that I, and I alone, must go! I already risk their harm by bringing you as an accomplice. I will not risk more by failing to appear at all!"

"Your presence will not be necessary, I assure you," he said, a mulish look about his mouth.

"How, pray, do you intend to redeem them without the payment?" she cried.

Sir Joshua took her arms in an ungentle grip. "There will be no payment, Genevieve! Am I clear?" He looked fiercely into her eyes. "The villain will give the girls to me or he will have great cause to regret, and that will be the end of it."

Mr. Ginsham jumped to his feet, suddenly reinvigorated. "He dashed well will! I give my word of honor to that, ma'am."

Sir Joshua glared over at him for an intense moment, then nodded briefly. "I will call my carriage."

Releasing Genevieve, he strode toward the door, but she darted ahead of him, opening it and standing defiantly with her hand on the knob. "You both fail to recollect," she said in a derisive tone, "that the great danger we must *avert* is the compromise of two young ladies, which will rather be *accomplished* if they are rescued from the clutches of one man, only to be seen coming into town in the early hours of the morning in the company of *two*!" She opened the door and sailed through, tossing back over her shoulder. "I go or all is vain!"

On this valediction, Genevieve went to Lady Cammerby, who waited in the drawing room in some bewilderment, having received the astonishing tidings from Cottam that three of her dinner guests were in heated argument in the saloon on account of the other two being gone missing. Genevieve swept into the room with no thought of disabusing her friend's mind, instead delivering herself of a whirlwind explanation of nothing, while expressing inadequate but heartfelt apologies for the ruined party, interspersed with assurances that all was as it should be, before sailing out the door.

This accomplished, Genevieve was the first to enter the chaise, and the gentlemen right behind, Sir Joshua, having had the forethought to avail himself of Lord Cammerby's stables to augment his team from two horses to four, instructing his coachman to make for Amersham with the greatest possible speed. Leaving behind them an intensely curious staff, who had observed just enough to conjecture wildly, the trio fairly flew through the busy evening streets and, to Sir Joshua's satisfaction, were clear of Kensington within half an hour.

The long road to Nordley stretching out before them, each nursed their separate anxieties in silence for several minutes. The thoughts of the two gentlemen Genevieve could only guess at, but had a shrewd idea from their grim expressions along what lines they ran. Her own thoughts were rather more convoluted, beginning with her fears for Lenora and Elvira, twisting through a maze of guilt, jealousy, and distress, and ending with the resolution of finally annihilating Lord Montrose's pretensions.

On this thought, Genevieve roused herself. "We must have a plan," she said.

"There is not much question what there is to do," said Mr.

Ginsham, glaring out the window. "We break in the door, and knock down anyone who doesn't give up Miss Chuddsley and Miss Breckinridge."

"That gem of idiocy is precisely why I had to come," replied Genevieve bluntly. "If that is all you can come up with, you are welcome to stay in the coach. Knock them down, indeed. You had as well offer your head for washing."

"They'd not get far!" Mr. Ginsham retorted, firing up. "I'm pretty handy with my fives, I'll have you know!"

She snorted. "I've no doubt you are, sir, in a fair fight, with one, or perhaps even two opponents. But at Nordley there are more than one or two who will take exception to a stranger forcing his way into their master's house, and you'd sooner find yourself trussed like a chicken and tossed into the cellar."

"They'll have Sir Joshua to reckon with as well," he pursued lamely.

She turned her head to look with raised brows at that other gentleman, who had remained conspicuously silent. "And what do you think of Mr. Ginsham's plan, Sir Joshua?"

Sir Joshua stared ahead, unseeing. "We have no way of knowing where he will be keeping the girls. Short of breaking into the house, I do not yet perceive how we can free them."

"You see?" cried Mr. Ginsham. "There's nothing else to be done."

"But Mrs. Breckinridge is right," said Sir Joshua sternly. "We'd not be doing the young ladies a favor by getting ourselves caught housebreaking. Lord Montrose would think it a mighty fine joke to hand us over to the magistrate while Miss Breckinridge and Miss Chuddsley languish somewhere in his house."

Silenced by this vivid image, Mr. Ginsham leaned back against the squabs, a belligerent crease between his brows.

"We must find out where he is keeping the girls," observed Sir Joshua, "and then we can make a plan to reach them."

"While alerting all the household staff to our presence?" said Genevieve, wryly.

Sir Joshua turned at last and regarded her gravely. "Mr. Ginsham and I may very well be able to reach them from an outside window or back stair."

"While I am to sit tamely in the coach?" she retorted through clenched teeth. "Oh! I am out of all patience with the pair of you! This is no novel, and you are no knights errant!" She took a deep, calming breath and then said, "Perhaps you forget that Lord Montrose was a long-standing friend to my late husband. I have stayed many times at Nordley, and know the house very well." She closed her eyes. "Too well, I think." With another deep breath, she continued, "The rooms where the girls are most likely to be kept are on an upper floor, and would be impossible to reach from the outside, and difficult to find from a back way, without drawing undesirable attention."

"Well, unless you know the chamber maids to be former contenders in the ring, there's no dashed reason why we shouldn't at least try!" exclaimed Mr. Ginsham.

"Mr. Ginsham," she said with dangerous calm, "Lord Montrose will be keeping a close watch on his prisoners. The stakes are too high for him to be careless. If even a hint of an attack comes to his notice, he may—he is very likely to—" She swallowed the wave of emotion that welled in her throat, and with a rather unsteady voice concluded, "The safest plan would be to convince Montrose to bring the girls into the library."

Watching her intently, Sir Joshua inquired, "Why the library?"

"It is an outer room, on the ground floor, with several French windows. A rescue from that room could be accomplished with minimal interference, and would be more likely to succeed."

"Then I should draw him to the front door," said a subdued Mr. Ginsham. "He doesn't know me from Adam, but he'd suspect Sir Joshua in an instant."

"There is no reason for him to suspect me," Sir Joshua contradicted him. "Montrose and I are acquainted, to be sure, but have never been on speaking terms. My appearance would be unexpected but not improper, and I have already conceived a plausible story to tell him."

"Sir Joshua," said Genevieve with desperate patience, "he must have been watching Lenora for some time, and will have noticed your attendance on her. It would be folly to present yourself at his front door as a friend, tonight of all nights."

"Then I'll go," declared Mr. Ginsham with finality.

"And with what power do you hope to persuade him to bring you the girls?" cried Mrs. Breckinridge. "Upon my soul, I could never in the whole of my life have conceived of the nonsensical notions the pair of you have put forward in the last thirty minutes! Do, I pray you, exert yourselves to think! Montrose is no fool, and would never have set forth upon this course without adequate preparation. The circumstance of his very neatly snatching both Lenora and Elvira from under our noses attests to this. He has, no doubt, planned for every expediency, and his note was clear as to his particular expectations. It would be the height of folly to assume that he would not be on guard against any aberrations."

Sir Joshua was eyeing her warily. "You are not about to suggest that *you* will present yourself at Montrose's front door?" he said, with barely restrained violence.

"The girls' safety is ensured when I, and I alone, come to redeem them." She persisted over their opposition by raising her voice. "It is of no use to cavil, gentlemen! The situation is dire, and will admit of only one solution. I must go."

"You speak of folly—" began Sir Joshua heatedly, but she cut him short.

"I am the only one he will not suspect. I am the only one who will be able to draw him to the library. I am also the only one with any chance of getting him to bring Lenora and Elvira into the room with me." She looked coolly out the window, brooking no argument. "I believe we are in agreement."

Chapter 28

A N HOUR LATER, the carriage could be seen to pause outside the gates of Nordley, and if anyone had been interested to watch, to have disgorged two shadows that crept into the shrubbery, while the coach continued up the gravel drive. Its remaining occupant, if she had been observed through the shadowed glass, would have given the impression of extreme hauteur, so disdainfully did she gaze upon her surroundings. This attitude was hardly appropriate, as the estate was beautifully kept, and boasted some of the loveliest views in the county. Its broad drive passed through a verdant park, up and over rolling hills, and finally through an avenue of stately beeches, to the sweep in front of the house.

The equipage had scarcely come to a halt when a groom came to the horses' heads, and a footman ran to the door of the coach, pulling it open and handing down Mrs. Breckinridge. Her stately silence upon setting foot on such hated ground betrayed none of the fear that held her nerves taut, and she paused on the drive to gaze solemnly about a scene in which she had hoped never to take part again. The handsome Georgian house reared up before her, with its meticulously groomed shrubberies, urns, and statuary lining the drive, and walks leading around the house to gorgeous pleasure gardens in the rear; the various servants standing at attention outside, and the promise of several more inside the house—all this magnificence impressed her only with the assurance that it was supported entirely by the folly of Lord Montrose's victims. In this place she had first become acquainted, during the countless house parties to which they had been invited, with the weakness and indecency of the man she had married, and with the utter shamelessness of their host.

The footman shuffled impatiently next to her and, with an effort, she suppressed the emotions that had accompanied her remembrances and turned to face the house, resolutely gathering her skirts and walking swiftly up to the door, which was waiting open for her. She had no illusions about what was in store for her inside the house, and had equally little hesitancy about her course. No matter the danger to herself, no matter the outcome, she would not leave Lenora to Lord Montrose's mercy.

She entered his house with a focus that exhibited as incivility. A request for her pelisse was refused, as was an invitation to step upstairs into one of the saloons. "I shall await Lord Montrose in the library, thank you," she declared, sweeping across the hall into that room, barely pausing long enough for the elderly butler to open the door for her.

As soon as the servant had closed the door again, leaving her alone, she immediately went to the long windows on the far side of the room, pulling back the draperies to unlatch two of them. Then she let the draperies fall back across the windows, leaving a tiny gap, and turned to survey her surroundings. The library was a stately room, with heavy oak shelves lining two opposing walls, a large, modern fireplace splitting one. The center of the room was rather crowded with furniture, mostly comprised of spindly chairs and tables, with a chaise lounge or settee here and there. She pulled off her bonnet, letting it hang against her back by the strings and, drawing off her gloves, she held them in one hand, agitatedly slapping them against her hip as she wandered the room, glancing at titles on the shelves and inspecting knick-knacks on the abundant tables.

After several minutes, she heard the door open and turned to confront the enemy. Lord Montrose entered, smiling with intense satisfaction, and with much ado, carefully locked the door behind him. Pocketing the key with a dramatic gesture, he advanced into the room, his hands out, his eyes drinking her in as though he were a starved man.

"My Genevieve. You have come to me!"

As he came closer, she perceived a short sword at his side. These precautions merely increased her resolution, and she replied coldly, "You gave me little choice, my lord."

He shook his head, tutting indulgently. "No more ceremonious names, my love. You must call me Carlisle now."

"Must I?" She moved out of his reach to another table, picking up a Dresden piece and looking it over critically. "And how will you threaten me to ensure it, I wonder?"

He laughed, low and long, a rumbling, triumphant sound. "Bertram truly was a fool to leave you." In two quick strides, he had taken her into his arms, one hand tilting up her chin. "I shall not make that mistake."

"You will not have that chance, my lord," she said, her arms wedged defensively between them. "For, if you are not to give me the honor of your name, how can you hope to keep me at your side?"

"Perhaps I have seen the error of my thinking, my darling." As he bent to kiss her, a sound outside the window made him pause, and he glanced toward it, but other than the whistle of wind, nothing more could be heard.

Genevieve raised her brows. "I expect nature suspects your duplicity, my lord, and gives you warning." She applied the pressure of her two hands against his chest. "Now, if you please, and even if you do not, we have business to attend to before anything else."

"Ah, of course." He let her go, perceiving the state of her dress for the first time. "You still wear your hat and pelisse! How comes it that you have not been attended?"

"Oh, I have been attended, but I have chosen not to attend. You will discover that I dispense my attentions most sparingly, my lord. I fear you will find this irksome, and have cause to repine your rash course."

He smiled knowingly. "Never have I been so sure of a decision in my life, Genevieve. How you can question that quite astounds me, given that you have submitted to my terms."

"You are too hasty, sir," she said with a scornful look. "I will be sure of my cards before I consent to any of your terms, including that of remaining under your roof." She sat primly on the edge of one of the spindle-legged chairs. "I would be most obliged if you will bring my daughter and Miss Chuddsley to me."

He crooked an eyebrow, standing as if he would refuse this demand, but at last seemed to think better of it, and went to the door, unlocking it with a flourish. "Without delay, my dear one. The sooner they are redeemed, the sooner we can be comfortable together." Leaning out, he called instructions to an unseen servitor, then he closed and locked the door once more. Crossing the room, he disposed himself on a settee near her. "As we are being so civil, may I offer you tea?"

"Somehow, I find myself without appetite, my lord."

"How unfortunate, my love. I shall make it my duty to tempt you with all the delights at my command."

"You behold me in raptures of anticipation, my lord."

He gazed lazily at her. "You think to daunt me by this manner, but you cannot know how it intrigues me. No woman has treated me thus." Smiling knowingly, he said, "I will make you love me, Genevieve. That is a promise."

"As you are incapable of keeping a promise, my lord, and I am even in doubt as to your knowledge of the word's meaning, such a determination in no way recommends itself to me."

He threw back his head and laughed, and was on the point of a rejoinder, when a knock sounded at the door, and he sprang up, rubbing his hands together. "Here they are, my love, and you will soon see that I am well able to keep the promises I choose." He unlocked the door and ushered in Lenora and Elvira who, upon spying Mrs. Breckinridge, ran to fall upon her neck.

"Oh, Mama! I'm so dreadfully sorry!" Lenora cried, her face stained with tears. "He told me he was Mr. Dupray, not Lord Montrose! I had no notion he could deceive me!"

"It is no fault of yours, my dears!" soothed her mother, who returned their embrace protectively.

"He saved us from a thief, ma'am, and was so kind!" added Elvira. "It never entered my head he could be the evil Duke!"

Lord Montrose, witnessing this affecting scene from the door, blinked at Elvira's words. "But I am not a duke at all!" he remarked, receiving for his pains two daggered looks, and circumspectly retired to a chair a little distant from the ladies.

"Are you hurt, my loves?" murmured Mrs. Breckinridge, quickly glancing over the girls as they clung to her. They shook their heads emphatically and she embraced them again. "Lord Montrose has agreed to release you. Are you ready?"

"Oho, now you are being hasty, my dearest," interpolated his lordship. "My promise was that they, and their reputations, would remain unharmed if you came to me. I have said nothing about releasing them."

Mrs. Breckinridge rounded on him. "Their remaining any length of time in the company of a gentleman of your reputation will do them harm, as you are fully aware!"

"Only if it becomes known," he said, with an unpleasant smile. "Now that you are here, the young ladies' reputations are safe from me, but I am persuaded it would not be entirely prudent to release them just yet."

The three ladies glared at him with such animosity that a lesser man would have quailed, but Lord Montrose merely stood and drew his sword, flourishing it carelessly before him. "Just as you wished to be sure of your cards, Genevieve, I wish to be sure of mine."

Something shook the window and he cocked an eyebrow mockingly at Mrs. Breckinridge. "Nature trembles as you do, my love."

"You snake!" hissed Lenora, releasing her mother and taking a step toward Lord Montrose. "You cannot keep us here!"

"Can I not?"

"No, you cannot," cried Elvira, moving to Lenora's side. "My family will have something to say to you if you try, sir!"

"I think not," he said, sauntering up to them and pushing each girl aside with the flat of his blade. Genevieve took a heavy step backward, but was impeded by a chaise lounge, and he raised the sword, pointing the tip at her neck. "For I am persuaded you would not wish to upset me."

The two girls watched in wide-eyed horror as he took Mrs. Breckinridge in his arms, tenderly placing the blade against her throat. "As you see, my dears, I hold all the cards after all."

He leaned in to take his kiss, but at that moment, several things happened in quick succession. Mrs. Breckinridge flung her head back and twisted to the side, wrenching Lord Montrose's sword arm down as she moved. The window then crashed open and a snarling figure flung into the room, closely followed by a second, effectively distracting both Lord Montrose and his fair assailant. As they gaped at the intruders, Lenora, seizing a heavy candlestick from one of the many tables near her, swung it down with a mighty thud onto the back of her captor's head.

Silence fell as Lord Montrose, with all eyes upon him, dropped in a heap onto the carpet. Sir Joshua, his chest heaving and hands clenched into trembling fists, glared hardest and longest but, at last, he mastered himself and looked up at the ladies. He stepped to Genevieve, taking her hand, his eyes at her throat where the blade had so lately been laid. "He did not hurt you," he whispered, in a husky, unsteady voice.

"No," was all the response she could muster, finally overpowered by the strain of the evening.

He inhaled deeply, eyes closing in the effort, and seemed about to speak again, but Lenora cried, "Sir Joshua! You came!"

"My dear girl," he said, smiling with mingled relief and admiration as he let go her mother's hand and took hers. "I see I was mistaken in the belief that you had none of your mother's blood in you. I never thought I should be so glad to be wrong!"

Lenora beamed at him until, recollecting that her other hand held something heavy, she considered the candlestick in bemusement. Sir Joshua relieved her of the weapon and deposited it on a likely table, neither of them aware that Mrs. Breckinridge had sat heavily into a chair, closing her eyes in what an astute observer would recognize as, not exhaustion, but dejection.

Mr. Ginsham, having received Elvira on his chest, encircled her in his ready arms. "Oh, my darling, you are safe!"

She looked up at him through tear-filled eyes. "You came for me! How could you know? Oh, never mind—it does not signify! You came, and you are my hero!" And she buried her face in his chest once more.

"Well, that's done," said Sir Joshua, looking about the room in satisfaction. "I propose we leave this place without further ado."

"What of him?" inquired Mr. Ginsham, nodding his chin at the heap on the floor.

"If Mrs. Breckinridge was not mistaken, there are plenty of servants here," answered Sir Joshua. "Let them deal with him."

Chapter 29

HOURS LATER, ALONE in Lenora's bedchamber, mother and daughter held each other tightly, neither willing to release the other too soon. Lenora had poured forth the story of the abduction on the coach-ride home, and now blushed to own her foolishness.

"I vow I shall never read novels again, Mama! I was never so taken in in my life! Being abducted was neither romantic, nor exciting, and I shall take care never to meet another evil Duke as long as I live!"

"My dear, you had no way of knowing he was an evil Duke. You said yourself that he seemed the perfect gentleman."

"Seemed, Mama, seemed! From now on, I shall suspect every perfect gentleman, until I know them to be true."

Her mother smiled and smoothed the hair away from her daughter's flushed face. "It may be enough never to entertain a man's attentions unaccompanied."

"I suppose so, Mama." She sat up suddenly, pushing slightly away. "I suppose that is why we must always have introductions! To save innocent maidens from meeting evil Dukes!"

Mrs. Breckinridge's eyes widened and she tipped her head, considering this profound notion. "I believe you must be right, my love! To think that we have been laboring under such strictures all our lives, without an inkling of the debt we owe. What ungracious creatures we are!"

Lenora narrowed her eyes at her mama. "You are roasting me."

"Well, yes, a little." She put a hand to her daughter's cheek. "But you are right, in that no young lady can be too careful whom she allows into the circle of her acquaintance."

"As Sir Joshua none too gently explained to us on the ride home."

Her mother lowered her eyes. "Anxiety has a strange way of making us gruff. Especially to those we love," she added, with some difficulty. "He meant it only for the best, I am sure. If your papa had been a man like Sir Joshua, he would never have given Lord Montrose the opportunity to be made known to me, and you would never have been in danger."

After a pause, Lenora said, with a commendable attempt at light-heartedness, "But we would have been denied such an adventure, Mama!"

Her mother achieved a smile. "Now you are roasting me, my love."

"Of course, I am," said Lenora, brightening. "It's that blood of yours, you know."

The smile wavered. "I am persuaded Sir Joshua meant that as a compliment to the both of us."

"To be sure, Mama!" Lenora cried with a beaming smile. "He is so droll! I hardly thought, when we first met him, that with all his gravity he could have such a perfect sense of the ridiculous. But I wouldn't change him for the world!" She looked up at her mother, suddenly conscious. "Would you, Mama?"

Mrs. Breckinridge transferred her attention to the knots on the front of her dressing gown. "I don't fancy I would, dearest," she said quietly.

Lenora bounced on the bed. "Oh, Mama! I knew it! He is perfect, is he not?" The murmured response merely encouraged her to give full vent to her raptures. "I vow I nearly fainted when he burst through the window—no, I do not think I would have fainted—rather, I nearly clapped my hands! It was so exciting, and so romantic for, you know, Mama, that I had no notion you had brought him, so I thought he had come all on his own, following his heart, and only just in time!" She tucked her knees up under her chin. "I am certain he would have knocked Lord Montrose down, if I had not noticed the candlestick and had the happy notion of doing it for him, and of course, you saved yourself by stepping out of the way, so Sir Joshua need not have come at all, though I would not have had him stay away for the world! Oh, Mama! What an adventure!" And she threw herself back onto her pillows with an ecstatic sigh.

Mrs. Breckinridge had forced herself to listen to this effusion with a smile, which valiantly persevered as she kissed her daughter goodnight and tucked her up into bed as though she were still a babe in the nursery. But the smile vanished completely as she closed Lenora's door and walked slowly into her own bedchamber, sitting mechanically at the vanity to gaze past her reflection in the large gilt mirror.

If she had met Sir Joshua when she was in London for her one and only season, would she have fallen in love with him then? He would have been still in his salad days, being three or four years her senior, and very likely may have been an entirely different man than he was now. Assuredly, she was an entirely different woman now than she had been then. Both had endured pain and heartache, and loss, though of different kinds. He had loved his wife and mourned her death, and still revered her memory and the memory of the years they had spent together. Genevieve had also loved her husband—had taken infatuation for love, at least—but it had worn off as the years had passed and his character, which she had discovered to be weak and selfish, had further deteriorated, and she had been made to regret her choice until the news of his death had come as a blessed release from an early Purgatory. No, she was not the same Genevieve Wainsley whom Sir Joshua would have met at Almack's, flirting up a storm with all her beaux, with her eyes firmly fixed on the prize of the season. Sir Joshua should not have had a chance with her, but she as equally may not have had a chance with him.

As she yet had no chance with him. Sighing, she picked up the brush and pulled it through her hair, having sent Sanford to bed, unequal tonight to her cosseting. She went about the business of going to bed with a detached awareness—loosening the ties of her dressing gown, laying it over the back of a chair, and pulling back the covers of her bed to slip under them and settle her head onto the soft pillow—as if she were separated from her body. It must be that she was exhausted after the trials and triumphs of this night, and of all the weeks leading up to it, but even as she closed her eyes and bid her limbs relax, she knew sleep would not come, for the trial was not ended. She faced the most daunting and painful task of her life, but she knew now, without a doubt, that seeing it to fruition was as necessary to Lenora's happiness as it was disastrous to her own. As a mother, she must steel herself to keep her own desires firmly behind the needs of her child.

So, when she woke late the next morning, Mrs. Breckinridge dressed and presented herself in the breakfast room with a very fair semblance of a cheery countenance and her usual lively chatter. Lady

Cammerby was shocked and amazed at the tale Lenora told of the night's events, and her mother interpolated such vivid details that none could suspect it pained her to do so. When Lady Cammerby had exclaimed her last, and the ladies had retired to the saloon, Mrs. Breckinridge evinced no dismay when the first of their morning callers was announced to be Sir Joshua, but seated herself purposefully in an armchair, to leave the remainder of the sofa beside Lenora free for her suitor.

Sir Joshua properly came to her first, greeting her warmly with a kiss to her hand and a glimmer in his eyes that belied the ardor he carried with him. He went next to Lenora, who jumped up to take both his hands and lead him to sit beside her, to receive her renewed transports over his heroism. These he politely disclaimed, glancing with embarrassed amusement to Mrs. Breckinridge from time to time, but she detected pride in his eyes as well, as though he was pleased at how his efforts had succeeded. She merely kept at her stitchery, as any good chaperone would do, and smiled, though as the interview wore on, this proved more difficult to do.

Luckily, the visit was interrupted at last by the arrival of Elvira, on the arm of Mr. Ginsham who, after the terrors of the day before, had determined that his dear one must never be unattended by himself—at least as often as could be contrived. This stricture she was only too happy to abide, and their two voices were added to Lenora's in recounting the events of the previous evening all over again, while Sir Joshua and Mrs. Breckinridge looked indulgently on.

At one point, the gentlemen rose to refresh themselves at the sideboard and became engaged in low-voiced discussion of their part outside the villain's window, and Mrs. Breckinridge, rigorously determined against attending to their conversation, naturally heard it all.

"It was all I could do to keep you from rushing into the room then and there," Ginsham exclaimed in an under voice, "which you must own would have been cork-brained in the extreme!"

"You saw what he was doing!" returned Sir Joshua, clenching his jaw. "That he should be even in the same room with her was enough to make my blood boil."

"But at the crucial moment, sir! All would've been undone if you'd burst in right then!"

"I'd have gotten the job done," declared Sir Joshua, tossing off his drink.

Ginsham snorted and refilled his companion's glass. "You would have planted him a facer, and knocked him into a table with all sorts of glassware on it, alerting the servants immediately! That would've gotten it done, alright! We'd have been ripe for the magistrate, just as Mrs. Breckinridge told us." He cast a respectful glance her way. "As it was, she played him devilishly clever, and got the girls without any interference from us frippery fellows, by gad!

"I own it worked, but I'll stand by it that we could have done it ourselves." Sir Joshua took another drink and stared grimly at the wall. "She had no business involving herself in such danger."

Feeling justly served for her weakness in eavesdropping, Mrs. Breckinridge withdrew her attention from them, becoming quite intent upon her stitchery while her brain fumbled over the ramifications of what she had overheard, but she soon abandoned any attempts at reconciling herself either to what had been said, or to he who had said it. She had been made aware what were his sentiments toward her during their outing to Vauxhall, and any energy she allowed herself to spend in feeling pained that they were unchanged would be wasted. With this lowering conviction, she tried to become absorbed in her sewing, but it held neither consolation nor interest for her, so her attention presently became transferred to the young ladies, who had huddled together on the sofa, quite within earshot.

"I felt a foreboding the day we met him, Lenora," insisted Elvira, "when he declared he admired you."

"That you did not!" cried Lenora. "You thought it as romantic as I did, and positively encouraged me to think him agreeable!"

Elvira blushed, but rallied, saying, "So I did, and I was right, for isn't that exactly what a villain does—deceives his chosen victim with flattery and attention?"

Lenora was obliged to agree with this assertion, but pointed out that Elvira had had no notion of Lord Montrose's being evil when she thought him romantic.

"At least I thought his manner suspicious at Hookham's," protested Elvira. "I distinctly recall saying so at the time. His coming up to us in so familiar a manner quite disturbed me."

"Your perturbation expressed itself most unsuitably, then, for I recall you flirting with him." Elvira disclaimed but Lenora pressed her, insisting, "You thought him charming!"

Sputtering a little, Elvira owned to it, saying, "So I did, for what else could I think? I could not be wiser than the rest of my sex, who take a gentleman at his word."

"Of course not, dearest," Lenora said in a conciliating tone. "You are no wiser than I, nor Emily or Adeline or Camilla, but you are a deal braver."

"You do not mean it," said Elvira, coloring again and lowering her eyes. "I thought my heart would stop when that horrid man put his knife to my side, and when I awoke in the hackney coach and we discovered ourselves to be in the countryside, en route to an unknown destination," she pressed a distressed hand to her bosom at the memory, "my blood ran cold."

"I believe it did, dearest," said her friend, "for you sat so straight and still that I fancied you to be in a fit."

"But you were not afraid, Lenora," said Elvira, raising her eyes admiringly to her face.

"Perhaps the shock made me braver than I otherwise would have been," admitted Lenora. "It was not the least bit romantic."

"No, but it was! To be carried off by force—"

"We were handed most tenderly into a comfortable hackney!"

Elvira revised her approach. "The romance was in the deception, Lenora," she said, edging nearer her friend and looking intently up from under her brows. "You must see that our trusting him so implicitly was our undoing, for if we had suspected aught before he had us in the coach, his plan would have been vain. He played his part of the evil Duke perfectly."

Pursing her lips, Lenora allowed that Lord Montrose was as vile a villain as ever there was, but insisted he had no notion of how an abduction should be carried off, and expressing severe disappointment in the state of the house, and the suite of rooms accorded them.

"Perhaps they weren't in a proper state of decay, or even of disuse, as they might have been, Lenora," reflected Elvira, moved by honesty to consider this assertion, "but the servants were positively eerie in their attentiveness, and they did lock us in."

"After serving us with a hot supper and warming pans in the bed!" cried Lenora, disgusted. "Not a ghost or a chain or a dim corridor to be seen, and no drafts to snuff our candles." She huffed, shaking her head. "I'll never believe in romance again, Elvira. It does not exist but in novels."

"Never say so, Lenora!" her friend implored her. "What of our valiant rescuers? When they burst through the window, I thought

I'd die! I could think of nothing but that dear Ginsham had come to rescue me, and then your mother freed herself and you knocked Lord Montrose over the head, and my head was in such a whirl that I nearly fainted!"

"Which would have been excessively unfortunate," observed Lenora drily, "Mr. Ginsham being across the room at that moment, so you'd have only fallen onto the floor." Sustaining a look of dislike from her friend, Lenora redeemed herself by continuing, "But you ended very sensibly in his arms, which I must say was terribly satisfying to witness. I can't conceive of even Mr. Barnabus having exhibited more heroism than your Mr. Ginsham."

Elvira sat up straight at that, blinking at her friend. "Mr. Barnabus? Oh, my. I have not thought of him this age." She looked down at her hands. "Oh, dear Lenora, I do believe you were right in warning me against letting my fancy carry me away. I was almost blinded by it, so much so that I nearly relinquished my one true hope of happiness." She cast an adoring glance Mr. Ginsham's way. "I could never meet with a more perfect match than Mr. Ginsham." Somehow tearing her eyes from her beloved, she laid a hand on Lenora's arm. "I relinquish all rights to Mr. Barnabus's heart, my dearest friend. I should have done so long ago. He is, and has always been, rightfully yours."

"Oh!" cried Lenora, astonished by her friend's misplaced generosity. "Your feelings are most noble, but I cannot pretend to a place in Mr. Barnabus's affections." She lowered her voice confidentially. "I must agree with you that romance lives in certain men, Elvira, but I believe it to be of a superior kind than that in the pages of a book." She cast a significant glance at Sir Joshua as she spoke.

Her mother, catching the look, swiftly lowered her own gaze back to the work in her hands. It was the ugliest work she had done in all her life. The stitches were uneven, and the fabric puckering. It would have to be picked out, and she could not but feel the afternoon to have been wasted.

But it was not to be an entire waste, it seemed, for Sir Joshua, apparently tiring of the topic upon which the young people were so intent, came to Mrs. Breckinridge's side and bowed to take her hand.

"I will take my leave of you, ma'am, but I wonder if I may have the honor of a few words with you tomorrow, in private."

Her mouth went dry and her hand trembled in his as their gazes met. Such ardent purpose in his eyes—it smote her to the heart. He would ask to pay his addresses to Lenora, he would ask for her daughter's hand, and how could she bear it? Oh, that the meeting could be postponed, even another day—but no, she must not attempt it. Her resolution wavered even now, and would only weaken with time.

She moistened her lips and forced herself to smile graciously. "Of course, Sir Joshua. I am at leisure tomorrow afternoon. Does that suit?"

"Perfectly." He kissed her hand, his gaze holding hers all the while. "Until tomorrow."

She watched him leave, only recalled from her frantically scattered reflections by a movement in the corner of her eye. Lenora was watching her with eyes brimful of joy.

The young people's chatter resumed and, excusing herself, Mrs. Breckinridge gathered up her work basket and went up to her room, prey to such dramatic yearnings as that she should fall victim to a sudden heart attack, or should be instantaneously rendered invisible. But an hour passed without any of these desires being fulfilled, and as she had no wish to excite Amelia's—or anyone's—curiosity or solicitude, she was forced to dress for dinner, resigned to play the part of delighted mama, until the forthcoming event broke her heart.

Chapter 30

IT WAS NOT to be supposed that with such perturbed spirits Genevieve would enjoy a night's repose. She tossed and turned on her pillow, first with guilt at her inability to feel joy for her daughter's upcoming felicity, and then with deep mortification at the feelings she had been too weak to banish from her breast forever. She gained no comfort from the knowledge that Sir Joshua knew nothing of her infatuation, for this assurance merely opened a new set of heart-burnings which turned upon the anguished question of whether the outcome might have been different had she made her attachment known to him. Could he have returned her affection, had he been made aware of hers? Or had his eyes been only for Lenora from the start?

No matter the convolutions of her thoughts, they returned again and again to her duty: it was clear that her desires must give way before her daughter's. Genevieve had had her day, had made her choice of husband, and had chosen poorly, and lived to regret and repair what she could. Lenora, she told herself, firmly and repeat-edly, must be allowed to make her own choice, and if hers was a hundred million times better than Genevieve's, what more could a mother ask?

Unfortunately, these assertions, coupled with increasing fatigue, had such an irritating effect that her inner voice quickly became recalcitrant, and her last reflections, before tumbling into troubled sleep, were far from resigned. She awoke cross, and no amount of self-chastisement could bring her to immolate herself upon the altar of motherhood without the air of a martyr. Possessed of just enough reason to accept the necessity of remaining solitary for a while yet, she took her breakfast in bed, but made a pitiful repast, only sipping at her chocolate while glaring at the opposite wall in a brown study.

She had done with sacrifice, of herself, her hopes, her dreams. Her entire life had been a sacrifice thus far. Lenora was young yet, she could find another man, a younger man, who would suit her just as well. Indeed, better! For the more she reflected on her daughter's and Sir Joshua's separate personalities, the greater the disparity she found between them, and the greater reason to keep them apart. As her thoughts turned, Lenora speedily dwindled into a fragile, trusting creature, while Sir Joshua quickly became a monster of inhumanity, whose very gaze must wither his chosen bride's self-es-teem. From thence, it was only a step to reasoning that in refusing Sir Joshua's solicitation for Lenora's hand, Genevieve would be pre-serving her daughter's life.

She did not turn her head when Sanford entered, and did not answer the first or second request for her orders, and when that faithful retainer touched her on the arm, she jerked back to herself so violently that the chocolate spattered onto her night dress. All at once, the spell was broken, and the idiocy of her musings struck her with uncompromising force. Uttering an oath that Bertram had been fond of using, Genevieve thrust the tray at Sanford and got up.

"There is little use in my remaining in bed now," she said petulantly, removing the stained garment and throwing it onto the floor. "I wished to wallow in self-pity, not in squalor."

Sanford eyed her narrowly, but kept her concerns as tight as her prim mouth as she helped her mistress to dress, not in the requested habit suitable for an execution, but in a pale-hued muslin morning dress that served to soften the drawn look on her mistress's face. Casting many a wary glance at the stormy reflection in the mirror, she brushed and styled her mistress's hair and placed a becoming lace cap over the curls, then curtseyed and asked if there was anything else Mistress required.

After a drawn-out pause, Genevieve replied, "I require a good, hard slap, followed immediately by a long, stiff drink, Sanford." The normally humorous blue eyes, which glittered alarmingly, met her maid's. "But I fancy you could not bring yourself to administer such things to me."

Sanford's lips parted to reply that she would never, ever, in a hundred years do such a thing to her dear mistress, but the fire in the blue eyes alerted her to danger, and she wisely lowered her own, bobbing a curtsey again, and hurried away to share her worries with Lady Cammerby's maid that Mistress had snapped at last, after pushing proper heroically through everything the old master, God rest him, she was sure, had seen fit to rain over her ears, but who could blame the poor thing, when Miss had got herself entangled in some terrible way just day before last, because that's what's to be expected in a great, wicked city like this, and they should all pack up and go home and sooner's the better!

Not being privy to her henchwoman's mutterings, Genevieve had no way of knowing how similar they were to her own. She spent the morning tugging away at her embroidery, hardly seeing the pattern before her as she yanked and pulled with fingers attuned to the violent thoughts in her head. Lenora did not deserve him—she was deserving of some other, faceless, future man, but not of *him*. She was just a girl—how could he think to be happy with her, who could be his daughter, who would need more to be reared by him than to be revered by him? Lenora thought him perfect, which was the worst way to start a marriage—as poor Genevieve had found out, and hadn't she imparted that wisdom to her daughter? How could Lenora ignore such important advice?

A sharp pain jolted through her as she inadvertently jabbed her finger with the needle. Gasping, she brought the injured member to her mouth, sucking on it with her eyes closed, her mind momentarily blank. As nothing else could, the pain had shocked her enough to throw her out of the sulks, but now her body quivered with pent up emotion, and before she knew what had happened, hot tears were spilling down her cheeks and splashing onto her embroidery. She sobbed and sobbed, her shoulders heaving, but no sounds escaped her except ragged breaths and pathetic sniffs.

After many minutes, the tears and the shudders at last ceased, and she felt emptied of every feeling, barren of humanity, as hollow and brittle as a fallen and forgotten tree. She wiped her eyes and cheeks, and her gaze fell upon her work on her lap. The hopelessly knotted and tangled mess was proof of her worthlessness, and she flung it away from her, just as the door opened, and Sir Joshua was announced.

He came in, looking more handsome than she had ever seen him, the flush of love enlivening his eyes, and his mouth turned up in that irresistible smile of his. She stood, her eyes locked on him, and he took her hand, bending to bring it to his lips, the kiss burning on her skin. She trembled, her heart pounding in her ears, and she wanted to cry out to him not to say it, not to ask of her what she could never give, but her throat was too constricted to make a sound.

"Mrs. Breckinridge, may I say you look lovely today." His words startled her into a nod, then he was leading her to the sofa and gently pressing her to sit beside him. Taking both her hands in his own, he said, "You cannot be ignorant of my intentions. My errand here today is a mere formality, for my attentions have been quite marked over the last weeks, and I flatter myself that I have been understood for almost as long. You must forgive me for taking so long to come to the point, but my nature is guarded, and at my age, one can hardly be expected to embark on a new estate without proper consideration. Especially in this case, I have had ample reason for caution, both on my part and on yours, for though Lenora assures me she has no qualms, and even Tom has given his sanction, I know as well as you that marriage must not be thoughtlessly considered."

She felt her heart shrink within her bosom, threatening to crumble altogether, and she instinctively tried to withdraw her hands, but he tightened his hold. "Mrs. Breckinridge, would you permit me to pay my add—"

Wrenching her hands from his grasp, she jumped up from the sofa, crying out, "I cannot! Oh, I cannot do it! I have tried—God knows I have tried to put myself aside, to forget my own desires on behalf of my beloved child, but I cannot!"

"I do not understand you," he said, rising and reaching out to her.

But she wrapped her arms around herself, turning her back to him and denying him access to her sensibility. "You would not suit! Can you not see it?"

"Would not suit?" His voice was fraught with disbelief.

His stubborn stupidity inflamed her to anger and she whirled on him. "You are far too old!"

He blinked at her. "Too old?"

"You said, yourself, just now, that at your age you must be cautious! And yet you persevere! Horrid man! Odious, impossible, provoking man!" she cried, whipping herself into a frenzy. "How can you deceive yourself that you, who could be her father, and will be doddering into your grave while she still struggles to raise your children, would make Lenora any kind of a husband?"

He stood still, staring wide-eyed at her for a pregnant moment, until a huff escaped him, and an incredulous smile tilted up the corners of his mouth. "Lenora?"

She wanted to hit him. "Yes, Lenora, my daughter, to whom you wish to pay your addresses! Of whom else would we be speaking, sir? Or are you already in the grip of senility?"

He stepped quickly forward to take hold of her arms, looking down with intense amusement at her. "Still, you do not fail to surprise me." He shook her a little as she struggled against him. "You adorable idiot, it is not Lenora with whom I am in love."

She stopped squirming and stared at him, stunned. "What?"

"You are correct in that Lenora could never fulfill my expectations for a wife. She is far too young, far too silly, and far too predictable." His eyes travelled over her face. "I want a delightfully dense woman who has made it her occupation to upset my peace, forever falling into scrapes, or even creating them, from which I am obliged to rescue her, except when she rescues herself. A mature woman whose courage is both an inspiration and a thorn in my side, whose sense is refreshingly impolite, and whose humor I cannot but describe as addictive."

"Sir Joshua—" she whispered, but more she could not say, for her whole strength was necessary to keep her suddenly nerveless body from collapsing.

"My dearest Genevieve, have I made myself clear at last?" he murmured, as he drew her to him. "I love *you*, and the happiness I have found in these last several weeks would at last be complete if you would consent to be my wife."

Her convulsive "Oh!" was accompanied by a burst of tears, and she found herself pressed to Sir Joshua's chest, sobbing not with heartache, but with unblemished joy. He held her, putting his cheek against her hair and saying nothing, for nothing was needed but his nearness and the assurance of his care.

When her tears subsided, she pulled away, accepting his handkerchief with a watery chuckle, and drying her face once more. "I fear I am horridly blotched, sir. What a spectacle I make of myself!"

"Were it only lamentation, my love, I may agree, but it provides me with the felicity of taking you into my arms, which more than compensates for any diminution in your looks—which, however, I do not perceive."

She chuckled again, but as he gathered her to him once more, she recollected a terribly disturbing fact, which threatened to overthrow all her peace. Holding him at bay, she cried, "But Lenora loves you!"

"Of course she does."

She hit a fist against his chest. "But how can you be so unfeeling? She thinks you are the perfect man! She told me so herself, only yesterday!" She covered her face with her hands. "Oh, her heart will break when she finds out—"

"I never guessed you could be so stupid, my love." He kissed her cheekbone, which was the only feature accessible to him. "Lenora thinks me the perfect man, for *you*." He laughed into her suddenly upturned and wide-eyed face. "We have spoken often of my feelings for you, and she has shared with me how she has long dreamed of a father who could give her mother all the happiness she deserves."

Again, she was shocked into an "Oh!" followed by a burst of tears upon Sir Joshua's breast. This time, she wept from shame at her selfishness all this morning, of her inability to think of her daughter, while her dear Lenora had been thinking only of her, in all her dealings with Sir Joshua. These qualms, however, were quickly resolved by the knowledge of the justice of her claims upon Sir Joshua's heart, and her tears, owing to the shortage of hydration in her eyes, dried comparatively quickly.

When she at last looked up at the man whose heart was securely hers, he cocked an eyebrow at her. "You have yet to answer me."

Wiping the remnants of her tears from her cheeks with the now sodden handkerchief, she smiled archly up at him. "How can I answer what you did not ask, sir? You merely stated that you would be happy if I would consent to be your wife."

Pursing his lips, he gazed down on her through hooded eyes. "Genevieve Breckinridge, will you marry me?"

"Sir Joshua Stiles, I will," she said primly, but her lips almost immediately parted in a most unladylike grin, and she closed her eyes as he bent to bestow upon her a breathtaking embrace, from which it was several minutes before she emerged.

Sighing, she melted against his shoulder. "There is no going back after that, Joshua! Whether you like it or not, I am now irrevocably yours."

He tightened his hold around her. "Oh, my Genevieve, I do like it."

Author's Note

The Regency era is such a delight to delve into that it was hard sometimes to decide between research and writing. Hopefully, the details I chose to include in this story were as interesting for you to read about as they were enjoyable for me to write.

Two in the Bush begins in the year 1816, "the year without a summer," as it came to be known in Europe. Strange weather patterns, including ceaseless rain and unseasonable cold, overspread Europe after the 1815 explosion of Mount Tambora, in Indonesia. This volcanic eruption, which is the largest in recorded history, caused all kinds of natural disruptions, poor air quality, a drop in average temperatures, and general gloom worldwide as clouds of ash remained suspended in the atmosphere for up to three years. Thus, the Breckinridges were not the only family to be set back, if not ruined, by the terrible weather that year.

One of Georgette Heyer's favorite haunts for her young heroines in London was the Pantheon Bazaar, a shop much like our present-day flea markets. Unfortunately, Heyer's information was incorrect; the Pantheon Bazaar did not come into existence until 1834, occupying a building that had previously been a theater and a meeting hall of the same first name. The Soho Bazaar, however, opened in 1816 in nearby Soho Square, and may well be the shopping center Heyer intended. This market was housed in a large warehouse made from three dwellings, and was created to allow widows, orphans, and relatives of soldiers who had died in the Napoleonic wars a respectable way to make a living. The market sold handmade items and other wares priced low enough to prevent haggling, and so gained a reputation for inexpensive but quality merchandise.

Elizabeth Fry, the wife of a banker and a Quaker, deplored the conditions of female prison inmates and, early in 1817, formed the Ladies Association for the Reformation of the Female Prisoners in Newgate. The association strove to return some dignity to the women by providing female yardkeepers and separate quarters, a cleaner and gentler environment—with no alcohol, profanity, gaming, or pornography—and gainful employment in the form of piecework and knitting. Many upper-class ladies, such as Lady Wraglain and Mrs. Breckinridge, joined the society in the hopes of being useful.

Vauxhall Gardens enjoyed a long and varied career as a pleasure garden, where the definition of "pleasure" changed over the decades. By 1817, it had been spruced up and built a decent reputation, which held for another twenty years. In the several pictures and paintings of the park that survive, only the large, main walks are apparent; however, many written descriptions imply that there were small, private walks where couples—and often unfortunate individuals—could lose their way in more ways than one. In my efforts to write only what was truly accurate, I visited the Victoria and Albert Museum in London, where I had hoped to view a meticulously crafted model of Vauxhall Gardens. Upon arrival, I discovered that my source had been outdated—the model now resides in storage and cannot be viewed. However, the kind curators of the storage facility provided me with pictures of the model, which convinced me that my conclusions regarding small paths in the groves were correct, making the scene between Lord Montrose and Genevieve possible.

Madame Saqui was a flamboyant figure who came to fame in Paris, and after the defeat of Napoleon enjoyed renown in England for decades. She performed many times at both Covent Garden Theater and Vauxhall Gardens from 1816 until 1845, and contributed greatly to the popularity of those venues. Her feats of agility, set against the backdrop of dazzling fireworks, awed audiences, and brought them back time after time.

One of the underlying themes of this story relies on the strict rules governing introductions in Regency society. Though many social rules were more relaxed in the Regency than during the Victorian era, writings of the time indicate that views regarding proper introductions were fairly serious, resulting in the lamentation of Mrs. Bennet that her daughters would never know Mr. Bingley if their father would not meet with him first. Interactions between strangers, especially between men and women, were frowned upon, and anything but the slightest accidental occurrences were avoided unless a proper introduction, from an existing acquaintance or a trusted leader in society, could be obtained.

Acknowledgements

First off, I'd like to thank Georgette Heyer for her short story, *A Husband for Fanny*, which was the inspiration for *Two in the Bush*. When I read this story, which is about 18 pages long, I thought it was tragic that such a great premise was confined to so small a scope, so I decided to take my own spin on it. While my story is significantly different than Heyer's, the idea of a mother falling in love with the man she believes to be her daughter's suitor is originally Heyer's, and I thank her for giving me the opportunity to tell it in my own way.

There are so many wonderful people who contributed to the success of this venture that I hope I don't forget anyone. I could not, ever, have done this without all of you!

To all of you who took a chance on a new author and read this book, and enjoyed it enough that you are still reading, thank you! I hope this is only the beginning of a long and exciting adventure together.

To Emily Menendez, Karl Hale, Lavinia Hale, Marintha Hale, Elizabeth Prettyman, Bobi Taylor, Marianne Harris, and my mom Signe Gillum, who were my beta readers and valiantly read draft after draft to give me valuable feedback, thank you for your patience and persistence. You helped me resolve my style and grow my confidence.

To my friend Nichole Van Valkenburgh, for all her excellent advice, cheerleading, and hand-holding through the process of self-publishing, and to my sister Laurel Hale, for saving my butt and sharing her amazing marketing, website building, and social media skills, you guys have my undying gratitude!

To my incredible daughter, Rachel Allen Everett, whose artistic prowess is displayed in the cover design, and to the awesome Rabbit Everett, who designed my stunning logo, your unbelievable talents amaze me!

To all my kids, who treat me like I'm a way better mom than I am, and who philosophically accept the tradeoffs of a messy house, cobbled together meals, and having to physically shake mom to get her attention, in order to support my being a writer.

And most of all, to the love of my life, Joe, for never tiring of building me up, telling me like it is, and believing in my work—whether you like it or not, I am irrevocably yours!

Sneak Preview of

Romance of the Ruin
Book 2 of the Branwell Chronicles

Lenora fled deep into the wood, away from the shadow cast by her dearest friend's joy. Even as she ran, the hood of her cape falling back from her head, she chided herself for being so mean as to resent Elvira's happiness, but every remembrance of her friend's delight set her yearning for something to happen—anything!—that would elevate her from her present humdrum existence to the realization of even the smallest of her dreams.

Pausing for breath against the knotty bole of a chestnut tree, she pressed her forehead to the rough wood, her eyes closed tightly. "You are selfish and ridiculous and... and totty-headed to act in this way," she sternly admonished the tree bark. "Life is not a romance, even if Elvira has achieved her heart's desire and you have not. You have no need to be jealous—you could not be more happy for her!" she insisted, hitting her gloved palm against the trunk in emphasis. "Marriage is no light matter—and a baby—" Here she found it necessary to swallow down a lump in her throat before continuing resolutely, "A baby is a serious responsibility, for all its plumpness and sweetness and tiny fingers and toes—"

But at this her slender self-control deserted her and she slid to the base of the tree, looking forlornly up into the branches. "Is there to be romance for everyone but me?"

The swaying branches above her murmured sympathetically, but she could take no comfort from them, instead pounding a fist into the soft, mossy ground at her side. "All my adventure in London, and what has come of it? I gained acquaintance enough, but no real admirers. Mr. Barnabus has forgotten all about me, and Lord Montrose was nothing but an imposter." She shrugged a shoulder. "Though I did hit him over the head, which was properly heroic. But that is neither here nor there, for nothing as exciting could ever occur here, I am persuaded."

Since Sir Joshua had first told her of Wrenthorpe Grange, describing the manor in thrillingly Gothic terms, Lenora had yearned to visit. Therefore, her first sight of the venerable house— tantalizingly obscured by the thick stand of the Home Wood, and then bursting upon her vision as the carriage emerged into the full light of afternoon—had been slightly disappointing. Sir Joshua had prepared her for lichen-covered stone walls and brooding casements, with undiscovered secrets lurking behind them, but her own eyes had told her that his was a biased description. Though it was blackened in many places, and one wall was entirely hidden by creeping ivy, the stone was of a much brighter hue—almost golden—than she had been led to imagine. And the windows, beside being fully intact, were sparkling clean in the afternoon sunlight, leading her to doubt the possibility of anything, most especially a secret, lurking within. In good faith, however, she had disdained her own judgment, and embarked upon her new life in the full expectation of mounting horrors—for what else could await her in such an ancient place?

But it was not many days before she was made to realize that she had never been so taken in. There was not a locked door nor an unexplained cupboard in the whole of the house, and search as she might, she could find no evidence of hollows behind the paneling, or of any flooring that could reasonably have been placed to hide an oubliette. She had even tried quite faithfully not to watch for ghostly figures vanishing from the corners of her vision, and had been justly rewarded—there were none. She was forced to the depressing conclusion that Wrenthorpe Grange, despite her persistent hopes and Sir Joshua's assurances, was everything that was proper and comfortable.

Her fingers had been pulling at a clump of moss, and it came away in her hand. "I am doomed to languish in the smooth seas of gentility!" she cried, throwing the clump away from her. But as the words left her mouth, a change came over her mood, as if a beguiling vision had opened before her. The cloud upon her brow eased, and she pushed herself to her feet, vaguely brushing off her dress with a far-away look in her eyes.

"I am cast adrift in unknown waters, friendless, penniless, and without a shore to call my own." She began to walk dreamily, moving deeper into the wood as she mused. "After untold hardships, my boat runs upon a desolate beach, where breakers crash so violently that the craft is broken asunder, and I am dashed onto the rocks." She moved onward, winding around trees and stepping over rocks and creepers as she continued, speaking aloud as if the wood were her bosom friend.

"I awaken in the hovel of a kindly hermit, who nurses me to health, before bestowing upon me a humble gift—" Here she paused to look about herself for a token suitable to the hermit's gift. Spying a burled stick poking up from the underbrush, she pulled it out, wiping the dirt and grass from it with a corner of her cloak and eying it critically. Its proportions, much like a wand, satisfied her, and she held it reverently before her as she continued, "He bestows upon me a humble gift, with the admonition to save it against a time of great need, which circumstance will reveal its magic powers."

Fortified by this knowledge, Lenora tucked the stick into the pocket of her cloak and strode more purposefully along the path. "Though I wish to repay his kindness, he accepts only a lock of my hair, and directs me into the forest, where he prophesies my destiny awaits. The forest is dark and ancient, full of mysteries and secrets, but my courage shines forth like a beacon, and the Spirit of the Wood guides me on my path."

She ran a hand along the low-slung branch of a tree, which she imagined was the arm of a faerie creature, and walked on, gazing regally about. "The faerie folk peek out from their hiding places to watch me with mingled hope and awe. I am, surely, the One for whom they have waited! Suddenly, a clearing opens up, and in the center, on a greensward like scattered emeralds, stands a prince, whose proud bearing nevertheless pronounces great suffering, and whose gaze pierces me to the very heart."

She advanced into the clearing, which was real enough, and stood in the center, her hand outstretched to the invisible prince. "'Your Highness,' I say, and extend my hand in peaceful greeting, but he falls to one knee before me, bowing over my hand in humble petition. 'My Queen,' he cries, 'I have long awaited thee, and bless the good fortune that has brought you at last to my side.'"

Raising her hand, and with it the gallant—if imaginary—prince, Lenora said, "My lord, I have traveled through untold hardships to find you, and will grant you the boon you seek."

But the prince uttered a groan. "You have already sacrificed much, my Queen! How dare I ask that you risk more?"

"My prince, not all the sacrifice in the world could—"

The prince moaned again, more loudly, and uttered a most unprincely string of curses.

In utmost astonishment, Lenora jerked from her daydream, her eyes darting right and left. The clearing was, indeed, empty, and the gloom of the trees had thickened the shadows beneath them, so that nothing could be discerned within the shapeless darkness. She had often supposed the woods to be haunted, and another moan, accompanied by the thrash and scrape of movement, caused her to take an involuntary step backward, her skin prickling. But fascination checked her, and as her gaze searched the shadows, a light breeze shivered through the gold-tinged leaves overhead, allowing a sprinkling of sunlight to penetrate the gloom. There, in the underbrush beyond the clearing, was the distinct outline of a man—a real and ordinary man—lying face downward in the dirt.

She blinked at the figure, weighing the prudence of investigating—for he was surely in distress, as the groans attested—against that of running away. Curiosity and concern, and perhaps, as her mother had lamented, intrepidity, convinced her feet to carry her forward, and she made her way to the man's side. He lay at the base of a low hill, his frieze coat and breeches stained and covered with dead leaves and other debris, as if he had rolled down the hill and into the brush.

"Sir?" she asked, and was mortified at the quaver in her voice. There was no answer, and Lenora, asserting herself, cleared her throat and said in a strong, brave voice worthy of a queen, "Sir, are you hurt?"

Another moan issued from the fallen man, and he tried to lift himself, but after an abortive effort, he again lay still.

"May I be of assistance, sir?" she pursued, taking tentative hold of one of his arms and pulling. This proved utterly ineffectual, as he was larger than she, and dead weight into the bargain, but, undaunted, she tugged insistently at the arm and urged in an encouraging tone, "Sir, if we both try at once, you may be able to rise—"

His arm suddenly swiped out in an arc, ripping itself from her grasp, and the man flung himself into a sitting position, facing her. "Don't need any assistance, you," he bellowed in a rough accent, with fumes of strong drink billowing on his breath and into Lenora's horrified face.

"Good heavens!" she cried, stumbling backward. "You're drunk!"

Her exclamation gave him pause, and he squinted hard at her, evidently making a discovery. "Ladies present!" he said, his hand going to the kerchief knotted about his neck, and patting down his coat in a cursory self-inspection. "Pleasure, ma'am. No wish to contradict, but only slightly disguised," he slurred, touching his cap. "Word of a gen'leman."

"Gentleman!" exclaimed his outraged companion, wide-eyed at this absurd speech. "No self-respecting gentleman looks—or smells—as you do, sir!"

He blinked down at his attire, then surged to his feet, achieving a bow that threatened to topple him onto his head. By dint of windmilling his arms in rather a haphazard fashion, however, he miraculously righted himself, and said, nodding in a conciliatory way to this angry, yet percipient young lady, "True. Not a gen'leman. Soldier."

"Well," huffed Lenora, her arms crossed sternly as she surveyed the disreputable personage before her, from his unkempt hair and overgrown beard to his mud bespattered boots. "Any man claiming to be in His Majesty's service ought to be ashamed to be seen in such a state!"

"Fallen on hard times," he mumbled sullenly, swiping at his nose with his sleeve. "Old Boney drew in his horns. Wellington gave us marching orders. Had to come here." He wheeled around and stumbled toward the path. "Nowhere else to go."

Lenora had heard of the sad lot of noncommissioned soldiers, who were turned out of the army with no pension, and often with no home to return to, after the long years of the Peninsular war. He did not seem to be so very old, either, which somehow made his plight the more pitiable. Discomfited, she watched him go, wavering between disgust and compassion for him. After all, how just was it to condemn this poor soul, who had sought refuge from his not insignificant troubles in drink?

His toe suddenly hit a root, pitching him forward onto his knees, and she cast aside her scruples, hurrying forward to help him to his feet. "Sir, take care," she said, holding tight to his arm as he swayed alarmingly.

He swatted at her hand, as if it were a fly. "Not fitting for a lady to take care of me."

"Certainly, under normal circumstances," she persisted, keeping step with him as he started once more down the path. "But you are not yourself, and I feel I should see you safely home."

He stopped again to gaze blearily into her face. "Much obliged, but can't be done. Raffles can't help me, and nobody answers my letters." He plunged onward.

Lenora, standing bemused for a moment at this cryptic utterance, hastened forward to right him as he nearly toppled into the brush, and stumbled alongside him as he wove from side to side along the path. The gloom of the wood deepened, and she glanced up through the burnished leaves at a cloudy sky, wondering how long she had been gone from home, and how much longer this ill-advised adventure would continue.

The third time she found it necessary to haul him to the side, to prevent him from breaking his head open on a low-hanging branch, she inquired in a tense voice, "How far is your home, sir?"

But her inebriated companion merely waved a hand in a vague forward direction and trudged on, obliging her to continue with him. Lenora, fast repenting the compassion that had decided her to accompany a stranger—and a drunkard at that—into the forest, was forming the determination to leave him to his fate and seek her own home, when the trees opened onto the most fantastic view she had ever beheld.

An undulating field of unmown grass, interspersed with patches of thistle, autumn gentian, and Queen Anne's lace, fell away from the wood, down a slight decline, and across a wide expanse, where it ended at the sloping and bedraggled walls of a hedge-maze. This was surrounded by a riotous garden of sweet pea and rambling rose, with spikes of hollyhock and delphinium, all tangled in russet-leaved bramble and ivy, with ragged clumps of lavender and geranium clinging about the edges.

But the vision that held Lenora dumbstruck was a fine old Palladian mansion that rose up beyond the gardens in four stories, its rain-blackened Cotswold-stone walls splotched with lichen and overgrown with vines, and its pocked roof line stretching the cracked teeth of chimney pots into the clouded sky. The building extended in a great, brooding block with the blank eyes of several boarded or bricked-in windows staring outward, as if in sightless resignation.

Her drunken companion trundled forward into the high grass, and Lenora, rooted to the spot, breathed, "You live here?"

But he shook his head ponderously. "Not the Big House," he mumbled. "Only ghosts there. Gatehouse," he finished succinctly, and swerved abruptly away from the mansion, onto an unseen path.

Lenora's heart leapt at the mention of ghosts, and she scarcely heard the rest. This could not be real—this could not be happening to her! An actual haunted house, within a walk of her home—she pinched herself to be sure, and the answering pain became a shiver of terrified excitement. Her eyes scanned the Gothic perfection of the mansion—all blackened stone and ivy and despair—and she resolved that she must know everything about this place. What was its history? How had it come to be abandoned? How was it possible that such a place existed at all, within miles of Sir Joshua's home—and why had he not told her of it?

She broke from her reverie to hasten after her drunken companion, who had weaved his way around the corner of the fantastic house. He must be the grounds keeper, or some such, and would have the answers to her questions. Indeed, he had owned himself obligated to her, for she had rendered him a signal service in ensuring his safe journey through the wood, without which he would surely be lying unconscious after walking smash into a tree, and would very likely have died of it. Yes, he felt he owed her a debt, which could easily be paid upon his satisfying her curiosity.

She followed after him through the grass, around the mansion, and finally caught him up on a weed-strewn gravel sweep at the front of the house. Here she was distracted for a long moment by the splendor of four ivy-wrapped pillars flanking the huge double doors at the top of a short flight of wide, cracked steps, and she gazed with unrestrained wonder upon its ruined beauty. Oh, to know the secrets of this house, perhaps to go inside—these thoughts forced her to command herself enough to drag her eyes from the mansion and address herself to the grounds keeper.

"Sir, I must ask you—"

He spun to face her, bristling in outrage. "Where'd you come from? Why're you following me?"

"Following—" cried Lenora, taken aback. "I did not follow

you—that is, I did, but you would have caught your death in the forest had I not attended you!"

The soldier's head reared back, his eyebrows, or what she assumed were his eyebrows under all that hair, drawing together over beetle-black eyes. "Why?"

"Why, because you are too inebriated to know—"

"Why did you follow me?" he elucidated, swaying slightly with the effort. "Do you know me? Do I know you?"

"No, you do not, for you are too castaway to walk straight, let alone allow an introduction," she answered with asperity.

He wagged his head as he regarded her. "Highly improper."

"I should say so, sir, and imprudent, too—"

"Lady shouldn't introduce herself to a gentleman. Highly improper."

Lenora was temporarily stricken dumb by the irony of this truth. "I—I would never press for an introduction. That is not why—Circumstances forced me to—" she stammered, but he reeled away and down the gravel drive.

She scrambled after him, hardly knowing why she did so, except that the notion that she must know the history of the manor had taken firm root in her mind, and she felt as strongly that she was perfectly justified in asking the grounds keeper of it now, though he was foxed, for she had no way of knowing whether he was not perpetually so, and she did not know when she should have the chance again.

"Sir, I beg you to stop, for only one moment, please, and hear me out."

To her surprise, he did stop, but he did not look at her, only standing, staring gravely ahead at the door of the cottage.

"Sir, though you do not seem to clearly recall it, the fact remains that you owned yourself obliged to me today, and you would be able to repay me in a very small way."

"No."

Only slightly daunted, Lenora persisted. "It would be only a trifling favor, and should not incommode you in the least—"

He turned on her again, towering menacingly over her. "I said no. I've troubles enough without vandals and trespassers wasting my time."

"I mean no harm," Lenora insisted, standing her ground. "I wish only to know about the house, sir."

"No!" he almost shouted, whirling to yank open the door and enter the cottage. "Go away!"

"Sir, I beg you to—" began Lenora, but he closed the door in her face, and before she could protest further, the bolt slammed home.

JUDITH HALE EVERETT is one of seven sisters, and grew up surrounded by romance novels. Georgette Heyer and Jane Austen were staples, and formed the groundwork for her lifelong love affair with the Regency. Add to that her obsession with the English language and you've got one hopelessly literate romantic.

Find JudithHaleEverett on Instagram, Facebook, and Twitter, or at judithhaleeverett.com.